KW-222-723

PLAYGROUND

PLAYGROUND

Samuel Bonner

eMPIRICUS
BOOKS

London, England

First published in Great Britain 2010
by Empiricus Books
105-107 Gloucester Place,
London W1U 6BY

www.januspublishing.co.uk

Copyright © Samuel Bonner 2010

British Library Cataloguing-in-Publication Data
A catalogue record for this book is available from the British Library

ISBN 978-1-902835-19-8

All rights reserved. No part of this publication may be reproduced,
stored in a retrieval system or transmitted in anyform or by any
means, electric, mechanical, photocopying, recording or otherwise,
without the prior permission of the publisher.

The right of Samuel Bonner to be identified as the
author of this work has been asserted by him in
accordance with the Copyright, Designs and Patents
Act 1988.

Cover Design: Gokhan Demirci

Printed and bound in Great Britain

Dedication

This book is for anyone who has ever had time for me,
encouraged me, or helped me when I needed it.
To those who are closest to me – I love you all.

Prologue

A cool breeze blew in from the air conditioning unit but he still felt too hot. He inhaled deeply to try and steady the trembling, his thighs vibrating. Rose touched the back of his hand and looked at him, and almost instantly, the tremors of panic began to subside.

'You alright?' she asked, stroking his skin with her fingertips. She looked worried and a little pale, though it was hard to judge her complexion under the white vibrancy of the backstage lights. He didn't reply verbally to her question, but instead, offered a weak smile and nodded; if he'd spoken his voice would've betrayed him in an instant.

The murmur of the current speaker onstage resonated through the narrow hallway where they sat. It sounded like the man was underwater, his words muffled and drowned by the concrete walls. Jonah unscrewed the lid of his water bottle and greedily took a gulp. He'd only just had a sip but his mouth was already dry again, like his tongue was coated in sawdust. He massaged the nape of his chafing neck with one clammy palm and suddenly became aware of how sick he felt. After undoing the top buttons on his shirt, Jonah clutched the crucifix eagerly.

'You look nervous,' Rose said softly. She reached for his hand that was twiddling with the little gold cross and squeezed it gently.

Jonah sipped some more water before he answered her. 'Nah, I'm not nervous,' he told her in a croak. With the words, a flare of heat rose inside him, stopping his breath short.

Troy, the event organiser, came down the hallway in an expensive-looking navy blue suit, holding a clipboard. He smiled at Jonah and Rose, and as his mouth curled up, the lights revealed the deep scar etched from his right nostril down to the bottom of his chin. From what Jonah had overheard, Troy got the scar fending off a bunch of skinheads that had trapped him on a train platform when he was in his early twenties and one of the racists managed to graffiti Troy's face with a Stanley blade before security intervened.

Troy greeted them both and shook their hands. 'Right, Eddie's just finishing up in there so you're on in five. That okay, Jonah?'

'Yeah, that's fine.'

'As you go through the curtain there's three steps leading to the stage that I forgot to mention. I've been so busy running around after everyone that it just slipped my mind. You gonna be alright getting up the steps by yourself or will you need some help?' Troy asked him, wide-eyed.

'I'll manage,' he replied.

A staggered, choppy applause signalled that it was time for the next speaker. The sound made Jonah's heart palpitate.

'I guess that's you then.' Troy said.

Jonah grabbed his crutches and began the agonising process of getting to his feet. Rose held his bicep as he grimaced, leaning on the crutches for stability. Troy watched over the exercise uncomfortably, unsure of what to do and wary of offering help for fear of causing offence. Jonah finally stood upright, panting from the effort. The numb twinge of pain echoed through his back and legs, but at least it took the edge off of the apprehension he was feeling.

The stage door was just a short walk, twenty seconds to an able-bodied person, but it took them the best part of five minutes to reach it. Jonah was breathless by the time he got there, his forearms throbbing from supporting his weight, his forehead gleaming with sweat.

'Okay, Jonah, if you need any help Cindy is just at the other end of the stage. There's a jug of water waiting for you on the table.' Troy patted his arm, careful not to unbalance him, and left them to it.

Rose looked up at him with that same helpless expression, like she wanted to burst into tears with pity. 'I'll wait for you right here, okay?'

'Okay.' Jonah leaned down to receive a kiss on the cheek, her peach scent strangely calming. 'Say a prayer for me.'

'Already have.'

Jonah hobbled across the stage, his legs dragging like wet spaghetti. His struggle to the microphone was met with a few sniggers across different sections of the crowded auditorium, before the care workers and police officials in attendance offered harsh, threatening whispers to the offenders for their disrespect.

He looked at the audience, squinting behind the blinding spotlight shining in his face, surprised at the diversity of the bunch. In that one glance, he recognised the look in their faces; the same steely, street-hardened stares. Jonah took his time, making sure he was completely comfortable before starting. He sat down in the chair provided, the microphone lowered just right. Next to him was the overhead projector that he'd requested. He placed the first picture on the OHP, looking behind him on the screen to make sure it appeared in focus.

He twiddled with his crucifix again, took a sip of water and began.

'What you can see behind me is a Tec-9 sub-machine gun. By the look of some of you here tonight I know that you're more than familiar with this particular weapon. Last time I checked, you could pick one up for around two hundred pounds, with ammo if you've gone to a good enough dealer.' He let the picture sink in, watching their gleaming eyes.

'It's a good little gun,' Jonah continued, then removed the picture and replaced it with another one. Before he even turned to face the audience again, groans of disgust filled the room.

'What you're looking at now is a picture of what that sub-machine gun did to my back, when seven bullets ripped through it nine years ago.' He looked up at the screen and recoiled despite his familiarity with the image; oozing red welts blistered over what had once been smooth, slender flesh.

'As I heard some of you noticed, I don't walk so good any more.' His honesty was met with a few more impolite giggles, which he didn't much mind. They wouldn't be laughing when he was finished talking, of that much he was certain. He was beginning to relax now as he got into the rhythm of speaking, though the nape of his neck still burned like summer heat was concentrating on it. That swirling, empty nausea still floated around in his stomach.

'I know none of you are here by choice, so I'm not going to lecture you about the dangers of carrying a gun or the effect guns can have on your family. I'm sure people have talked your ears off with that one. Everyone in here knows that guns were designed to kill people, and the number of guns that are on the streets of London tonight is so staggering that it's not even worth getting ourselves paranoid about.

'I've been informed that you guys had to attend as part of your parole programmes, and that you're all involved in gang activity,' Troy, the manager and founder of the Help Save London campaign, called Jonah personally based on an interview that he did for a short gun-awareness documentary. Apparently, Troy was so touched by the programme that he believed Jonah would be 'invaluable' to these kids' lives. Maybe he was right.

'I was seventeen when it happened, younger than a lot of you in here. I never really took the thought of God seriously till that night – ' he heard an impatient deflation of air from an agitated listener, probably bored to death of the same old *How I Found God* speech, ' – don't worry, I'm not going to preach at you or try and force my religious beliefs on any of you. All I will say is this; those bullets made me aware of real evil. And, whether you want to believe me or not, there's evil in this very room with us tonight.'

'Yeah, the police!' an anonymous joker shouted, inspiring a round of applause. Even Jonah laughed. At that age, he didn't much like them either.

'You're absolutely right,' Jonah continued, addressing the comment. 'There are too many crooked police officers that abuse their power,' this time, *he* got a round of applause along with some angry glares from the officers that were maintaining security. 'But don't get me wrong. Without police, London would be a bigger zoo than it already is.' The cheers fell silent.

'But the evil I'm talking about is a different kind. It's the thing that puts the knife or the gun or the bat in your hand and makes you kill someone – and it's here sitting amongst us. It'll be on the street when you leave here tonight, and, it might even be in your own homes.'

There was a sense of confusion among the boys in the audience. While some sat slumped in their chair asleep, others with drooping eyelids, a small percentage of them were actually paying attention, as if the words *gun* and *knife* were some kind of anchorage. All Jonah had to do now was keep them interested long enough to tell them the whole story.

In the corner of his vision, Jonah saw Troy standing with his arms folded across his chest nervously, worried that all this talk of guns and evil might spark some kind of riot among the rival gangs in attendance. Rose stood behind Troy, watching intently.

'I don't have any religious agenda here tonight,' Jonah said, his voice lowering to just above a whisper. 'All I want to do is tell you a story of how that evil found me. It's up to you to listen or not.'

MONDAY

1

Jonah knew things were different the minute he stepped off the train and was greeted by a vaguely recognisable figure. Since moving to Nottingham the year before, a depression and homesickness had consumed him. He'd argued with his mother to stay but he really didn't have much of a case to present. For every Pro he thought of, she had five Cons. But the main factor that swayed in her favour was that they had family in Nottingham, so his mother decided to move him away from the estates and the crime, before the city swallowed him.

And that was that.

He'd enrolled in a course that he didn't care about, studying advertising in a predominantly Asian college. From the moment he walked in his first class he could feel the tension between the black and brown-skinned people on the campus. Stare-out competitions issued from groups of boys, along with a few sly comments just audible enough for him to hear, became a regular test as he queued in the canteen or waited for a bus.

During the third month of being there, Jonah became friendly with a girl in his computer literacy class called Nathalie, who was of Kenyan and Indian descent. Though she looked black, she was claimed by the Indian crowd due to her long hair and blue eyes. She seemed nice enough, always saying hello and asking him how he was, that kind of thing. She'd even helped him with his coursework during class because his computer at home was a relic from the Jurassic period, incapable of keeping up with his demanding studies.

Outside the lesson though, was a different story. During a morning break, Jonah set out to the tuck shop to grab a Kit-Kat and a strawberry milkshake, as such things were customary before facing a two or three-hour lesson, and passed Nathalie smoking with a group of her friends by the back entrance of the building. Naively, he made the mistake of saying 'hello' to her outside of class, a gesture which was met with deliberate silence. He felt like an arsehole, even more so when he heard one of the boys mutter *black cunt* behind a curtain of laughter.

The fury that surged through him was unbearable, but the embarrassment burned twice as hot. He wanted to grab whoever made the comment and just kick the shit out of him – punches, kicks, head-butts, whatever – but he knew the group would've swarmed all over him before he could raise a fist.

So, he began carrying a shank to college with him. From his observations of Nottingham, he'd noticed that the police harassment wasn't so bad as long as you didn't hang in a big crowd and weren't shouting your mouth off. The steak knife he kept concealed in his jogging bottoms pocket was small but reassuring. He'd never dared to carry one in London, not when you could get stopped and searched by a policeman – plain clothed or uniform – as regular as eating breakfast. Plus, in Nottingham, being a loner gave him all the incentive he needed to wield his knife, for show more than anything else. He had no intention of using it of course, but he figured that if he got into a spot of bother he could just pull it out, yell a bunch of convincing swear words, and they'd get the message: Don't fuck with me.

That little four-inch blade was all the bravery Jonah needed. With it, he could glare back at someone who was staring at him awkward, could puff his chest out in a heated confrontation with a guy who might have a fetish for working out. *Try it* he thought, imagining someone twice his size pushing up against him, *try it and I'll stab you in the fucking bicep and send you flying like a deflated balloon.*

Jonah hadn't even realised that he had the knife on him when he got to London. He'd gone to buy a croissant from the buffet car and felt the sharp edge of the blade as he reached in his jeans for some change. Paranoia immediately flushed through him. He knew from past experience that the police had a tendency to randomly stand posted at train platforms ready to pounce with sniffer dogs. They'd pat you down all over, grab a guy's balls to see if he was trying to hide a tool or drugs, and then scan you all over with the hand-held metal detectors. Last he'd heard, they were really cracking down on knife offences. Just getting caught with one was two years in the pen, previous history or not. Luckily, the blade fit into an empty crisp packet. He threw the knife in the bin by the train doors as he got off; he wouldn't need it now anyway, he was home.

Dwayne was on the platform waiting, just like he said he would be. He'd grown taller since Jonah saw him last, and was now sporting neatly trimmed facial hair and draped in an outfit so dapper that he looked as though he was in a boy band; black designer shirt, dark denim jeans and a pair of white Nikes that looked like they were on their maiden voyage – fresh out of the box that morning.

Lugging his bag behind him, Jonah shuffled up to Dwayne with a huge grin slapped across his face. They embraced briefly, both of them laughing for no apparent reason, before Jonah pulled away to appraise the chain that Dwayne was sporting around his neck.

'What the fuck is this?' Jonah said, tugging at the necklace with a broad smile.

'Platinum,' Dwayne told him, matter-of-factly.

'For real? You're lying. Is it really platinum?'

'Nah, it's white gold and diamond, but still, most people don't know the difference.'

Jonah punched him on the arm and they strolled toward the station exit, joking along the way. When they reached the road, Dwayne pulled a key out of his pocket and pressed the button. A shiny black BMW flashed its lights to signal that it was now unlocked, its bodywork gleaming in the sun.

BMW? They were seventeen years old.

'You're kidding me,' Jonah said in disbelief, marvelling at the pristine vehicle that looked as though it'd just rolled off the showroom floor, 'this can't be yours.'

'Course it is.' Dwayne smiled. 'I *acquired* it yesterday. You can drive if you want.'

Jonah succumbed to a fit of giggles, shaking his head. 'I don't know how to drive. I ain't even got my provisional licence yet.'

'Alright, just get in and enjoy the ride.'

Dwayne grabbed Jonah's bulging holdall full of clothes and tossed it in the boot. Jonah knew he should've been hesitant to get in the car, but he was lured by the fresh leather upholstery, that *new* smell seducing him to drown in the seat. It occurred to him later, when he was over the initial joy of being back home, that two seventeen-year-old boys sitting in a stolen vehicle worth over twenty thousand pounds without so much as a licence was about as inviting to a copper as beer to a darts player.

Dwayne drove like an experienced pro and the power steering made doing a three-point turn with one hand look like he was wiping a window.

'Boy-oh-boy this is a nice car. When did you learn to drive?' Jonah wondered, still stroking the seats and analysing the dashboard. The interior was how he imagined a spaceship to look like – full of dials and electronic read-outs. The stereo was playing some Barry White type song on a low volume.

'Me and Billy decided we was sick of getting the bus everywhere and one day we saw this clapped-up little Ford in the front of this guy's driveway for sale. He wanted a sixer for it but I got him down to a hundred and a big bag of weed. We just took it to a car park and messed around in it. It ain't that hard when you get used to it.' With one hand on the wheel, Dwayne leaned back like he was in a sun lounger, a chunky gold bracelet hanging heavily from his wrist. When he realised that a soppy love song was on, he changed the CD in the car with the flick of a button to a menacing rap anthem.

'Shit, forgot I had that CD in there. You'll have to forgive me, had a girl with me yesterday night.'

Leaning over, he opened the glove box with his other hand and showed Jonah a tangled pink thong sitting on a pile of CDs. Jonah giggled with a childish excitement and was immediately embarrassed. Dwayne was acting so grown-up and mature and there he was laughing at a pair of panties like he'd never seen a girl in his life before, so he made a mental note to try to keep his composure in the wake of these adult revelations.

As the car travelled along, Jonah became fixated by all the landmarks of the different neighbourhoods, all the little things that he'd forgotten about while he was away; there was the corner shop with the Cadbury's Milk headboard; the dirt-crusted plastic bubblegum machine outside the wedding-cake shop that never seemed to have any customers; the chipped red paint on the swings in the park of a passing estate. He looked at it all with fresh eyes, the conflicting happiness and sorrow he felt was dizzying, surreal.

They cruised past Kenny's Chicken and Chip shop, and just a glimpse of that cartoon cockerel in the window evoked the taste of the 99p deal which consisted of one piece of chicken, chips and a coke. It seemed like such a good offer when he was younger, even though it had a more explosive reaction than any over-the-counter laxative you could get at the chemist. Despite this, he suddenly had an urge to go in and ask dirty Ken for his addictively nauseating chicken, disregarding the dreaded hive of acne that would usually sprout afterwards or the projectile vomiting that would occur as a result.

He just wanted to go back and do all the old things they used to, like buy cheap beer and drink it in the park as the sun went down, play dominoes on the porch and holler things at girls as they walked by. Excitement tingled through his body and his lungs ached like he had too much breath in his body. It was a good feeling.

'Everybody's missed you, man,' Dwayne told him as they pulled up at a red light. The school kids hadn't broken up for summer holiday yet and wouldn't do for another fortnight, so the roads were virtually empty. 'I'm telling you, Jonah, I've got so much planned for us that you're not gonna wanna leave.'

'I didn't in the first place.'

'Well why don't you stay down here now? You're old enough,' Dwayne suggested as the light turned green.

'You know I wanna stay. You think I like it up there being in college with no mates? It's gonna be even worse now I know you guys are driving around in cars and shit like that, having fun without me.'

'We do have fun, but it ain't the same without you.' Then, the tone in Dwayne's voice seemed to lower with unexpected seriousness. 'But things have changed. It's like before, I couldn't even get a girl to give me a smile in the fuckin' street, right, but when they see me driving a brand-new car and wearing expensive shit, they get all interested. So now I know how they operate, I treat them even worse. Like this girl I had in here yesterday night. I made her blow me outside of her own house and right before I came, I pulled out and busted all over her fuckin' T-shirt. You know why?'

Jonah laughed nervously and shrugged, not quite sure how to answer.

'So that when she went inside and her Dad's all like "why were you out so late?" and he sees this great big come stain still sticking to her clothes, he beats the shit out of her for being such a nasty slut. And the best part is ... she's Muslim! Her dad probably chopped her head off.' Dwayne slapped the steering wheel and cackled wildly; the sound vibrated through Jonah like a heavy bass line.

'But don't worry about that, Jonie, I got some girls lined up for you. And I do mean lined up.'

Embarrassment pricked the skin of Jonah's cheeks. He avoided encouraging the conversation for fear of revealing that he was *still* a virgin. Unfortunately.

Before he knew it, they were at the Drakeford Road Estate, known as The Dracula Road Estate to the locals. It was made up of two large tower blocks facing each other with a small courtyard in between. Jonah and Dwayne lived in the green building, and Billy-Lee lived in the blue building.

When he saw the smog-soiled yellow paint, the satellite antennas spotted here and there like the many eyes of some hideous sea monster, a thousand snapshots fragmented in his mind like a shattered mirror. The familiar melange of grease and smoke filled the air, helping to animate the memories.

'Some Somali family moved into your old house,' Dwayne said as he slowed to a stop, looking up at the building. 'A whole bunch of kids cramped up in that little place. It's funny 'cos whenever they leave their house, I bet they wonder who D.T., B.L.P. and J.W. are when they see it written all over the roof outside their door. Remember?'

Dwayne Tamer, Billy-Lee Porter and Jonah White, autographed in magic marker. How could he forget?

'Seen enough?' Dwayne asked.

'What do you mean? Ain't we staying at yours?'

'Yeah, but I don't live here no more,' Dwayne told him with a smile, putting the car back into gear and continuing down the road. 'I told you, Jonah, everything's changed.'

'What, you guys moved house?'

'Nah, my mum still lives there but I got my own place. We don't really talk that much now.'

A while later and Dwayne parked up by the garages of a modern apartment complex. The architecture gleamed in the sun and was far more dynamic than the crumbling relics from Dracula that were built during the sixties. The picturesque courtyard flourished with multicoloured flowers and healthy inch-long grass that someone had taken meticulous care and pride in trimming to ensure that every blade was the same length. Each floor flaunted pristine, sparkling windows, with enough clarity to see the pores in your skin from twenty feet away. No graffiti ... No graffiti! Not one squiggle of permanent marker or a single bruise of spray paint. Jonah couldn't believe his eyes.

The humidity made Jonah feel grimy like he was saturated with all the train and car pollution of his travels. Man, did he need a shower; his balls felt like lychees in syrup.

'Ah shit, I forgot my bag in the boot,' Jonah remembered as they reached the massive foyer.

'Forget about it, we'll get it later.'

The cool air blowing through the building was just lovely, soothing Jonah's scorched flesh. Who was in charge of cleaning this place anyway? The guy deserved a knighthood for his services. It was so clean in the hallway that if he were eating a piece of Kenny's chicken and dropped it on the floor, well, he'd just pick that son of a bitch back up and carry on eating. Shit, he'd even lick the grease spot from where it landed. In Drakeford Road, he felt like he might catch an airborne STD just walking through the stairwell.

'Here we are,' Dwayne opened the door and they went in.

Jonah was amazed at how spacious the place was; it had two floors, and five people could live there comfortably. But his attention was abruptly snatched by the topless blonde woman walking out of the kitchen and into the living room.

His trousers pitched a tent immediately.

'This is Genie,' Dwayne said with a mischievous smile, pointing at the woman now sitting on the couch with a plate of toast on her lap. She was slim with small, fried egg breasts, with her hair tied back in a ponytail. She waved at Jonah nonchalantly with her mouth covered in crumbs, then carried on watching the TV. Jonah, with his dick hard enough to support a wonky table from seeing his first pair of tits in the flesh, tried to play it cool and nodded back to her. Dwayne tossed his keys and phone on the table by the door, patting Jonah with the back of his hand to get his attention.

'I'll show you where you sleep.' Jonah followed Dwayne down the crème-carpeted hall and into a large bedroom that looked like something out of a hotel brochure. There was a double bed made up with fresh sheets next to a large window with venetian blinds, a wide-screen TV fixed to the wall, and a wooden wardrobe in the corner.

Ignoring the room, Jonah shut the door behind him and whispered, 'Who is she?'

A grin stretched across Dwayne's face. 'I told you, that's Genie.'

'How old is she?'

'I don't know. Thirty or something.'

'She just had her boobies all hanging out and everything,' Jonah said excitedly, dropping his facade. 'Is this her place?'

'No it's mine. It's in her name but for all intents and purposes, this is my flat.'

'Why ain't she got no clothes on?' Jonah asked, still hung up on her intimidating promiscuity.

'Shit, I don't know. Why don't you ask her yourself? Anyway, fuck that, check this out.' He opened the wardrobe revealing a whole range of packaged clothes, T-shirts still with their tags on, folded jeans and boxes of trainers. 'I couldn't remember what size shoe you were so I just got a whole bunch.'

Jonah exhaled, flattered and amazed. He fell on the bed laughing, bouncing on the springy mattress.

'And if you want Genie to suck your dick just ask her. I wouldn't advise fuckin' her though.' Dwayne told him without a trace of humour, like he was telling Jonah about asking her for a sandwich.

Jonah sat up. 'Ain't that your girlfriend?'

'No!' Dwayne was almost disturbed by the question. 'That fuckin' coke-head? No way. Solomon gave her to me and said that as long as I fed her coke and shit like that I could do whatever I wanted with her. I only keep her in this house 'cos she tidies and irons and all that other shit.'

'Who's Solomon?' Jonah asked, flicking through the choice of shirts in the wardrobe.

'Ah, you need to meet this guy,' Dwayne said enthusiastically. 'I'm telling you, this guy Sol can get you anything you want. *Anything.* Straight up, that's how we got all this stuff. Like check this out – how much money do you have on you right now?'

Jonah reached for his back pocket and pulled out his wallet, fingered through the notes and counted ninety pounds plus a few bits of shrapnel in the coin compartment. 'Almost a hundred.'

'Here,' Dwayne pulled out his wallet from the front of his jeans and threw it on the bed. It bulged with money, the leather cracked and stretched from maintaining the wad. 'Count that.'

Jonah picked it up and removed the cash, feeling the difference in weight immediately. The notes, mostly fifties, amounted to four hundred and thirty pounds. No coins.

'You wanna be careful carrying that kind of money around with you,' Jonah warned, holding the folded notes in his right hand and absorbing the texture of the paper.

'I don't need to worry,' Dwayne told him. 'The money's yours. Take it.'

Immediately, Jonah put the money down for fear of growing too attached to it. Dwayne was obviously taking the piss and Jonah wasn't about to get suckered.

'I'm being serious, take it,' he urged.

'Stop bullshitting,' Jonah said with a laugh, turning the TV on with the remote by the side and idly surfing through the channels until he reached a music video he liked.

Dwayne shrugged, reached into his pocket and pulled out a rolled joint, then lit it up. 'I'm being deadly serious, that's your money. Pocket money compared to what we'll be making.' He blew a poignant green plume of smoke into the air and watched it dissipate, then passed the joint to Jonah. Inhaling hard and struggling to contain the choking fumes within his chest, Jonah coughed once, then released. His head floated away like a helium balloon. With that one pull, he felt his body begin to fall, like he was in the process of lying down too quickly.

'That money isn't anything, believe me. Do you work up in Nottingham?'

'Yeah,' Jonah replied, the word coming out slower than he intended. 'In a bakery.'

The smoke got caught in Dwayne's throat as he exhaled. He began coughing hard to regain his breath from the sudden unexpected burst of laughter. 'A bakery?' he asked, making sure that the weed wasn't affecting his hearing. 'A bakery? As in making cakes?'

'Yeah,' Jonah managed to say with a giggle, his hand extended for the joint. He took a longer drag this time, filling his taut lungs and making his heartbeat accelerate. The bed tilted like a see-saw. 'Only on Saturdays though. College four days a week, bakery on Saturday.'

Sitting down on the bed, Dwayne covered his face with his hands to muffle his laughter and leaned against the headboard. 'Jesus Christ ... A bakery? Do you like it?'

'Do I like what?'

'The bakery!' Dwayne yelled with a smile, amused by how dopey Jonah had become with his virgin lungs. 'Do you like working there?'

He shook his head. 'Hate it.'

'Then quit.'

'I can't do that,' Jonah told him, mesmerised by the way the pixels seemed to be blurring on the TV screen like a child's clumsy attempt at colouring in. 'I need the money.'

'Shit, if I knew you were working in a bakery I would've sent you some money every week. What about college? You like that too?'

Jonah shrugged, undecided, remembering the large portfolio that needed to be completed by the beginning of the new term, worth forty per cent of his overall grade. He had complete control over what he chose to base his project on, as long as it showed how different advertisements entice consumers to buy their product. He decided to go with the fast-food industry, thinking about all the subliminal flashes and tactical wording that they must use, and figured that as a fast-food consumer himself – partial to the occasional Big Mac or Variety Bucket – the work would be somewhat interesting.

On his course they taught him that adverts for all types of products ranging from kids' toys to women's clothing, had intricate methods of almost hypnotising the intended consumer. There was this one ad with a woman in a red bathing suit talking about how much weight she'd lost from eating a particular cereal, which just so happened to have big red writing on the box. So when a woman watched it, with her nagging insecurities about her mummy tummy or how much weight she'd gained over Christmas and saw something red afterwards, her mind would be triggered back to the thin model in the red bathing suit and how good she looked. Jonah appreciated the psychology of that kind of thing, how people could be brainwashed into buying something without even knowing they'd been affected. So when Jonah gave his proposal to his teacher, Michael Ravens *(but you guys can just call me Mike)*, he was welcomed with an enthusiastic pep talk designed to encourage him.

'Yo Jonah, I think that's a really cool idea,' Mike, a mid-thirties suburban white male whose only real experience with black people had been MTV and the occasional 'hello' he gave to Grace the post lady, still thought it was acceptable to use the word *cool.* Fair enough, he was trying to talk to the kids on a level they understood, but addressing him with *Yo* was such a parody that it was almost offensive, not to mention the inadvertent racism ('hello' for whites, 'yo' for blacks? Fuck that). But Jonah thought nothing of it. He could see that Mike was at least trying to show some interest in the future of the anti-social, unhopeful bunch that slouched over their computers every day and would probably never amount to shit. Mike, who wore trendy trainers with corduroy trousers and colourful t-shirts that always had different witty slogans or sometimes just plain weird shit written on them like 'Nobody Knows I'm a Lesbian' or a silhouette of a beer glass with 'I don't drink water, the fish piss in it' slapped across it.

'They use that subliminal stuff all the time. No word of lie, my man. Mac Dee's are crazy on that stuff, probably why those Americans weigh more than their sofas, am I right, Jonah?' he'd said with a nudge and a wink. Then he got all excited and carried away, showing Jonah a website that revealed some of the famous subliminal adverts from all the big corporate companies like Coca Cola and Pizza Hut, with tiny blurs that popped up so fast on screen you didn't even know they were there until you slowed the frame rate down and saw that those quick blurs were actually the company's logo being imbedded into the back of your mind. *'You gotta watch out for that kind of stuff, my man – they still do it today, even though they ain't supposed to. Anything that's there and below the threshold of awareness is subliminal. It's evil shit, man.'*

It was that same notion of deception that intrigued Jonah, the audacity of being compelled into craving a burger, or a box of fried chicken or a can of drink that made him want to uncover the secrets of how it was done. According to Mike Ravens, the more familiar with the techniques of subliminal advertising you became, whether it was the way the text appeared on screen or some other super-quick hocus-pocus, the more you started to notice it being used, and not just in advertisement, but in the newspapers and magazines, too.

'Mind manipulation, man. Scary stuff.'

But after the morning he'd spent back in London, the thought of having to do any kind of college work depressed him. As for the bakery ... Jonah quickly reached for the herbal remedy.

'Anyway, forget about studying now, you're on holiday,' Dwayne told him. 'Come with me a second.' Jonah went to get up and follow him out the room but his unresponsive legs wouldn't obey him on the first attempt. He felt like a baby giraffe as he wobbled to his feet, blinking hard to clear his vision. Dwayne disappeared into one of the other rooms leaving him to feel his way through the hallway, using the walls as leverage. He swayed to the front room where Genie was still topless and still watching TV.

'You seen Dwayne?' he asked her, his earlier shyness lost in a haze of marijuana. She pointed to a room behind her, looking somehow older than she first appeared to him and a lot less attractive than his initial hard-on led him to believe. The enormity of the TV in the front room left him momentarily stunned as he stared at the titanic screen, able to see the hairs on the chat show host's arms.

Dwayne reappeared carrying a drawer that he'd pulled out from a dressing table.

'What the hell you got in here, a cinema or something?' Jonah said, his eyes hurting from the sheer detail and vibrancy of the television.

'Big, ain't it?' Dwayne snorted, holding out the drawer. 'Here take whatever you want.'

It looked like a treasure chest filled with different kinds of jewellery; golden orbs danced around the room as the sun shone off the contents. It took Jonah a few seconds to focus. The diamonds twinkled like a kaleidoscope. Mesmerised, Jonah reached out and sifted through it to make sure it was real.

'Shit boy,' the disbelief written across his gawping face. 'You got a cinema and Aladdin's cave in this flat!'

They both broke up with an uncontrollable fit of giggles, though Jonah's laughter arose from sheer excitement. He was high, had a new wardrobe of clothes, enough cash to papier mâiché Big Ben, a naked woman at his disposal and his pick of the bling.

And it wasn't even lunch time.

2

Billy-Lee was a lunatic. Of course, to his childhood chums it was a simple quirk they'd learned to overlook because, crazy or not, Billy-Lee had the ability to have you pissing yourself on the floor with laughter and not even mean to do it. Whether or not he should be sectioned, though, was simply a matter of opinion.

While playing a game of tag when they were eleven, Billy jumped off the third-floor balcony of his flats to escape getting caught, and broke both his ankles trying to land on the car below. He missed the Ford by a clear metre and crumpled on the concrete. Neither Jonah nor Dwayne could believe their eyes when Billy flew off that balcony with his arms spread out like he was skydiving. To them, it looked as though Billy thought he was actually going to glide down to the floor and evade his pursuer, and as they later debated, maybe he genuinely thought he'd be able to fly away.

In any case, he was wrong.

It was easy to just say that Billy was another wrong 'un or that he was just another backward estate kid too stupid to know the difference between flying and falling. But the formula to fucking him up completely was a general concoction of drug abuse, violence, and cheap booze.

His mum Debbie, a bleach-blonde with black roots (which was funny because although her hair was naturally dark as was his father's, Billy's hair was bright ginger), began the day with a can of beer and cigarettes, glue for lunch, and usually had the shit beaten out of her for dinner. Yum Yum. His dad, Teddy, who was known as Teddy Strange in the eighties because he looked like something out of the Neanderthal era, all wild hair and stubble, was a thief, a fiend, and a genuinely mean bastard.

Billy was nine when he watched Teddy Strange batter his mum around the face and back with an iron, leaving her looking like the Elephant Man with black welts the size of tennis balls all over her head. Teddy was later found sleeping in a public toilet with a heroin needle in his foot, and arrested. Billy hadn't seen his dad since.

Debbie, not unfamiliar with hands-on discipline, used to hit Billy with just about everything in the room when he played up; if she could lift the couch up and swing that at him she would have, until Billy grew to almost six foot by the age of fourteen, and ended all the beatings one afternoon when he returned from playing football in the park.

She'd had a go at him about something to do with slamming the door too hard when he came in, though with her drunken ramblings it was often hard to decipher exactly what was said. She charged at him, her hands at his neck ready to dig her nails in his skin like she always did, when one swift punch to the nose stopped her in her tracks. Red mist exploded between them.

'Don't fucking touch me, you cunt,' was all he said after the fist connected, then he casually side-stepped her as she cradled her bloody face, and went to his room. After Teddy's savage beating a few years before, she'd often black out when she was on the bottle. She woke up the next morning hung over with a broken nose, assuming that she'd just stumbled over something and cracked her face open.

In the dusty pool hall, Billy stood with his cue waiting to take his shot wearing a white England T-shirt with St George's cross splashed across the middle, a pair of red shorts, and a red woolly hat pulled down over his eyebrows despite the heat. He had a thing for the colour red ever since any of them could remember. When they all bought Ice-Poles, Billy had to have the red flavour. He always wore red trainers, always with red laces, and God only knew how much trouble he had to go through to find red trainers every time he needed a new pair.

As he bent over the table, Jonah noticed a beige-pink scar running from the corner of Billy's mouth to his ear, hideously clear under the pool-table lights. He took his shot, concentration cementing his features into a stone mug, and managed to sink the six-ball in the side-pocket.

'Hey, Bill,' Jonah called to him after he'd taken his shot, the weed making him focus on Billy harder than usual and stare at his scar. 'What happened to your face?'

Billy looked up and smiled, his pale blue eyes piercing through the fog of green smoke. He took another shot and sank another ball, the clash ringing through the place and cutting across the low hum of the radio. 'Got sliced up in a fight.'

As the smoke drifted, the scar became even more prominent. It was an ugly, savage thing that tainted his face like a twisted half-grin. In the dull gloom of the pool hall, Jonah hadn't spotted it immediately, but now that it was in plain view he couldn't divert his attention from it. Billy explained that he'd been wrecked at the Dog and Sparrow (by himself), calmly sailing through his eighth or tenth pint of Stella, when another guy fell onto the edge of his table and flipped it over. It wasn't Billy's table so he didn't give a shit. It was only when this other drunk dude, a tall, skinny Albanian-looking guy who'd stumbled and made a heap of mess with all the glasses and bottles, got up and grabbed Billy by the head, probably for stability, that the action kicked off. The second the Albanian's fingers made contact with his face, Billy – who was funny about being touched in the first place – reared his head back and slammed it in the Albanian fella's nose and he collapsed by Billy's side unconscious. Well, by the time the pub staff got the guy to his feet, his nose like a smashed tomato in his blood-splattered face, he'd already regained enough smarts to reach for the Stanley blade in his pocket and snag it on the inside of Billy's mouth like a fishhook, tearing his cheek wide open. As the melee was broken up and the paramedics attended to the both of them, Billy caught a glimpse of his mutilated face in the ambulance door window; you could see his teeth while his mouth was closed, the flayed skin flapping comically.

'Jesus Christ, he fucked your face right up,' Jonah said, revolted yet compelled by the disfiguration.

'Yeah I know!' Billy began to laugh, his head bobbing up and down like he was nodding enthusiastically. It creeped Jonah out because Billy rarely laughed at anything. Usually, it took something bad to happen to crack him up, like when he jumped off the balcony and broke his ankles, for example. As soon as his feet made contact with the concrete, producing a sickening crunch with much the same intensity as the pool balls knocking together on the table, he began howling in pain and laughter. Another time, when Billy and Jonah were on their way back from the park, a bunch of little Turkish kids were playing football in the street when a moped zoomed down the road and hit one of the littler boys, practically doing a wheelie over his face. Everyone else raced over to help the kid who was screaming with a black tyre mark running from his forehead, but Billy just fell on the floor, cackling spastically.

Dwayne returned from the bar with a tray full of condensed beers and placed it on the table next to where they were playing. He glanced at the table, noticing the array of striped balls still scattered across the felt. 'Shit, Jonah, you're getting cleaned-up!'

Slamming the eight-ball away, Billy threw the cue on the table. 'Finished.'

'You want a real game now, Bill? I'll show you how to wipe this table up.' Dwayne drained a whole beer in one go. 'Now watch closely, Jonah, you might learn something.'

'Yeah right,' Jonah mumbled, seeking refuge in the neck of the bottle. He took a sip then rubbed the bottle over his forehead, his grasp on the beer seeming too loose, like the weed had turned his hands into clay dough. He quickly put it down before he dropped it.

'Don't they have pool halls up there or something?' Dwayne teased. Billy racked the balls up, potting three on the break.

'Yeah they do, but what am I supposed to do, go down there and play by myself like some kind of arsehole?'

On the table, Billy put the balls away in rhythmic succession, whitewashing Dwayne in one sitting. Pissed off and embarrassed, Dwayne quickly groped around in his jeans pocket and pulled out a bundle of notes and tossed them on the table. There was easily three hundred pounds.

'Play me again, this time I break. Play me for money if you think you're that good.' There he was again – Mr Competitive. Jonah had forgotten all about him.

Billy scrounged around in his shorts, which on closer inspection were suspiciously high-cut; what Dwayne would often call 'bollock scratchers'. He pulled out a bunch of scrunched-up notes, along with a lolly-pop and a miniature car figurine. 'I don't know how much is there.'

Dwayne didn't bother to check. They re-racked the balls and played again.

'All that money you got in your pocket there, Bill, you could've bought yourself a new pair of shorts,' Jonah said giggling.

'Yeah, a pair that fits you so I don't have to see your cock every time you go to tie your shoes up,' Dwayne chimed in, joining Jonah's laughter.

Either he was purposely ignoring their jibes or he was in his own world. Billy limped to the table and snatched up a beer, chugging from it like a baby on its mother's tit.

'Careful, Bill!' Jonah shouted covering his eyes. 'You're gonna blind me with your legs!'

A fountain of beer sprayed from Dwayne's mouth and stained the felt on the table, soaking the money as he burst into hysterics. 'Look at the state of you, Bill, all you wear is shorts and T-shirts and you still look like Casper the Ghost! You would've thought you'd have caught the sun by now in this heat.' He strolled around the table to the beer tray, knocking the dead soldiers away until he found a full bottle and slurped it down. The rickety old fan in the corner of the hall did little to diffuse the itchy warmth that clung to their skin.

Zoning in and out, being part of the conversation and then staring into the smoky darkness of the hall, Jonah realised that he was now very high and very drunk, and it felt very good. His chair seemed to sway from under him like the legs were marching on the spot, and he bent down to check them constantly. The sun poked in through holes in the blacked-out windows and sparkled across the room, fairy-like dust motes fluttering in the rays. He stood up and almost toppled, the edge of the pool table in front of him offering nice solid support. His fingers felt rubbery and numb as he shimmied along the table and began his journey toward the sunshine. The first unassisted step was like walking in one of those madhouse rooms at a funfair that tilted against your weight, or like in those old films set on a cruise ship sailing on rough seas, where the screen tips and all the tables and chairs slide with the motion. After almost falling over, he realised that he had to use his arms like a counter-balance to his disobedient legs if he wanted to reach the gold. One step, two steps, he was beginning to get the hang of it, but it was like his legs were polystyrene blocks treading on sponge. As he neared the window, which seemed to take far too long considering the distance, he put his hand through the magical translucent glow, trying to catch the little fairies in his palm. As he basked in the marvels of the tiny flecks of dust floating around in all their yellow glory, a beer bottle struck him on the foot.

'Havin' fun there?' Dwayne asked, smiling from what seemed like miles away. Jonah nodded at him and made his way back to the table. When he finally got there, Dwayne patted him on his back and sent him tumbling forward, but Billy caught him before he fell.

'Feel good?'

'I feel fucked.'

They all laughed.

3

Pool seemed too exhausting after a couple of games, and a grimy coat of sweat and dirt covered their skin. Before they left the hall, Dwayne put a pound that he had left over from the beers he bought into the pulsing slot machine. The machine was far too bright for Jonah, like the light was radioactive. He held on to a nearby change dispenser and worked on his breathing, blinking profusely, trying to steady his balance. The clunking noise of coins raining out of the slot machine distracted his meditation, an annoying alarm whooping to signal a big payout. Jonah turned wearily, shielding his eyes with his hand. Dwayne was crouched down by the mouth of the machine collecting his winnings, the kaleidoscope of colours giving him a brilliant aura.

Thirty seconds later and coins were still dropping out of the damn thing like hailstones. He couldn't be sure, not in his state, but Jonah guessed that Dwayne had won over a hundred pounds in one pound coins.

'How the hell am I going to carry all of this shit?' he complained, trying to keep the coins from spilling onto the floor. He grabbed a metal tray from a nearby table, the same kind he'd carried his beers on, and poured the majority of the coins onto it. Billy scooped the rest up and used his t-shirt as a net, and the two of them waddled over to the counter to get it changed up.

A young, washed-out-looking Polish girl sauntered over to serve them behind the counter, her face a picture of bored irritation.

'Get this changed up,' Dwayne ordered. She silently obeyed, counting the coins out two at a time.

'One hundred and sixty-five pounds,' she said with a hint of amazement in her voice but not on her face. She spilled the money into a small sack and heaved it to the till. 'I only have thirty pounds here in notes,' she told Dwayne in a dull, yawning tone.

'Why have you only got thirty pounds in your till?' he asked her, annoyed.

She shrugged. 'It's not busy on Monday afternoon. Everybody is down the park maybe.'

'So what the fuck am I supposed to do with the rest of the money? Carry it in a wheelbarrow?' Jonah laughed nervously, shocked by Dwayne's sudden ferocity. He began to feel sorry for the girl as she scrambled to separate the money, counting out thirty pound coins and giving him the notes leaving the remaining money in a small sack.

They left through the graffiti-splashed hallway and re-emerged into the smog-heavy street greeted by a busy high road of pram-pushing young girls and groups of horny boys with Super-Soakers. Dwayne swung the heavy money bag as they walked, sidling through the human traffic. 'Hey, you lot,' he called to the other two, 'quick detour.'

He cut through an alley way around the back of the high street and led them up a flight of metal steps leading to the roof of a butcher's. The stench of rotting flesh being baked grabbed them like a clawing corpse, and they covered their noses with their shirts to keep from being overpowered by the odious odour.

'Jesus Christ, it stinks,' Jonah complained while spitting a thick wad of saliva onto the tarmac of the roof, which was so hot it seemed to stick to the soles of his trainers. 'What we doing up here?'

They walked to the edge of the roof and looked down at the street three storeys below. In the sun, the girls seemed prettier to Jonah, like they'd just come out of hibernation. Either that or he was just pleased that they wore less than usual. As he spied on the ladies a strange vertigo suddenly overcame him. He reeled back from the edge, frightful that the alcohol might make him topple over.

'Check this out,' Dwayne said, holding the bag of money up. 'Oi!' He shouted down at the packed pavement. 'Money!'

Dwayne emptied the bag of coins out onto the street below, pelting the girls and boys and babies. At first, everyone began to run for cover, staring up at the roof and swearing, that is, until they realised it was literally raining money. Within twenty seconds the pavement was swarming with people climbing over each other to pick the coins up, like a flock of pigeons around scattered breadcrumbs. They were running from the other side of the road, in front of cars, risking getting hit by mere inches for a few measly pounds. A heavy, sweaty, dark-haired woman was casually strolling with her little son, but was down on all fours scouring the concrete like it was coated in chocolate when she saw the coins. Near her, a tall, flimsy man was knocked down awkwardly, cracking his head on the floor, and although a puddle of sticky blood was slowly oozing out of the wound a teenage boy still trod on the side of his face as he clambered over to join the scavengers. Car horns went berserk and the traffic came to a standstill as two vehicles collided in the pandemonium. The drivers got out of their respective cars and marched toward each other, ready to duke it out.

Sirens soon cut through the thick air, though even the annoying pitch of the approaching law wasn't enough to deter the frenzy.

'Look at them,' Dwayne said, shaking his head. Billy's eyes became transfixed on the expanding puddle of blood, *red* blood, his mouth a horseshoe of happiness. Some of the people looked up at Dwayne and smiled and cheered like he was a celebrity.

'Sounds like the pigs are coming,' Jonah said groggily. An etching fear of getting harassed and chased by racist policemen settled in his mind. He was in no fit state to run. His lungs felt like the next cough would make them explode, and just walking scared him with a nauseating dizziness. The two beers he'd killed back in the pool hall had gone right through him, and now his bladder was pressing against the wall of his stomach, the tip of his dick aching for want of relief.

Manoeuvring down the spiral metal stairwell as carefully as he could, Jonah leaned one arm against the wall for support while he urinated. The pee gushed out of him like a fire hose, spraying the wall and running down between his legs and splashing his thighs. What was it about trying to piss whilst drunk that just made it a complete and utter shambles? It was an eternal battle between him and his prick whenever alcohol was involved.

The sirens were now loud enough to suggest that the cops had pulled up and were trying to divide the crowd, and now the ludicrous weed-induced paranoia set inside Jonah's head: *What if they give me a piss test? What if they chase us and I get caught, and the policemen are racist and they just beat the shit out of me and dump me somewhere all fucked up and bleeding? What if my heart stops when I run? It sure is beating fast at the moment.*

Inhaling deeply, he shook his cock dry. Dwayne and Billy trotted down the stairs, still laughing at the carnage they'd caused.

'You okay, Jonah? You look paler than Billy.'

Jonah nodded and attempted a weak smile, still wary of getting sprung by the patrolling feds. Past experience warned him that no policeman was colour blind, and that if you were black and near the scene of the crime, you were guilty. They weren't all like this of course, he knew that much. But it was like trying to tell someone with a phobia of dogs that not all canines are vicious; yeah, you believe it, but they still got teeth and can still bite you in the arse. *Just keep them away from me and I'm cool,* he thought.

A few months before he moved away, the three of them had been stop-and-searched by Lofty, the angriest white copper on the streets of London, who looked like he fought crime during the day then went home and kicked the shit out of his wife by night. The stop-and-search was routine stuff in London, and by the age of sixteen they were more than used to the inconvenience of being made to empty their pockets and go through the details of where they'd just been and where they were now heading.

But this time was different.

It was on one of those late afternoons when it felt hot enough to send Lucifer himself in search of shade. They were coming back from a water fight in Haidon Park, which was nicknamed Hades Park because of all the stabbings and gunshots that were let off. Apparently, as legend goes, the decade before they were all born some kid was shot and paralysed while he was playing football by a guy who'd climbed a nearby tree with a hunting rifle. The kid was shot in the arse but the bullet ricocheted and fragmented into his spine, crippling him for life. The rumour was that this young boy was so depressed from sitting around all day in his wheelchair and watching all the other kids play football that he hung himself from the climbing frame by the big banana slide. Like most urban myths the story was hyperbole based on facts. Yes, Fredric Sanderson was paralysed from being shot by a rifle. Yes, Jimmy Mortimer, the twenty-six-year-old paranoid schizophrenic who was wrongfully released due to lack of government funding and insufficient space for other higher risk patients at St Helen's Mental Institute, went crazy with a hunting rifle and was convinced that shape- shifting panthers were trying to kill him. But did Little Freddy really hang himself in the park when he'd gone from being a sporty little whippersnapper to a fat, bitter teen confined to a chair for the rest of his life? Probably not. Whatever the truth was, the unsavoury reputation stuck.

Jonah, Billy and Dwayne were drying off under the orange sky. It'd been mostly teenagers from the area at the park, armed with Super-Soakers, water balloons, empty Coke bottles, buckets, and sponges that they replenished in the community drinking fountain (that no member of the community would dare drink from with all the spiteful bastards that pissed and did God knows what else in there). Most of the girls wore white t-shirts which was good news for the boys that wet them because it meant a cheeky glance at their nipples as their developing breasts were accentuated by the water. A bit of playful groping, which would usually be frowned upon depending on which of the girls you tried it with, was permitted on this one occasion as part of the fun.

The sun was setting and their stomachs were rumbling. It was at about this time when they would briefly disband, get some food at home, and meet up in an hour or so to see what the night had to offer. Their smiles faded when they saw Officer Lofty coming towards them, hands on his belt like some kind of podgy Sheriff.

Now, they knew what to expect from your usual routine stop-and-search, but with Lofty the rule book went out the window. Lofty always patrolled the park alone, and they thought this was so he could hit them and hurl as much racial abuse at whoever he searched without the hindrance of having to act professional in front of a colleague. The thing that was most menacing about him though, was his plain unlucky ugliness, which wasn't helped by his beer belly and boozy red face.

Lofty saw the three of them and leaned against the railings of the park, waiting for them to cross his path. The three of them knew that he planned to stop them but carried on walking anyway, because to do anything else might suggest a guilty conscious, which would be more than enough reason for Lofty to give them a slap.

'Where the fuck are you little pricks going?' Lofty said as they walked by in silence.

'Home,' Dwayne said, trying to maintain composure.

'You lot been to the park yeah? Throwing all that water around?'

They remained silent – Jonah and Dwayne out of fear of answering the rhetoric and catching a slap in the jaw, and Billy out of heat exhaustion and sheer boredom; he couldn't be bothered with all this twenty-questions bullshit that Lofty always pulled because they still ended up wrestling with him. It was better, as Billy saw it, to stay silent and save his energy for a tussle.

'Why're you throwing water around in the park, making all that noise? Making a nuisance of yourselves? Don't you know that there's kids in Africa who ain't got any water to drink, and you lot are throwing it all over the fuckin' grass?' Lofty said, unpredictably calm. 'Come on, up against the fence. Shoes off, socks off.'

The three of them faced the fence, taking their footwear off, praying that nobody they knew would walk by and witness the inevitable humiliation that was to ensue. Jonah, being first in line, was unable to control his quivering legs. He could feel Lofty breathing on his neck as he spoke to them, raising the hairs like static.

'You lot throwing water around with your brothers and sisters in Africa dying with flies all over their faces.' Lofty's insincerity was sinister. Jonah felt nauseous, and he became fearful that he'd throw up all over the pavement and be made to lick it up. 'You just waste all that water. All your lot do is waste and make noise.'

Lofty slowly ran his hands up underneath Jonah's T-shirt and over his bare skin, slowly tracing his nipples with his fingertips. A soft grunt trickled from Lofty's mouth as he pressed his erection against Jonah's back. Tears began to well up in Jonah's eyes, but he tried his best to refrain from crying. Instead of dwelling on the thing prodding him from behind, Jonah tried to distract himself by looking around. He was hoping that someone would get shot in the park so that another patrol car would swing by and make Lofty stop. He didn't care who got shot, just as long as Lofty stopped.

'Any weapons on you, coon?' Lofty whispered, his bitter breath tickling the back of Jonah's neck. Jonah shook his head. Lofty slapped him in the ear and said, 'I asked you a question, you little shit.'

'Nah, man,' Jonah managed, his voice cracked and wavering. Tears were rolling down his cheeks now as he struggled to keep his breathing steady.

'Nah, man,' Lofty repeated in his best Jamaican accent. 'Nah man, me want go home and eat me rice and pea.' Lofty ran his hands up the inside of Jonah's leg, stroking his thighs and finally squeezing his cock. Now, Jonah began to sob. 'Go on. Put your fucking shoes back on.'

Jonah quickly moved away from the fence and wiped his eyes with his t-shirt, embarrassed to be crying in front of his friends. His skin crawled from where he'd been touched, his belly curdling like he'd drunk a pint of old milk. As he put his trainers back on and moved away from Lofty, Jonah suddenly realised something awful; nobody was in the streets and it had turned dark. The trembling progressed through his body and evolved into cataclysmic shockwaves.

Lofty came to Billy and slapped him around the head. Billy stiffened up, staring straight into his eyes.

'You trying to eyeball me, boy?'

'Don't hit me again,' Billy warned; his voice void of intimidation. As Billy and Lofty squared off, Dwayne held his breath.

'What did you say?' Lofty cocked his head to the side in disbelief. 'What the fuck did you just say, you little shitkicker?' Lofty put his hand over a compartment on his belt and gripped something tightly.

'I said don't you hit me again. We ain't done fuck-all wrong, so don't bother trying to hit me or feel my dick up 'cos I'm not on that gay shit – '

'– Billy!' Dwayne yelled out, trying to interject and stop his runaway mouth before it got him killed. Lofty looked at Billy wide-eyed with his mouth gaping, as though Billy had just performed the most amazing magic trick he'd ever seen.

'I ain't afraid of you,' Billy continued. He was going into cowboy mode and once he got there, nothing could stop him. His complexion began to redden, and his tongue poked through his clenched teeth like he was trying to blow a bubble with it. 'If you didn't have all them weapons I'd fuck you up right now.'

Lofty stomped down on Billy's bare foot, sending him sprawling on the pavement in agony. The revolting, crunch of Billy's foot shattering bounced off the houses on the opposite side of the street. Billy screamed with pain, spitting out every swear word he knew in an angry jumble.

Dwayne and Jonah's eyes met, their worried expressions mirroring one another; *this is bad. This is so fucking bad.* Later, it occurred to Jonah that they should've made a run for it earlier, as Lofty never did name-checks, but instead, preferred to just grope them up and smack them around a bit and at that age they were naive enough to still believe that the police had that kind of authority. But there was no way that they were going to run off and leave Lofty alone with Billy. If one of them got molested and stomped on, then they all did.

Struggling on all-fours like a grizzly in a bear-trap, Billy looked up at Lofty and burst out laughing.

'You fucking pussy cunt! Fuck your mum, you fucking piece of shit!' Spit flew out of his mouth, foam bubbling and coating around his curled lips.

Then, something incredible happened. Lofty took one step backward from Billy like he'd stumbled across a rabid dog. Jonah saw it and so did Dwayne; Lofty was frightened. The expression may have only lasted for a couple of seconds, but in those seconds that aura of menace was shattered completely. Billy had backed him down. The result for Billy, of course, was half a can of C.S gas in his face that swelled his eyes closed for three days and left him looking like the loser of a bare-knuckle fight.

But all of them knew it was worth it. Jonah had been sexually assaulted and Billy couldn't walk or see so good for a while, but it was worth it.

Fat Lofty was afraid.

He finally left them alone, muttering something about having wasted too much time on niggers and little white kids who want to be black. Billy's face swelled up real bad and although he could only hobble on his injured foot, it wasn't badly broken. After that, none of them were stopped by Lofty again. Dwayne and Jonah had just hoped to high heaven that he didn't catch them alone.

'See all that blood?' Billy asked Jonah excitedly, tapping him on the arm and bringing him out of the daydream. 'Jesus Christ, that guy was pouring his brains out all over the street. Did you see that, Jonah?'

'Yeah Bill,' Jonah said. 'I saw it.'

4

At four o'clock, Dwayne told them to get changed as he was taking them to a barbeque. Jonah showered and as the water washed over him he began to regain some of his senses. He could breathe better now, and having urinated about a paddling pool's worth of beer out of his system, the wobbliness was beginning to reorganise itself.

He smiled as he dried off, leafing through the clothes in his wardrobe for a suitable outfit to wear. He found a yellow t-shirt with a Japanese anime drawing of a woman with purple hair splashed across it, and slipped it on; nice and summery, he thought. The jeans were all pretty much the same – baggy denims with differing designer logos on the back pocket. Indiscriminately, he put a pair on, and looked at the transformation in the full-length mirror on the wardrobe door. Having had his hair neatly shaped before he left Nottingham, and now wearing a bunch of fresh and expensive clothes that he hadn't forked out a penny for, he was feeling good. A virgin pair of white Air Force One's from the many Nike boxes served as the finishing touch to his ensemble.

'Nice,' he commented to the reflection, bouncing on the spot in the comfy trainers. Down the hall in the front room, he could hear Billy and Dwayne playing on the computer, the loud gunshots from the video game thundering through the house. Jonah rushed out to join them, passing the kitchen where Genie was bent over the side counter snorting coke. Shock stopped him in his tracks as he watched her sniffing up the powder greedily and rubbing her nose furiously each time she came up for air. She saw him looking at her and wiped her nose again.

'Alright?' she asked, beaming a painfully stretched grin.

'Yeah,' he nodded and carried on, the discomfort from watching her face-down in the powder like a pig in a trough making him cringe. Shamelessly, she bent over and continued snorting up big white clumps, exhaling with ecstasy after each line.

In the lavish living room, Dwayne had changed into a pair of white jeans and a plain white t-shirt, with his chain still draped around his neck as he concentrated on the video game. Billy sat next to him on the leather sofa, still in his short-shorts and scuffed England shirt. On the coffee table next to them, sat a crystal decanter filled with rum among a messy pile of scattered banknotes. A few stray notes lay on the carpet, swept from the table amid the excitement of the game.

The television screen was split down the middle as Billy and Dwayne played; two androids were running through a city street at night, shooting at each other with assault rifles. The gunfire boomed all around the room like they were having a real shoot-out in the house.

'What game is this?' Jonah asked, shouting above the racket, each gunshot and explosion making him jump.

'Tech Marines,' Dwayne yelled back without taking his eyes off the screen for fear of giving Billy leverage. Jonah fell into the armchair and watched as the mayhem unfolded on the screen. Billy, playing as some kind of all-black, featureless, super-robot, was flying in the air and firing two hefty cannons down at Dwayne, who was this little schoolgirl with half her face revealing a metallic skull.

'This shit looks insane.'

'Yeah, it is,' Dwayne replied as his schoolgirl got her arms and legs blown off by some kind of shrapnel grenade that Billy had thrown. Blood poured down Dwayne's half of the screen and a dead-pan, monotone robot voice echoed "You have expired" over and over again.

Dwayne threw the controller onto the floor in a huff. Billy grinned, leaned over and scooped up his winnings next to the decanter, stuffing them untidily into his pocket.

'Wanna play again?' Billy asked him while pouring a selfish volume of rum in his glass.

'Fuck this game,' Dwayne said bitterly. He poured out two big glasses of rum and handed one to Jonah. The sharp fragrance of the alcohol lingered among the faint weed aroma the minute the lid was removed from the decanter. Jonah had just straightened out, and although he wasn't much of a drinker, he gulped from the rum in a hurry to get drunk again; everything was so much more fun when he was drunk.

Billy and Dwayne sipped it casually, savouring it. Billy's eyes were glassy and red as he stared at the ceiling. He was away in his own hazy world, his mind drifting into orbit.

'So whose barbeque is this we're going to?' Billy asked. 'Is it far?'

'Some girl's twentieth birthday. It's in Haddonberry.'

'Haddonberry?' Jonah repeated, not expecting it to be that far away. In the background, Genie coughed and began sneezing continuously. Jonah turned around and faced the direction of the kitchen anxiously, thinking *surely her nose is gonna explode the way she's snorting up that Coke.* 'Is she okay?'

'Cokehead,' Dwayne mumbled absently. 'For that powder she'd suck a complete stranger's dick if I told her to. Can you believe that? A grown woman like her, sucking a guy's dick just because I told her to? She's like a zombie.'

A wave of guilt began to wash over Jonah as the alcohol took effect, mellowing him and heightening his emotions.

For a split second, he missed his mum. 'Is it really that bad? How did she get hooked?'

'I don't know, man.' Dwayne swirled the rum around in the glass and looked into it like he was trying to see a vision in a crystal ball. The sunlight caught the decanter and created a fragmented rainbow on the walls. 'I just told Sol that I was sick of living at home and he hooked this place up for me. Genie was living here and had a good job in the city.'

'Doing what?'

'She was a stockbroker, and you know how all of them stock people do a bit of blow here and there 'cos it's such a high-pressure job? Well, she was just the same, doing a line here and there to keep up. Sol introduced me to her and gave me this big pack of coke. The shit was big enough to build a snowman. Sol just said, "Use this like a magic lamp. Sprinkle some out and make a wish." Eventually, she just did more and more blow and stopped goin' to work completely, but it's cool 'cos the mortgage still gets paid so it don't matter. Anyway, after she used up all her savings from buying coke off me – and she only bought from me 'cos I gave her freebies all the time, giving her more than she paid for and stuff like that, she just does anything that I tell her to and I reward her.' He necked the rum and wiped his mouth, finishing the tale with a surprising lack of emotion for the woman whose life he'd ruined.

The rum kicked in Jonah's heated chest, making his heart pump double-time. His melancholy for Genie was beginning to subside. After all, she'd made a choice to get hooked on that stuff and in a way, he gathered that it was smart of Dwayne to capitalise on it and exploit her weakness, from a business perspective anyway. Still, there was something really disturbing about having a grown woman happily enslaved in a house. At first, the idea of being able to do whatever he wanted sexually with Genie turned him on, and he'd made a conscious decision to have a little five-knuckle-shuffle when he went to bed that night.

But seeing her hunched over the counter, a fiend with a flushed face and emaciated body, utterly repelled him.

'The funny thing is, I don't give a shit about her,' Dwayne continued, rolling up a joint on the coffee table. 'She could get hit by a bus today and I wouldn't so much as go to the funeral. But, 'cos she loves that blow, she loves me, 'cos I'm in control of her habit. Y'see?'

Jonah looked over at Billy, interested in his opinion, but Billy was still analysing the ceiling like he was trying to discover a new constellation. Jonah could've yelled in his ear with a megaphone and Billy wouldn't have broken his concentration.

'If you don't care about her, why don't you just let her go?' Jonah asked with a shrug.

'And do all my washing and ironing?' He began to laugh at the idea. 'Look, I'll show you why I won't let her go.'

Dwayne stood up and yelled for Genie to come in the room. A moment later she shambled through the door, red-faced and scratching her nostrils. 'What is it, babes?'

Dwayne stood up, unzipped his fly and pulled his dick out. Jonah gasped and looked away; that brief glimpse was enough to make him feel gay.

'Oh,' Genie said and got on her knees instinctively, not ashamed to perform oral sex in front of a crowd. She went to grab his limp shaft when he stepped back.

'What're you doing?' Dwayne asked her.

'I thought you wanted me to suck you off.'

'Nope,' Dwayne said, grabbing the empty glass and pissing inside it. Jonah's mouth dropped open when he realised what Dwayne was doing.

'What the fuck – ' Jonah said absently as Dwayne filled the glass with piss nearly as dark as the rum they'd all been drinking. It brimmed to the top and spilled over, staining the carpet – a chore she'd have to attend to later. An unhealthy combination of shock and repulsion grabbed Jonah like a bear hug.

'Drink,' Dwayne ordered.

'What?' Genie looked up at him perplexed.

'I said drink it. All of it.'

She stared at Jonah with a pleading glance but he was unable to avert his eyes from the glass, unable to speak or voice his objections like he was watching a caged freak at some backward country circus.

'Are you serious?' She asked, staring up at him, his dick near enough resting on her chin.

'Do I look like I'm playing?'

She looked over at Billy, but Billy's head was still tilted toward the ceiling. Dwayne thrust the glass into her reluctant hand, spilling even more of his urine on the carpet.

'Baby ... I don't want to.'

'Then don't drink it, and see if I ever give you any more blow again. You think I'm playing?'

'How about I just let you all fuck me instead?' She asked enthusiastically, promoting her body like it was her ace in the hole, her bargaining chip out of this depravity. 'All three of you at once? It'll be good, you know it'll be good.' She said the last part looking at Jonah, and once again his naive penis began to uncoil from its slumber.

'Maybe after,' Dwayne said. 'Now drink.'

A part of Jonah wanted to intervene, but another sick part of him wanted to see how low she'd really go. Had the white stuff really fucked her head up so much that she was willing to swallow a glass of piss?

Seeing that he wasn't joking, she hesitantly put the glass up to her lips, screwing her face up.

'Stop,' Jonah told her; she froze instantly. He pulled himself out of the chair and looked at Dwayne. 'Don't make her do that shit. I don't want to see it.'

Dwayne looked back at him with a strange smile on his face. It wasn't a friendly smile but instead, one of amusement. 'Let her do it. Who gives a fuck?'

'Come on man,' Jonah said waving his arms. 'That's enough. I get it, she's rough, she'll do anything.'

Dwayne tucked himself back into his trousers and zipped up. The alcohol was making Jonah feel breathless and angry. He looked down at her and shook his head like a disapproving parent. She stared at the floor, almost ashamed of herself, as if for that one second she remembered she was still a human being.

'What're you doing? Get rid of that glass, go on.' Jonah ordered.

Genie got to her feet and carried the glass out, trickling pee in her haste.

'That's why I keep that crazy bitch around, 'cos she never ceases to amaze me.'

Jonah exhaled hard, relief splashing down on him like he'd just cut the right wire to deactivate a bomb. The brief moment of silence before Dwayne nudged him back in his chair seemed to last hours.

'Take a seat and relax, playboy.' He lit up the joint he was rolling and held it to his lips. 'Don't be so serious.' Dwayne grabbed the control pad to the computer and began a new game by himself as Billy was still in La La land. The gunshots began again, along with the cacophony of bullets piercing metal and the surrounding city atmosphere being blown to shit by the killer robots. The surround-sound speakers made Jonah feel like he was sitting in an Iraqi war camp.

The apartment buzzer rang three times and was barely audible above the hectic computer action. Dwayne heard it and tapped Billy. 'Come Billy boy, it's time to roll. You got everything?'

He nodded back at him sheepishly like he'd just been stirred from a deep sleep.

'Ready, Jonah?'

With a grimace, Jonah swallowed the last gulp of rum.

When he stood up out of the chair his legs almost buckled, so he grabbed onto Dwayne for leverage, letting go as soon as he was balanced. The room was blurred and slow, like he was viewing it from inside a goldfish bowl. Dwayne led them out of the living room, Jonah behind him palming the wall for support. As they passed the kitchen, Genie brushed at her nose frantically, standing away from the pile of coke and pretending to busy herself with some other kitchen duty – a fiend trying desperately not to look fiendish.

'Don't wait up for me, honey,' Dwayne called out sarcastically as he opened the door without looking at her.

When Jonah walked past the kitchen, Genie smiled ever so slightly.

5

It was cooler outside now, the sky a palette of swollen reddish-orange clouds. The neighbourhood sounds brought back brilliant flashes of something quite similar to déjà vu in Jonah's mind; he remembered that annoying ice-cream-van jingle on a distant street and the murmur of teenagers yelling and laughing as they soaked each other with water guns. He recognised the dull, echoing thud of a football being kicked around in the street and bouncing off the parked cars. In the very outskirts of his hearing capacity, police sirens faintly wailed like a red alert, warning the residents not to get too carried away in the sweaty madness.

A boy dressed all in black leaned against a white jeep. Around his neck hung the most dazzling and detailed crucifix that Jonah had ever seen; a golden Jesus bleeding on a diamond encrusted cross. Jonah's initial thought was that this kid must've been sweltering wearing those dark, heat-absorbing colours, not to mention that his hooded jumper would've kept him snug in the middle of December. The crucifix glimmered, forcing Jonah to shield his eyes as he neared the jeep. When he was close enough, Jonah could make out the boy's features beneath the hood that shrouded his face; he had a thick, curly black beard and bushy black eyebrows that looked like they were drawn on with a magic marker. However, his skin was an enigma, a peculiar shade that Jonah couldn't pinpoint to one specific ethnic origin. Jonah realised that the boy must have a rainbow heritage when he saw his greyish complexion and startling green eyes that shone like emeralds in fog.

He smiled at Jonah and extended his hand.

'Hello,' the boy said, startling Jonah with what was quite easily the weirdest voice he'd ever heard; it was soft and low, like a child whispering. 'I'm Solomon. You must be Jonah, yes?'

Jonah shook his hand, trying to recognise the accent but failing to align it with any nationality that he knew of. He wasn't from London, that much was obvious. At first, Jonah thought the accent had the twang of South African, but he quickly changed his mind. Perhaps the boy was Brazilian? Wherever he was from, it was bugging the shit out of Jonah.

'How you doin'?' Jonah asked him, stumbling over his words. 'That's a nice Jesus-piece you got there.'

A velvety, almost musical giggle came from Solomon's closed mouth, sending a low volt of irritation through Jonah. It was like this programme he saw while flicking through the channels one day. There where these two posh old men laughing their heads off about something in the middle of some field. Turns out they were cracking-up about this really expensive wooden carving that one of them bought for something close to a half a million pounds, but when they went travelling to India they saw cheap replicas of the same carving on a market stall. The story wasn't funny at all, and in Jonah's opinion, you'd have to be some kind of arsehole to laugh that hard at something that lame, but there they were, wiping the tears away from under their glasses.

'Yeah, that's a nice chain, ain't it?' Dwayne added. 'Bastard won't tell us where he got it from though.'

'Ah come on now, that isn't fair.' Solomon said, his voice void of any kind of bass or volume. 'I have to keep some things secret don't I?' He winked at Jonah and got into the driver's seat. The gesture made Jonah shudder softly.

The kid was creepy; a gentleman dressed like a thug. There was also the air of fraudulence about him that made Jonah feel wary. Wary, and a bit afraid.

Maybe it was the drink, Jonah decided after a moment of thinking about it. After all, this Solomon guy had been perfectly polite and welcoming. He'd even gone to the trouble of picking up a crate of cold beers for them to kill on the way to the barbeque.

If Jonah was honest enough to admit it to himself, he was jealous of his replacement in the group and resented his new status as a *visitor*. But to be jealous of another guy seemed kind of gay so he quickly shunned the thought.

They drove through the yellow haze of the approaching sunset, the summer very much alive and personified in the streets and gardens. Smoke billowed up from the barbeques in all the different neighbourhoods they passed, the irresistible smell of grilled meat seducing Jonah's nostrils. A shaky, drunk train of thought began to pull up in his mind; the sun, he thought, was almost like a kind of magic in London. Nothing else had more of a profound effect on the moods of Londoners than a bit of sunshine. He watched the streets in awe as neighbours sat on their front porches drinking together, or as a girl braided a boy's afro on her doorstep. Everybody dressed down to accommodate the humidity, even the fat people.

Conversation and laughter rotated around the car, but Jonah excluded himself, choosing to soak up as much atmosphere as he could before he had to go home instead. A strange, vibrating excitement welled up inside him as he built a memory bank full of happy thoughts to take back to Nottingham with him. These were the essential thoughts he'd need to battle depression with when he got back to the real world.

At that moment he wanted to cry as a quagmire of emotions overwhelmed him. He looked at Billy sitting next to him downing his second beer. Billy had this little gun-lighter that he kept playing with, a blue blowtorch flame shooting out of the barrel when he pressed the trigger. Jonah watched Billy as he ran his fingers through the flame, concentrating on it like a puzzle, mesmerised by the mysteries of the fire. You only had to look at him to realise he didn't give much of a shit about anything. Like that scar on his face for example; most people would be distraught about having their face ruined with that kind of savagery, but not Billy; he just did what made him happy.

In the front passenger seat, Dwayne was messing around with the CD player, blaring out tunes and hollering at any girls that they passed, then yelling abuse at them when they failed to acknowledge him. Fair enough, they all liked girls and even Jonah admitted to being guilty of propositioning the ladies while they waited for a bus or while Solomon pulled up at the traffic lights, but usually when they rejected his offer, it would be a giggle. Now, Dwayne hissed at the females and spat derogatory comments at them like some kind of woman-hating rapist.

'Yo, darling,' he shouted to a girl wearing bright yellow leggings and a red t-shirt. She walked beside a boy who could well have been her boyfriend, but this didn't deter Dwayne. 'Yo, darlin', you got a fucking arse like I've never seen before, you know that?'

The girl tried to ignore him, and to his credit, so did the boy, though his eyes locked onto Dwayne with an intense ferocity.

'Yo, darlin' we got space in this car if you wanna come sit on my dick.' Solomon drove extra slow along the high road so that Dwayne could have his fun.

Understandably, the boyfriend got pissed. The boy, who was tall and skinny and didn't look capable of any real damage, still had to defend her honour. 'Fuck you!' He shouted, straightening up and puffing out his chest. The girlfriend had one hand on his stomach in an attempt to restrain him.

'Stop the car, Sol.' Dwayne ordered.

Solomon laughed that eerie, raspy giggle but continued driving slowly. 'Forget him.'

The boy remained still, one stride in front of his girl with his arms out inviting a fight. Jonah had to admire his bravery; he didn't appear frightened by the probability of getting stomped down in front of her.

While focussing on the boy, Jonah missed Dwayne reach in the glove compartment and pull out what appeared to be a real gun. It took a few seconds for Jonah to adjust his wavering vision, but when he was able to clearly define it as a .38, the same gun the cops carried in the old American films, Jonah froze with a paralysing astonishment that left him speechless. He was forced to sit there and watch the scene unfurl in slow motion; Dwayne leaned the gun out of the window and let two shots off in the boy's direction.

Bang Bang.

Jonah's heart stopped.

It sounded like fireworks going off and Jonah thought his eardrum had ruptured from the sheer volume of the gunshot.

Jonah quickly spun around in his seat to see if the kid got hit. The boy and girl were sprawled out on the pavement covering their heads like they were under a desk during an earthquake procedure. The relief that Jonah felt was indescribable; his heart slowly began to pulse and he remembered how to breathe again.

Billy was laughing.

'What the fuck's wrong with you, Dwayne?' Jonah screeched, sounding more whiny that authoritative. His ears felt like they were submerged in water. All of them were laughing at Jonah now, even Solomon, who kept glancing at him in the rear-view mirror.

'Is that thing real?'

'Course it is. The fuck am I gonna have a fake one for?'

Luckily, the shops on the high road were closed and the street was pretty empty. All the people who were still wandering the streets had now scattered into the nearest alley or behind a parked car for cover.

'Jesus Christ! Were you aiming to shoot that kid?' Jonah asked him angrily. 'Were you trying to hit that fuckin' kid or what?'

When he managed to stop laughing, Dwayne replied: 'Why not?'

'If I had the gun he'd be dead right now.' Billy added casually. 'Dwayne can't shoot for shit.'

'Fuck you! I bet I can shoot better than you can. I bet you three hundred quid that I can shoot the lights out of the next five lamp posts that we see.'

'Alright,' Billy smiled at the challenge.

'What are you guys, insane or something?' Jonah covered his face with his hands, stressed with frustration and shock. 'You guys are carrying a loaded heater and letting it off in broad daylight! Someone'll report that shit and a fuckin' Swat Team'll shoot this car up with us inside it.'

'Relax – ' Dwayne began.

'Don't tell me to fuckin' relax. This is bullshit! I don't wanna do a bird for this dumb shit and I ain't trying to get sniped by some police chopper. So don't tell me to relax.'

Now they were cracking-up at his words like he'd just dropped the punch-line of some hilarious joke. Even Billy was doing his donkey laugh and shaking his head. In the rear-view, Solomon's green, feline eyes twinkled at him.

'Why are you guys laughing at me? You think I'm a pussy just 'cos I don't wanna get arrested?' He turned to Billy and punched him in the arm.

'Ow!' Billy complained mid-chuckle.

'That hurt? Good! Why are *you* laughin' at me, Bill?'

'Cos what you said was funny, about the police and that stuff.'

'How was it funny? You're pissing yourself laughing over here like I'm Tommy fucking Cooper or something. What's so funny about what I've said?'

Dwayne turned around in his seat and faced Jonah, speaking calmly. 'He's laughing because the police can't touch us. They won't catch us – '

'Bullshit. Don't talk like some kinda frigging cowboy to try and impress me, like I'm some country bumpkin who ain't never been to London before, okay? If the fives saw what you just did, they'd arrest us and beat the shit out of us and we'd all get sent down.'

Still holding the gun, Dwayne kneeled on his seat. 'If the police saw what I just did, I'd've shot their tyres out so they couldn't drive no more.'

'Yeah right.'

'Yeah, right.' Dwayne repeated, his face deadly serious. 'You don't need to be afraid of that kinda thing any more, Jonah.'

'Who's afraid? I ain't.' He lied.

'Maybe you don't understand right now, but you will.' Dwayne told him with a smile. 'Ain't that right, Sol?'

Jonah turned to face the rear-view mirror angrily, the pre-fight adrenaline turning his blood to lava. 'What? What you gonna tell me? What the fuck you gonna say to me. You don't know me.'

Solomon smiled in the mirror, revealing perfect white teeth. 'I know I don't know you,' he said calmly. 'I'm not your enemy. I don't know you. But I think you've all had a bit to drink and you're all a bit high, and there's really no need to fall out over this. It's nothing.'

'What d'you mean *it's nothing?* He could've killed that kid.'

'I understand,' Solomon said calmly, his perfect gentlemen act slowly grating on Jonah. Right then, Jonah wanted him to pull the car over and for the two of them to slug it out in the road. 'Dwayne, you're making your friend uncomfortable. Maybe you should put the gun away, what do you say?'

Dwayne nodded and returned the gun to the glove box. 'You're right,' he said to Solomon. 'Sorry for freaking you out, Jonah. I was just fuckin' around. I'm drunk as shit, don't think nothin' of it.'

The scowl on Jonah's face began to soften; he was pretty wasted too.

What a day it was turning out to be. In the space of an afternoon, he'd seen more crazy outlandish stuff than he had in his previous seventeen years. The anger inside him was beginning to dampen, but that miniscule part of him that was still able to think rationally knew this whole thing wasn't right. Either his friends had just lost their minds, or they'd grown mighty brave in the space of a year.

And why was this Solomon dude still smiling at him in the mirror? Was he queer, was that it?

You shouldn't have smoked so much weed he kept thinking. *It's got you paranoid and you know it.*

'Forget about it,' Jonah waved it off, leaning further back into the seat. 'I just don't wanna get arrested, that's all.' Jonah tried to relax and ignore what'd just happened but couldn't keep his mind off of it. Visions of a riot van screeching around the corner and unloading some kind of chain-gun at them, spilling their brains all over the hot pavement, made his temples throb with anxiety. Getting caught with a handgun was a standard five-year offence as far as he knew, and he'd heard you got an additional year for each bullet inside it. As accomplices, he wasn't sure of how much time he could get sent down for, but he didn't want to find out. In his mind, prison meant one thing; buggery. He was only five-nine and weighed just over ten stones, his meagre frame completely oblivious to any kind of gym activity; the perfect candidate for some inmate arse-raping.

If we get pulled over, surely I'll be able to talk my way out of it. I got my train tickets back at the car, and my mum can verify to the police that I've been living in Nottingham for the last year. They couldn't just throw me in the slammer without any evidence, could they? He opened his beer-blurred eyes wider to see if he could spot anything up ahead, any glimpse of rotating blue light, but only the orange-red sunset glared back at him. His concentration span lasted all but a few seconds, and by the time he'd stared at something long enough to define it – a shop sign, a car licence plate – it obscured by the time he blinked and he'd have to start all over again. Not to mention that Solomon was speeding at sixty miles an hour down a thirty strip, making the smoggy breeze sting his vision. All he could try and do was regulate his breathing and calm down. A part of him wanted to try and laugh it off and pretend like it didn't mean anything to him, like shooting a gun at a person was to be viewed in jest; like 'Oh so what, it's hot and we're shooting people. Who cares, it's sunny!'

Maybe when he sobered up he'd see the funny side.

They heard the music from a block away. The car pulled up as the sun burned out, silhouetting them in a dry dusk. A scattered crowd of people spilled from the vibrating house holding plastic cups and munching away on chicken wings from greasy paper plates.

The alcohol made Jonah dizzy and light, but now he also felt breathless in the dark humidity. It seemed that he'd forgotten the basics of balanced movement as he stepped out the jeep. The process of tripping over his heels and slamming into the parked cars – breaking the mirror clean off an old Ford – was reminiscent of learning how to ride a bike for the first time; you wobbled all over the place and fell on your arse a great number of times before you really got the knack of pedalling. A disgusting taste lingered in his mouth like he'd been sucking felt tip pens.

Dwayne sauntered ahead with one hand on his extravagant, gun-shaped belt buckle. Oh the clichés! Despite the maroon sky that was rapidly inking into a black sea, Dwayne wore a pair of big round sunglasses on the bridge of his nose like a State Trooper. Solomon walked with his hands in his pockets next to Dwayne, saying something in his ear that was making him laugh like a naughty schoolboy. He must've been whispering at a frequency only a dog could hear, because Jonah was only a few steps behind and couldn't make out a word of it. Next to Jonah, Billy was still flicking his lighter flame on and off, concentrating on it like an optical illusion. Boy, Billy was hammered! In the thirty-minute drive, Jonah watched him finish four beers, but after that whole fiasco with the gun he stopped counting, so it was probably more like six.

Each step Billy took looked as though he was about to wander off in a completely different direction as he staggered in a zigzag. Jonah grabbed on to his arm to stop him from reeling off but ended up using him as stability for his own wayward stumbling. Both Billy and Jonah fell into the side of a car and tumbled awkwardly on the floor, the boom of drunk-human-on-metal grabbing the attention of the people gathered outside of the house. Dwayne and Solomon turned around startled, laughed, and carried on walking, suddenly too mature to be seen with the adolescent drunkards.

'What ... is ... we're on the floor,' Billy mumbled, rubbing his bleeding elbow. He tried grabbing the door handle to pull himself up to his feet but gave up through lack of motivation and decided to rest instead.

'Sorry, man, I'm smashed. I can't even walk.' Jonah propped his head against the door and looked over the road at a couple of sexy girls that were laughing at them.

'... need to piss,' Billy managed, his eyelids drooping closer into an alcohol-induced slumber with every second they spent on the floor.

Jonah shook him. 'Wake up, Bill. You okay, you straight?'

Billy's mouth opened and closed like he was sucking on an invisible tit. 'I can smell the food. You reckon ... you wanna call up Dwayne and tell him to bring us some food out here or what, Jonah?'

'Not really. He probably won't do it anyways. Why don't you call him?'

'... ain't got no phone, do I? I don't keep no ... phone!' Billy's volume rose and dropped at random sections of the sentence, sounding aggressive then sleepy in the same breath.

'Shit, Bill, I've seen you throw around about five hundred quid today and you don't even have a frigging mobile, you crazy fuck. I was beginning to get offended when you hadn't text me while I was away.'

Billy spotted his lighter next to the car tyre, where it had fallen from his hand and leaned over to pick it up. Pulling his t-shirt out of his shorts, Billy flicked the lighter on and ran the flame through it. The cloth slowly began to burn and by the time Jonah realised what he was doing, there was a large hole rapidly spreading in Billy's t-shirt.

'Bill!' Jonah yelled. 'You're gonna set yourself on fire.' They both began laughing as Billy patted the flame away.

'I've missed you, Bill.'

'Miss me when I go and take a piss in one of those girl's mouths over the road.' Although Jonah wasn't quite sure what he meant, he laughed anyway. 'I need a piss.'

The music was so loud that the car they were leaned against vibrated like a railway track with an inbound train approaching. In the hedge outside of the house, multi-coloured Christmas lights knotted in between the twigs adding a magical ambience to the muffled samba that was playing. That familiar, teasing whiff of food wafted by, but getting through to the garden where the meat was being cooked looked like it might be impossible, especially when standing up was about as difficult as a tight-rope walk. The girls, who seemed to be in abundance and scantily clad in brightly coloured skirts and tight-fitting tops, further tempted Jonah's progress toward the house. In his current state, he'd be lucky to slur his way into getting a pity kiss with an equally boozed-up slapper, let alone stumbling into the arms of a half-decent-looking female.

'Come on, Bill, let's get the party started.' Being the sturdier of the two, Jonah struggled to his feet, spat on the floor to clear his throat of that nasty acrid taste, and leaned down to help Billy up. On his third attempt, Billy managed to rise, and leaning on each other like Siamese twins joined at the hip they bobbed toward the music.

The watchful stares of onlookers did little to ruffle Jonah; he always felt safe with Billy. When they were about thirteen, a bunch of kids got on the same bus as Billy and Jonah as they were on their way to the cinema. One of these other kids tried some bullshit, taunting Billy because he was wearing a bright red raincoat in the middle of a dry April day. One of the kids, who was older than them by at least a couple of years, struck Billy around his head with an ugly sucker punch. Instead of falling back under the weight of the blow, Billy fell forward and head-butted the boy in his eye, and landed on top of him on the floor. All of the boy's friends were trying to pull Billy off as he rained head-butts down into the boy's face and bloodied it to a pulp, and even Jonah grabbed hold of Billy to try and pull him up, but it was like trying to calm a pit bull who'd locked its jaws. These other guys, who were panicking and yelling at Billy to let go, turned white as porcelain when they tried heaving Billy off their friend and realised that he had the boy's bottom lip inbetween his clenched teeth.

There was blood everywhere, and while it was happening, Jonah truly believed that Billy had head-butted the boy to death. Whether he was alive or not, Jonah knew one thing; that kid was going to need a damn fine plastic surgeon to fix his mug.

Then another thought struck Jonah as he was remembering that day; Billy was mighty fond of head-butting people.

They managed to reach the queue in front of the house and boogied their way in. The place was absolutely rammed and hotter than an oven. Wall to wall, people crowded the small confines of the living room, the body heat sucking the air out of the house and making even breathing seem like a workout. The lights were dim as the sweaty couples groped in the darkness and writhed to the rhythm of the Samba. Excitement fizzed through Jonah as he sidled past girls with fat arses, gently stroking their cheeks with his idle fingers – a forgivable sin in such a packed environment. A short, chubby, but not unattractive girl felt Jonah's hand press on her bum and upon contact she backed it up in his hand, welcoming him to dance. He gave her a little squeeze but felt far too cramped and off-balance to get into any intimate dancing; just walking without passing out was challenge enough.

Jonah led the way, patiently waiting for the human traffic to unclog itself as they approached the kitchen. Food was the first priority. Just two minutes inside was like being in a sauna, his t-shirt clinging to him. He may have been wrong (as his boozy vision usually was) but Jonah was pretty sure he could see steam rising off of the glistening flesh of the dancers. With concentration and care, he turned around to check if Billy was still with him – and he was, one step behind, now bare-chested and carrying his t-shirt around his sunburnt neck. There was something slightly worrying about the way he had his head tipped back, his face flushed red.

'Don't puke, Billy.' Jonah shouted pointlessly; the music was far too overpowering for verbal communication.

The kitchen was less hectic. Empty rum, gin, and vodka bottles lay scattered around on the side counters along with a community of plastic cups, some empty, and some still containing alcohol. The sudden light was magnificent, and despite the clamour coming from the eruptive speakers in the front room, there were still a huddle of people who used the little space as a chill-out area – mostly girls who wanted to rest their feet from all the wigglin' and shakin'. A few girls glanced over at him in between their conversation, the gesture becoming an unspoken invitation in Jonah's swirling mind.

'The girls here are so sexy it's unbelievable,' Jonah shouted to Billy, loud enough for the two frizzy-haired vixens by the sink to hear.

Billy nodded with his eyes now closed, grabbed hold of Jonah's shoulder, leaned in and slurred: 'Some beers and piss first, okay, Jonah?'

'You want more beer?' Jonah couldn't believe it. The boy was a machine.

'More beer!' Billy chanted with his fist in the air, pushing Jonah through the kitchen door and into the garden. The air was fantastic. A welcome breeze whistled gently through them. More Christmas lights entwined the washing line and ran the length of the spacious garden, tall trees looming outside the glow like ominous black towers. A fat black guy with a naked lady apron on stood behind the barbeque with a San Miguel in his hand, chatting away to a skinny white dude with sandy blonde hair. A few people were stretched out in deckchairs with their beverage and plate of food on their lap, chatting away in another language. Three ice buckets filled with all kinds of different beers sat by the fence, and Billy was drawn straight to them like he was magnetised. Up ahead, under a webbing branch that leaned over the fence from the tree next door, Solomon and Dwayne stood with a couple of girls.

'What's happening, Jonie?' Dwayne called to him over the shoulder of one of the girls. He had a big grin on his face and his eyes were gleaming little slits behind the cloud of marijuana smoke. All Jonah could see of Solomon was a smiling mouth, the rest of his features were shaded by his hood. Jonah smiled back at them and shambled toward the grill.

'Grab yourself a plate, young man,' the hefty chef told him. Jonah thanked him and happily received two wings, three ribs and a burger black as charcoal, a little more well done than he'd usually like but he wasn't about to complain.

'Smells good, man,' Jonah told the chef. 'You've done a good job with this food.' The over-friendly, unnecessary bullshitting began to flow like it always did when he drank heavily. But he didn't care, because even if he wasn't drunk he would've thanked the guy for his hospitality the same way. Billy joined him by his side with a beer in each sweaty palm and one tucked in the pocket of his shorts. For the first time that day, Jonah noticed how Billy's belly bulged out below his ribs, like he was carrying a litter. When they used to play football, Billy could breathe the outline of a six-pack out with every exhale. Now, his physique was a flabby mess, the muscles drowned and softened under the excess fat.

After Billy loaded his plate, they walked over to Dwayne who promptly introduced them to his latest girlfriends. 'This is my dear old friend Jonah, and the ginger white boy is Mr Billy-Lee.'

The girls smiled and said 'hi'.

'Yo, Jonah, guess how old these two are,' Dwayne said, slinging his arm around the pair of them. They wore too much make-up and were podgy trying to pass as curvy.

'I dunnoe ... How old are they?'

'Billy? You wanna take a guess?'

Billy necked half his bottle and wiped his mouth. ' ... I couldn't give a fuck.'

Solomon sniggered, and the softness of it sent a shiver through Jonah. The girls laughed too, at his audacity and the sight of Billy's bloated, swaying body and his clumsy speech.

'Take a good look,' Solomon said to Jonah. 'Have a guess.'

Reluctantly, Jonah appraised them. It would've been hard enough trying to tell what colour they were with the amount of foundation they had caked on their faces let alone how old they were. He shrugged. 'What are you, eighteen?'

Dwayne slapped Jonah on his arm, nearly pushing him over. 'Fourteen. Fourteen years old, drinking and smoking weed.' He shook his head with mock disappointment and they found it hilarious. 'What I want to know is, have you two ever been fucked before?'

They giggled, and this time they showed their age. But to Jonah, they looked pretty developed for fourteen-year-olds. Dwayne honked one of their boobs with each hand.

'I'd be careful with that if I were you, Dwayne.' Jonah warned. 'When they sober up they could report you and get you done for statutory rape or sexual harassment or some other shit like that.'

'You two ain't gonna do that are you?' Dwayne asked the girls. Still giggling, they shook their heads innocently.

'You're looking at a long bird if you get prosecuted for that shit,' Jonah told him. Had he been a little less drunk he would've felt sick at the sight of his friend molesting two young schoolgirls.

Like Jonah knew he would, Dwayne shrugged off his advice. 'I'm going to the car with 'em. You wanna come?'

Instantly, Jonah shook his head and looked away, feeling perverted just for being asked that kind of question.

'Bill?' Dwayne offered.

Without replying, Billy shuffled over to them and grabbed one of the girls by the arm and pulled her toward him; he looked like a zombie advancing on a damsel in distress. Jonah thought about trying to talk Billy out of it, but knew it was a waste of breath. Billy was going to do whatever he wanted, and the worst thing was, Jonah knew that those girls could've been even younger and he would've still gone with Dwayne.

They walked off, Dwayne swaggering lazily with his little tart, and Billy slouching on the poor girl who was trying to keep him upright while he spilled beer out of his mouth and over her top.

'Have fun.' Solomon called as they ventured through the kitchen.

Great stuff, Jonah thought. *Now I'm alone with this fucking weirdo.*

Even though a nice mellowness welled inside of Jonah, he still felt the jarring awkwardness of being in the proximity of someone he didn't like. So instead of trying to make small talk, Jonah took his food to a deckchair, not wanting to be caught in the middle of a laboured conversation with Solomon. When he sat down, Solomon was already sat in the deckchair next to him, moving as quietly and smoothly as he spoke.

'You don't like me, do you, Jonah?' he said eerily like he'd just read his mind.

The question caught him like a punch in the head, startling him with its brutality. 'I don't know you.'

'But you don't like me. I can sense it.'

'That's too bad,' was all Jonah could manage. The syrupy texture of Solomon's voice raised goosebumps on his forearms.

'Maybe this'll change your mind. Watch this.'

Jonah looked over to the deckchair next to him, where Solomon had pulled out a five-pound note from the inside of his jacket. He handed the note to Jonah and told him to check that it was real. Once he did, Jonah handed the note back to Solomon.

'I practise magic in my spare time. I practise all these little tricks and I show them to Billy and Dwayne and they go crazy for it. See if you like this one.' He held the note in his open palm and with his other hand he drummed his fingers in the air above the money. After a second, the note fluttered upwards, apparently twirling by its own accord. When his fingers stopped moving, the note floated back down to his palm like a feather. 'What do you think?'

As random and bizarre as the trick had been, it was impressive.

'Do you know how it's done, other than magic I mean?' he asked Jonah, his white teeth shining out of the featureless black void of his hood.

'If I had to guess, I'd say fishing wire. You poke it through the note and put it up the sleeve of your jacket. In this light it would be impossible to see. Was I right?'

Solomon nodded and pulled the note through his sleeve and out of his jacket with the wire, which was still invisible in the darkness. 'Okay, what about this one.' He smoothed the note out in his open palm once again and asked Jonah to check it. Jonah grabbed the note and placed it back in his hand, satisfied. Solomon made a fist, and then rolled the sleeves of his jacket up.

'Cup your hands,' Solomon instructed.

Jonah did as he was told, and Solomon held his clenched fist above Jonah's cupped hands. Silver and copper change began to drop down at Solomon's command. If he said 'Five pence,' then a shiny five-pence piece fell.

'What coin do you want to fall next?'

'Fifty pence,' Jonah said, baffled, trying to get his mind around the illusion.

Fifty pence fell down and clinked onto the shrapnel in his hands. Solomon opened his hand and the note was gone. Jonah jingled the change for a moment, trying to unscramble the trick in his head. At once, he thought that the change must've come out his sleeves, but Solomon had rolled them up to show that there was no funny stuff happening up there. 'Let me see your hands a second.'

Solomon leaned in and held his palms out like he was about to receive a psychic reading. Not wanting to be beaten, Jonah scanned his hands along every line and callous. Jonah had a theory that the money might've fallen out of one of those small plastic change bags like they give you at the bank and that Solomon might've discarded it before he upturned his palms. Even if that was vaguely correct, then how did Solomon manage to call what coin was going to fall out, or more to the point, how did he make the fifty pence piece come out when Jonah asked it to?

'If you count it out, there's exactly five pounds in your hands there.' Solomon told him, a hint of smugness in his tender voice. 'Now, for the second part of the trick. Pour the money back into my hands.'

Again, Jonah did as he was told, making sure not to spill any coins onto the floor. When it was all there, Solomon chucked the money up in the air and clapped his hands in the middle of the metallic cloud. As soon as his hands clasped together, the wayward coins vanished – and as far as Jonah could tell none had fallen on the grass. Jonah breathed in sharply, not sure of what he'd just witnessed, and slightly frightened at the mystery of it. He quickly searched the floor, raking the grass with his fingers.

Solomon opened his hands, and inside, was the five-pound note. 'Magic.'

The alcohol took the edge off the astonishment of what would have otherwise been an amazing trick. Instead, a specific anger flared up in Jonah. He wasn't surprised when he felt the irritable heat scraping under his skin – in fact, he was familiar with this feeling.

He'd only been this annoyed at being conned once before. The first time was when he was about ten or eleven. His mum had sent him to the corner shop to get some bread with a ten-pound note because she had no change.

Taking the bread, which cost 69p, to the counter, Jonah proceeded to pay for it with the tenner. The old Indian woman behind the counter, who he remembered as being a miserable bitch that was always asking him why he wasn't at school and stuff like that, gave him four pounds and thirty one pence change.

'Hey, this money's wrong, I paid with a tenner,' He told her, not raising his voice as he assumed she would see the error that she'd made.

The woman, chewing her gum annoyingly loud and making a revolting slurping noise every time her mouth closed, huffed uninterested. 'You gave me a five-pound note, check your change, okay?'

'I never gave you a five-pound note, I gave you a ten,' he said again calmly. 'Check your till, I gave you a ten, I promise you.'

'You gave me a five,' she retorted bluntly.

Then, her refusal to even give him the courtesy of checking, accompanied with the notion that she was just trying to exploit him because he was a kid, made his temperature rise. The inside of his chest began to ache as his heart beat manically, his neck stiffening.

'Look, I gave you ten pounds. Now give me the rest of my money back.'

'You gave me five – '

'– You fucking Paki bitch! Don't try and con me, just gimme the rest of my money back before I fuck this place up.'

Her chubby face was flabbergasted like he'd just thrown a bucket of freezing water over her. She stormed from around the corner, her jowls wobbling like a bag of custard, with one hand raised like she was going to give him a mighty slap with all her body weight behind it. As soon as he'd called her the 'P' word, he regretted it; that shop was his local. Where would he get his fizzy sherbet straws from if he got banned from the corner shop?

Eventually he left, tipping over the stand that held the crisps and giving the window a good kick from the other side. Just for good measure, he called her a bitch again and then went home to report what'd happened to his mother, editing out the part about him calling her a bitch and a Paki.

His mum marched him straight back to the corner shop to get to the bottom of what happened. The Indian woman said that Jonah had paid with a five, but Jonah's mum reassured her adamantly that she had definitely given her son a ten-pound note because that was all she had in her purse.

'Your son swears at me and tips things over and calls me a Paki. And you want me to give you your money back?' the woman yelled, the pink glob of gum bouncing around her mouth like a second tongue.

'Is that true?' his mum asked him. When he didn't answer, she grabbed the collar of his neck and threw him forward in the direction of the shopkeeper and ordered him to apologise. It was only later, after a lecture of treating people the way he wanted to be treated, did Jonah find out that his great-grandfather was actually from India. By that time, he'd already got a slap across his face – hard – by his angry mum who said he *'should've known better'* about saying something so racist, especially to another person of colour. In the end, the shopkeeper gave Jonah's mother her money back after he apologised, but said that he was banned from coming back inside (though Jonah's mother was still free to buy her ten Marlboro and *Sun* newspaper).

It didn't matter that much to Jonah about not being allowed back, after all there were other shops he could get his sweets from. But he knew she was trying to con him out of money and take advantage. So fuck her.

Anyway, things seemed to balance out about five years later when Billy went in there drunk one winter afternoon and fell into the drinks refrigerator, smashing the glass door and most of the bottles inside it, which as Jonah saw it, made them even.

Now, with Solomon smiling in his face after pulling off what was otherwise an airtight, impressive illusion, Jonah began to get the feeling he was being conned again; his inebriety was being taken advantage of. There was no way that what he'd just seen was possible – drunk or not. Even though plausible magic tricks relied on that kind of deception, Jonah knew there was something else, something obvious that he'd missed.

'How'd you do that?' Jonah asked him sternly.

'Like I said ... ma –'

'Fuck that!' Jonah stood up with his fists clenched. 'Don't tell me, *magic*. Don't try and bullshit me to my face. You better call it a trick. Don't bother calling it magic and trying to play me for some kind of prick, okay?'

Solomon looked up at him, emotionlessly. 'Why are you getting angry, Jonah?'

'Because I know that what you just did wasn't a trick. There's no way that was possible.'

'Then I must just be a really good magician, what do you say?'

In through the nose and out through the mouth; Jonah had to remember to breathe. He felt like one of those cartoons with steam coming out his ears.

'Look, man,' Jonah said, sitting back down, already regretting getting so amped up. It showed poor character to get so riled about something so meaningless. 'I'm sorry. I'm drunk and everything, and I'll bet you anything I'll be able to figure that trick out if you do it in the daytime when I'm sober.'

'Maybe.'

'No. No maybe. I'll bet you anything.'

A low, shivering chuckle escaped from Solomon's mouth as he leaned back into the deckchair, resting his hands behind his head. 'I showed that same trick to Billy and Dwayne and a few other people. And they always clap like happy seals being thrown some fish. You're determined that it is *more* than a trick, and it is. But you're the first person who's figured that out.'

'I just don't like being lied to. Magic is like lying. But what you just did, I don't like it. I'm sorry. It looked good and everything, but I know there's something wrong with it.'

'You are absolutely right, Jonah. Absolutely right. I bet you've noticed how much money your friends have now, haven't you?'

He didn't answer. Something about being so desperately broke and working in a bakery was mortifyingly embarrassing to admit to a complete stranger, so instead, he exhaled through his nostrils and looked around, pretending he didn't hear.

'You can have more money too. I can show you how to make as much money as you want.'

Jonah let his eyelids slowly close and a yawn sailed out of his mouth. 'What are you into? Some credit card scams? No offence but I knew a kid who tried one of those scams and got arrested for fraud the day before his seventeenth birthday, so forget about it.'

'I'm not talking about cheap scams, Jonah. I'm talking about *taking* what you want. That car that Dwayne was driving, the jewellery, the flat you're staying in. All of it was just taken. In this world, we get the fear of God put into us about prison and jail time, right? But the truth is everything is there for the taking. This city is a playground. We take what we want, and we do what we want. We're free. And being free is the only way to live.'

The eloquence of Solomon's words was so elegant that it was almost poetic; the silky sentences rolled off his tongue as though they'd been rehearsed to perfection. He seemed fiercely intelligent, far too smart to be bumbling around with Dwayne and Billy on an intellectual level. As condescending as it was to admit, Jonah always knew he was smarter than them, but they'd grown up together, gone through puberty together. Now, a sour thought poked at him; he wondered if he'd be friends with them if he'd just met them in college or bumped into them at work. He doubted it.

'And what happens when you guys get caught? When the police pull you over and find a handgun, or they raid the flat? What happens when they finally get to you?' Jonah challenged, nibbling the gristle of a spare rib even though the meat was long since devoured.

'That's where the magic comes into it,' Solomon replied, so quietly that later that evening when he remembered the conversation, Jonah wondered if he'd imagined Solomon saying it.

The music suddenly cut off from the speakers and was replaced with a jumble of shouting and arguing. Jonah sat up in the chair with his ear pointed to the kitchen door, trying to make out what the racket was all about. 'Sounds like something's going down in there,' he said.

A mingle of male and female voices protesting in Portuguese rose from inside the house.

'Billy's done something,' Solomon said staring into the kitchen.

'You know Brazilian?' Jonah asked, surprised that he was able to decipher the chorus of yells. As he looked at him, it was quite probable that Solomon could be from somewhere in South America. Maybe he was an illegal immigrant who was adopted and was fortunate enough to get a decent education in England, but if so, why was he so into criminal activity? Maybe, as Jonah's mother often said, some people were just born bad.

'What're they saying?' Jonah asked him, already struggling to his feet and re-realising how drunk he was. As he headed toward the kitchen the volume increased to a violent pitch. The people in the kitchen were huddled around the door leading to the front room, tiptoeing to see what was happening in the middle of the crowd. Solomon followed Jonah close behind. A little too close.

'What's going on? What're they shouting about?' Jonah asked again trying to squeeze into the kitchen.

'Well, it seems that Billy's had an accident.'

'What do you mean?'

'Apparently, he was desperate to urinate and relieved himself all over the floor trying to leave the house.'

A shudder of fear wracked Jonah. This was bad ... extremely bad. They were strangers at this party and drastically outnumbered by South Americans, who communicated in a tongue that only Solomon understood. There was bound to be a couple of guns in the house, and more than a kitchen drawer's worth of sharp artillery in some of the pockets. Plus, from what Jonah noticed in the brief forty minutes or so he'd spent in the house, the people in there were very much segregated in their own community and branched off away from everyone whose first language was English. Being at that party, they were tolerated but not completely welcome. Suddenly, Dwayne's pistol wasn't such a bad idea after all.

Forcefully, but not audaciously, Jonah squeezed into the front room where he became wedged between a muscular, sweaty, vest-wearing Colombian and a smaller, beady-eyed teenager with a dark blonde moustache that was too light and furry to be anything more than bum-fluff. The backdraught of body heat hit Jonah in a suffocating wave; his face, arms and legs dampened with warm, itchy sweat.

In the centre of the kerfuffle, Billy was propped up against Dwayne, who was laughing as the whole side of the room cursed at him and shouted foreign abuse in his face, spraying spittle in angry showers. The leader of the mob, a tall, lean character called Ernesto (indicated by the short girl that was pressing her hands against his chest and trying to keep him calm and away from Dwayne, repeating 'No, Ernesto!' followed by some incomprehensible Portuguese), was squaring up to Dwayne and staring through him like he was trying to stab him with his eyeballs. The whole room buzzed with the imminent excitement of pre-fight nerves, and the odds didn't look good for Dwayne. Billy's were even worse.

Ernesto was covered in tattoos; the doodles and names of relatives scrawled over his arms and neck like agitated spiders. He looked like he'd just served time in a South American prison and been grazed on a diet of stodgy food and push-ups. Needless to say, he looked as though he'd had his fair share of scraps (probably over scraps of food, ironically enough) and had as many scars as he had tattoos. To make matters worse, Billy was wobbling around like he was attempting to balance himself on a skateboard and Dwayne was laughing his head off like he was watching a comedy sketch show, and the more the two of them did this, the redder Ernesto's eyes became. The only thing that was stopping him from flipping and beating the shit out of Dwayne and Billy and possibly killing them, apart from the girl in his way trying to calm him down, was the bizarre curiosity of their sheer bravery.

With the intensity simmering and threatening to implode in the tiny sweat box of a living room, Jonah's heart began to physically ache with worry. His lungs burned with apprehension, and although he wanted to try and keep a mean poker face, he felt flushed and sick.

'What're we gonna do?' Jonah asked Solomon anxiously, surprised that he was now confiding in him. He didn't want to, but in the midst of being outnumbered and surely trapped in what only ten minutes ago seemed like the party of the year with all the winning elements – drink, girls and, of course, free food – now turning into a nightmare of violent potential, Jonah realised he'd need all the allies he could get.

'Nothing,' Solomon replied. 'Just watch.'

Dwayne's laughter ricocheted around the room, and the louder he laughed the quicker Jonah's heart thumped.

Billy staggered back and fell into Dwayne's arms and they both burst into hysterics. The two girls that were with them were on the far side of the living room with easy access to the front door in case the looming carnage sprawled out in the room and the angry Brazilians began targeting anyone associated with the prick who just pissed all over the crowded dance area and the even bigger prick that thought it was hilarious.

Ernesto was shouting and pointing in Dwayne's face, and it reminded Jonah of a science experiment he saw on TV showing the effervescent effect of vinegar and baking soda in a coke bottle. Even with the lid on, the reaction of the two opposing ingredients eventually blew the lid clean off of the bottle. And now, Ernesto looked as though his blood was vinegar and baking soda and any second he was going to blow his lid.

'What is he saying?' Jonah asked Solomon over his shoulder, receiving an ice-cold stare from the Colombian guy in the vest.

'He's saying "You fucking English niggers coming into my house and pissing over my floor, I'll murder you like a dog", or something to that effect.'

Without warning, Dwayne straightened Billy on his feet and tried to balance him like a tall stack of books, then amazingly, if not stupidly, rolled his shoulders and got serious. He looked Ernesto in his face and clenched his fists, and then uttered two simple words that made everybody gasp in fear of his safety, the way a crowd might gasp staring up at a man threatening to commit suicide by jumping off a building and losing his footing : 'Shut up.'

The girl, who until this point was keeping Ernesto at bay, backed away from him as if to say, *you've done it now. He's your problem*. It was like she'd unlatched the fence to let an angry bull out.

'You understand me, you English Fuck?' Ernesto snarled with a psychotic glint in his eye.

'Just about.' Dwayne replied sarcastically, smiling like he was having a conversation with a good friend and not fully understanding the peril of his words.

'Unless you wanna die I suggest you take your fucking bitch here and get the fuck out before I kill you.'

The room was silent except for the low hush of panicked breathing around the room.

Dwayne was still smiling.

Billy puked on the floor.

A Mexican wave of disgusted groans circled the room as Billy finished vomiting and staggered out of the room, leaving Dwayne giggling and covering his nose from the smell of the sick. Ernesto, as big as he was, swung his arm to throw a punch but amidst the clutter of people in the room, his hand got tangled in the body of a nearby girl, and that was all Dwayne needed. Like he'd practised the move a thousand times in front of the mirror, Dwayne whipped out the .38 snubby and stuck its muzzle into Ernesto's cheek.

'What you saying now? You want me to blow your face off, *Ernesto?*'

Behind him, Jonah heard Solomon snigger.

'Dogs who can't bite should never show their teeth, know what I mean?' Dwayne said, pushing Ernesto's head back with the gun, his face a new shade of maroon.

The whole time while this was happening, Jonah held his own breath in fear of exhaling too loud and accidentally provoking Dwayne into pulling the trigger. The room trembled in an uneasy unison, not sure if they were about to witness a murder or a serious physical beating.

'Give me your phone,' Dwayne told Ernesto, who, after a second's hesitation, did as he was told. Dwayne patted him down, and not finding a wallet, noticed the rings on Ernesto's little and middle finger of his left hand. 'Take 'em off.'

Ernesto remained still. Dwayne shoved the gun into Ernesto's mouth and pulled the hammer back; a small cigarette-burn sized mark left imprinted in his cheek from the muzzle of the .38. Ernesto took off his rings and handed them over.

'Good boy,' Dwayne said. 'Who stopped the music?'

Nobody confessed.

'This is a party, right? Let's have the music on!'

When they realised that if Dwayne was surely serious enough to pull a gun out on a man in a room full of people, he was surely serious enough to use it, the music began again. It was happy dance music that belied the tension of the room. Then, out of nowhere, Dwayne shot Ernesto in the foot, but behind the cloak of loud music the shot went unheard by the neighbours, probably mistaken for a moped backfiring or a speaker blowing out.

With a scream that slashed across the music, Ernesto fell to the floor and gripped his toes, blood pouring out of his foot and mingling with the piss and puke puddles next to him, turning into a sticky beige soup. The second Ernesto dropped – like his legs had been hacked out just below the knee cap with a chainsaw – the party-goers began scrambling out of the house at the nearest exits. The front and back doors got rushed at once. Even Jonah, who knew he was in no jeopardy from Dwayne's trigger finger, bolted out the back in fear of another bullet being fired and ricocheting around the room.

The garden filled with hysterical people and Jonah knew that pretty soon, either another vengeful gunman was going to be spraying up the house or an armed swat team was. He leapt over the garden fence and continued running through and jumping fences until four gardens later he reached the side street. Jonah froze for a minute but wanted to keep moving, the adrenaline coursing through him like an electric shock. His knees wobbled as he slouched against the brick wall, panting. Somewhere close by, a siren was wailing. It was probably a meat van headed to the party, or maybe an ambulance on its way to atend to Ernesto's shattered foot. The obvious thing to do was jog back around to the street and get in the car, but doing so meant he'd have to pass the house again, and he wasn't about to risk getting shot at by a Brazilian who wanted to just kill a British kid ... any British kid. Plus, the police could be lurking and he might get pointed out by one of the people at the party and get hauled off to jail.

Either way, fuck both those options.

Jonah wiped the sweat from his brow and slowly crept to the end of the backstreet like a Neanderthal who hasn't grasped the upright position yet. Behind the cover of a nearby car, he peered down into the road trying to see beyond the swamping darkness. All he could make out were the anonymous people wandering around in a daze on the pavement and in the middle of the road like bewildered cattle who'd just escaped a wolf attack.

The night-time stillness fell on him like a weighted quilt, making his arms heavy. His chest was a wooden birdcage splintering his lungs with every breath, but viewing the pandemonium from afar filled him with nerves so bad he wanted to laugh.

The laughing stopped when he heard tyres creeping behind him.

6

'What're you doing down there?' a strangely gruff voice called from the vehicle, concealed from view behind the blinding headlights.

Squinting for a half-second, Jonah realised that every moment he spent sitting on his haunches was a moment closer to premature death or a night behind bars. He sprang from his spot and darted off, his legs suddenly thumping down like motor pistons harder than they'd ever run before. The people in the car behind whooped and shouted at him, accelerating faster and screeching round the corner to keep him in their sights.

Jonah, realising that he was running down a long, straight road with no possible turns for another two hundred yards, quickly dived behind a truck parked under a tree with big leafy branches. Hitting the concrete on his elbows, Jonah hissed-in the numbing pain that was shooting through his wrists. *Funny Bones,* he thought, not remotely humoured. Still seething, he rolled under the truck and sprawled out flat on the road taking shallow breaths, his eyes wide and peeled like frantic surveillance cameras scouting the location of his pursuers. He hoped, *prayed,* that whoever was in the car didn't see him G.I Joe his way under the truck, otherwise he'd be a sitting duck, a crab in a bucket.

The car slowly rolled up to the truck, and as the headlights began to bleed onto the road, Jonah recoiled and tried to squirm his way closer to the back tyre, thinking that if he could curl up a little bit that he might be mistaken for part of the car, or a cat maybe.

The headlights shone over his face and he closed his eyes shut instinctively, the old childhood theory of *If I can't see you, you can't see me* cringing through his brain. As the sound of the engine came closer, Jonah held his breath, the rapturous laughing from inside the car seeming like they were right beside him now. The car stopped next to the truck. Jonah's stomach plunged like it was coming loose from the rest of his innards and he felt as though he were going to pass out, all the energy and pulsing adrenaline zapping from his body.

Guttural chokes of laughter fell on him.

'What you doin' under that car, jungle baby?'

Jonah slowly opened his tear-blurred eyes to see Dwayne leaning out of the passenger seat of the jeep. In the back, Billy was slumped against the window in an alcoholic coma.

'You motherfuckers,' Jonah managed to croak through his crackly cotton-mouth. The relief he felt was something close to an orgasm, the ripples of fear softening into tickly feathers making him giggle and moan in exhaustion.

Dwayne looked down at him, extending an arm out of the car with an open beer bottle. 'Hurry up, Jonie, get in. The law are gonna be looking to arrest a bunch of black kids and one passed-out white boy, so move your arse.'

Scooting out from under the truck, Jonah jumped in the back of the jeep; Solomon drove off before the door was even slammed shut. Sweaty, breathless, and with what felt like two fractured arms, Jonah stared at Dwayne, who was grinning back at him.

'You had a good day or what?'

Jonah reached for the seatbelt. Billy slept against the window with his mouth wide open like a set bear trap with vomit caked to his beer stained t-shirt and fresh piss stains on his shorts. He smelled like a homeless bum who'd soiled himself; it was a bitter, acrid smell.

'Did I have a good day?'

'Yeah. Did you have a good day?'

The harder Jonah tried to force back a smile, the more he wanted to laugh. For all he knew, police were on their trail as they spoke. Ernesto could bleed to death. Billy could choke on his sick in the night from all the beer and weed he'd smoked. And still, despite this, Jonah had to admit it: 'Wasn't bad.'

In the morning, though he dreaded the revolving hangover, he knew he'd see the funny side of all of it. When he thought about it, all Dwayne had really done was shoot the kid in the foot, the most he'd have is a limp. Surely the police wouldn't give a shit about a little shooting at a rowdy party that all the neighbours probably complained about anyway. With this knowledge, he relaxed.

And saw Solomon grinning in the rear-view.

TUESDAY

7

Getting to sleep was one of the most frightening things Jonah had ever done in his life.

Not wasting any time on such formalities as washing or brushing his teeth, he flicked off the light, stripped and got into bed. That horrible free-falling feeling was simply unshakeable. Yeah, he could gulp down a few glasses of water and hope that they helped with the dry mouth in the morning, and he could even scoff down a bit of bread (because he was surely too drunk to construct a sandwich of any worth). But no matter what precautions he took, the minute he'd decided to have that one drink too many, that was it. He would suffer the shaky night-time haunting. There was, in his opinion, nothing worse than that feeling of being smashed-out-of-his-head-drunk and trying to sleep.

Except, being smashed-out-of-his-head-drunk and high-as-a-kite-stoned.

The general rule, as he knew it, was that two things you never mixed were weed and alcohol. You could blaze away and smoke, or you could binge away and drink, but you should never do the two at the same time. Generally.

Yet, that's what he'd done. So now, he was drunk with the bed feeling like it was spiralling from underneath him, but he was also stoned, and his body felt like it was drifting upward toward the ceiling in a vortex of intoxication.

He'd tried for about two minutes to lie flat on his back, but that breath-taking feeling of dropping through the bed like he was sky-diving was just too intense. The window next to him was open and he tried breathing in the cool air but found himself drifting asleep with his head rested against the ledge.

After ten minutes of spinning, jerking, floating and falling, Jonah was now unsettled enough to sit wide awake and realise that he wouldn't be able to make it through the night without eating something to absorb all the alcohol, and maybe then he'd be able to relax a little.

The rest of the house was silent except for the soft snoring that stirred from down the hall. He got up out of bed, and used his arms to balance himself out like a tightrope-walker at the circus. His mouth was bitterly dry, a symptom no doubt that would be amplified to an unbearable degree in the morning.

Fumbling around in the dark for the doorknob, Jonah slammed the door open by accident. Tracing his fingers along the wall he managed to feel his way to the bathroom, where he emptied his bladder of what felt like a week's worth of piss and washed his face again, trying to shake that numb, stoned feeling away. In the mirror his eyes looked droopy and bloodshot, so he slapped his cheeks to see if they still registered feeling.

When he made it to the kitchen, he was relieved to find the fridge well stocked. Jonah grabbed the sliced bread from the counter, where it had sat nonchalantly next to the white crumbs of a leftover line of coke, and stuffed two slices into his mouth without butter. Stodgy food was good for soaking up booze in his belly, and he'd heard that milk was good for settling the stomach, so he grabbed the semi-skimmed bottle and filled himself a couple of glasses that he backed in one gulp, spilling white streaks down his chin. The food and drink didn't help immediately, but he guessed that it might take time to work its way through his body. There was a bunch of other things in the fridge that were appealing but also looked like too much effort to make. On that note, he chewed up one more slice of bread, returned the milk to the fridge and made his way back to his room where he fell into a deep, still slumber.

8

The grey, desolate atmosphere before him bore all the familiar traits of a nightmare; he was barefoot in the middle of an empty street and enveloped in the murky twilight, the creeping darkness of the night still lingering.

It was cold. Wearing just a pair of boxer shorts, the seething winds lacerated him with each violent gust. As he took a step forward, the concrete pavement seemed to pull back in the other direction like he was walking on a treadmill.

A smoky-charcoal smell filled the air and filtered the white clouds above him, turning the sky a strange smudged colour; it looked like an old television set tuned into a scrambled channel. Somewhere behind the long row of decrepit houses, was an unidentifiable, monotonous droning.

Jonah tried a light jog on the uncooperative pavement, and was slightly relieved when he noticed a bit of progress. His legs felt too flimsy for running – boneless flaps of skin fighting against the wind to advance forward. Repeatedly, he assured himself that it was only a nightmare, which was odd because the knowledge of this didn't make a bit of difference. It felt real. So real in fact that he looked down at his arm and could see the goosebumps covering his skin like the pimples on a basketball. A smoky odour scratched the back of his throat.

'Hello!' he bellowed into the long stretch of nothingness and cringed when his voice reverberated off the surrounding houses. The idea behind shouting out was to snap him awake, hoping that maybe Dwayne or Genie would hear his distress call and come into the room to shake him. He yelled again for good measure, but this time no volume came out of his mouth, only a strained whisper. Dread began to shake him like a Rottweiler clinging to his legs; *what if I'm in a coma,* he thought. *What if I choked during the night or if I had a heart attack from all the weed?*

He screamed.

Responding to his noise, a goat trotted out from behind a nearby car and stared at Jonah as it chewed on what looked like the wires to some kind of electrical appliance, with its head cocked to the side. When it finished its meal, the goat bleated its objections to Jonah's presence within the nightmare, but it sounded more like laughter. The goat appeared to have a smile on its face.

'Can you talk?' Jonah asked it absently. Obviously, he knew that real goats couldn't speak. However, matted, scabby goats with disturbingly humanoid faces that appeared out of nowhere chewing on wires and laughing like robots, he wasn't so sure about.

The goat grunted out some kind of backwards sentence in a low, human voice that sounded like a subliminal message in a rock song. Another noise filled Jonah's ears, the eerie moaning of a whale call, which seemed to be coming directly out of the sky above him. Jonah looked back at the goat, which had begun eating the tarmac off the road as easily as it would grass in a field.

Pain shot through the soles of his feet; his toes felt like glass, his ankles aching and numb all over. Ignoring the goat, he tried to walk forward but his step began tilting to the side like he had a club foot. The floor had taken up a ludicrously soft quality, sinking beneath his weight like a mattress.

When he managed to pull his attention away from his spastic attempts at walking, he looked back up to the goat, which had squirmed and morphed into a person. Before him was a tall, gangly figure in a baggy black shawl. Two horns that funnily enough looked like two ice-cream cones stuck out of the stranger's head. Though most of its face was shrouded by the shawl, Jonah saw something that looked just about as weird as anything he'd ever seen in a dream before. It was certainly provocative enough to make him avert his eyes and stifle a scream. God knows he wanted to shriek out for help, but his voice was low and raspy and couldn't cope with the demands of his terror. Though the horns on the creature's head were enough of an abnormality to warrant a certain degree of fear, there was something comical in them. Maybe it was their resemblance to ice-cream cones that took the edge off of them. But the nose ... that was a different thing altogether. There was nothing funny or remotely cute that Jonah could compare that nose to.

It reminded him of a book that they used to have at his nursery, and coincidentally, was one of his earliest memories. During story time the teacher (what was her name? He'd never be able to remember that far back. She was white, middle aged, looked like a lesbian) often read one of the classic fairytales that started with Once Upon A Time ... to get them settled at the end of the day. Usually, he enjoyed them. What he found particularly interesting about those books was the illustrations that accompanied the text. They were extremely detailed pictures that depicted the events in the story, but drawn in a way that didn't patronise the child or try and baby it down, which even at that young age, he respected. He remembered *The Three Little Pigs,* and enjoyed the way the mean old wolf fell into the hot water at the end, its face a feral, snarling grimace of pain and anger. The teacher would hold the book up after she read the page and show it to all of the engrossed little children, and they'd smile and stare back at it amazed. But one day, while reading *Hansel and Gretel,* the teacher showed Jonah something that sent him into a fit of panic. When she read the part about the candy house, he listened eagerly, beguiled by the blooming possibilities in his imagination, wishing that he'd been the one who stumbled upon it so he could eat his way through the walls. It seemed like just another great story with really nice pictures, until the teacher showed him the witch that lived inside the candy house.

Oh-me-oh-my, how he screamed. Good thing his mother was outside the class waiting for the three o'clock bell, because otherwise it might've taken a sedative to calm him down. He was all caught up in the lovely thought of living in the candy house (which at that age seemed like the only heaven there could possibly be), when he saw the grotesque witch and shattered the fantasy for good. She was hideous, all fat and bent out of shape, with boils over her face and long, gnarled fingers that looked like limp carrots. But the worst part about her, the most terrifying thing about the crazy old hag, was her crooked witch nose. It looked like some kind of deformed turnip that was more beak than nose, and stood out far too long on her face. She looked like a bird-woman, a psychotic vulture with pale, beady eyes.

What kind of twisted bastard was that artist anyway, didn't he realise his target audience was four year olds?

The hooded atrocity recognised Jonah's fear and revelled in it, hobbling toward him like a crippled maniac, while Jonah was bound to the spot, cemented to the pavement.

It opened its mouth/beak to say something to Jonah, but blurted out a bunch of nonsensical words like a child who's just grasped the basics of speech and tries to improvise the rest. Somehow, those babblings were far more sinister than any demonic threats that it could've uttered. Jonah closed his eyes so tightly that the pressure from his squeezed lids hurt the bridge of his nose. His ears popped from the effort, his bladder a balloon filled with too much water.

The gargling creature was advancing closer. Tears began to stream down Jonah's cheeks, warm and salty. He lashed out with his arms, which felt like elastic bands, droopy and pathetic, swinging wildly but gathering no strength behind the punches. Exhausting from trying to strike his assailant, he pulled his fists to his face and decided that some kind of defence was better than a pitiful offence.

Through his loose guard, he peered out, barely able to see past the watery lashes.

The hooded shape-shifter continued to rustle onward, though now it seemed that it had the head of a goat, its black lips slobbering. Inhuman yellow eyes the size of yo-yos glanced back at Jonah curiously. Flapping wings surrounded him and he could feel soft insect-like limbs stroking his exposed flesh. He shuddered, gagged and crumbled in a pile on the floor under the weight of a sudden thick air pressuring him.

Piss began to flow freely now. He was terrified as the rough farm animal stench oppressed him, the anomalous slaughterhouse groaning turning his blood sour. The palms of his hands bled as his fingernails embedded into them ... Oh God he couldn't bear it, couldn't stand it for much longer. It felt like he was drowning, gasping, swallowing too much rancid air.

'Please ...' he managed in a hiccupping whisper.

When he opened his eyes the figure was still there in front of him, except now beneath the hood, Solomon stared back at him. Solomon began to vomit and puked out huge lumps of clumpy bile that collected in large soupy puddles on the floor. His mouth opened so wide that Jonah could hear his jaw crack and dislocate. Squirming out from inside Solomon's throat was a bald, limp dog that plopped onto the floor wetly.

The dog, with all its misshapen limps and facial retardations, staggered around with a smooth coat of sick trailing down its back. When the dog got a grip of its surroundings, it snarled at Jonah and charged toward him with the speed of a greyhound, snapping and scratching at him viciously. Jonah didn't feel pain, but instead, a tense sort of relief that he might actually be able to wake up from the madness.

Behind the jagged jaws of the dog, Jonah could see Solomon parading around, opening his shawl and flapping it like he was imitating a bird in flight. Past the angular teeth of the hellish beast, Jonah saw something that terrified him enough to make him wake bolt upright in his bed, something deranged enough to make him physically jump off the mattress:

Beneath the shawl, Solomon had both a penis and a vagina, and teats that ran down his chest like a rat.

9

It was still dark outside, and before running off to yak his guts up in the toilet, Jonah searched his clammy arms for scratches and bite marks. Though drowsy and delirious, he was coherent enough to realise that he was safe now; the abject atrocities he'd just witnessed were nothing more than figments of his drug-altered subconscious. He sat on the edge of the bed breathing hard, feeling the vomit slowly work its way up from his bowels and begin coating the back of his throat. His wet biceps slipped against his chest as he hugged his stomach, his boxer shorts sopping wet with what he hoped was urine; any other liquid would raise questions about his sexuality that he didn't know if he could answer.

The inside of his head was filled with the rocks of a good old-fashioned hangover that stockpiled on top of his brain and ground against each other with every slight movement he made. To choose which was worse would be a painfully impossible decision; the imminent violent vomiting that was about to ensue or the thundering migraine that felt like his brain was swelling against the walls of his skull. The combination of both made him quiver uncontrollably, his muscles turned to jelly and void of any strength.

Standing up was no small effort. The room began to sway around him like he was in the middle of a Fun House at the fair. All he could think about was projectile vomiting as his stomach gurgled with bubbly anticipation. Vomiting is good, he thought, because it'll clear all the shit out of his system and he'll start to feel better. Wasn't that the way it worked? When he was in his second year at senior school, he'd had a terrible stomach ache all through the first periods of the day and through first break. Halfway through Mrs Atkins' English class, he quickly excused himself from *Of Mice and Men* and ran to the toilets to hurl his guts up. When he'd finished, he felt brand new again and even had a bit of spring in his step, until one of the girls in his class announced to everyone that his breath smelled like sick.

For the first time in his life, Jonah actually looked forward to throwing up. Jesus, anything had to be better than the wood shavings taste he had in his mouth. It hurt to swallow and he desperately needed some water. But first things first –

The puke forced its way out of Jonah's mouth in a hot, sour tidal wave. When he got rid of it all, the dry heaves came, his stomach muscles clenching and tightening like he was doing a strenuous ab exercise (binge drink your way to a six pack, he thought). With every retching motion, his head tensed and squeezed, sending him blind with tears.

'Oh Jesus,' he moaned miserably when the first bout had finished. He leaned against the radiator and tried to regain his breath. The stink coming from the waste in the toilet was hideous. As he wiped the tears away from his face he wondered about alcoholics. How the hell could those bums drink so much every single day? Just from this one little session of sickness, Jonah was quite positive that he didn't want to drink ever again. The thought of alcohol made him squirm, and he rejected the idea just the way his body had rejected the alcohol.

Poison.

The cold water tap offered some momentary relief as he splashed handfuls onto his pulsing forehead and into his ashy mouth. Using a rolled up towel as a pillow and another towel for a blanket, Jonah decided to try and get comfortable, lying completely still with his feet by the radiator. He may as well sleep there, he thought, because there was absolutely no point in going back to his bed and having to run to the bathroom every five minutes. Jonah realised that if he kept his movement to a complete minimum, then he could keep the brain-ache and even the sickness at bay. If he moved around, his head would be back in the toilet before long.

Sleep was the only respite his body could afford, yet the thought of slipping back into one of those inescapable comas was enough to send him back on the bottle. Now that he was reasonably sober (he still walked and smelled like a drunken person, but his mind was positively that of a sober person regretting the night before), he had a chance to think about the evening. And then it came – the hazy alcoholic guilt and shame of his behaviour. Little snippets of the previous day came back to him, mortifying him into a foetal position.

All he could think about was how Solomon had tried to be nice to him, and how in return all he'd done is try to start a fight, and when he remembered the whole fiasco with the magic trick ... he leaned over the toilet again, wanting to climb inside the bowl and die of embarrassment.

Ah man, what the fuck happened last night? Little by little, Jonah worked at piecing the previous day into a coherent and viewable reel. Starting from the beginning:

I got off the train. Came to the flat. Went and played some pool. Got ready for the barbe –

Dwayne shot that guy in the foot!

Jonah's stomach swirled again and rumbled spitefully. His heart began to thump like the drum line in a techno song. Any more stress on his heart and he was sure he'd have a stroke. Surely, the police would be looking for all of them right this second, and just for the fact that he was there at the party with Dwayne and now sleeping in his house, they could probably throw him in the lock-up too.

Before he left for Nottingham, the Metropolitan Police were running an awareness campaign to try and crack down on the rapidly increasing gun activity in the city of London, using posters and slots on the news to get their message across. Officers would go around the secondary schools and give lectures on what would happen if you got caught with a gun, having family members of the victims of shootings giving their moving testimonies and pleas for peace. Gun amnesties were set up throughout certain dates, so that anybody with a gun who was worried about the effect it might have, could hand it in to the police with no questions asked and no arrests made. Yeah right. Big metal banks like the glass and paper recycling bins that were set up all over London, were planted in inner city 'problem' areas, where people could just drop their gun off like they were putting a letter in a post box. Jonah knew, even despite the Police reporting, the campaign was hugely successful, but that there were 'still too many guns on the streets'; nobody who was serious enough to own a gun was dumb enough to hand it in. And not all the heartfelt pleas from tearful mothers or promises of a better London from all the white policemen in the city was going to change that.

The only thing that Jonah thought had quite an impact was a couple of posters that they issued around hot-spots and schools that basically broke down the facts of owning a gun. The first one read: 'A gun gets you Five years, plus a year for each bullet inside it. No ifs, buts or maybes.' If it was true that just getting caught with a firearm got you the time it said it did, then that would be enough to put a scare up in him, he thought. The other poster, which was a lot better, just had a picture of a regular handgun and underneath was like a shopping list that read: 'No Phone. No girls. No Internet. No Partying. No new trainers. No going out. It's your choice.' Who would want to risk all that lovely freedom for a hunk of metal when the end result would mean getting leered over by a gang of hungry bandits? Not Jonah, he knew that for free.

But now, he was sleeping in a house that had at least one gun that he knew of, and by the way that Dwayne thought he was The Terminator, Jonah would bet a whole day's wages from the bakery that there were more firearms hidden throughout the rooms, maybe even his. The thought of this triggered a trip to Pukesville.

Dark liquid fell out of him, burning his stomach. He spat a thick wad of saliva into the brown soup in the toilet, then drew more phlegm from the back of his mouth and got rid of that too, flushing after it. As he rested his head on his forearms, his stomach muscles felt as though they were going to burst through his skin like that scene from *Alien*.

'Jesus, help me,' he groaned.

He fell asleep slumped over the toilet. It must've been some time later, judging by the warm daylight that shone through the bathroom window, when Genie woke him by lightly stroking his back. Jonah lifted his head off his arms, which was like trying to bench-press a heavy weight with his neck, and turned to see her holding a glass of water for him.

'Are you okay?' she asked, genuinely concerned, still stroking his back.

'Feel like shit,' he croaked without raising his voice above a whisper in fear of his head exploding.

'I heard you being sick in the night,' she said, handing him the water and sitting on the edge of the bathtub. 'Good night?'

'Great,' he replied sarcastically. 'You?'

'Just watched a bit of TV,' she replied, her pale cleavage exposed shamelessly beneath the flimsy silk robe. 'Are you hungry at all?'

Now that she mentioned it, he was famished, but the thought of bringing anything solid near his mouth repelled him. He waved her question away and rose to his knees and washed his mouth out with the Listerine by the sink. 'What time is it?'

'Almost seven.'

'How come you're awake so early?' Jonah held his palms over his head like he was trying to stop his skull from expanding.

'I'm always awake early. I don't sleep that well,' she said, and even though she was smiling there was more than a hint of sadness behind her tired, red-rimmed eyes.

There was a moment of awkward silence that Jonah managed to fill with grunts and groans. 'Is Dwayne awake?'

She shook her head and stared at the floor. More silence. Then: 'I er ... I wanted to thank you. For yesterday.'

'What for?' he asked, although he knew what she meant. But something in him wanted her to see what the problem was, why she should be able to realise that she was sending herself to an early grave.

'For stopping Dwayne,' she whispered. 'He likes to show off when other people are around, but he's not really like that.'

'Oh?'

'Yeah, he's normally really nice to me. He just likes to give it the big man in front of his friends.'

'Tell me something,' Jonah began, sitting on the floor opposite her. 'Were you going to drink it?'

She didn't answer, but bit her nails.

'How old are you?'

'Twenty-nine. I'm thirty in December.'

'Can I ask you another question?' He continued without her response. 'Why are you hanging around with Dwayne and taking orders from a seventeen-year-old?'

She shrugged, and that was enough of a gesture for Jonah to read into. She obviously wasn't the sharpest tool in the box, naive and definitely lacking in self-esteem. She'd been picked apart by drugs, looking more like a haggard forty year old than someone pushing thirty, and the way her collar bones protruded from her skin showed obvious signs of malnourishment.

He looked at her and tried to imagine her before she met Dwayne, what she might've looked like wearing a suit on her way to work with a bit of make-up on. It seemed too unbelievable, too distant to be pictured. There were no sanitary towels in the cupboard in the bathroom because Genie hadn't had a period in the best part of a year. She was literally drying up, decaying in front of him.

Jonah's head throbbed again. He was stressing himself out with all these sentimental thoughts about this poor woman. Poor? A (small) part of Jonah thought *Fuck her,* she allowed herself to get like this. She had a good job and a good home and was already dabbling in the china white since before she even met Dwayne, so why should he feel sorry for her? Because she was weak minded? Because she was insecure? Fuck both of those reasons, he thought coldly. He hated women who used insecurity as an excuse to stay with a guy who beat the shit out of them, or allowed themselves to be cheated on dozens of times because they genuinely believed that the guy loved them. And it was the same here. She allowed a kid like Dwayne to waltz into her twenty-nine-year-old-good-job-with-great-pay life, and completely destroy it. She *let* him do it.

With his tummy empty, he wanted to try and eat something but he just wasn't sold on the idea of Genie preparing him food. She could barely look after herself let alone fix him something to eat, but he wasn't about to be rude enough to tell her that. Plus, he'd probably throw up if she handed him something to eat with those dirty fingernails of hers.

'So what've you guys got planned today?' she asked, grasping at conversation.

'I dunno. He hasn't said anything.'

She nodded, looking down at her long, bony feet.

'What about you? What you doing today?'

She tittered, embarrassed. 'Probably nothing.'

'What about work? You gonna get a job?'

She shrugged, and her body language summed her up perfectly – someone who just gave up caring about their future, who took each disastrous day as it came. Jonah wanted to slap her across her Goddamn head or just shake her until she came to her senses, but didn't have enough power in his arms for the job. And even if he did, he could slap her until his hands fell off and shake her until he ruptured his biceps, and none of it would do any good.

'Hey, would you mind waiting outside, I gotta take a piss kinda bad.' he said with an aching urge to drain the rest of the beer out of his system.

'Yeah. I'll be in the front room.' She seemed surprised, as though none of the guys in the house had ever given her the courtesy of asking her to leave so that they could piss in private.

When the door closed he managed to relax, then peed for what felt like a decade, the urine worryingly dark. The sun beat against his back; it was gonna be another roaster for sure. The weatherman wasn't kidding when he said it might be one of the hottest weeks in London's history. Over the last day he must have shed at least a couple of stones in sweat alone. That was probably why he'd been getting so agitated, and even now as he shook his dick dry, the lack of air was beginning to grate on him.

Come on, relax. You're on holiday.

'You're right,' Jonah muttered to himself as he rinsed his hands. All that negativity was going to spoil his week if he wasn't careful and the last thing he wanted was to fall out with any of his friends, especially since everyone was being so hospitable. But he simply couldn't help thinking about the domino effect that the shooting was bound to have, and as he stroked the craters under his bloodshot eyeballs he had to tell himself to relax, repeating it like a mantra. The bitter residue of angst remained in the pit of his sore stomach, regardless.

There had been a time when the phrase 'worried sick' took on a whole new meaning with him. Billy had stolen a hunting catapult while on his way to the arcade, from the back of this old sailor guy's van, who sold fish at the market. It seduced him with its shiny red chrome as it lay next to a tray of iced tuna steaks. Well Billy, being as slippery as the eels that that old sailor jellied and sold on his stall, slid up in that van like one of the fish market workers and just helped himself to it.

After a few games of Riot Night, Billy met up with the others at Hades Park with the catapult to give it a test run, and immediately realised that it was far more powerful than the shitty little ones that they got for a pound down in the crap toy section of the corner shop. They could hurl a stone from one end of Haidon Park right to the other side of the football pitch like a gun expelling a bullet.

'I reckon this thing could kill someone, easy,' Dwayne noted after they took target practice on a tree, ripping away the bark from about twenty feet away. So the next natural step after Dwayne's insightful revelation was to test the catapult on a living target. A part of Jonah had wanted to object, but a more prominent part of him was curious to see what would happen.

Not too far away from the Drakeford Road manor lived this big crazy black guy who always had half a dozen dogs on a lead whenever he walked down the street. They didn't know his name but Dwayne always referred to him as Donkey Kong, and due to the uncanny resemblance to the character, the name stuck. The thing about Donkey Kong was that he looked like he would just fucking kill you on any day of the week. He was about six-two, and must've weighed at least eighteen stone, with a big gut that always stuck out like a pregnant woman's belly, and because of this he would lean back when he walked giving him this strange swagger. Jonah would be the first to admit that he was scared stiff of Donkey Kong and would not want to trouble him for any amount of money, so now when he was thinking back about the incident, he couldn't quite remember where he got his bravery from.

Donkey Kong's house backed on to a side road, and it was one of those gardens that a passer by could see into because the walls weren't that high – hence the burglary epidemic in that area. But just from looking at Donkey Kong's back garden, you could tell he was absolutely, irrevocably insane. The weeds grew higher than the back wall and always reminded Jonah of the vines that prevented the Prince from getting to Sleeping Beauty. All the other gardens seemed maintained to a reasonable standard, not that they were neatly trimmed or trying to win a horticulture award or anything like that, but there was some level of care that went into it. But when you looked in Donkey Kong's garden, washing machines, sofas and old gas canisters lay scattered about, tangled in weeds and choked by nettles. They were familiar with Kong's garden because you could take the back road as a short cut to the arcade, and on more than one occasion when they did that, they saw his mangy dogs yapping with gawping, toothless mouths. They looked like the kind of animals you see on the RSPCA adverts about animal cruelty, their skin covered in raw blisters, their eyes gooey and weeping. They were so senile from their bad diet and general lack of care that half the time they just fought with each other, tearing lumps of flesh away with untamed savagery.

So when Dwayne suggested they try the catapult on a living creature, Billy, quite eagerly, said that he would kill one of the dogs in Donkey Kong's back garden. Quite honestly, Jonah hated those little bastards. They looked evil. Jonah bet that if they ever managed to get over that back fence – which without the huge tangle of shrubs and overgrowth sitting against it they'd easily be able to – those dogs wouldn't give a second's thought about biting someone or mauling a little kid to death. So in Jonah's mind, they needed to be put down for the sake of the community, which made him feel better.

Luckily for them it was winter and the early darkness worked in their favour, the hoods of their coats shrouding their faces.

Billy had been adamant that he was going to be the one who shot the dog with the stone, and there were no arguments. When they came to Donkey Kong's back garden, the gloom was sufficient to cover any distinction that may have given them away to any potential witnesses to their crime. Jonah kept an eye on the back window, like he always did when he passed Donkey's house. Through the grey blanket of dust on the glass he could just about make out the interior of the room; no curtains, no furniture, bare floorboards. It was like a squatter's den in a condemned building, but he kept his eye on it anyway just in case a shadow should appear.

The only audible noise was Dwayne's nervous, excited snickering, bubbling in the confines of the narrow road. Billy, however, remained completely serious, like he was hunting. With that catapult and rock clutched in his hand, Billy transformed into a ginger-haired Rambo. With the hood of his red Puffa jacket up ('Red, Bill? I mean why would you wear a red jacket? You may as well knock on the cunt's door and tell him you're gonna kill his dog,') Billy marched to the back garden. The frenzied mutts sensed his presence and fought their way through the swamping green overgrowth to attack him. One of the dogs, a little scrappy thing with broken teeth that looked deranged with rabies, got so worked up by Billy just standing there that it had got stuck trying to poke its head through a thick wall of foliage. Perfect.

Like a sniper, Billy took time and care in aiming the catapult. Jonah held his breath.

'Go on, Bill,' Dwayne encouraged with a whisper.

Just before Billy let the rock fly, Jonah wondered what was going through his head. Did Billy see a ratty, vicious animal or did he see his dad holding the iron, or his mum sucking on the neck of a vodka bottle?

The rock whistled toward the tangled dog, splitting its head wide open. It seemed to go cross-eyed for a second, then its tongue rolled out of its mouth and lay limp like a rasher of bacon. One last cloud of breath puffed from the dog's mouth before it flopped onto its side and lay still.

All three of them took off down the road, sprinting at full speed until they were a safe distance away from the garden. The maniacal howls from the remainder of the pack tore through the air with frightening intensity.

When they hit the high road, they made their way toward the arcade and played a bunch of games, finding solace in front of the flashing screens. Although they were surely safe now, the comforting electronic orchestra shielding them from the realities of the cold outdoors, Jonah had never felt more like a bastard in his life. He'd never been a part of killing a creature before, and now that he had, he felt like shit for it.

Primarily though, a feeling of paranoid dread outweighed his guilt. Jonah was sure that just as Billy let go of the rubber strap and the rock flew out, he saw a shadow in that empty room. He'd got it in his mind that Donkey Kong saw what they did to his dog, and was going to hunt them down and feed them to his remaining pack. When Jonah told the others what he thought he saw, they were already past the whole thing. It was just another case of Jonah thinking too much. But for a week after, Jonah found it incredibly hard to sleep. He had visions of Donkey Kong bursting through his front door and going absolutely ape shit in the house and attacking his mother.

Christmas came and went, winter thawed into spring. By March, the whole thing was forgotten. Jonah only saw Donkey Kong once after that – stark-bollock-naked in the middle of the high street, walking with that same leaning swagger with his stomach bulging out. He wasn't on the street for long. The police came and attempted to arrest him. It was then that Jonah saw just how strong this Donkey Kong guy actually was. Four officers were on him, clobbering him with their flick-out batons, but the blows bounced off him like moths on a light bulb. Donkey Kong hit an officer so hard that he literally flew into the air. He grabbed another officer, picked him up by his neck and attempted to strangle him to death, when another sergeant came from behind and raked his eyes. Five wagons and three cars later, they managed to subdue him, much to the applause of the shoppers. During the whole time this was happening, though Billy and Dwayne found it amusing enough, Jonah kept one thing in mind: *If that's what he did to a bunch of armed police officers, what would he have done to us?*

10

At eight thirty in the morning, Jonah just about felt strong enough to leave the bathroom without toppling over or needing to hurl. After a shower, which he thoroughly enjoyed primarily because it managed to get rid of the beer-sweats, he changed into some fresh clothes. As soon as he went back into his room, the smell of stale alcohol hit him like evil conditioner. The bed was a shambles, the sheets in complete disarray as if someone had tried break dancing on the mattress.

On the floor in the living room, Billy was laid out in his boxers, despite the sofa bed right next to him. Genie was in the kitchen sitting at the table, and Jonah was surprised that she had a cup of coffee in front of her rather than a pile of powder. He nodded to her as he came to the front door, and in return, she smiled weakly then averted her eyes back to the mug.

Though there was absolutely no refuge from a hangover that angry, he wanted some fresh air to walk off the sickness and regain some strength in his legs, and now that his body was completely void of liquids and solids (he'd had a temporary bout of diarrhoea) he felt like trying to eat something light.

As he walked through the courtyard and onto Doris Avenue, he began to feel more and more like his old self. The headache was slowly subsiding and devolving into a slight murmur. There was something about being awake so early on such a nice day that he'd never be able to fully explain to his friends, and he doubted that they'd want to hear that philosophical shit anyway. It was a private feeling to truly appreciate the city when it was still half asleep. In a few hours, the streets would be full of people trying to absorb as much sunlight as they could, but now, he had it all to himself.

He came across a big park opposite the string of shops that he was strolling past, with several trucks and lorries parked on the grass. Stapled to the gates of the park were posters advertising that the fair was in town and would be opening tomorrow night for one week only. Squinting past the sunlight that felt like pins all over his skin, Jonah tried to see if he could spot what rides they were setting up. There was a big ferris wheel, a waltzer, a sizzler, and of course, the bumper cars.

The fair brought back all kinds of fun memories, but at the same time, the fair could be the most dangerous place in the city. People from all areas would congregate in there and use it as an excuse to go around mugging people or starting fights, and more often than not, kids got stabbed, rushed-down, and shot. The funfair would usually turn into the Blood Fair, which was a shame because without all of the silly bullshit, those fairs could be a riot, but it was usually a riot one way or another. Dangerous or not, he was determined to go there before he headed back to Nottingham. After all, when would he get the chance to go to the fair again? In Nottingham? He doubted it. You needed friends to go to the fair.

In mid-trance, his stomach growled like an angry creature. The urge to fill his belly with a greasy Full-English overwhelmed him and he began to fantasise about the texture of scrambled eggs on toast, the saltiness of the bacon. When he spotted a coffee shop hidden away down an obscure little side road, his wobbly legs quickly got their act together and near enough dragged the rest of his body toward it. With all the money he still had stuffed in his pocket from yesterday he could afford anything he wanted for breakfast, so why settle for a cheap fry-up at some greasy spoon when he could blow his cash on some over-priced panini and get extorted for a regular latte? He was on holiday wasn't he? Why shouldn't he treat himself?

The shop had a brass sign that read 'The Mocha Inn' with a subtle painting of a hand cradling a large mug of steamy coffee. Despite what he thought to be an early hour, there was a healthy crowd of people; a businessman sat tapping away on his laptop in the corner, two housewives with their babies fresh out of the oven in prams next to them while they talked about nothing in particular, and a few others sat reading newspapers or working on their dissertations. The low hum of Italian opera swirled in the room, complementing the brown leather sofas and stained hardwood floors exquisitely. Jonah imagined the place being like heaven in the winter, packed full of people sipping on marshmallow-topped hot chocolates. The fragrance of roasting coffee was gorgeous to him, and he breathed it in deeply, sucking up the aroma. His body felt nicely loose, like the tension that he'd carried was unable to permeate the door. Even though he looked like shit and his body still bore the scars of that dreadful hangover, he felt oddly at peace, like he'd reached Nirvana.

Taking his sweet time, he scanned the chalkboard menu. Everything seemed good. Pricey, but good.

'Hello there, what can I get you?' the waitress asked him. He broke away from the menu, his mental list of food compiled, and turned to her.

Wow.

He'd been so involved in choosing an appropriate breakfast that he didn't even notice her, and now his tongue tripped over his gums as he tried to give her some kind of reply. The more he fumbled his words, the more obvious it became that he'd been thrown off-guard by her looks, so after a few mumbles that made it appear that he had some kind of severe stutter, he just smiled and nodded. Not the most appropriate gesture to give to a pretty girl, but it was the only one he could manage while his mind argued over whether he should *be cool or look cool*.

What was she, Spanish? Wherever she came from, she was so sexy that it hurt him, it physically hurt him.

'Hey!' he said, far too loudly, and then began to laugh. She looked at him like he was a weirdo, not a dangerous weirdo, but a funny one, which he guessed was slightly better.

'Um ...' He began, trying to muffle a giggle.

'Do you need more time to order?'

'No. No I'm good. How are you this morning, anyway?' Normally, he wouldn't bother with trying to inquire how a girl was feeling, especially a pretty one. He decided long ago that the prettier the girl, the more of a complete bitch she was likely to be. And, if his theory was correct, then this waitress was bound to be a completely self-absorbed, money-grabbing slut. His temporary braveness had been inspired by her chirpy attitude at such an early hour, and the fact that win, lose or draw with this girl, he was back in Nottingham next week. So while he was in a good mood, why not share it with a beautiful girl?

'I'm not bad. A bit tired, but I can't complain.' She smiled, and it was one of the prettiest and most unique things he'd ever seen.

'You don't look tired at all. In fact, you look fresh as a daisy. You should get a promotion for looking this good this early.' The words flowed from his mouth now without hesitation, this new found bravado pouring out of him like some kind of romantic Tourrette's syndrome. He thought that he might still be a bit drunk and in the knowledge that whatever he said from this point onwards would have to be blamed on the alcohol, he continued. 'I mean, it's unnatural for human beings to be awake this early, right? We should still be tucked up in bed and not have to wake up till at least ten. Then we can function better. I think ten is a good time, what'dya think?'

'If only,' she said rolling her eyes. 'That'd be the life.'

'Wouldn't it just? But seriously, well done for your presentation. I really do think you deserve a promotion because it shows a certain kind of dedication to the business to which you're employed. Like for instance, say I wasn't gonna buy anything, I was just in here to browse – '

'Who browses in a coffee shop at eight in the morning?' she asked, tickled by the thought.

'Good question. I dunno, some weirdoes out there probably do. You know London's full of weirdoes.'

She raised her eyebrows with mock surprise. 'It is?'

'Yeah definitely. I'm not one of them though, just to clear that up. But say I was just browsing, and I didn't know if I wanted to buy anything, but then I see the waitress looking nice and presentable and ready to serve me with a smile on her face, then I think "maybe I *will* buy something".'

By this point, she was already giggling away at his abstract tale and thankful for the comic relief. Her smoothly rounded cheekbones were the anchorage that tied the rest of her features together, the eyes, the nose, those plump lips (*don't stare at her lips!* he told himself). On top of all that, her brown hair seemed to reveal different shades of black and red as it flicked in the sun, and as he tried to concentrate on that, he became drawn to her ears, her neck ...

'So, are you just browsing or did you just come in for a chat?'

'You know what – ' he looked down at her name badge, ' – Rose, I think you've persuaded me. Okay, I would like an orange smoothie, a black coffee, an Italian club sandwich, and ... what pie can you recommend?'

'Blueberry is quite nice. I like that one.'

'Blueberry it is then.'

She went to the till to add it all up. 'That'll be £9.30 please.'

He gave her a twenty. 'And the change is for you, okay? Don't stick it back in the till either, I want you to have that'

'A whole ten pounds?' she asked him, shocked. 'You are crazy aren't you? Have your change, I can't take that.'

When she extended the note toward him, sadness overcame him like a sudden downpour of rain. It wasn't that she refused his tip, but because in that gesture of not wanting to take such a large amount of money even though she was probably only on minimum wage, he realised that he *really* liked this girl. It'd gone beyond harmless flirting, because now she'd affected him and he knew he wouldn't be able to have her. Even if she said yes to a date, which would be a miracle to begin with, he had to go back to Nottingham in a few days. He had to do his assignment. He had to go back to the bakery.

'No honestly,' he said, moving away from the counter and out of arm's reach. 'I want you to have that. I know what it's like to wait on people and feel unappreciated. Take that money and treat yourself, you're doing a great job.'

Her expression changed from one of bemusement to one of ... was it concern? 'Well, thank you,' she said sincerely. 'Go grab a seat and I'll bring the food right over.'

And there it was again, that nagging depression that was bound to set in unless he distracted himself. Thinking about Nottingham could only be compared to a dental appointment, he thought. You know you're going to have to go there and get your teeth drilled, and you know it's going to hurt like a son of a bitch. But because it's later in the week, you don't have to keep thinking about it. He sat at a sofa in front of a little table with a chess board painted on it and watched her prepare his food. Every so often, between blending his smoothie or toasting his sandwich, she'd look over at him, and seeing him looking back at her, divert her eyes. As he waited, Jonah leafed through a nearby newspaper, but it was one of those business broadsheets that never had anything interesting in them except politics and economic statistics.

When Rose came over with the tray he sat up automatically and smoothed out his t-shirt. The smell of booze still lingered, and he was consciously aware that his face was flushed and pale. She placed the tray on the table and told him to enjoy the food. He thanked her and assured her that he would, following her back to the counter with his eyes before he took his first bite.

A little tulip sat in the small vase that she'd put on his tray. He looked around to see if all the people had a tulip, and almost leapt on the table cheering when he realised they didn't.

Behind the counter, Rose tried her best to be discreet when looking over at him, but not discreet enough for her careless glancing to go unnoticed. Jonah ate his food slowly and deliberately, savouring the bitter coffee and enjoying the sweetness of the pie. When the food vanished, there was only one thing left to do. Jonah turned to the business man with the laptop.

'Excuse me, sir,' Jonah called to him. The man looked up from the screen but didn't say anything. 'I was wondering if you had a pen on you that I could quickly borrow.'

The businessman went into his inside suit pocket and pulled out a Parker and handed it to him without a word. Jonah thanked him regardless and wiped the crumbs off his napkin, then paused while thinking of something to write. For a good minute, nothing came to mind. He could've just put his phone number down he supposed, but that was too standard. After his eccentric little bout of spontaneity with her, it would seem like such an anti-climax to just write his number down and hope she'd call.

Then it came to him, something so perfect and random enough to be charming.

Would you like to go the fair with me? he wrote in his best handwriting, followed by his mobile number.

'Thanks.' Jonah said, handing the man his pen. He got up with the note on his plate and left it at the counter while Rose was serving another customer.

'See you later, Rose,' he called as he left, hoping she wouldn't spot the note until he was out of sight.

'Thank you. Bye!' she replied behind the whirl of the frothing milk.

11

After breakfast and a walk around the town, Jonah came back to join the others rehabilitating, or 'vegging out' as Genie had put it in her bourgeois way. He'd browsed around the rather unimpressive shopping centre and avoided the watchful stares from the security guard who'd followed him around in one of the upper class shirt shops. He'd also scanned the CDs in the record store and had a good look for some DVDs to watch, picking out a few action thrillers, the kind of films that would've sounded really intense in Dwayne's front room with those surround sound speakers, but put them back on the rack after a moment's thought. Although he'd been given a wad of cash that he could quite easily have frittered away on films and junk, he thought it best to make it last for the duration of the week, just in case they wanted to go out or something. Plus, if Rose called him and accepted his offer to the fair, he'd want to buy some nice cologne and have enough cash to take her on every ride and get her candy floss.

The afternoon was strictly a period of relaxation. Every window was open in the apartment and Genie hooked the revolving fan up in the front room. A breeze worked its way around, and the low burr made everyone even sleepier than the heat had previously. Dwayne found his usual spot on the leather sofa and lay in his boxers under a white bed sheet. Billy was spread out on the floor with his hands behind his head like a pillow, in the same shorts he wore the day before. They were watching television, too hung over to concentrate on playing the computer.

Jonah fixed himself a glass of lemonade from the fridge and came to the front room to join the others. Conversation was limited to the most essential of words; in the wake of yesterday's alcohol binge, even breathing too hard caused bodily trauma, though with a bellyful of grub Jonah was over the worst of it. Dwayne covered his forehead and eyes with the crook of his arm, grimacing at regular intervals as the flares of electric pain shot through his head, groaning and inhaling sharp breaths through clenched teeth. Where Billy remained silent, gawping up at the crap daytime dross on the television, Dwayne fussed and panted like he was dying of a brain haemorrhage. After a while, his indiscreet gasping and sucking of his teeth became unbearable for Genie, who came rushing to his side with a wet flannel to put on his head and a glass of water for him to sip.

'Try and drink the water, you need to rehydrate,' she told him, dabbing his sweaty forehead with the flannel like some kind of drugged-up Florence Nightingale. 'You should try and eat as well. Maybe some dry toast or some porridge to help soak it all up.'

Dwayne groaned and leaned over onto his side like he was going to puke in the bucket on the floor. 'Stop going on about food,' he whimpered.

'Okay, okay,' she cooed in a calming whisper, rubbing his back.

'Make me some food,' Billy said without looking at her.

'Sure,' she replied immediately and got up to fix him some lunch.

'Make Jonah something too,' Dwayne whined from underneath the flannel.

Genie stopped on her way to the kitchen in mid-stride, looking back and forth between Dwayne and Jonah like a confused infant.

'No I'm fine, thanks,' Jonah told her. She nodded and for what seemed like a few seconds too long, smiled at him. Ignoring her creepy face, Jonah got up and walked to the balcony. He peered out at the endless sprawl of houses and tower blocks, the building complexes and industrial sites. It looked like there wasn't an inch of space between the congestion of brick and concrete for the city to breathe. Everything seemed so tight, so squashed up. It was no wonder there was so much crime and people going crazy all over London when there was hardly enough room to swing a cat, let alone live comfortably; if you put too many fish in a bowl they will eventually eat each other.

It looked like a giant labyrinth, one enormous maze with no entrance or exit, just miles and miles of snaking roads. He began to wonder what it might've looked like a hundred years ago, before all the buildings raped the scenery. Maybe there would've been thousands of trees and fields of lush grass, and instead of looking like a concrete jungle it might've looked like an enchanting forest. He closed his eyes trying to visualise it, the sun slowly pinching at his flesh. Exhaustion grappled him with suffocating warmth, his neck aching from sunburn. On street level the clamour of traffic clogged up the airwaves, and horns beeped and sirens wailed like a snare and baseline to some hectic urban symphony. *All those cars* he thought. Since they began broadcasting those adverts about pollution destroying the ozone layer and how people should be more aware of the carbon footprint they're leaving on the earth, he realised just how many cars there must be in London alone. They said on the news that the planet is overheating from all the fumes in the air, and he could see it too. In the distance by the horizon, where the last estate building in view met the skyline, a solid, dirty grey cloud streamed across like cigarette smoke hanging in the air.

'And we're breathing that shit in ever day,' he muttered to himself.

'What?' Dwayne asked from behind the flannel. 'You say somethin', Jone?'

Maybe the planet would just explode one day. 'Nah, I was just thinkin' out loud. How'd you feel?'

'I feel like somebody's using my head for a frigging bongo and the inside of my stomach for steel pans. I feel like absolute shit.'

Jonah laughed and sat on the arm of the sofa by Dwayne's legs. 'Well you drank enough.'

'You can talk, you violent drunk. Shit, give him a few beers and he wants to fight everyone.'

Even though it was intended as a joke, Jonah cringed with embarrassment; if there was one thing that made him want to just crawl up in a hole and die, it was acting like a dick when he was drunk.

'I know, I know. Look, I'm sorry about flyin' off the handle yesterday.'

'Forget about it. I have.'

'No seriously, I shouldn't have been shouting my head off like that.'

Dwayne managed to stifle a chuckle. 'Stop acting like a pussy and forget about it. Do you know how many times I've pulled a gun on Billy over some dumb shit while we've been drunk? That crazy bastard over there nearly made us take a dive off the top of a fuckin' twelve-storey rooftop once from clowning around too much. Don't worry about it.'

On the floor, a deep hiccup-laugh rolled out of Billy.

'Where the hell did you get that gun from anyway?' Jonah asked him, sipping the lemonade.

'Sol hooks 'em all up.' An uncomfortable flashback invaded Jonah's mind, as unwelcome as a bum wandering into a wedding reception buffet. 'One time I got rolled up on by a bunch of boys with knives and shit like that and got scraped for a few quid. That same day, Sol comes to the house with a bag full of guns and clips and simply says "let's go and find them".'

Genie came back into the room with a tray and placed it on the floor next to Billy's flabby stomach. He grunted some kind of thank-you at her and turned to get stuck in; toast, porridge and a side of bacon and eggs. Dwayne looked down at the tray, distracted by the food.

'Actually I will have some food, Gene,' he called out to her. 'Anyway, Sol gets the guns from his guy. I don't know who it is.'

'Ain't you frightened about shooting that guy's toes off?' Jonah asked him. 'What was all that shit about anyway? What if the police get onto you?'

'Fuck them guys,' Billy shouted through a mouthful of toast, his voice like hardened earth. 'He should've shot him in the face. If I'd had that gun I would've put a bullet through his fucking face.'

'You guys are nuts,' Jonah said, shaking his head.

'The police won't care about a guy getting shot in the foot. And even if they do, so what? Look, no one knew us at that party, and the jeep isn't registered in any of our names. With all the other shit that's going on in the city you think they're gonna try and hunt down a person who shot some illegal immigrant in the foot. Boo-fucking-hoo, they're probably glad.' Dwayne gulped back the whole glass of water and sat up on the sofa, changing the channel to some skateboarding competition. 'There is something very simple that regular people have overlooked for centuries. Even Billy and me did until we met Sol.'

'Yeah? What's that then?'

'That you don't need to work your arse off in a bakery for a peasant's wage. You don't need to do a nine to five making just enough to keep your head above water. Sol showed us that if you're brave enough, if you can breach that line between civilian and so-called criminal, then you can have anything you want. *Anything.* It's all about bravery Jonah, understand? It's like, if I keep thinking "Oh shit the feds are gonna burst through the door and arrest us" then the likelihood is that I'll behave in a way that will get me thrown in jail. But, if before I do something like break into a person's house or steal their whip, I think "fuck it, whatever happens, happens". I'll never get caught because I'll always be one step ahead", then I stay confident. I can do whatever I want.'

On the TV, one of the skateboarders flew about eight feet above the half-pipe and did a triple spin, but landed awkwardly and scraped across the wood, cutting the side of his face to shreds. All three of them winced.

'We've been doing moves for months with Sol. Would you believe that we haven't even been stopped by a policeman in the best part of a year? A year, Jonah!'

Now that was impressive, Jonah thought. But his theory on criminal success had more holes in it than a Connect-4 board. What they were having was a prolonged lucky streak that would inevitably come to an end. Either that or they were just too dumb to realise that they'd been given an inspirational bunch of bullshit from a petty crook looking for a couple of stooges to join his crusade.

'What's the story with Solomon anyway? Where'd you meet him?' Jonah asked, subtly trying to elicit information about this so-called mastermind.

'He came up to me one day outta the blue,' Billy said, spooning the porridge in his mouth, 'just after I got the sack.'

'What'd you get the sack for?' Jonah asked him curiously, a smile spreading across his face awaiting the humorous tale. Billy had only had a couple of jobs in the past, all of which he got fired from. He worked for an outlet store as the delivery boy, getting there at five in the morning to unload and sort all of the stock. When stock started to go missing or not match the quantity on the order form, Billy got fired for it because he was the easy target to blame. So in retaliation, because on this one occasion he was genuinely innocent, Billy took a crowbar to the company van's windscreen.

'After I got into that fight and got the scar,' Billy pointed to the beige mark on his face, 'my boss said that I couldn't go and do deliveries because people wouldn't want me in their house looking like a football hooligan.'

Jonah's smile faded. Billy had only been delivering beds to elderly people and fitting them up – the only job an illiterate kid with no GCSEs was just about qualified to do.

'Anyway I'm off my tits at the pub, I'm so hammered I can 'ardly even remember any of this. All I do remember was leaving the pub and making it to a phone box to try and call for a cab, but I just pissed myself and fell asleep in there on the floor, and at the time it was winter so it seemed like the warmest place to be. It must've been a few hours later when Solomon came in the phone box trying to help me to my feet. He took me to a pie and mash shop in Walthamstow and bought me some food. We just got talking and that was that.' Billy burped and scraped the last splodges of porridge from around the bowl and shovelled them away.

'He was telling me about being unemployed and all that stuff. He thought I was homeless at first but when he realised I wasn't, he started talking about ways that we could get rich. He asked me if I wanted to make lots of money, so the first thing I'm thinking is that this guy's some kind of bender. I thought he wanted to pay me money so he could bum me or something.'

Both Jonah and Dwayne giggled.

'But when he explained that we were just going to go on a raid, then I understood.'

The bluntness of Billy's words hit Jonah like a rolling pin upside the head. He was quietly struggling to believe that Billy got talked into being an accomplice to crime so easily. But Jonah supposed that if anyone was going to embark on a career in crime, why not Billy? He had all the classic hallmarks of a developing criminal, like it was rooted in his genetic make-up from generations of tyranny.

'What did you do?' Jonah asked him, a false smile covering the discomfort he felt.

'The first thing Sol wanted to do was to raid a jewellery shop.'

'A jewellery shop?'

'Yeah,' Billy snorted. 'I didn't think there was any way we'd be able to do it because of all the security and shit like that. But he said we could pull it off and I believed him. He tells me to meet him in some alleyway at midnight – '

Dwayne cut in: ' – Sol told me Billy was wearing a pair of red shorts and shoes and a balaclava when they hit the place! Talk about discreet. Like anyone else wears red fucking shoes!' The image of Billy standing in an alleyway with his pasty white legs and a balaclava to disguise his face was just about the funniest thing Jonah had ever thought of. Laughter rendered him breathless for the best part of a minute.

'So he gets there and has a big duffel bag over one arm and a shotgun in his hands,' Billy continued. 'We go to the end of this alleyway, climb up this fire escape, and without warning Sol just blows the shit out of this back door that to me just looks like a regular door. It took about three blasts at the door for it to soften. The alarm starts going crazy but we just ran up in there smashing cabinets and pouring all kinds of jewellery in the bag. There was this well nice leather jacket in there as well, in like the staffroom, so I took that for myself.' He kept on nodding while he spoke about the heist and Jonah couldn't quite put a finger on why. When they were younger Billy used to rock back and forth and they used to tease him for it. Only later when Jonah caught a bit of this programme about autistic kids and saw them rocking in the exact same way that Billy used to, did he stop making fun of him.

'We only got about eight grand when we sold the jewellery on 'cos most of it was just gold. No diamonds or anything like that. But Sol let me keep the lot.'

Jonah was blown away. As he sat there, a college student – sorry, college student and part-time baker – he couldn't help but feel like the world's biggest dummy. Why the hell was he bothering with education when it would take him three more years at university, which would put him in a world of unaffordable debts and sleepless nights trying to meet deadlines, when his starting job would pay him peanuts even with all his qualifications. Was that fair? No, of course it wasn't fair and that is just the way this bastard world works. *Without risk there is no reward.* Who said that? Jonah couldn't remember but he figured it was just about the realest thing he'd ever heard in his life. Was it fair that footballers got paid thousands a week – A WEEK – when your average nurse got paid far less a year and worked all the hours God sends?

Slowly and subtly, anger was beginning to vibrate through Jonah, his shoulders feeling tight and painful.

'When Billy told me about all that cash, I was like "I want in". Then I went with them on the next run and we turned over some rich guy's house. We even made the papers,' Dwayne said, the flicker of excitement flashing in his smile. 'Sol tied this guy up and held a shotgun in his face while me and Billy cleaned his house out. He had a safe behind a bookcase with a shitload of cash in it and just gave it up straight away. He thought we were going to kill him.'

'I don't blame him,' Jonah replied. 'I'd have thought the same thing.'

'Fuck him anyway,' Dwayne said and curled up under the sheet. 'His house looked like a friggin' castle. You could fit this whole flat in his kitchen, so he deserved to give away some of his cash. It's not like he needed it.'

When all his breakfast was finished, Billy got up and wandered off to the kitchen and closed the door.

'It's so easy, Jone,' Dwayne began, sipping his water. 'You'd think by hearing about all these dumb pricks that get caught doing robberies that the police are like Superman or something. They're not. They're human, just like you and me.'

'I don't know, man. I just think that everyone's luck will run out sooner or later. Know what I mean?'

'I know what you're saying, but it's not true in our case.'

'I bet everyone thinks that until they get caught,' Jonah said stubbornly, aware of his condescending tone.

'We don't just go on robberies, y'know. With the money we make we can buy up a load of stuff – coke, heroin, speed, whatever – and sell that shit and then make twice and three times as much as we had to start with. It's like a little business in itself.'

'And it's the police's business to try and catch you, right?'

'Absolutely.' He finished his water and wiped his mouth. 'Hey, Jone, do me a favour. Would you get me another glass of water?'

'Sure.' Jonah grabbed the glass and went to the kitchen. When he opened the door the first thing he saw was Billy's chalky white arse shining back at him like a torch. Billy had Genie bent over the counter, thrusting at her like a man trying to nudge a pin ball machine. Genie looked back at Jonah, her head bobbing from the violent force, with an expression of both pain and sadness, her eyes welling up.

'Ah fuck,' Jonah mumbled, disgusted, and turned away. Dwayne doubled up on the sofa, howling with laughter. Genie yelped from Billy's rough handling, and then cried out. Something smashed in the kitchen soon after.

'You guys are fucking sick.'

'Stop being a faggot, Jonah. She loves it.' Dwayne rose from the sofa and crossed the room. Billy walked out of the kitchen moments later holding a beer, Dwayne patting him on the back as he passed him like he was being tagged in to take over.

Before the door closed, Jonah looked in and saw Genie with her face buried in her arms.

Billy got comfortable on the sofa and began necking his breakfast beer.

Jonah knew he shouldn't have even cared about that silly coked-up bitch. She didn't give a shit about herself, not one ounce of self-respect in her. So why did he feel so queasy, so sick with guilt?

Because they're raping her, Jonah. That's why.

Dwayne was grunting like a pig and it was met by equally disturbing shrieks from Genie, the clamour of their movements booming through the living room. Despite the heat in the room, Jonah shivered. There was something sinister behind the way Dwayne was pounding on her and making sure that both Billy and Jonah could hear him, and something equally ominous in the way Genie was squealing in pain instead of moaning with pleasure.

There was a time when Dwayne had his mind set on being a footballer, with more than a damn good chance of realising that dream. He'd get up early and go training three times a week, and wouldn't so much as eat sweets or drink fizzy pop for fear of it slowing him down on the pitch. He'd even been scouted by Chelsea youths and had a promising stint as their midfielder.

One of the head coaches, Terrence Duff, who was an ex-professional footballer and played for Millwall between 1971 and 1975, saw the potential in Dwayne from his first touch on the ball – quick feet, incredibly smart, always thinking moves ahead and passing accurately enough to set traps for the opposition. Plus, Dwayne could shoot with both his left and right foot, rare among boys of that age.

Terry would take Dwayne aside during each training session and work on different things to sharpen what was already becoming a very dangerous tool on the pitch. He'd set out agility ladders for him to sprint in between the rungs on his tip-toes, and cones for him to dribble around, and then target boards for him to aim at. Soon, this practice became too *standard* for Dwayne, so Terry would further test his ball control and accuracy.

One rainy, miserably cold Sunday, Dwayne showed up to training breathing on his quivering, gloved hands to keep them warm. After the usual jogging and stretching routines, Terry once again pulled Dwayne out of the team drills to the other side of the pitch where he'd set up something of an obstacle course for him to complete, much to the envy and dislike of his teammates. There were the usual dribbling poles set up in a straight line that he'd have to zigzag in between with the ball, but this time at the end, there were passing arcs stumped into the ground like upside-down horseshoes. A silhouette board of a player that stood about six feet tall waited a few feet in front of the goal.

'Right,' Terry began with one hand on Dwayne's shoulder, the other on his clipboard. 'All I want you to do is weave in and out of them poles – easy. When you come to the passing arcs, I want you to put the ball through each one and collect it round the other side to pass it through the next one. If I see one of the dribbling poles move or you miss the passing arc, its twenty push-ups and you start again. Got it?'

Dwayne nodded, unthreatened by the thought of failure. Terry noticed this as well, and was glad the lad had that cockiness about him, that fearlessness that he saw in all the special ones.

'When you get to the penalty box, all I want you to do is put the ball behind that cardboard dummy over there. Okay?' Dwayne nodded again, blowing on his hands. 'Good. Off you go then.'

Terry blew the whistle which signalled for Dwayne to begin, but on the other side of the pitch it sent daggers of spite through the rest of the team. Sometimes during the routine five-a-side kickabout game they played at the end of training, some of the boys often went in for hard tackles on Dwayne with their studs up. Because of his speed and gazelle-like guile, Dwayne often avoided the challenges. But every now and then he'd get clipped, and luckily it was never anything serious enough to render an injury, but if he'd been tagged with just a fraction of the malice with which the tackles were intended, Dwayne would need more hardware in his legs than a jumbo jet to keep him walking.

Weaving through the dribbling poles like he was figure skating, the ball always stuck to the end of his foot with adhesive control. Then, he proceeded to usher the ball through the passing arcs and was there to retrieve it in blurring speed, with the smoothness of a puck on an ice rink. When he got through with all that, he took a swipe at the ball with his left foot.

'Incredible,' Terry uttered to himself, like he'd seen a magnificent sunset for the first time. The ball curled around the dummy and into the bottom right hand corner of the goal with similar dynamics to a boomerang.

'Done,' Dwayne said, blowing on his hands.

'Collect the ball,' Terry ordered, trying to conceal the stun in his tone, his voice too flustered to harbour authority. Dwayne jogged off and obeyed the command and placed the ball at the beginning of the obstacle course. Terry walked to the front of the goal and stood at the opposite post to the dummy, leaving even less room for the ball to bend. 'Do it again, and if the ball touches anything – poles, arc, dummy and especially me, you're gonna do so many laps round this pitch the caretaker will 'ave to plant new grass.'

This time Terry got to observe his performance head-on, watching Dwayne's feet closely. Again, he twirled around the poles, threaded the ball through the arcs, and then launched the ball. It whipped toward Terry's face and somehow ('impossible' Terry thought) dipped just before it hit him and into the back of the net. A short, sharp exhale rushed out of Terry's mouth as the ball rustled the net. He looked at Dwayne. Dwayne looked back and grinned.

'Thirty squats,' Terry called. 'Chop chop.'

Each week, Terry would come up with new obstacle courses for Dwayne to complete, and as each new week came the tasks became more challenging. 'This'll help keep you sharp on that pitch when it comes to the big game,' Terry would say to Dwayne, constantly analysing his balance, studying his control. 'If you can complete these drills perfectly, then the game becomes nothing but a dress rehearsal for what you've been doing all along. There'll be no player you won't be able to outsmart, no keeper responsive enough for your attack.'

On his first big league game, Dwayne scored five goals. The opposing team weren't mugs – they were disciplined, strong on the ball and aggressive. But it wasn't enough. Every pass was intercepted, every potential shot ruined by Dwayne's crafty positioning. The maverick performance was enough to confirm to Terry what he'd thought all along. That football, as a game, as a sport, as a hobby, just made sense to Dwayne. The same way a musical prodigy could just sit at a piano and play the theme to a soap opera before they're even able to speak a fluent sentence.

When the final whistle blew on what was a single-handed massacre, the players of the other team walked off the pitch with their heads hung, exhausted. A few of them glanced back at Dwayne like they were checking to see if the kid was really human, as he paraded around topless showing off his sweaty physique despite the bitter air.

The first slip-ups were easy to spot. After establishing a formidable reputation as a skilled and brilliant footballer, and gaining something of a celebrity status on his side of London, he got The Ego. Terry had seen it in a hundred other talented players who'd banged in a few goals. They begin to feel special, as if the general rules of turning up to training and straying from partying and boozing didn't apply. So when Dwayne arrived almost forty minutes late staggering like he was still drunk from the night before and inhaling deeply through his nose like he was going to spew, it was easy for Terry to wave it off. He'd give Dwayne the lecture about not throwing his God-given talent away and resisting the temptation of hanging out with his friends and indulging in all manner of things that would ruin him.

As usual, he sent Dwayne to jog around the pitch a few times and put him through the usual exercises. When Dwayne finished his penance for being late, Terry put him through his paces with a few drills but everything was off; the dribbling poles wobbled from when Dwayne brushed them, and he misjudged the distance of every pass through the arcs. As for the shooting, Dwayne hoofed the ball like an abusive father kicking his stepchild. When the heartbreaking display was over, Dwayne crouched on his haunches, spitting onto the grass and panting.

'Come here,' Terry called him angrily. 'You know you're not meant to be going out on the piss don't you? What do I always tell you about beer being the Devil?'

'Yeah, I know,' he replied groggily.

'And you see what it's done to your game, don't you? You weren't sharp today. You didn't convince me.' Dwayne was looking away, staring into space so Terry slapped him on the cheek to gain his attention. 'Listen to what I'm telling you. There is a good chance that you'll get picked up to play for a big club and go on to earn a shitload of money. And when you're in the position where you can afford to blow a grand on a bottle of champagne, then yeah, you can miss training and it won't matter that much. But until then, you've got to stay sharp. You've got to stay humble, understand?'

'Yeah,' was all Dwayne could manage. *You're lucky I fucking turned up at all* was what he was thinking.

'Don't let it happen again. I mean it.'

It was like the forbidden fruit; after his first taste of getting a lie-in on a Sunday morning in what seemed like forever, he found it harder and harder to resist. And why – why should he have to go to bed early on a Saturday night when everyone else was out enjoying themselves. Why did training have to start so early in the first fucking place?

The next time Dwayne turned up late, Terry knew it was gone. He didn't even bother making him run the pitch or do his drills. When Dwayne didn't turn up at all, feigning some kind of cold when really he was hung over as shit, Terry still couldn't find it in him to drop Dwayne completely.

The next match Dwayne played was against Watford Youth FC. It wasn't that Watford had a terrible team, because they didn't, but this was a game that everybody, including Doug Phillips the assistant coach for Watford, was expecting to lose. They'd been plagued with injuries all season and their first team was made up of subs.

Despite everything, Dwayne was part of the starting line-up, much to the dislike of his fellow teammates. Terry was angry at himself also, for not having the courage to sub Dwayne like he'd threatened to.

The anger didn't last long.

After ten minutes, Dwayne stopped running for the ball. He was sluggish and looked heavier around the gut than he had just a month before. It was depressing to see him getting run ragged chasing after strikers that weren't half as fast as he used to be. When he did get the ball, Dwayne was easily muscled-off by defenders who ganged up on him due to his notorious rep as a real dazzler. But all those flashes of brilliance he'd previously shown had faded into mediocrity. After twenty-five minutes of looking like shit, Dwayne was subbed.

And he never played again.

When he was finished with Genie, Dwayne returned to the room with sweat running down his face in oily rivulets. As he passed Jonah he slapped him on the chest, and immediately, Jonah wanted to run off and change his t-shirt.

'Your turn, Jonah,' he said slumping in the armchair.

'No thanks,' he replied, his skin crawling. They could think he was queer for all he cared, but he was not about to lose his virginity to some drugged-up old slapper. In the kitchen, he was quite sure he could hear Genie sniffing.

Whether it was powder or tears she was sniffing up, Jonah wasn't sure.

12

The orange intensity of the sun began to mellow. This freak heat wave had sapped all the juice out of the city of London, and now, even the police sirens seemed lacklustre, as if they were yawning instead of sounding the menacing wail that sent panic through the community.

Jonah was back on the balcony, mesmerised by the endless sea of buildings, the scatter of cars and dots of people; its ugliness was almost poetic. The summer air was thick and weighty and did nothing for his heat-induced headache. A glass of water would surely sort it out, but he couldn't pull himself away; not yet. He was entranced by what he could see, and enchanted by what he *couldn't*. There were beautiful girls hidden behind some of those buildings, he thought. There were people having sweaty early-evening sex under a bed sheet with their windows wide open. There were people getting fucked-up on crack, heroin, weed, speed, booze. Maybe there were girls getting forced to do things they didn't want to like Genie. Maybe there were *boys* getting forced to do things they didn't want to. With that train of thought, Jonah began thinking again about that anti-gun campaign and feeling sorry for anybody unfortunate enough to be locked up on a day like this. Maybe that could be a campaign in itself, he wondered. Just take snapshots of the city on a day like today and put them on posters warning that this is what you leave behind when you go to prison.

There would be a thousand crazy stories on a night like tonight, he thought to himself. There was something in the air that tickled him with each rare kiss of breeze. The citizens of this city need a lift every now and then from the piss-poor miserable weather and vibes so bad that they made your skin itch like flea bites. Of course they did, and when there was that scarce feeling of ... of peace, of relaxation, then it was worth celebrating like Christmas or any other holiday.

In his pocket, Jonah's phone began to vibrate against his leg. When he took it out and saw that the screen displayed a number that he didn't recognise, he knew it was *her*. For a second, his belly turned over, breath got caught in his throat; a painful and uncomfortable combination that came with that gratifying mix of excitement and nerves. To go with it, he suddenly had the urge to urinate even though he knew his bladder was empty, the tip of his penis aching like he'd tried to stop peeing mid-flow.

He answered the call, trying to sound as cool as he possibly could. Husky and easy-going was the vibe he was going for: 'Hello?'

'Hello?' the voice said back, like she'd been the one answering the call.

'Hello.'

'Is that Jonah?'

'It is indeed,' he replied, his tummy settling but his dick still aching with anticipation. 'Who may I ask is calling?'

'This is Rose. You left your number?' Ah, very clever. She'd managed to turn the game around and force him onto his back foot. Yes, she'd called him up, but he'd left his number in the first place signalling that he was the one who wanted to speak to her. So now, instead of just trying to play it cool and pretend like he was the one in demand and she was the eager beaver, he had to turn on the charm to reel her in. It was a complicated game.

'Oh hey!' He immediately regretted the transgression from laid back to over-the-top enthusiastic. *Relax, just be yourself.* 'Hey, how you doin' Rose?'

He opened the balcony door and hurried off to his room, avoiding the curious looks from Dwayne who was sharing a bong with Billy and Genie on the sofa.

'I'm good, bit tired.' Her voice was soft but weary, the texture like honey on toast.

Closing the door, Jonah stretched out on his bed and got comfortable. 'I felt sorry for you earlier, all cooped up in there on such a nice day. It's criminal.' Her laugh was like a flute played underwater. 'So, what you up to?'

'I'm just at home, just had some dinner.'

'Oh yeah? What'd you eat?' he asked, genuinely interested.

'My mum made a potato salad and some salmon.'

'Nice?'

'Lovely.'

'Sounds it. I ain't eaten anything yet. You just reminded me that I'm hungry. You reckon you could open the cafe up and make me a sandwich?'

'Yeah right!' she said sarcastically. 'What, can't you cook?'

'No I can cook,' he lied 'I just can't be bothered right now. It's too hot.'

'Mmm. Heard it's going to rain soon. I hope it doesn't though.'

'I hope it *does*. When it gets this hot, a bit of rain is needed just to wash everything away. Freshens the air up.'

She sighed. 'No, I hate the rain. I want it to stay hot like this all the time. It's funny how people always complain that it's too cold in this country, then when the sun comes out everyone moans that it's too hot.'

He giggled. His stomach settled and he no longer felt the need to fill the bath with the contents of his bladder. He snuggled against the pillow and looked out onto the street through the blinds. The sky was turquoise-purple, turning the scenery grey in the hazy twilight.

'So ... What's all this about the fair?' she asked him with what sounded like a smile on her face, and this in turn stretched his own smile even further until the skin on his cheeks felt like it was going to split.

'Well,' he began like he was about to pitch a business proposition. 'I saw the fair being advertised and I thought you might wanna go.'

'Why'd you think *I'd* wanna go?' she replied in an equally business-like tone.

'Because the fair's fun.'

'Is it? All the fairs I've been to are filled with too many gypsies and too many thugged-out blacks. No offence.'

'None taken,' he said with a snigger. 'I know the fair is pretty ghetto, but they're kinda cool as well. Don't you think?'

She paused. 'I'm in two minds.'

'Please elaborate.'

'Well on one hand I'm thinking "It's been a long time since I went out on a date" and on the other hand I'm thinking "This guy wants to take me to some rusty old fair with those creaky old rides and a bunch of mad gypsies running wild all over the shop".'

'And?' he asked, knowing that he must have it in the bag now. She'd given him all the right signs, the first and most obvious was that she called him.

'I'll think about it.'

'You'll think about it?'

'Yeah. I don't even know you yet. What d'you think I am, a moron or something? You got to charm me a bit first.'

Something about her invite to charm her gave him an erection. It was an innocent enough thing to say, but it was also seductively suggestive enough for him to read between the lines. He knew if he played his cards right he could take her out. And if that went well, who knows? A kiss and a fumble? Maybe, just maybe, if he was a lucky boy and was sweet enough to make her laugh or win her a stuffed bear at one of those rigged shooting ranges, it could have a happy ending.

'Fair enough – no pun intended,' he said and was pleasantly surprised when she seemed to find it hilarious. 'What's your favourite film, musician and food?'

'Erm ... favourite film ... I like that movie Training Day. You ever seen that?'

'Yeah. Once.' He'd watched it round Billy's flat the day before New Years eve after getting smashed on some absolutely foul white wine that his mum had stashed in the kitchen from Christmas. It tasted like vinegar and was about as easy to swallow down as nail varnish remover.

'I like that film. My favourite musician is ... I don't know I like all kinds of music. I bought Beverly Knight's album the other day. That's quite good.'

'Oh I like her,' he chimed, though he'd never heard any of her songs and only knew the name from hearing her briefly interviewed on the radio. 'What's your favourite food?'

She paused before a gentle chuckle escaped from her mouth. The sound went through his ears like a musical note on the other end of the receiver. 'I don't know. I just eat whatever's in front of me. I'm not that fussy.'

'So if I take you out for dinner at McDonald's that'll be okay?'

'Yeah, if you don't mind wearing a Big Mac on your head and a milkshake down your shirt, then by all means take me to McDonald's.' They both laughed in sync. Jonah's muscles were loose like he'd just received a massage from her voice. As long as he didn't say anything stupid, which he hoped to God he wouldn't, his guess was she was ready to be reeled in and hauled onto his love boat.

'What about you?' she asked.

'Me?'

'Yeah. How come you were so chirpy when you came in to the shop this morning?'

Her question caught him off guard. The truth was, he didn't really know how to answer it.

'I don't know why I was so happy. See, I don't live in London at the minute –'

'– You don't?' she interjected, more disappointed than she'd like to have let on.

He quickly bounced back so he could fully explain. 'No. I'm from London originally, but I had to move to Nottingham a year ago.'

'How come?'

'My mum has a whole bag of sisters up there and she thought it would be good to get away from London because of all the black kids that are getting shot up and stabbed to death, and I suppose she didn't want me dead too. My cousin got shot in the back a few years ago – '

'– Did he?' she gasped, shocked but morbidly intrigued.

'Well yeah,' he continued, knowing the rest of the tale would disappoint her. 'It was an accident. Him and his friends had this pellet gun, but they got some guy they knew to drill the barrel out so that it could fire live rounds. Don't ask me why they wanted it, but they did. Anyway, my cousin Marcus was sitting in the front seat of the car and one of them was fucking around –' as soon as the swearword left his mouth, he cursed himself silently. '– I mean they were playing about with the gun in the back, like aiming it out the window and stuff like that, then one of them had it on his lap when it suddenly just went off. Missed Marcus's spine by half an inch, so I guess my mum was all stressed about the fact that they were able to get hold of a loaded pistol so easily.'

Was he giving her too much information? That was a risk he didn't want to run over the phone. He didn't want to fill her up with horror stories about his life for the sake of entertaining her, but at the same time he thought maybe she'd appreciate him being so open with her. This first time phone stuff was tricky.

'Wow,' she said in a low voice. 'Can he walk?'

'Yeah. It hurts him like hell in the winter but that's the price he pays I guess.' He was glad he didn't tell her how the guy who accidentally blasted Marcus in his back broke his own wrist from the recoil of the treacherous weapon.

Jonah began telling her about college and what he was studying and was flattered when she began to ask him questions about the course without being prompted. She seemed to find the whole subliminal advertising thing as fascinating as he did. If only she was on that course with me, he thought to himself and then became almost overwhelmed with the thought of leaving her and London behind. With his eyes closed, Jonah sketched her face in his mind. He needed that happy thought as a distraction;

he was going to hit the bottle if he kept thinking about going back.

She told him she was studying to become a beautician, and although she loved learning how to make people pretty, the bitchiness in the classroom was almost intolerable. 'We have these dummy heads that we had to cut and layer for part of a mock exam,' she explained, 'and this one spiteful bitch called Helen snipped a chunk out of my dummy's hair when I went to the canteen on my break.'

'How did you know it was her?'

'She's just a cow. It was written all over her face when I came back. She had this little smirk while she was cutting her own dummy's hair and I was wondering why she was so happy until I realised that my dummy had been tampered with. I would've loved to have caught her doing it though. I'd've grabbed her and cut her eyebrows off. But instead, I just went into the toilets and cried,' she admitted sadly, and ironically, they both seemed to sigh at exactly the same time like two tuneless bagpipes. 'I just get really fed up at college, know what I mean?'

Jonah wanted to tell her that he knew exactly what she meant, but instead just nodded silently. She explained that she was thinking of dropping out because although she loved what she was studying, the tools were just too expensive and she was barely keeping her head above water working at the cafe. She received a grant from her local council because only one of her parents was working, but that was just enough to pay the fees.

'What's so expensive that you need to buy?'

'Oh God ... Scissors, curlers, tongs, make-up, clips, pins, dummies, hair dryers. It's a really prestigious college y'know. The list is endless. Did you know I bought a pair of scissors for seventy pounds?'

'What?' Jonah exclaimed, astonished that such a common instrument could be so costly. 'What were they made out of, gold?'

'Nope. Stainless steel, industry standard, and I've still got another year of this to go.'

As their dire situations seemed to parallel each other, there was a moment of complete and comfortable silence, before Jonah said something that breached even his new found courage: 'I really feel like giving you a hug.' Like a delayed reaction, Jonah realised what he'd just said and his body stiffened like rigor mortis. 'I didn't mean it like in some kind of pervert way, I just ...'

'It's okay, relax!' she assured him. 'I know what you mean. It's a bit forward though. You haven't even officially asked me out.'

'I wrote you the note.'

'I don't care. I want an officially worded verbal invitation to go out on a date with you. And, I want a detailed plan of what time, where you're thinking of taking me, and what time you're going to have me home.'

Considering that he had a wad of cash, his pick of clothing and flashy jewellery, he realised he could afford to be as extravagant as he wanted. The only problem was he didn't know many restaurants outside of the fast food chains and he certainly had no intention of taking her to dirty Ken's.

'I'm waiting.'

'Okay, well I could pick you up at seven –'

'I haven't agreed to go out with you yet.' She said cheekily.

'Oh, sorry. Rose, would you like to accompany me to dinner at seven tomorrow evening?'

'Make it eight and you might have a date.'

'Okay,' he said shaking his head, steadily getting turned on by the game of cat and mouse. 'Would you like to accompany me to dinner tomorrow night at eight?'

'Where?' she asked immediately.

'To ... um ... a nice Chinese restaurant?' He hesitated. 'Do you like Chinese?' He added quickly before she could gather her words to shoot him down with.

'Love it.'

'Phew! Would you like to go to the fair too?'

'What's your obsession with the fair, boy?'

'I just like them. I haven't been to one in years. Come on, it'll be so much fun, we can eat candy floss, go on the ghost train, it'll be a laugh. That's a money-back guarantee.'

'Your guarantee means nothing to me. You're the one paying for all of this,' she said nonchalantly.

'I'll have you home by ... let's say eleven? What d'you say?' It sounded a reasonable enough hour, more than enough time for her to get settled into bed and get a good night's sleep if she had work the next day.

'Make it midnight and you got yourself a date.'

She gave him her address and advised him to phone her when he was on her street and wait on the corner; her dad was something of a ball-breaker and if he knew that a (black) boy was taking her out, he'd probably set their Dobermann Chooko to maul him on the spot. Jonah didn't take it to heart. If his mother knew that he was taking out a girl that wasn't black, she'd be ... disappointed.

To say the least.

Jonah ended the conversation on what he thought was a nice touch: 'It's been lovely talking to you, Ms Rose. We're gonna have a fun time tomorrow, I can tell.'

'We'd better,' she replied.

When they hung up, Jonah was glad that none of his friends could see him hugging the pillow and smiling at the ceiling. Shit, he wanted to jump up and down on that bed and sing at the top of his lungs. Endorphins pumped overtime, numbing the stress that'd knotted up in him during the day. Without even being consciously aware of it, Jonah found himself humming some old eighties love song only usually shown on VH1 classics, though he couldn't remember the words or who it was by. For half an hour after that conversation he sat relishing that exquisite excitement that made every breath seem like a gift from God. He revelled in that anomalous joy for as long as he possibly could, because he knew he was experiencing one of life's true highpoints, and most definitely the pinnacle of his summer. No, not his summer, his year. Come to think of it, that very moment may have been the happiest of his life.

When he realised that he'd spent about an hour in his room and that they probably all thought he was trying to have some private time with his palm, he danced back to the front room. But when he got there his smile fled his face.

Solomon was sitting in the armchair with a briefcase held to his chest. Across from him, Dwayne was crumbling weed onto the table, and Billy was playing that noisy robot computer game again with the neck of a beer bottle in his mouth.

It was like the emergency brake got pulled in his head. Jonah came to a complete halt when he saw Solomon in such a dramatic fashion that the momentum almost pulled him backwards and off-balance. His heart jolted upwards into his oesophagus and his throat clogged up like a sooty chimney. For a second or two, while his fingers ached from what seemed to be sudden bad circulation around his heavy hands, Jonah couldn't move or breathe or even swallow. He thought that he might pass out at any moment if he didn't sit down, his blood rushing through him in a boiling tidal wave.

Jesus Christ, am I having a stroke? Jonah thought as he fumbled for the door frame and gripped it for support. It was a ludicrous thing to think, because only old people had strokes, right? But what else could it have been? A heart attack? Oh, dear lord, now he was scared. The feeling in his hands slowly came back, that horrible pins-and-needles seeming to slowly roll away like a sea tide going out, and air was passing through his mouth okay now. He took a deep breath just to make sure, and as he looked at the carpet beneath his feet, the stars began to wink away from the orbit of his vision as it reorganised itself. When he looked up, only Solomon had noticed Jonah's presence in the room, and his lips curled up at the corners as if he'd just witnessed Jonah's discomfort and had found it ... amusing.

Jonah quickly retreated from the living room and into the kitchen. He'd tried to look natural, but his haste only drew more attention, as Dwayne looked up in time to see him vanish from the doorway. Once inside the kitchen Jonah charged past Genie sitting at the table with a cup of tea in her hand, and scrambled for an empty glass to fill with water. It took two whole glasses for the dryness in his mouth to subside, but that bitter taste still lingered, like he'd swallowed some raw coffee. Again, he inhaled through his nose, held it, and released through his mouth. He repeated the process a few times until he started to feel somewhat normal again, but the scenery was still blurry and wobbly.

'You alright?' Genie asked him sheepishly, staring at the fridge. She slowly sipped from the mug, not even bothering to look at him as if she didn't expect an answer.

'Yeah, just came over a bit dizzy there,' he replied wetting his hand under the tap and wiping his brow. He leaned against the counter, the lights in the kitchen harsh and aggressive. Under the forceful glow, Genie looked like a translucent skeleton – a pile of bones trying to appear human with a bad disguise of waxy skin. Her eyes were dark, beady and unblinking, like that of a mentally disturbed person. Under that light, Jonah was able to see the extent of how much humanity she'd given the drugs, and realised at the rate she was going, she didn't have long before she'd OD.

He didn't know where he was more uncomfortable, in the living room or in the kitchen. A panicky, surreal claustrophobia began to constrict his respiratory system. His first thought, and it was a plausible enough theory for him to run with, was that he was having some kind of bad reaction to all the weed he'd smoked last night, and because he'd mixed it with alcohol, his body was still just a bit wonky. There had been times when, after a heavy night of blazing and boozing, he'd get these chronic headaches that would just attack the interior of his skull and then disappear at random intervals. He'd also suffered loss of breath before, but that was more because the beer was ruining any kind of cardio tolerance he'd developed than anything else.

Another thing that might've been possible was that the weed was laced with something spicy that Dwayne hadn't let him know about. He'd heard that certain drug dealers in London would actually sprinkle cocaine over the weed in a joint to make it more addictive, and thus get the client hooked on their product. Not to mention that the combination of the different-class narcotics would send you to another planet and give you a high that Jack and his beanstalk would have had trouble reaching. Well, he'd been about one degree of meditation away from an out of body experience from what he was smoking, and he guessed that if you got *that* high, you would have one hell of a bumpy trip on the way down. But turbulence wouldn't even describe what just happened to him, it was more like something had gripped hold of his heart and was trying to wring it dry, slowly draining his life force. And why had it happened so suddenly? He was fine just seconds before. In fact, he couldn't remember the last time he was ever that happy (or if he'd ever been that happy before in his life to begin with) and he'd got over the worst of the hangover by about six that evening. So what triggered it off?

Solomon. Solo man. Solo. Sol. Soul.

Jonah realised it was only when he saw Solomon sitting in the front room that he began to spin out. Was he afraid of Solomon? That was insane. No, it was stupid to even think that he'd be afraid of Solomon, and more to the point his male pride wouldn't even consider it a possibility.

So what was it? Because, if he began to feel that way again when he went back in the front room, he may very well just drop dead on the spot.

As he rinsed his glass and refilled it, Jonah felt plain nervous. Nervous like the dentist was going to hammer his teeth out or nervous as though a doctor was going to tell him he had cancer. It was the nerves that lay at the other end of the spectrum from the ones he'd had just moments before when butterflies danced around near his groin while on the phone to Rose. But where did they come from? Maybe it was embarrassment from how he'd behaved and responded to Solomon's courtesies that clawed away at him. His mind began piecing together memories through the foggy haze of the previous evening, and one that continued to flash up was of him yelling at Solomon that his magic tricks were nothing more than fraudulent bullshit. It was with the realisation that he'd have to apologize in some way to Solomon that made his body shut down with mortification. Apologising for acting like a drunken yob was always a difficult and shameful chore, but once done it would help lift his burden of guilt; a dozen hangovers in the past had proved this theory.

That wasn't it though, or all of it anyway. Something niggled away at his mind like he'd just packed his suitcase and left the house wondering what vital thing he'd forgotten to take with him (he later remembered that while in his hurry to leave Nottingham, he'd forgotten to take his rosary. It wasn't anything essential in the way a toothbrush or a comb is essential for his daily routine, but he never really slept without it hanging over the bedpost).

He remembered the nightmare. Aftershocks of unease shook him as he wondered how he could've possibly imagined something so disgusting. What would a psychiatrist have made of the dream? They'd probably tell him he was some kind of sexual deviant and felt a strong anxiety about not having done the deed yet at almost eighteen years of age. But it didn't matter what a psychiatrist would've thought because he'd be damned if he was ever going to reveal those dreams to another soul.

Or that he was a virgin.

Did I just have a fucking panic attack? Men didn't have panic attacks, did they? What else could it have been? He wasn't ill (touch wood) and the more he thought about the weed and the drink, the more he began to disregard the negative side effects, because Billy and Dwayne seemed normal enough and they got wasted every day.

'Yeah right. Normal enough, he snorted under his breath, feeling drained and flimsy.

'Did you say something?' Genie asked, gaping up at him with her gaunt features.

He snapped away from his daydream, surprised that she'd heard him under the din issuing from the next room. 'I was just thinking. Do men get panic attacks?'

Her tight, sunken cheeks stretched into a painful smile as she began laughing. 'Of course they do. It's a human thing not a generic one. It's not like having a period.'

Genie's vulgarity made Jonah wince, and at the same time she seemed to have the exact same reaction; she hadn't had her period in months.

'But why do you get them?' he asked her, quickly realigning the conversation's direction and away from the abject.

'Could be anything,' she shrugged. 'If you got a phobia about something or if you're nervous it could happen. Some people get panic attacks about being in debt or some people even have problems about leaving their house and the thought of it brings an attack on. It's just one of those things.'

'Have you ever had one?'

She looked at him suspiciously, as if she were trying to work out where this line of conversation was headed. 'Yeah,' she said reluctantly.

'What about?'

She tucked a loose strand of hair behind her ear, distracting herself from his gaze. 'When I used to work with the stocks,' she recalled the memory with bitter nostalgia, 'if I was given the responsibility of being in charge of a certain number of stocks and I invested the money wrong, the bank could've lost thousands. Millions on one occasion.'

'Did it ever happen?'

Shaking her head, she sipped her tea. 'No. But that's the way it always is. The fear of something happening is always worse than the event itself.'

The more they conversed the more Jonah realised just how intelligent Genie had actually been. The thought was always in past tense because she no longer had that same intelligence that made her operate in such a high pressure job. Instead, she'd become a robot reliant on the oils of her cruel creator. He wanted to ask her if she ever had panic attacks about running out of coke, but he knew that what she probably experienced on those occasions was far worse than a mere panic attack. It would probably be like Hell.

They were silent after that. He looked down into his water and she stared at the side of the fridge in a miserable trance. There was part of Jonah that wanted to go over and shake her out of it, just grab her and make her see how she was up to her neck in the sands of life's hourglass. But what was the point? She was lost forever, and being in the same room as her was like being in the room with the terminally ill, watching them withering away before his eyes.

He backed the water and shambled out the room without a word.

13

The thing to do, Jonah thought, was just relax and try and have a bit of fun. What was the saying? Boys will be boys? Wasn't that what they were all doing? After all, most red-blooded males got drunk, had fights and used women like playthings as they saw fit, and that was just the way it worked. If he was going to bitch, moan and worry through the rest of the week, then he may as well just go home now and he certainly didn't want to do that.

Continuing to breathe in through his nose and out through his mouth so that his heartbeat stayed nice and even, Jonah went into the front room, which was now littered with candles. Shadows danced on the walls as Billy, Dwayne and Solomon sat around the coffee table.

'Ah, just the man to get the party started,' Solomon said as Jonah walked into the spooky ambience. The briefcase, along with three bottles of red wine and several glasses, lay on the table, flanked by two cylindrical candles.

'What's in the case?' Jonah asked suspiciously.

'I can't show you until the girls arrive, apparently,' Solomon said, pouring wine for everyone.

Jonah walked over and took a seat next to Billy, whose lips were already purple from his third glass of wine. 'What's with all the candles?'

'You'll see,' Dwayne replied, sipping the wine. 'It's gonna be so fun. Especially when the girls get here.'

'What girls?'

'Three girls from around the way should be here any minute,' Dwayne told him, dipping his finger into the pool of hot wax collecting just beneath the flame.

Solomon was organising the cushions around the table, fluffing the pillows and making sure that everyone would have adequate space to be comfortable. The secrecy of it all was beginning to excite and at the same time frighten Jonah. So far, all the secretive things he'd discovered this week had shocked him into paranoia of potential jail time. But, reluctantly sipping on the wine even though the mere fragrance of it made his stomach writhe like a nest of angry snakes, he began to calm down. Whatever was in the case couldn't be that bad if a bunch of little estate whores were coming over to indulge in its contents. If it was drugs then Solomon would already have them on the table, and the same went for guns. Maybe they were going to have a quiet game of Cluedo.

Dwayne began telling them about the plans for later in the evening. He suggested that after they got nicely toasted on wine and, inevitably, weed, that they go into the centre of town and hit a club. Jonah wanted to bring up the fact that they didn't have any ID to prove they were over eighteen (or twenty-one as more of the up-market clubs deemed it necessary), but chose to keep a lid on it. They'd probably just laugh at his naivety and he'd get pissed off, so why bother? Jonah agreed that Dwayne's plan seemed like fun, and he began to genuinely look forward to it. If they went to a club, it meant that Dwayne probably wouldn't be able to sneak a gun in, and therefore nobody would get shot. It also meant maybe, just maybe, they'd be able to have some regular fun without any violent hassles. They had plenty of money after all, and Jonah always wanted to go out for a night on the town without worrying about spending too much of his weekly budget, or feeling insecure about his lack of jewellery and designer clothes. Now he didn't have to worry about any of that, because everything was sorted for him. All he really had to worry about was drinking too much, which was a problem his immaturity hadn't seemed to be able to curve yet. But, as he drank the wine, he decided that no amount of peer pressure was going to make him take a hit on a joint. No way Jose – especially since he had a promising date with a sexy girl the next evening. By sticking to getting drunk, he could weather the hangover in the morning and duration of the next day until he had to start getting ready to see Rose.

The doorbell rang and Genie answered it with a face so sour that she actually looked like one of those crappy little cheap Halloween masks made of plastic. The three girls, Mary, Helen and Shamilla, who turned up wearing trashy market clothes and looking like Kings Cross hookers, became quite uneasy at the sight of Genie and hesitated to ask for Solomon, even with their street-hardened attitudes.

Genie let them in and told them to go through to the living room with the enthusiasm of a piece of dry toast. The girls hurried ahead, treating Genie with the same wariness that they treated every crack-head they saw. Of course, there was the unspoken rule you lived by when it came to people on drugs – don't trust them as far as you can throw them, and if you stuck to that and kept a relative amount of distance from them, then you were cool. The girls were more than familiar with the stories of crack-fiends who went around trying to jab people with diseased needles. Now, these may have just been urban myths but even so, to treat a crack-head with any kind of humanity was to run the risk of getting poked with a HIV needle, so it was best to avoid where possible.

Jonah gave them the once-over as Solomon introduced them to everyone. Mary was a rather butch, dark-skinned black girl, who wore a silver skirt about five inches above her knees, a green boob-tube top, and leather boots. Helen was plain and mousy, and about as exciting to the eye as a cardboard box. She wore a skirt too, but due to her ginger hair, her skin remained milk-bottle pale. Shamilla, who Jonah supposed was the most attractive of the three (which wasn't hard to be) but was still no prize turkey herself, wore a long imitation-fur coat, and under it not much else. She was Indian or Sri-Lankan, curvy with a big chest and flabby stomach to match. If she lost a bit of weight, Jonah thought, she might be attractive, if not for her long side-burns.

'What the fuck are they supposed to be?' Billy slurred as he looked at the girls, shutting them down as they entered the room.

Although he hated being discourteous, even to a bunch of cheap slags such as these, Jonah joined Dwayne and Billy laughing. Mary and Shamilla began to protest, running their mouths with colourful expletives in that classy way only girls from the estate seemed to be able to do. Helen remained quiet and instead made herself comfortable on the sofa next to Solomon.

After commenting that Billy wasn't more than a trampy-looking drunk with a beer belly, Mary reached down to the wine to fill up a glass.

'What're you doing?' Dwayne asked the girl.

'What's it look like? I'm getting a drink.'

'Didn't Solomon tell you to bring your own bottle?'

'Are you being serious?' Mary protested in an annoyingly cockney accent that didn't somehow fit her appearance.

'Deadly.'

Taking her coat off and revealing a pudgy stomach that seemed to fold over the top of her jeans, Shamilla joined in fighting for the cause against sobriety. 'You got three bottles over there, why don't you stop being stingy?'

'Billy bought them, so it's down to him,' Dwayne lied.

'Can we have some of your drink?' Shamilla asked Billy.

'What do I get?' he said, the sentence so mumbled that it sounded like one word.

'What do you want?' Mary asked.

'My cock sucked,' Billy told them unflinchingly. 'Then you can have as much wine as you want. And we got weed too.'

Not quite believing the audacity of what Billy had just said, Jonah began cracking up though part of this was down to embarrassment. The three girls all looked at each other and burst into laughter.

'You're drunk!' Shamilla said, then began howling with probably the most annoying laugh that Jonah had ever heard. It was a cross between high and low pitch, like a machine gun sped-up on a tape player. 'Go on, Mary, I want some wine.'

'Bollocks!' Mary said, her muscular arms flexing. 'I'll go to the off-licence and stick a bottle down my knickers if I have to. If you're thirsty you do it. I hear you're the best at it anyway.'

'Shut up!' Shamilla said, nudging Mary.

'Is she the best cocksucker in London?' Dwayne asked Mary.

'Best cocksucker this side of England,' Mary yelled before being pushed onto the sofa by Shamilla.

While all the joking carried on, Billy interjected: 'No. I want the white one to do it.'

There was a moment of stunned silence before everyone in the room broke into laughter – Jonah included. He put his hand over his eyes and sipped his wine. Helen, who'd barely said a word to anyone or smiled since she arrived, seemed to cringe into her seat, an uncomfortable centre of attention.

'Look, if you get us drunk, who knows what we'll do?' Mary said, quickly flashing her small breasts to the boys then pulling her top back up. Dwayne began pouring them some wine, then grabbed Mary and pulled her on his lap. Once there with her wine in hand, Dwayne casually put one arm around her shoulder and began fondling her boobs. Shamilla gulped at her wine, took her shoes off and sat cross-legged on the floor next to Jonah. When everyone was settled, Solomon opened the case.

'You've gotta be kidding me ...' Jonah said, realising what they had in mind. 'A Ouija board?'

It looked ancient, like it'd been carved from Eden's apple tree. The letters were in a faded italic text that was so old he could barely recognise what they were. 'It's been in my family for generations.' Solomon informed him.

Shamilla placed a hand on the inside of Jonah's thigh, and squeezed it gently. 'Don't be scared, it's only a bit of fun.'

'I'm not scared,' he protested, scanning the room. Everyone seemed to be smiling, and this comforted him a little bit. Whatever superstitions Jonah harboured about the supernatural were somewhat calmed by the feeling of shared consequence; If something bad was going to happen as a result of the Ouija board, it was going to happen to all of them.

'It's only a bit of fun, mate,' Mary told him while Dwayne tweaked her nipple. Clinging to the arm of the sofa and curling up against it, Helen drank down the remainder of her glass and proceeded to pour another. When Billy saw this, he used the table to pull himself to his feet and slumped down in between Helen and Solomon, even though there was clearly no room for three people on the couch. Solomon got up and sat where Billy had been. Billy began to emulate Dwayne's movements, whispering in Helen's ear as he draped one lazy arm around her. After the initial apprehension, Helen began to relax. She'd been in this predicament dozens of times before and learned how to block out the bad stuff.

'Okay, has anyone ever played this before?' Solomon asked, his voice charming and distinguished. None of them had meddled with a Ouija board before, so he continued. 'It's really easy. All we have to do is touch our fingertips to the glass and call out to see if any spirits are there. If they are, the glass will move around the board and start to spell stuff out. But once it does, don't take your fingers off the glass or we'll break the connection.'

'And why's that bad?' Dwayne asked him.

'Well if we're in the middle of contacting a spirit and the connection breaks it could wind up just staying in the house. And you don't want that do you?'

'Yeah right,' Dwayne replied sarcastically.

'Don't be a sceptic, Dwayne. You'd be surprised what kind of freaky things happen when it gets going.'

'Like some Exorcist shit!' Billy managed, mumbling like he had a mouth full of food.

'I don't believe in all this stuff, it's all a load of bollocks anyway,' Mary chimed in. 'Who gives a shit if a spirit gets trapped in the house?'

'You scoff at it now,' Solomon said gently, 'but see how hard it'd be trying to eat dinner when all the plates in your kitchen are flying against the wall because you've got an angry ghost living with you.'

'I believe you, Sol,' Billy added, raising his glass. 'My mum used to have one of these things.'

'She did?' Jonah asked. This would probably be the most coherent thing Billy would manage to blurt out before he got completely wasted and just started swearing at everyone. 'What was it like?'

'I only saw them play it once. All I remember was this one time when I woke up and her and my dad and some other guys were all fucking around with it in the kitchen downstairs, and they all started shouting. I heard my dad shout out something about contacting Elvis, then one of my dad's friends ran out the house. It must've scared the fuck out of them whatever it was.' He sipped his wine and nodded to himself, and his face became locked in the most unusual expression; he just stared through Jonah with glassy, bloodshot eyes, as if he were remembering something else that he didn't want to share with the rest of them. 'I remember that guy coming back to my house a few weeks later and telling my dad that he kept hearing the Devil talking to him, but my dad didn't believe it.'

'Great,' Jonah mumbled. A shudder slid down his spine and his head became heavy with the next gulp of wine, like the one glass he'd consumed rekindled the alcohol from the previous evening and accelerated the intoxicated feeling. He put his glass on the table and waved Dwayne away when he tried to refill it.

Ignoring Billy's worrying little parable, Solomon cleared his throat. 'Shall we begin, ladies and gentlemen?' he said, placing his fingers on the large triangular glass. There was a hole cut out in the middle so it could circle a letter when spelling something out. Everybody crouched closer to the board and sat on their knees around the table, Billy wobbling on the spot. 'Don't take your fingers off the glass, Bill.'

'Right you are, skipper,' Billy replied.

When everyone had their fingers on a part of the glass, careful not to burn themselves on the flames of the candles, Solomon began.

'Is there anyone there that wishes to talk with us?'

Nobody spoke. The girls all looked at each other with smiles of unpredictable excitement. Shamilla bit her bottom lip, just waiting for someone to break the silence and frighten her.

'Is there anyone who –' before Solomon could finish his sentence, the glass slowly slid to the word 'YES' on the right side of the board.

'Oh my God,' Helen whispered. An excited giggle wriggled from Shamilla's mouth even though she bit her lip with anxiety.

'One of you lot pushed it,' Mary said defiantly. 'I felt it.'

'Shh!' Solomon ordered. 'Spirit, can you tell us your name?'

Slowly, the glass slid across to 'B'. Helen gasped like someone had stolen the breath out of her mouth.

'One of you lot is pushing it –' Mary said again, her loud voice contradicting the eerie atmosphere.

'Shut the fuck up!' Jonah demanded in a harsh whisper, focussing all his attention on the board like he was witnessing a miracle.

From 'B' the glass moved to 'I' and then began to move quicker. Dwayne whispered each letter out loud as the glass settled. Jonah felt tingles rise and drop through his torso like his stomach had pins and needles.

'B-I-N-L-A-D-E-N. Binladen?' Dwayne said, confused, then looked up at Billy who was looking back at him and grinning. 'You prick! You had me going there.'

Jonah felt his chest loosen up and the oxygen release from his lungs easier. Everyone, including Solomon, was giggling, but Jonah was mostly laughing at the fact that Billy was able to spell the name properly.

'Okay, okay. Joke's over now, let's get serious,' Solomon said, and then instructed them all to replace their fingertips back on the glass. He cleared his throat and tried again. 'Is there anyone there who wishes to talk with us?'

This time everyone was less tense. They were all still amused at Billy's little prank, and that took the edge off of the potential fright of contacting the dead. Now the Ouija board just seemed more silly than scary to Jonah, not that he believed in any of that supernatural mumbo jumbo to begin with.

'Are there any spirits out there that wish to contact us?' Solomon repeated with his eyes closed, his voice low and even for dramatic effect.

After maybe twenty seconds of complete silence, the triangular glass began spinning around the board in a large circle making them look like they were all trying to clean the table with one sponge. A nervous laugh escaped from Mary as she looked down at the board with unblinking eyes. She knew now that nobody was pushing the glass just from the way that it spun out of control like an unfettered garden hose on full blast. Dwayne watched with intense concentration, following the circle with awe. While this was all happening, Jonah removed his gaze from the board and looked over at Solomon, who was staring at Helen without her knowing – a subtle and peculiar smile on his lips.

Then, as if magnetised from beneath, the glass flew to 'YES'.

'Spirit,' Solomon said, averting his attention from Helen and staring at the ceiling. 'Can you tell us your name?'

With the pace of a slug the glass began to spell something out, the anticipation adding to the unpredictable anxiety around the table. The glass suddenly darted to the last letter, completing the word.

B-E-R-R-E-T-T-A.

When it finished and they realised what it spelt, Helen's hands shook like a Parkinson's sufferer.

'Don't take your hands away,' Solomon told her softly.

'Berretta? We've contacted a fuckin' gun?' Dwayne said, puzzled.

Now, Helen's fingertips flushed white as she pressed down on the glass. Jonah noticed that her mouth had twisted into a grimace of horror. She was gasping, overloaded with trepidation.

Before her friends could enquire what was wrong, Solomon began to speak up again.

'Is Berretta your name?' The glass went to 'YES'. Solomon continued, 'How old were you when you died, Berretta?'

The glass slid to the top row of numbers, flicking to '6' then back to '2'.

Helen emitted a frightened sigh with the movement of the glass.

'Ask it how it died,' Dwayne said enthusiastically, ignoring Helen's obvious distress.

'How did you die, Berretta?' Solomon called out calmly, like he'd performed this ceremony several times in the past.

Slowly, ever so slowly, the glass drifted across the letters and screeched over the wood like someone running their fingernails down a chalkboard. It spelled out 'H-E-A-R-T-A-T-T-A-C-K'.

A short, concentrated breath came out of Helen's mouth like she was trying to blow out one particular candle on a birthday cake.

'What's wrong, babe?' Shamilla whispered to Helen, who refused to take her eyes away from the glass.

'Is there someone among us you wish to talk to, Berretta?' Solomon called to the invisible guest. Jonah watched the board in a sort of daze, quickly becoming convinced that nobody was tampering with the glass's flight path. It seemed like it'd got darker in the room, the candle flames incredibly still.

Once again, the glass scraped to 'YES'. Solomon asked it: 'Who would you like to speak with?'

As the glass went to 'H', Helen whimpered like an injured cat. Tears burst out of her wide eyes and rolled down her cheeks and her lips curled into her mouth like she was trying to swallow them. When the board finished spelling her name, she cried out. 'I don't want to play any more. I don't wanna play!'

'It will be extremely dangerous to break the circle now, Helen,' Solomon informed her. 'Let Berretta speak and then we can finish.'

Helen began to sob quietly, and Mary, who'd been so tough in the beginning of the game, now looked ready to start crying herself. Jonah found it hard to breathe, like he couldn't swallow down a good inhalation of oxygen. His head began to throb. Well this was a good idea, he thought, a great way to relax.

'Berretta, what would you like to say to Helen?'

The glass spelled out 'W-H-O-R-E'. Just as it settled on the last letter, a smash from the kitchen made Helen jump up on the spot like she'd sat on a live rail and got an electric shock through her arse. She screamed, and it was a loud, long and hideous sound. Helen began shrieking now, her hands quivering as she tried to hold them over her face.

'You broke the circle. That is extremely bad,' Solomon said, indifferent to her trauma.

'Fuck you!' she yelled and fell onto the couch wailing. Shamilla and Mary quickly rushed to her side and put their arms around her but she wasn't having any of it.

Dwayne looked stunned and perplexed. Then, he began to scowl as he got up and charged toward the kitchen. Though he closed the door, everyone could hear what was being said.

'Did you drop this glass?' Dwayne shouted at Genie.

'No, it fell out of the cupboard,' she replied childishly, offended at his tone and accusation.

'How can a glass just fucking fall out of a cupboard?'

'I don't know but I was nowhere near it!' she told him, raising her voice to match his.

When Dwayne returned to the room, Helen was getting up to leave. Her face was blotchy and puffy around the eyes from crying. Mary and Shamilla tried to get her to stop walking, just long enough to calm her down, but she thrashed against them with flailing arms.

'What's wrong? Them things are bullshit, you know they are,' Mary said, blocking her path to the front door.

'Berretta was my grandma's name! She died last year of a heart attack! She was sixty-two!'

Dwayne went into the hallway and put his arm around Helen, offering phony sympathy. 'Look, come back in the front room. We'll put the game away.'

She violently squirmed out of his grasp and pushed him. 'No! I'm going home!'

'Well fuck off then,' Dwayne told her simply. He looked at Shamilla and Mary. 'Are you two going to go as well because of this little prick or are you gonna stay and have some fun?'

Helen was already out the front door, the sound of her relentless sobbing echoing through the hall. Dwayne slammed the door after her and put his arms around both Mary and Shamilla. Jonah glanced over and saw both the girls looking down at the floor as they rejoined the room, ashamed of abandoning their petrified friend.

'Does that mean I'm not getting my dick sucked then?' Billy said, uninterested in the drama of the last five minutes or by the possible spirit they had just contacted. He had half the bottle of wine in his hand and was draining it from the neck of the bottle as casually as a glass of soda.

On one glass of wine Jonah had been tipsy, but the fright from the Ouija board scared him sober. As there was apparently no rational explanation behind what had just happened, he was forced to accept that they might've just been in touch with a ghost. With that discomforting notion and the weird atmosphere of shock that seemed to loom in the room, Jonah reached for the other bottle and began to refill his glass.

With the wine finished, they brought out a bottle of Jack Daniel's. Dwayne ordered everyone to do a mandatory shot – house rules. The girls didn't like the whiskey because it was too harsh, and began to chase the rum with Coca Cola from then on. Then, the weed got passed around. Even when Solomon held out the joint for Jonah, there was elegance to his gestures, like he was handling an ivory cigarette holder instead of a joint. It then occurred to Jonah at that moment that Solomon might be gay. After all, there was something distinctly disjointed about Solomon, something a little too gentle about his mannerisms.

'No thanks,' Jonah told Solomon. 'I mixed last night and ended up in the middle of a hurricane when I tried to go to sleep.'

'I know what that's like,' Solomon said, offering the joint to Billy.

'You know,' Jonah began, 'I've been trying to work out how you did that magic trick yesterday and for the life of me I can't.'

Solomon shrugged with the kind of smile you might find on a little boy trying to be cute and adorable. 'You're not supposed to figure it out. That's the point.'

'I was drunk last night, that's the only reason I wasn't able to work it out,' Jonah tried to say casually but ended up sounding confrontational. 'I'm not so bad now. You got any other tricks up your sleeve?'

'What's this?' Shamilla asked, butting into the conversation after taking a long, deep hit from the joint then passing it to Mary.

'Sol here does magic tricks,' Jonah said, pointing his thumb at Solomon. 'They're really good. I've been wracking my brain trying to figure them out.'

'Let's see one,' Shamilla asked.

'Maybe later,' Solomon told her modestly.

'Oh come on! Just one little trick,' Shamilla pleaded, her eyes slanted from the weed making her face seem even chubbier.

After a pause, he considered it. 'Okay. Just one.'

Dwayne interrupted his kissing session with Mary and told her to watch Solomon carefully.

'I'll need a volunteer.'

Shamilla waved her hand excitedly. 'Me!'

'Okay, you'll do,' he said. She clapped her hands at being chosen and stood up to join him in the middle of the room. 'Now, Shamilla, can you reveal to us that you're wearing a bra? You are wearing one, aren't you?'

Shamilla, loving the attention being drawn to her big ol' hooters, slowly pulled her top down to show her black bra just about keeping her boobs at bay.

'Okay good,' Solomon said. He picked up the imitation fur coat that she'd taken off earlier and wrapped it around her body, covering her chest. 'Jonah, I'll need you for the next part of the trick.'

Jonah, who'd been keeping an intense watch on Solomon's hand movements, stood up and walked over without taking his glance away from them. 'What do you need me to do?'

'All you have to do is place your hands over Shamilla's chest here.'

At his direction, Shamilla began flicking her tongue at Jonah, 'Come on baby, don't be shy.'

Jonah groped her chest and gave her breasts two honks, mainly to amuse his friends.

'Okay,' Solomon said. 'Billy, will you just pat Ms Shamilla on the back there.'

Billy got up, banging his knee against the edge of the coffee table in the process, and whacked her on the back with more force than necessary.

'Ow!' she complained.

'Okay, Jonah you can move your hands away now, I know that's going to be difficult, but try,' Solomon said with a smirk. Jonah's hands dropped, thankful that they didn't have to be there any longer. The public promiscuity was beginning to unsettle him.

Solomon removed the coat from around Shamilla's body. Already, Jonah could see it. He couldn't believe it, but he could see it. The line of Shamilla's cleavage and the surrounding flesh was bare under her low-cut top, where before her bra had peaked through to give a seductive glimpse of her goodies.

'Would you be so kind as to pull your top down again, my lady?' Solomon asked her, ever the gentlemen, even when asking her to show off her property to a room full of people.

She pulled her top forward and looked down, giving herself the first secret glimpse of Solomon's magic. 'I don't believe it.'

'What? What is it?' Mary asked, fascinated, craning her neck to try and see down Shamilla's top.

'My bra's gone!' Shamilla said, and then released a machinegun burst of annoying laughter, the effort of which knocked her back onto the sofa and sent her legs flying in the air, showing Jonah that her remaining underwear didn't match the item that'd magically vanished.

Jonah squinted at her chest then quickly scanned the floor. Again, he felt that anger slowly creeping up through him like burning hot mercury. He leapt to his feet, crossed the room and grabbed Shamilla, who was still cracking up too much to realise what was happening. Jonah grabbed her top and pulled it forward, looking down for himself; he saw two big breasts with nipples the size of Pringle lids and stretch marks scraping to her armpits, but no bra.

Around him, the room turned into a cacophony of laughter, at first because of the seemingly miraculous trick and then because of Jonah's audacity. The more everyone laughed, the angrier he became. Shamilla's face showed a mixture of shock and arousal as Jonah flipped the pillows and the sofa cushions in search of the missing garment. Dwayne was giggling so much he fell onto all fours on the floor, his mouth open and gasping for air, the alcohol and weed in his system obviously making Jonah's actions more hilarious.

'Lift your feet up!' Jonah ordered Mary, who was leaned back into the couch with her mouth around the rim of the wine glass filled with whiskey. Instead, she spread her legs wide open as Jonah bent down to look underneath where she was sitting, and he saw that she too was missing a piece of underwear – but that wasn't due to any magic. Jonah didn't care for pussy at that moment. All he cared about was finding that dumb girl's bra. Dwayne, who was still scrambling on all fours himself, fell onto Jonah, sucking in air like he might actually suffocate from laughing so much. Jonah nudged Dwayne off him and stood up.

'What're you looking for, Jonah?' Solomon asked, his voice just about audible. Billy's chuckling seeming to dominate the din as Jonah approached Solomon and patted him down like the law. 'Do you have a warrant?' Solomon joked without the addition of humour.

'Where is it?'

'Where's what?'

'Where's that bitch's bra?'

Shamilla feigned offence, but gave up the act to rejoin the chorus of hyenas. Jonah and Solomon were the only two people in the room who weren't smiling. They squared off to each other, eye to eye. Jonah clenched his fists, the drunken adrenaline pulsing through him and making his chest tight.

'What did you do with her bra?'

'I did a magic trick like you asked me to.'

Jonah had a premonition of attacking Solomon with a barrage of punches if he continued with his game.

'I watched you the whole time and there was no fuckin' way you could've unhooked her bra. Absolutely no way,' Jonah told him, trying to restrain himself from launching a verbal assault of swearwords and showering him in saliva. For some unexplained and completely uncharacteristic reason, Jonah hated Solomon at that moment. He felt as though he could quite easily pull his head clean off his neck with his bare hands.

'You watched me the whole time?'

'Yeah,' Jonah snapped back.

'Even when you had your hands on her body?' Solomon said with a raised eyebrow.

Jonah quickly realised that he might've been distracted for a split second, but even that wasn't long enough to go up her top, undo her bra and remove it without her or anyone else in the room seeing it. So he lied; 'Even when I had my hand on her tits I was watching *you.*'

'Even still,' Solomon began 'it wouldn't be a magic trick if you knew how I did it, would it?'

'You should be on television with that kind of stuff, Sol,' Billy interrupted. 'I bet you'd be more famous than David Blaine.'

Solomon smiled his appreciation and then turned to face Jonah, his eyes wide and ready to defend any other claims Jonah had to fire at him.

'I don't know how you did that,' Jonah confessed after a long, painful pause of silence. He was exhausted from having to exercise that much self-restraint when every vein inside him burned with ... was it envy? He couldn't tell at that point, but all he knew was that whatever the feeling had been, it was strong enough to make his body vibrate beyond his control.

'That's why it's magic,' Solomon replied.

Jonah almost fainted. He felt the room jerk away from him and then suddenly restore to normality a breath later. The laughter began to mute in the room. He sat down quickly, the smirking faces around him bobbing and floating before him like some kind of comedy ghost train. After catching his breath, Jonah reached out for the whiskey and poured himself a glass.

'Well done,' Jonah said raising his glass. 'You're a fine magician, Solomon.'

'Thank you,' Solomon said with a bow.

'I don't have the faintest idea of how you did what you just did,' Jonah said, swirling the whisky around and staring into it. 'And you lot are all laughing your heads off like it's funny. What you just saw was impossible and none of you seem to realise it.'

The more Jonah tried to unravel the mystery behind the trick, the more hilarious they found it; all except for Solomon of course, whose face remained calm throughout but with that ever so subtle curl in his top lip like he was battling to keep a smug grin at bay.

'What's so impossible about it?' Mary asked, the volume and pitch of her voice intensified from the alcohol. 'If you think that's good you should see how quick some boys have made her knickers disappear!'

Shamilla responded by slapping Mary across her bare legs, leaving a purple hand mark on her dark skin. Mary yelped and rubbed her thigh while Dwayne brazenly withdrew her breast from her top and jiggled it like a dead fish, then announced: 'Okay, you guys all ready to go? Sol?'

Solomon nodded.

'How're we getting down there?' Mary asked Dwayne with her arms draped around his neck, one boob still hanging out.

'We're driving, obviously. You ready to go, Sol?'

'Ready when you are.' Solomon replied with the obedience of a butler.

Dwayne necked the whisky and chucked Mary off his lap with the all the chivalry of a wild boar. She fell onto the seat sideways and spilled a drop of Jack on her green boob tube, leaving a dark stain ironically near her nipple. Her complaints fell on deaf ears, which Jonah found surprising for a girl with a voice that annoying. Dwayne rushed out of the room and jogged back with a six pack of bottled Budweisers. He lay the Buds down on the table and cracked one open for everyone except Solomon.

'You're not having one?' Jonah asked. Not accepting a beer was just suspicious enough for Jonah to regard him with even more caution, especially when he'd just realised that for the two days he'd spent with him, Jonah hadn't seen Solomon sip one alcoholic beverage or inhale one lungful of weed.

'I'm the designated driver,' he said, smiling.

'Oh,' Jonah replied, but he could see that there was something more to it than just him being the driver. Before he could chase up the train of thought, Dwayne pulled a little polythene bag out of his pocket. All at once he was hot, like the thermostat inside him had been cranked all the way up. His shirt clung to the back of him with an outbreak of sweat. He wiped his brow with the back of his palm, then took the Budweiser and rolled it across his neck, staring at the bag in Dwayne's hand.

'Ever done X, Jone?' Dwayne asked him, handing the pills out to the rest of them like sweeties. Billy flicked two in his mouth without hesitation, and after he gulped enough beer to wash them down, grabbed two handfuls of Shamilla's arse while she was taking her pill.

Jonah's mouth felt tomb-dry when he tried to speak. He cleared his throat with a sip of Budweiser, his eyes remaining on the little white pills. 'No, can't say that I have.'

'You'll love it,' Dwayne told him, placing a pill in his palm and extending it toward Jonah. 'Trust me on this, Jonah. You'll have a wicked time.'

Once again, Jonah sought refuge in his bottle, hoping that a distraction would fall into place between them, but the longer he waited the hotter he became. The horror stories of people doing ecstasy, collapsing in a club and dying in a coma ran through his mind. He'd heard about how the pills made you thirst like a vampire and people who had actually killed themselves by drinking too much water trying to rehydrate.

'I think I'll be alright on the beers for now,' Jonah said weakly, shying away from the bag like he was retreating from a phobia. He was drunk, and for the last year of his life that had been a good enough buzz for him.

Dwayne swallowed the X like an aspirin. 'Jonah, honestly, this makes your night better tenfold.'

'Take two, it'll make it better twentyfold,' Billy said, licking behind Shamilla's ear while she giggled.

'I don't know,' Jonah hesitated, trying to structure the sentence properly in his head before he said something that made him seem afraid. 'They put a lot of bad chemicals in those things.'

'They put chemicals in weed, too. Studies show that some forms of schizophrenia are directly linked to cannabis abuse,' Solomon added from behind him. The comment, like most of what Solomon said, angered Jonah.

'Yeah so? I don't abuse cannabis.'

'And you don't have to abuse this,' Dwayne told him simply. 'At least try it and see if you like it.'

Now, too much time had been spent dwelling on Jonah's refusal to take the drug. The girls were getting restless and harping on, trying to encourage Jonah to get on with it and stop holding them up. Billy remained neutral, content with nibbling Shamilla's lobes.

'What is it you're afraid of Jonah?' Solomon asked, trying to sound genuinely concerned. 'Is it the stigma that ecstasy carries with it?'

Jonah looked around and saw everyone staring back at him. 'Who said I was afraid?' he snapped.

'Of course not,' Solomon said in a cool, non threatening tone, 'it's your mind and your body after all.' He backed away and stood by the hallway door, saying his piece and then butting out of the situation. Jonah knew exactly what Solomon had just done – he'd stuck a fork in and then innocently sauntered off as if it made no difference whether or not Jonah took the damn thing in the first place. But he'd made a point of explaining that the drug was basically harmless, so if Jonah didn't take this virtually safe endorphin-enhancer, he would be seen as a pussy by everyone there. Jonah allowed his eyes another quick glance around the room; he was already on his way to being full-blown drunk. He knew for a fact that weed and alcohol had disastrous affects – the aftermath of which still lingered in the back of his throbbing mind. So what the hell would alcohol and ecstasy be like? Worse. Much worse.

But there was only one way to find out.

14

The car journey to the club flashed by like a passing train. Later, Jonah only remembered little fragmented snapshots of the memory like a lucid dream; he remembered *being* in the car but not getting in. He remembered both Billy and Dwayne fingering Shamilla at the same time and her smiling away as they did so. He also remembered Mary singing along to the stereo and waving her arms in the air, and thinking 'shit, her arms actually have more muscle than mine'. And, if it wasn't for the effects of the pill he'd taken, Jonah might've asked Solomon why he continued to stare at him throughout the journey in the rear view mirror when he should've been watching the road.

In what seemed like a blur of seconds, they were inside the club. Jonah was able to see that there was in fact a queue but that they didn't have to wait. When they wriggled out of the foyer and made it down onto the main floor of the club, the pill really started to kick in. It felt as though the music was pumping *through* him; it wasn't that the base was too heavy or that the volume was too loud, it was that each tiny detail of the song seemed to be a separate entity, serenading him personally. Jonah didn't even care what song was playing because they all seemed to have the same effect. The snare showered him with delicate kisses in his ears while the baseline had a conversation with his internal organs and made them vibrate and before he could control himself, he was dancing away.

At one point a song came on and Jonah was convinced that the female vocalist was talking directly to him.

Everything seemed to go silent and slow around him, and in that moment the woman's words were all that mattered to him in the world. An intense feeling of love came over him as he listened to the high pitched chorus, and at that particular moment, Jonah felt as though he could marry the woman behind that voice just on the strength of how she was making him feel.

'Oh, don't be wastin' my time, boy, you better tell me you're mine.'

'I'm yours!' Jonah was yelling at the speakers, spinning around, jumping up and down. The strobe lights were going nuts, lighting the room up for split seconds then leaving it in total darkness. Every time the light came back on, the people around him seemed to be in a different pose; Billy was topless, and dancing in such an unusual fashion. His feet were firmly rooted to the spot and he refused to move any part of his body, including his head, but instead, he clenched his fists and thrust his arms up and down. Dwayne was off and away – trying to compose himself with some kind of rhythm even though it was virtually impossible with the frantic pace of the music.

When the lights flashed on, Shamilla and Mary were kissing each other like a pair of full blown lesbians getting it on in the middle of the crowded dance floor and the sight of this made Jonah burst into laughter. He wasn't laughing at them, but he was simply laughing because he was happy that they were expressing their love for each other. Jonah felt as though he'd known them his whole life, like they were as close to him as sisters.

The vibes were soaking Jonah with orgasmic joy. It was so intense he wanted to physically have sex with the music. Everyone around him was cavorting, canoodling, caressing. Strangers acted like relatives with each other, friends acted like lovers; boys on girls, boys on boys, girls on girls, whatever. It was all love. He went over to where Billy was planted and put his arm around his sweaty shoulder.

'You okay, Bill?'

'Yeah, I'm smashing, mate, smashing.' The reply in Jonah's ear was too loud and felt as though it had just perforated his eardrum.

'Listen, Bill, I love you. You know that don't you?'

'Course mate. I love you too.' Billy put his hand around Jonah's face and gave him a kiss on the cheek. Normally you ran the risk of looking gay doing that kind of thing in such a crowded place, but not here. Everywhere Jonah looked he saw that people were dancing together, smiling and generally having the best time of their lives.

When the room lit up for that brief second, it was brilliant; the club came into complete focus and all the colours from the ceiling to the varnished floor were vibrant and alive. Each time Jonah saw a poster on a wall or the pattern in the wallpaper, he was positive that it was the best example of interior decorating that he'd ever had the privilege to lay his eyes on. It was like the building was animate, every inch of the structure fuzzy and alive.

Everything was just perfect. No wonder they called it ecstasy, he thought.

Then ...

... Whoa. In the act of peeling his shirt from his sweaty body, his fingers felt something slam in his chest.

What the fuck was that? He pressed his palm against his heart; it was thumping like crazy, beating like he was running a marathon. Oh man, the last thing he wanted right now was to panic because that would only make things worse. He put his hand underneath his shirt to try and count the beats, but they were going too fast.

Weaving hastily, he scrambled to get away from the cluster of people and stand to the side of the dance floor to catch his breath. The inside of his mouth tasted like he'd eaten a bag of flour, and as he tried to move through the crowd, he was continuously stopped by people who wanted to say hello, or by girls that wanted him to dance with them.

'Just a second, I'll be back,' he kept saying, but before he finished his sentence they'd lost interest and been distracted by something else, another pretty person or shiny object. With every step he tried to take, he was knocked off-balance by the other ravers leaping about. The dance floor, which at first seemed cosy with the excess of dancers, was now dangerously crowded. He sidled past the wall of people muttering 'excuse me', but couldn't see a clear space. Now, his heart was pin-balling around his chest as he nudged bodies out of his way, his head mopped in sweat. The lights weren't helping much either. Every time he found his footing or it seemed like he was going to get a clear pathway, the room went black and the strobes did their epileptic-fit routine.

'Please don't die,' he mumbled as he clawed to get past. 'Oh God, I'm so sorry, please don't let me die.' With every morbid premonition of collapsing he could see his mother's distraught face as the police told her that her son had died from a drug overdose. 'Oh sweet Jesus ...' he moaned again, cringing away from the thought of leaving the earth after a ... he couldn't even phrase it in his head again. *Drug Overdose* sounded too scabby, too much of a filthy way for a reasonably smart kid like himself to end up.

'Jonah!' Dwayne was standing in front of him with a girl under each arm and a grin like a half-moon on his face. But when he saw Jonah, Dwayne's arms dropped from around the girls and grabbed hold of him. 'Shit, Jonah, you okay?'

Tears began to well up in Jonah's eyes. 'I think I'm dying, man.'

'Calm down,' Dwayne ordered, softly slapping his cheek. 'You're not dying, you just need a drink.'

'My heart –'

'What?' Dwayne put his ear closer to Jonah's mouth trying to hear him over the boom of the music.

'My heart ... too fast.'

'Don't worry about it. That's what's supposed to be happening. Look, feel mine.' Dwayne grabbed Jonah's hand and put it on his heart, and sure enough, it was thumping like a maniac. 'Just relax, Jonie. Let's get some water.'

The main hall bounced and quivered as Dwayne ushered him to the foyer, nudging people out of his way with aggressive authority. When they got there, Jonah had to shield his eyes from the lights which seared through him with brilliant intensity; it was like staring into the full-beams of a car a few inches away from his face.

'Here, sit down,' Dwayne said, helping him into a chair. An acrid whiff of B O and vomit drifted through the room like a yellow-brown ghost, permeating everything. If he'd been sober, the smell alone would have repulsed Jonah to gagging, let alone the fact that someone had quite obviously puked down the wall not three feet away from him. A chubby blonde girl sat crumpled on the floor by the slimy vomit while her friends tried to get her on her feet before the bouncer came over and threw their arses out onto the pavement.

'Dirty bitch,' Dwayne muttered, looking over. Jonah took a deep breath and chanced a look through his fingers. The light in the room calmed down, mellowing into a much more rational ambience, though the walls still vibrated like they were coloured with lava. He saw the sick dripping down the wall, the same colour and texture of porridge, and covered his eyes again.

'Jesus Christ ...' Jonah mumbled, his stomach lurching. 'Dwayne?'

'I'm here, bro.'

'What the fuck's happening? I thought you said that stuff was meant to make you feel good.'

'It is ... supposed to do that.'

'I feel like shit.'

There were no illusions about what happened in Club Xplosion. The owners, managers, staff and bouncers were all aware that it was a pill spot. Yeah, everyone got *searched* at the door, and as long as you didn't stuff a pill down your throat in front of the wrong person then everything was fine. A lot of the bouncers actually sold pills themselves because they knew that for a decent little tab they could get ten pounds a pop, and considering the amount of pill-heads that filled the venue, you could make anywhere between five hundred pounds to a grand a night. However, when somebody 'monged-out' from doing a bad pill or was just a greedy bastard and did too many, then there was trouble. The unwritten law was that people could do pills in the rave, but please don't overdose. Hence, the foyer had a free water dispenser with plenty of plastic cups so people could help themselves.

For a good half an hour of panicking while Dwayne went to get some water, Jonah stared down at the carpet as it wrapped itself around his feet. To him, it looked as though the carpet was alive and breathing, and reminded him of when he used to stroke his pet cat Sellas. Some days, Sellas would curl up in his lap while he watched a film or played a computer game and as the cat fell asleep, her warm chest would inflate against Jonah's forearms. That's what the floor looked like it was doing – purring against the soles of his feet. Dwayne returned with two cups of water and handed one to Jonah.

'That's good,' Jonah said, gulping the water and trying to realign himself with his surroundings. The more he focussed on things and worked on controlling his breathing, the less he seemed to feel like his heart was going to implode.

'You okay? You looked a bit scary back then,' Dwayne told him, crouched by his side.

'Yeah ... I'm starting to come back down to earth now.'

'Your eyes looked like two black coins. I've only seen a couple of people look like that at these kind of raves and it was usually a bad sign. Drink this one.' Dwayne passed him the other cup.

'Thanks.' The colours in the foyer were still too bright and every couple of seconds the room would become lop-sided, but apart from that, he was beginning to calm down. Though it seemed almost impossible to concentrate on anything, Jonah realised that the more he thought about dying the worse the room would appear. He convinced himself that he was perfectly fine and thanked God for allowing him to live through that stupid mistake (he'd quickly come to the conclusion that ecstasy was not for him, in fact, if he had a headache in the future he would grin and bear it because no amount of money was going to get him to take so much as an aspirin). 'For a second I thought I was gonna die.'

Dwayne patted him on the knee, and sat down on the chair next to him. 'You're fine.'

The bouncers finally came over to remove the silly girl who'd collapsed on the floor.

'Where are those girls from earlier?' Jonah managed to say, still getting accustomed to the mechanics of talking.

'I don't know. Maybe they're with Billy.'

'You sure I'm not going to die, Dwayne?' It sounded pathetic to even ask, and as the sentence materialised it seemed too quick and high-pitched like it'd been sped up on a tape recorder. He wasn't even sure that Dwayne was going to be able to understand what he'd said, because he barely did himself.

'Nah man, you're fine, trust me. It's a mental thing, y'know?' Jonah nodded. 'It's like – if you think something bad's gonna happen then it's gonna happen. Like if I acquire a car that doesn't belong to me, and all I can think about is the pigs pulling me, then I'm going to act all twitchy and attract the copshop. See where I'm coming from, Jone?'

Again, Jonah nodded and laughed at Dwayne's choice of words. *Acquire*, like it wasn't the same thing as stealing. Did Dwayne really have it in his mind that everything that he could get his hands on actually belonged to him? Jonah wanted to tell him that he was on a slippery slope with all this crime stuff, and because he'd been getting away with it for so long it would make it about as easy as trying to piss with an erection trying to explain that nobody – not even a criminal mastermind such as Dwayne the Great – was exempt from the law. They would catch him and haul him into jail with the strongest possible sentence. Why? Because that's what *Jonah* would do, that's why. He knew that Billy was a lost cause, probably from the minute the poor kid was born, and that he had those jail bars in his blood like a genetic trait.

But it didn't have to be like that for Dwayne. And both of them knew it.

'How you feeling now?' Dwayne asked him with a light sheen of sweat on his forehead; the body heat had turned the foyer into an sauna with all the people queuing up for water.

'Yeah ... not too bad. If you wanna go back inside and dance, you can. I'll be fine.'

'Nah, we'll go in together. Think you can manage it?'

The thought of going back inside sent a dull dread through his fragile body, but the shock of the experience had scared him sober. Rubbing his face like he was washing in the sink to wake himself up, he nodded and used Dwayne's body as leverage to get to his feet. After the first few steps, the rhythm of walking returned. With his chest heaving as he breathed in deep, Jonah silently thanked God that he was still breathing at all – and he even tried to bop a little bit to the music. As his equilibrium returned, the music was too loud, like one long blast in his eardrums.

The strobes flashed and he could feel his heart palpitate slightly. He didn't want to mong-out again, because for one thing he didn't think Dwayne would be so attentive if he was interrupted from his partying a second time round.

The crowd parted as Dwayne muscled his way through like a shark fin bobbing in a sea full of swimmers. Jonah placed a hand on Dwayne's shoulder in front of him so that he didn't get marooned with the smiling strangers whose complexion under the lights appeared so waxy they could've been used as shop window mannequins.

In the centre of the hall, Billy's flabby gut was bouncing as he spun in a circle with his arms outstretched. There was a clear perimeter around him that the other dancers didn't dare breach for fear of getting struck by his arms. Dwayne strutted toward Billy and grabbed him mid-spin. Entranced, Billy went to throw a punch before he'd even stopped his legs from rotating another 360 degrees, but due to a lot of previous experience dealing with him, Dwayne knew this kind of reaction was only natural. He hugged Billy like a referee does to a boxer who has just been knocked out and wobbles to their feet to try and fight on. Billy looked at Dwayne with an expression of confusion as Dwayne whispered something in his ear.

Billy nodded.

Dwayne took out two pills from his pocket and handed one to Billy, then tapped the man standing next to him. The man, who was taller and a good three stone heavier than Dwayne, greeted him with a smile – one which abruptly faded when Dwayne snatched the bottle of Stella out of his hand and shared it with Billy as they took the pills. Dwayne handed the man his empty bottle and continued dancing.

The man, who looked uncannily like a fat John Travolta in *Saturday Night Fever,* began scowling and inflating his chest. Jonah saw it all unfold like slow motion: Travolta, mouthing his silent outrage under the volume of the music like some kind of pissed-off mime, gripped hold of the bottle and was about to smash it over Dwayne's loaf. Dwayne was oblivious to the whole thing as he thrashed his head away like he was in a mosh-pit with Billy, spinning out in his own little world.

'Oh sugar,' Jonah whispered as he raced toward Travolta, still feeling too humble to risk annoying God by swearing. Travolta's sweaty girlfriend, whose eyes were rolling into her head, hadn't even realised he was about to get into a whole heap of drama because she was too busy raking her fingers through her hair and trying to stay alive. Jonah reached out and grabbed the man's hairy wrist, but his hand was so clammy that his clasp slipped away. The man spun on his heels and faced Jonah with eyes glowering like two magic eight-balls.

'Sorry, mate,' Jonah shouted in the man's ear, patting him on the shoulder.

'What's going on?' he yelled back, looking down on his wrist where Jonah had touched him.

'Can I get you a beer?' Jonah asked.

'What?' he asked over the din.

'Your beer ... Do you want another one?' This time Jonah gestured with his hand up to his mouth. Travolta pulled away, his face twisted with disgust.

'I'm not queer, mate!' he yelled, his anger turning into embarrassment with an awkward grin. He grabbed hold of his zoned-out girlfriend as if to solidify his point; she stumbled backwards into his arms all stiff like the zombies in black and white films.

'No, no, no,' Jonah waved his hands in front of his chest. It was obvious that conversation was about as pointless as a butter knife, so instead, he reached in his pocket and pulled out a tenner. 'Here,' he said and did the same hand gesture which he guessed was the beginner's version of saying 'drink' in sign language.

Finally, Travolta understood and took the note. He beamed a smile so wide it looked as if it would unhinge his jaw. Jonah nodded and managed to release a shaky little laugh despite his shredded nerves.

You just don't know how close that was, do you? Jonah thought, finally catching his breath.

By the main stage, Dwayne and Billy were dancing to the hyper-tempo music like there was an earthquake and the floor was shaking, or like they were trying to show people how to stay balanced on a surf board. Their faces shone with perspiration. Now that the situation had calmed down and Jonah didn't feel like the room was getting smaller and darker, he decided that he could afford to wiggle and jiggle himself a bit. He joined Billy and Dwayne without an ounce of self-awareness to how dumb the three of them must've looked. The baseline slammed to the rhythm of his erratic heart while he did some kind of windmill motion with his arms like a drunken pub fighter.

After the next couple of songs, he stopped looking over his shoulder to see if Travolta was still planning to start some shit as the snare shot little electric currents through his body. He closed his eyes and felt a complete dislocation to his environment, like he was far and away from his real life, from his worries. The sweat pooled in his chest worked as the perfect adhesive to stick his shirt to him, and even though the balls of his feet ached something chronic and his shoulders and neck felt like they were about to unscrew themselves from their nearest joint, he couldn't stop dancing.

It had begun to get a bit ridiculous now. Sweat was pouring down from his forehead and stinging his eyes. He frantically wiped it away, but moments later, a new downpour would occur. Jonah opened his eyes fanning his shirt in an attempt to generate some air in the stuffy club.

Then he spotted something that made his sweat turn into ice cubes, halting his feet instantly.

He squinted, thinking that maybe some sweat was still blurring his vision, an optical illusion brought on by the strobes flashing in the darkness of the club. But it wasn't. He'd managed to spot Solomon in the distance mingled with a crowd of ravers toward the end of the club. He would never normally have been able to spot him and just pick him out of the crowd at first glance like that – not with the amount of people that were jammed in there. It was only because it appeared that Solomon had blue lights shooting from his eyes that Jonah was able to fix his attention on him. He'd briefly wondered where Solomon had been since they'd got into the club, but his thoughts were continually distracted by other things, like staying alive. But there he was, still in his black hoody, with rays of light coming out of his face. Even with an unbuttoned shirt on and without dancing like a lunatic, the club was hotter than hell, and there was Solomon just standing there in a thick black hoody ... just staring at him. Jonah rubbed his eyes and looked again, but Solomon was no longer there.

Blue Lights? Jonah couldn't believe how badly that pill had begun to affect him. His emotions and senses were up and down like the inside of a heated lava lamp. Slowly and carefully, he sidled through the crowd and found the foyer again, where the light was more familiar and his ears and eyes weren't being gang-raped by volume and contrast.

He curled up in the armchair, and waited to go home.

WEDNESDAY

15

It's funny how kids always retreat under the bed when they're frightened. But Jonah guessed that if you're in a house and you're scared, under the bed actually isn't a bad idea. So it was only logical that, being in a room with nothing but a bed, Jonah would scoot under there when he felt like he was going to scream with fear or have a mental breakdown with the tension of the situation.

He was dreaming again and this time he recognised it by the strange grey quality of the environment. Everything seemed drained, like an old photograph. He didn't recognise the room, although he had some degree of awareness that he was again trapped inside sleep with that heightened and irrational fear of the unknown. His body couldn't stop shaking. Maybe if he got worked up enough in the next few moments then he would spring wide awake with a scream and a stiff dick and that would be the end of it, but somehow he knew this nightmare wouldn't be that easy to elude.

He put his ear to the floor and tried to listen – to what, he didn't have a clue. All he knew was that there was something or somebody outside that room and it was scaring the fluid out of him. Clenching his teeth, he slid from underneath the bed deciding that if there was a window to climb out of he would rather take his chances with that than stay in there.

Nauseously, Jonah glanced around. Above the bed was a small circular opening with a glass panel, not even big enough for a magpie to pass through. There wasn't a single part of his body that remained still – even his teeth chattered like those wind-up ones you find in joke shops.

In the corner there was a door, but to open it was to face the source of his terror and he wasn't sure if he could take the shock of seeing it materialised. To stay put was to have the inevitable horror seek him out and have its wicked way with him. Thoughts of being sodomised by a large piggish creature began to wrack him, yet he knew that whatever lay beyond the confines of the room was somehow worse.

'*This is a dream,*' Jonah tried to say aloud but the words came out like wet burps. He attempted to scream thinking that the effort of doing so would jolt his body into snapping out of this situation, but when he opened his mouth, a faint dry whisper came out. As he stepped toward the door a foreboding prevented his advance. The door led to something awful, he felt it with every nerve in his body. He turned back to the circular window, and this time, there was an eye looking through, the size of a mango. It was a yellow reptilian eye with a swirl of black iris that looked like the inside of a marble. Jonah refused it another glance. His body tensed up like every muscle was attached with a weight far heavier than he could manage.

Okay. The window was a bad idea. A very, very bad idea. Somehow, he neared the door, struggling against his own body. From behind him, he could hear whatever was looking through the window breathing; it sounded like it was trying to whisper thousands of simultaneous sentences under its breath.

Jonah fumbled with the knob, his arms too weak to turn it. With both hands, his entire body's weight and concentration behind it, he managed to open the door; a gust of stale, cold air hit him in the face.

Cautiously, he entered the hallway of the dilapidated building. The walls crumbled like old sponge cake as he inched forward. The slick floor led him to a rusty metal staircase, but he was unable to see below. He heard talking. Whatever was speaking in that low, gargling voice was at the bottom of the stairs.

'Spaghetti bolognese ...'

Jonah stopped in his tracks and held his breath.

'In my belly you will find spaghetti bolognese ... and a sausage.' The voice was sickening, like somebody trying to have a conversation while drowning. Jonah looked behind him – the door of the room that he'd emerged from was gone; the surroundings had just silently morphed and turned into a dead-end.

The only way out was forward.

Coming to the edge of the first step, Jonah peered down into the gloom of the floor below. Something was down there, hidden in a patch of shadow just in front of a door that looked as though it led to outside. The thing was making slow, deliberate movements just outside of Jonah's visual range.

Gripping the slimy, rickety banister, Jonah took a careful step down.

'I have spaghetti bolognese, a sausage, and ... What else do I have in my tummy?'

The thing's voice made Jonah's balls tingle with fear. The feeling ran up his sack and down his legs, draining the strength out of their stability.

The small, round figure scooted around in the grey shadows, making a wet, slurping sound with each movement. Awkwardly, it poked its head out of the darkness.

'Spaghetti bolognese, a sausage, and there is something else in here ...'

Jonah gripped the rail of the banister so hard that pain shot up his forearm. It looked like a baby with neon green eyes, trailing some kind of electrical wires out of a large, seeping wound in the back of its head. It crawled out of the darkness into full view, paralysing Jonah.

'I have spaghetti bolognese, a sausage, and ...' the baby put its hand inside of a tennis-ball sized hole in its belly button, and pulled out something red and flapping. 'A fish!' the baby exclaimed excitedly like it'd just received the present it'd always wanted on Christmas morning.

Jonah screamed silently. The baby ignored Jonah's presence in its dank lair, and this gave him enough courage to make a run for it. Deciding that since it was a dream and the laws of reality could be bent and broken, the best thing for Jonah to do would be to clear this hurdle in one giant leap. It would take all his nerve to gather enough strength in his treacherous legs to be able to jump, but anything had to be better than spending another second with that baby. Anything.

Just as he attempted to leap, Jonah lost his footing on the slippery metallic step, and tumbled painfully downwards. As his jaw made impact with the grimy floor, pain shocking through his face and teeth, the baby advanced toward him with athletic speed, pulling itself along with its arms like it was paralysed from the waist down. Those neon eyes trailed little rays of green light in the darkness as it approached, the tangled wires flicking from side to side like electric dreadlocks.

'Spaghetti bolognese, sausages and fish, spaghetti bolognese; sausages and fish; Spaghetti bolognese sausages –'

16

'Please ...' He woke up tangled in the sheets of his piss-sodden bed. He felt like shit, just as he had the previous day, but now he was hyperventilating.

After a brisk, tepid shower and change of clothes, Jonah left the flat and went for a walk. He didn't want to be inside any longer, gasping for air like a fish out of water. Guilt sat on his chest and weighed down each step he walked along the pavement, but the more he tried to realise why he was guilty, the further it eluded him. He did know one thing though – he'd almost died last night of a heart attack while experimenting with ecstasy – an endeavour he knew he would never venture into again. It wasn't one of those half-arsed pledges that he made to himself like 'I swear to God I'm never gonna drink again' after a bad hangover and then getting pissed the very next weekend, it was a solid oath.

The sun was out and putting the hurt on his scrambled brains, his head spinning like a ceiling fan. It felt like everybody he passed was watching him, so he kept his eyes to the pavement. When he remembered his nightmare it made his flesh crawl and he wished more than anything that he could've just packed them in a box and thrown them down a well in the farthest corner of his memory.

It was another postcard-perfect day, which was surprising since he'd heard on the radio there was meant to be a storm the previous evening. He hoped that it would, though, because all the heat was beginning to sap his strength. Either that or all the alcohol, drugs and late nights were beginning to take their toll. He thought about his 48 hour binge, groaned, and made a promise to stay clean for at least the day.

'Shit!' he yelled, then immediately regretted it when a brick of tension bounced all over the interior of his head.

He'd forgotten all about his date with whatsherface ... Rose! That was it. Instantly, depression grabbed hold and almost wrestled him to the floor. He didn't understand why, but all he wanted to do was crawl beneath a duvet and sleep forever. He was tired, sure, but this was different. The thought of having to see a pretty girl later on that day made him more nervous than he could ever remember being.

When he found a corner shop he went inside and searched for the freezer; he wanted an iced-lolly to rub across his head and neck. The place was nicely air conditioned and he almost couldn't bring himself to leave. He stayed for a few seconds longer, leafing through the limited magazine section, taking in huge gulps of cold air.

Maybe he'd cancel on her. After all, he was in no condition for sweet talk and all that other smoochy bullshit. Knowing his luck he'd probably fall asleep in his kung po chicken and she'd storm off and that'd be it. Then again, if he cancelled on such short notice, she'd think he was a piece of shit all-mouth no-balls wannabe player: the worst possible outcome of the date, he decided.

All he needed was sleep. A lot more sleep. But he didn't want any part of those crazy dreams again. No sir. He'd woken up from his last two nightmares aching all over, and both times he thought he was going to die without so much as enough breath in his lungs to call for help. Maybe when he got back he'd crash out on the sofa in the front room and fall asleep to the sound of the computer games, at least then there would always be someone near him, even if it was only Genie.

As he sucked on the Rocket, welcoming the sticky-sweet purple flavour (not quite blackcurrant, not quite grape, just purple) the fatigue started to set in. The sun weighed heavy on his neck and back, baking him inside his clothes. Looking down toward the end of the road that led to the flat, he began to dread the journey. The heat began to sting his forearms and scalp, the sunlight pierced through his eyes forcing him to bow his head painfully with each step. He wondered how those soldiers in Iraq managed to go around the desert all day wearing their uniforms and backpacks without flipping out and going berserk. That clip from *The Good the Bad and the Ugly* continued to pop up in his mind as he hobbled forward, the one where Clint Eastwood was being led through the desert by the Mexican bandit and his lips are all chapped and his face is coated with dust. Jonah guessed he was beginning to know how old Clint must've felt.

It seemed to take ages to reach the front door again, but as soon as Jonah was inside, he tore off his shirt and flicked off his shoes. His body was oily but he didn't care enough to wipe himself down. He just went to the kitchen, ran the cold tap, splashed his face, and then marched toward the front room.

'Morning,' Dwayne greeted him, reaching the sofa with an unusual smile on his face. He was sat in his boxer shorts, with a cup of tea in his hand. The television was on in the background, but the volume was almost mute.

'Morning,' Jonah replied, finding the other sofa and collapsing on it. He stretched out and placed his head on the arm rest. 'It's too hot,' he groaned.

Dwayne sipped his tea and nodded. 'Indeed it is. Where did you go?'

'Just for a walk. Needed some air.'

'How did you find last night?' Dwayne asked him, his left eyebrow slightly raised. Jonah noticed that he was a lot more subdued this morning, probably from the late night, or maybe just because there was no one around to show off in front of. 'Did you have fun?'

'Apart from being scared nearly to death – literally – then yeah. But I don't think X is for me.'

Truthfully, Jonah didn't even want to talk about the previous evening, especially the part with him trying ecstasy. It made him feel dirty and ashamed.

'What about you, did you have a good time?' Jonah asked him through a yawn.

'I always have fun. *Always.*'

An awkward silence wedged between them. Jonah looked up at the ceiling fan and watched it spin silently, relishing every gust of air that it created.

Jonah closed his eyes and wriggled to a comfortable position. 'Where is everyone?'

'Billy's down the cafe getting something to eat, Sol's at home and the girls are upstairs sleeping.' The reply was mumbled, like he couldn't be bothered to relay the information. Deep crevices circled Dwayne's eyes. Maybe he hadn't slept yet.

'The girls are upstairs?' Jonah opened his eyes. 'Did you ...'

Dwayne shook his head with a reluctant grin. 'Nah. They're in the spare room – together. It seems the old ecstasy brought the lesbian out in 'em both. Either that or they're gonna have one hell of an awkward moment when they wake up.'

A small, weary laugh managed to escape Jonah. Now that he was lying down, he realised how exhausted he actually was. He couldn't have slept more than a couple of hours before his little *accident* woke him up. The clock on the wall said it was only eleven. There was still a long time before he had to shake a leg and get ready for his big date, so he could surely afford a nap.

'Ain't you tired?'

'Not really,' Dwayne replied, a little louder than a whisper. 'I caught a couple of hours sleep but once I'm awake, that's it, I'm awake. I'll probably feel like shit by about three o'clock.'

Again, the silence. Jonah felt himself slowly begin to drift, when an unusual noise made him open his eyes. It was a light thud, followed by a quiet clicking sound. Jonah looked up at the T.V, but he was sure that it hadn't come from that blonde girl in *Bewitched*. He decided to ignore it – and then heard it again a second later.

'What was that?'

'My rabbit,' Dwayne told him.

'Rabbit?'

'Yeah.'

Jonah sat up and cocked his head to the side, confused. 'What're you talking about, rabbit?'

'I mean in the box by my legs –' Jonah bent down and looked under the coffee table between them and there it was, a cardboard box '– there is a rabbit.'

It was just random enough to be hilarious. Jonah temporarily forgot about his exhaustion and stood up to investigate. Inside the box, nibbling away on a leaf of lettuce was a fluffy white bunny rabbit. Jonah laughed with childish glee. He'd wanted to remark how cute it looked with its little red eyes, but he managed to contain himself. It was so extraordinary to see just how fresh and pure the creature looked, like it was a ball of fallen snow. He crouched over and petted its head.

'What's its name?'

'Name? I just call it rabbit.'

'Ah man, you gotta give him a name,' Jonah prompted.

'*Her*. It's a girl.'

'Oh.' Jonah stroked the rabbit's floppy ears back, and then quickly moved his hand away. 'Does it bite?'

'Not that I know of,' Dwayne told him.

For a minute, they just played with that rabbit not saying a word to each other. Jonah was grinning from ear to ear as he held the lettuce for the rabbit to eat.

'I got a dog, too. Wanna see it?'

'I didn't know I was staying in Noah's Arc.' Jonah said, his spirits lifted by all these nice surprises.

'It ain't here, I keep it somewhere else. I gotta go feed it soon anyway. Wanna come?'

Genuine happiness rushed through Jonah at that point. Maybe it was just because he was fond of animals, and the unexpected sight of the rabbit threw him off guard. After all, his cousin had two rabbits and Jonah absolutely adored them when he was younger. Or maybe it was because for the last couple of days he'd been trying really hard to act grown up, and the rabbit just forced the kid out of him, but whatever it was, he didn't care.

'Yeah, I'd love to see your dog.'

'Calm down, I'm not gonna let you have sex with it.'

Jonah punched him in the arm, then ran off to find a clean t-shirt.

17

They walked for about ten minutes until they reached a street where another one of Dwayne's cars was parked. The sun was so dazzling that it tinted everything with a yellow glow – the road, the houses, even the people. Flies and wasps bobbed around in a drunken zigzag, while smaller, more annoying insects explored the landscape of their faces. All the different shades of green on the leaves and grass were electrically vibrant.

The car was an old white Mercedes from the early nineties – the type common among old Greek men in their area. It was ancient, something Jonah thought was far more subdued than a diva such as Dwayne was used to, but it was clean and well-maintained nonetheless. Dwayne explained that the car had belonged to Genie's father, but as a debt payment, now belonged to him. Jonah didn't ask – he knew it was something seedy and rooted in powder, but at this stage he was no longer surprised or sympathetic. Dwayne had made an absolute fortune by being a businessman of sorts, hiring people to sell drugs for him and reaping the profit. And, as Dwayne delicately explained, anyone who tried to pull a fast one got *dealt with* accordingly. He didn't go into the specifics of what exactly that meant, but Jonah guessed it was some heavy shit. After all, Dwayne was giving orders and delegating work to men five and ten years his senior and he must've done something to earn the kind of reputation that would keep men twice his size at bay. Maybe, as Jonah suspected, it was nothing more than flashing his money around – nobody would hurt their employer who was consistently providing a heavy cash flow for them, would they?

Even though Dwayne didn't have a licence or any kind of insurance on the car, the vehicle wasn't stolen and this put Jonah somewhat at ease. The one thing he did find strange, however, was that Dwayne had brought his rabbit with him along for the ride, and that was just unusual enough to put Jonah right back on edge and have his nerves jingling and jangling. He had asked why – but Dwayne simply told him it was too hot for the rabbit indoors and as they didn't have a garden it was nice for it to get out for a bit.

Dwayne was mostly quiet as they drove except for the odd story about something that had happened at certain spots that they passed. He had the box with the rabbit inside on his lap as he drove, with one arm leaned out of the window.

'Ain't you scared that it's going to jump out into the road?' Jonah asked him, slightly worried about the way the rabbit had settled its front paws on the edge of the box, peering over at the passing cars inquisitively.

'Nah,' Dwayne replied. 'It's fine.'

Jonah realised just how confident Dwayne had become over the last year. It was his refusal to allow the worst case scenario into his head that had given him this new ego, and in addition, made him totally free; free from classrooms, jobs, debts, or the usual esteem-shattering hassles like being turned down by girls. That rabbit could get scared, fly straight out into the road and get flattened by a passing car, and if it had been sitting in Jonah's lap it probably would have. But it was as if Dwayne's relaxed demeanour had a calming effect on the creature and physically prevented it from doing that.

Half an hour later they pulled up to an allotment so far from the main roads that not a car honk or radio could be heard for miles. It looked like a long stretch of farmland with sheds erected here and there, and rows of sprouting vegetables poking through the earth.

When they got out of the car, Jonah burned his hand trying to close the door. 'Jeez, I bet you could have a fry-up on the bonnet of this thing.'

Dwayne cradled the rabbit in his arms like a baby, and locked the door. Ignoring Jonah's remark, they continued walking, and Dwayne told him something that both frightened and excited Jonah: 'I want you to work for me.'

'What d'you mean?' Jonah almost stammered, somehow shocked at how serious Dwayne had become. For the last couple of days, he'd been joking around and smiling. Now, his eyes bore a steel glare like a prisoner hardened from years of incarceration.

'I wanna be completely honest with you, Jone. You reckon you can handle it?'

Jonah knew he couldn't. 'Yeah, of course.'

'I care about you a lot, not in a gay way, but I mean, you're like a brother to me. Understand what I'm saying?' When Jonah nodded, he continued. 'It broke me up hearing that you're working in a bakery.'

'It's honest work,' Jonah interrupted, sounding more defensive than he wanted to.

'No it isn't. It's honest slavery. The wages you get paid for the hours you do are probably an absolute disgrace. And what about your college?'

'What about it?'

'You bust your arse getting all that work done, studying all them books, then you gotta go university, am I right?'

'Yeah,' Jonah replied.

'That's what ... two or three years more of studying? In which time you'll accumulate a heap of debts and if you graduate, you gotta find a job that's gonna start you off on some wage that would make a sweatshop in Thailand look like a dream come true. Then, when you work for enough years to build up enough money to finally pay off what you owe, you'll be in your thirties.'

The rabbit stared up at Jonah as Dwayne spoke, like it was interested in hearing his reply. They came to a knee-high mesh fence that separated the allotment and stepped over it.

'Not necessarily,' Jonah said feebly.

'But most likely.' Dwayne kept his eyes trained in the distance, stroking the rabbit's head like a James Bond villian. 'I'm telling you now you could earn a shit load of cash with me. Ask Billy, he'll tell you.'

'I know what you're saying Dwayne, believe me I do. But ...'

'But what?'

'There's a right way and a wrong way to do it,' Jonah said finally, the words almost stinging him with spite. He knew that he could be rich beyond his imagining, but the risk would always be on his mind like a constant migraine, so the money would be pointless if he didn't have the peace of mind to enjoy it.

'Then let me ask you this,' Dwayne began, pland weighty. 'Do you think it's *right* to work all the hours God sends, studying in your free time, to not be able to enjoy life? We have the easiest way of making money, Jonie, the money practically makes itself. That's the beauty of it.'

'I know, I know, I know,' Jonah said, like a son being lectured. 'I just ...'

'What? You just what?' Dwayne stopped walking and faced Jonah his expression tensed like he was getting ready to be offended.

'I just don't think it will last.' He looked away as he said it, then quickly added. 'But believe me I want it to. I'm glad for you guys that you got money and all that stuff, but you know how it goes ...'

'No I don't, Jonah. How does it go?'

'The police crack down on everything. I hope it doesn't happen, but I think sooner or later something's gonna catch up with you.' Dwayne looked away, disgusted by what his friend was saying. 'Hey, I'm just being real with you, Dwayne. The cars, the guns, the drugs, I mean you shot a kid in the foot the other night. That kind of thing doesn't go unnoticed.'

Dwayne walked on and Jonah followed in silence. They came to a reasonably large shed that backed onto a wilderness of overgrowth. Dwayne fiddled with the padlock and opened the door. A hot waft of stale shit hit them. Jonah turned away and gagged immediately, spitting onto the soil trying to clear his mouth of the taste.

Inside, a monster of an animal was crouched in the dark corner, chained to a bolt in the wood. Upon seeing Dwayne, it perked up, standing on all fours and growling like a helicopter propeller was stuck in its throat. It had a head the size of a basketball, and shoulders as broad as a doorway. In the dark, it looked more like a pony than a dog.

'This is Champ,' Dwayne said, trying his hardest to stay oblivious to the stench waves that rose from inside the shed. The dog lurched forward at once and managed to get far enough to poke its head into the spilling sunlight, its jaws snapping ferociously.

'What the fuck have you done to it?' Jonah asked, appalled at the dog's temper. It tugged so hard against the chain that for a second, Jonah thought it was going to pull the whole side of the shed down. It had yellow, watery eyes that were uncannily human, and scabs all around its mouth. Piles of crusted excrement sat around the dog's feet like lumps of brown clay. 'He needs some water.'

'This is my attack dog,' Dwayne said, simply. He handed Jonah the rabbit and then bravely entered the shed, prancing by the beast like it was a half-dead mule. Out of sight from Jonah, Dwayne grabbed a bottle of water from somewhere in the shadows and filled Champ's bowl. The dog ceased its maniacal snarling routine and limply strolled to the bowl. The white foam from the dog's drooling lips dripped into the water and lay on the surface like algae on a pond. As it drank, it no longer seemed like the threatening hound from hell, but rather, a pathetic and sad creature, distraught in the heat. It reminded Jonah of those 'protect the bear' adverts that used to come on TV quite frequently a few years back, that just showed an anonymous, grey bear with its fur eaten away all over its body, thumping its front paws on the ground with a chain around its neck.

An image of Billy cracking that gummy dog's head open popped up in his mind.

Dwayne crouched beside the animal and stroked its head and behind its ears. 'Good boy,' Dwayne whispered. 'You're the first person I've ever taken here, Jonah.'

Jonah's stomach rolled over. He wasn't sure if it was because of the wooden-shit smell or because he was now the only other person involved in the cruelty of the animal.

'Billy's never been here. Neither has Solomon, even.' That surprised Jonah. 'This is where I keep a lot of bad things, and Champ guards it all for me,' he turned to the dog, 'don'tcha boy?'

'The dog looks absolutely fucked. Do you ever walk it?' Jonah asked stepping back with the rabbit just in case it decided to get brave and do a Superman routine out of Jonah's grip.

'When the dog comes on patrol with me it walks. Otherwise, no.'

'What kind of dog is it?'

Dwayne shrugged, pouring more water into the bowl and over the dog's head. 'It's a mix. It's got a bit of Staff, a bit of Pit, a bit of Rot, even a bit of Doberman. Basically all the worst dogs you could hope to have biting your arse. I got him when he was a pup. This white guy called Frazier in east London was breeding dogs and doing dog fights for years. I went to one and mentioned that I needed something to take with me if I need to do some business with someone I don't know so that they know not to fuck with me. See, a dog like Champ is a lot more intimidating than a gun. I mean, everyone and their mum has a gun these days, it don't mean shit.

'One time I had Champ in the back of this van when he was only about a year old. I was coming back from a deal and I accidentally collided with this other guy who was turning into the road I was coming out of. I jumped out to see the damage to my car, and this big Nigerian nigga jumped out of his car and was going absolutely fucking berserk. He went straight for his boot, and when I saw that, I went straight to the back of the van and let Champ out.'

'What happened?' Jonah asked eagerly.

'Champ was on this guy in two seconds. Have you ever seen a dog lock its jaws on something, Jone?'

Jonah shook his head.

'There's a rumour that the only two ways to get a dog to release its lock is to break its jaw, or stick your finger up the dog's arsehole. Luckily for that Nigerian prick, Champ locked onto his foot and not onto his calf or his arm. This Nigerian dude was stomping the shit out of my dog with his other leg but Champ wouldn't let go. Champ was actually dragging the cunt across the road. I wasn't about to stick my finger up its arse so I just guessed at that point that he was never going to dance again. Luckily, and I don't think he knew just how lucky he was, his foot slipped out of his trainer and he managed to get back into his car and drive off. Champ mauled that fucking Nike into a mess of fabric, spinning his head around all nuts like he was trying to shake the shoe to death.'

Watching Champ drink the water, Jonah took another step backwards. It was like looking at the American Werewolf in London. The dog seemed to shy away from the sunlight as it touched him, but with every glimpse of the dog's body outside of the dingy corner showed Jonah just how strong it really was. Knots of muscle rippled along the dog's back and legs, and as it breathed out, new muscles seemed to surface. It looked unnatural, like Dwayne had been injecting the mongrel with steroids.

But Dwayne hadn't been exaggerating. Champ could probably pull a car along the road with its mouth quicker than The World's Strongest Man.

'Business is expanding, Jone. Solomon has got bigger and better plans for us, and I want you to be a part of it.'

'Oh yeah?' Jonah asked unenthused, shielding his eyes from the sun with his free hand. 'Like what?'

'Like rolling over a bank.' Dwayne looked up at Jonah and studied his face with a mannequin-blank expression.

'Are you kidding me, or what?'

Dwayne shook his head. 'Of course not.'

'Then you're a fucking idiot,' Jonah told him, feeling a tide of anger rise up in him. 'What is it with you and Bill? This guy Solomon could tell you to suck each other's dicks and you'd both think it was a good idea.'

A low, creepy laugh drum-rolled from Dwayne's chest; the kind of laugh you'd expect to hear from Dracula in one of those cheap old vampire flicks. Champ slobbered and panted in his hands, and after recognising that Dwayne held the key to its food and water it became even more pathetic and melancholy. Two seconds ago it was ready to tear the testicles off of the nearest man to him and now it looked as though it was ready to catch a Frisbee in the park.

'You don't know what you're talking about, Jonah.'

'Don't I?'

'No.' Dwayne stood up quickly and faced him like he was preparing to throw blows. 'In the last year I've made over a hundred grand because of Solomon. He took me and Billy and showed us how to get paid, so we didn't have to break our back all day doing a nine till five. He showed us how to intimidate people, how to manipulate people with their weakness –'

'Like Genie, you mean?'

'Yeah, just like her. I manipulated her weakness and now look – I'm not living with my mum in some fucked-up little shanty where I can't swing a cat. I got a nice place. If I want a car, I got them too. So what's your problem with that, Jonah? What's your problem with us getting money that's there to be got?'

The heat of the sun along with the heat of the tension between them had begun to exhaust Jonah. He puffed out a long breath, tired of going in the same circle. 'Whatever, man. Look, I'm glad you put me up for the week and gave me all those clothes and that money, believe me, it means a lot. But I'm not like you and Bill and Solomon. I ... I don't know.'

For a long moment, Dwayne didn't say anything, his facial expression neutral. Then, slowly, a proud grin crept across his mouth. 'That's why I want you to come in with us. Because you're better than us. You're smarter than me and that donut Billy put together, and I think you may even be smarter than Sol.'

Champ yelped with a husky series of barks like it had no fluid in its mouth to lubricate the sound, and then attempted to pull against the chain once more. A maroon ring of dried blood covered the dog's fur from its previous encounters with the chain.

'You think I'm smarter than the almighty Solomon, do you?' Jonah said sarcastically, still annoyed that Dwayne had lost his temper.

'Yeah, I do, in certain things. Look man, I'm sorry.' Dwayne extended his hand. To avoid any further tension, Jonah shook it reluctantly. 'We cool?'

'We're cool, but Jesus man, you need to slow down with all this shit. I mean, knocking off a bank will send you down for twenty-five years.'

'You're right. And I know you've heard it all before from every little crook that's ever spoken about crime, but if you only knew what you could have if you were brave enough to go for it. But I know you're different, and that's why I wanted to talk to you about maybe taking a backseat position with us. You'd still get paid like crazy, Jone. In one day I can give you more money than you'd get from working in that bakery full-time for a year.'

A sick, greasy feeling sank in Jonah's stomach. Just the thought of never having to go back to that bakery or back to that college felt beautiful. But realising that it was just a fantasy was horrible. Horrible and cruel. 'I can't do what you guys do.'

'You won't have to. But you'll have to have the balls to take some chances. You can't become a successful businessman without taking chances, right? And I promise you, I won't get you in deep. I just want you to be a part of this, cos you're from the estate and you're my brother. Solomon and I were thinking –'

Solomon ... Solomon?

'– that you could earn with us because you've got the street smarts, but also because you think things through. You're not impulsive like Billy and me. You see through a lot of bullshit. And once you see just how anything can be taken and how easy it all is, well, you could use the money to start your own legitimate business, which is what I'm gonna do.' Jonah knew that Dwayne was lying about wanting to go legit at some point; he was too addicted to the buzz of crime to do anything constructive. 'Trust me, Jone. The police can't catch us because they don't know what we are. They need clues to find us and need proof to arrest us. It's so easy, Jonah, all you need is to see just how easy.' He finished his rally with a curious, almost pleading expression, waiting for Jonah's response.

Jonah felt his insides crawling. Dwayne spoke to him with all the promise of a pimp trying to talk a reluctant pre-teen into her first blowjob. He sounded like Solomon.

'It sounds good. Really, it does.' And, against Jonah's will, he felt himself welling up with envy. In a couple of days the summer would be over for him. He had an essay to write, revision to do, cakes to bake. 'I know I'd be no good to you, Dwayne. I wish I was brave enough and I wish I *didn't* care. But like I said, I'm not like you guys.'

The grin returned to Dwayne's face. He bent back down to Champ and began to scratch the sides of his face, muttering baby talk under his breath. Without looking at Jonah, Dwayne said something that ended a big part of their friendship on the spot, and right then in that spontaneous transgression, Jonah knew things would never be the same between them again.

'Solomon suggested that I test your bravery, something to boost your courage.' He dug into his jeans pocket and threw his fat, cracked-leather wallet behind him at Jonah's feet. 'There's almost one thousand pounds in that wallet in fifty pound notes. All you have to do is feed Champ the rabbit.'

'What?' Jonah looked down at the wallet, disgusted, hoping that Dwayne was joking but knowing that he wasn't.

'I only feed Champ raw meat, especially living things, so he develops a taste for living tissue. He's eaten dozens of rabbits. Solomon thinks that if you get past this little phase of thinking you're scared, then you'll really start to bloom. I agree with him.'

'Are you joking or what?' Jonah asked him angrily.

'We all had to do these little tests to get past that scared phase, Jone. You got an easy one. It's only a rabbit.'

Jonah kicked the wallet away from him and a little cloud of earth spun around his foot like a brown tornado. 'You're sick. Keep the money.'

'It's only a rabbit, Jonah. Foxes kill these fucking things all the time. Once you start to see that, you'll have no idea what you can do.' He looked up at Jonah, wide-eyed.

'Nah, I'm not doing it. No way. Not for any amount,' Jonah told him firmly, covering the rabbit with his other hand.

Dwayne just stared at him without blinking or speaking. Jonah stared back.

'Last chance. For one thousand pounds, are you *sure* you don't want to feed Champ?' Dwayne asked him like a game show host.

'I'm positive,' Jonah spat, disturbed and drained.

'Fine. Then give me my rabbit and I'll do it.'

'No.' Jonah shook his head and backed away.

'What do you mean, no?' That grin slithered back over his face reducing his eyes to deceitful slits. 'It's my rabbit. I paid for it.'

'I don't give a French fuck. You're not having it.' Jonah backed away further. 'You can pull a gun on me or whatever you want but I'm not giving it to you.'

Dwayne clapped. 'Then you're a thief. Well done.'

'Whatever. I'm not going to let you kill this thing and I'm being serious. Look at the state of that dog, for God's sake. You're torturing it!'

'I'm training it.'

'Good for you. When it turns around and bites your arms off I hope you'll be as proud.'

Dwayne sniggered. 'You're really not going to give it back are you?'

'No.'

'Alright.' He poured the remainder of the bottle in the bowl for Champ who proceeded to lap it up thankfully, its snout stuck in the water. Dwayne began to close the allotment door, and as the inside of the shed began to darken away from the pouring sunlight, Champ let out a long, miserable howl. The sadness of the pitch made Jonah's insides feel cold with pity and he could've quite easily cried right then. It was strange to well up over an animal that looked so lethal and evil, but that vulnerable howl put everything into perspective. It was like the first time he watched King Kong on TV and saw the gorilla get shot to bits by all the fighter planes. All through the film,

Jonah had been scared to death of that jerky abomination, but when it fell off of the Empire State building and breathed its last breath in the middle of the road, Jonah blubbered like a baby.

'What now?' Jonah said, still feeling pissed off and edgy, not knowing what exactly Dwayne was going to do. At that point, if Dwayne pulled a shank or a gun out and threatened Jonah with it, he wouldn't have been surprised.

'What now?' Dwayne repeated. 'Well, I guess you've just bought yourself a new rabbit. It cost me eighty quid yesterday, so seeing as you're so desperate to have it you can pay me the same amount. I'll expect my money by tomorrow though, okay?'

Was that a threat? Jonah wanted to ask what exactly Dwayne was going to do if he didn't pay, but decided against it when a fresh moustache of sweat weighed heavy on his upper lip. He couldn't believe this was happening. Right then was the first time that Jonah had truly experienced the way people just grow apart. People *change*. It was now apparent that the person that he'd been friends with just the year before, was no longer there, and would only ever exist in his memories.

A new sadness replaced the anger inside of Jonah; the emotion of the last half an hour had mounted to a crescendo and underneath the smiling orange sun, Jonah surrendered. He dug in his pocket for the money that Dwayne gave him the other day and held the scrunched and balled-up notes in his sweaty palm. 'Here. Take it all. I think there's about two hundred pounds there.'

Methodically, Dwayne selected three moist notes from Jonah's clutch; one fifty, a ten and a twenty, then turned and headed back toward the car. Without looking behind him, he asked; 'You coming?'

Jonah looked around. He was in the middle of a dry allotment in an area he didn't know, with a fluffy white bunny rabbit under his arm in the blazing sun. He needed a drink, he needed some sleep. The *last* thing he needed was a hike across a foreign landscape to find a bus stop or a tube station.

'Nah, I'm cool. I'll probably just stay here and play with my rabbit.'

So he decided to brave it and find his own way back. Because anything would be better than an awkward and sticky drive with a stranger.

18

When Jonah reached home with Snowy (he decided on the name while on the bus. The name seemed unoriginal but fitting) he gathered his things from his room in the apartment and placed them in a carrier bag. There wasn't much – just the clothes he was wearing on Monday because his suitcase was still in the boot of the car that Dwayne picked him up in at the station. He flicked through the rail of t-shirts and rummaged through the drawer of jeans; he was only going to take one item of each and didn't want to seem like a hypocrite by taking a whole bunch of stolen clothes with him after their little dispute at the allotment. As he was trying to make up his mind on which T-shirt to take, the expensive-looking polo top or the 'I Luv London' graffiti shirt that was obviously cheaper but a lot more exclusive, Genie knocked on the door softly before poking her head around.

'Do you want a cold drink?' she asked him wearily.

'Nah, you're alright.'

'What's wrong?' She frowned, inviting herself into the room.

'Nothing I'm just getting my stuff ready.'

'What's this?' Genie looked down at Snowy curled up in Jonah's arms. She bent down to take a closer look, but he pulled away instinctively; he'd got into too much bother over that little animal to risk it being hurt now that it was safe.

'It's a giraffe.'

'He's cute,' Genie said, ignoring the sarcasm, reaching out to the rabbit with her gnarled hands, stroking its floppy ears. 'Is it yours?'

Jonah nodded. 'I bought it off of Dwayne just now.'

'It's lovely.' She palmed the rabbits head and twiddled with its ears. Just then, Jonah thought he saw a spark of humanity in her for the first time since he'd been introduced to her.

'Did you know that Dwayne was gonna ...' Jonah thought about finishing the sentence but decided against it. The silly bitch would probably just run off to Dwayne and blab what she'd been told and cause even more friction between them.

'Gonna what?' Genie asked eagerly. Her ears pricked up like a dog when she heard His Royal Highness's name.

'Never mind.'

'What? Tell me.' Something about the way Genie was trying to pry the information out of Jonah made him feel uneasy.

'Look, do you like this rabbit?'

'Yeah. I had two when I was little,' she told him, still occupied with Snowy's ears. 'One died of cancer and one got eaten by a fox.' She relayed the news of her pets' deaths with a flicker of sadness in her oily eyes.

Before continuing his line of questioning, Jonah paused to ponder on how weird it was that an animal could die of the same thing as a human, then said: 'The one that got eaten by the fox. What was its name?'

'Sheeba.'

'How did it feel when Sheeba got killed? Tell me about it.'

She turned to him, her face a mask of stone. He was expecting something along the lines of *'you sick fucking arsehole how do you think it felt, it was horrible!'* or *'how could you ask me such a thing?'* but months of mental and physical abuse had rendered her as emotionally charged as a plank of wood. 'I found it in the garden ripped apart. My little sister Karen cleaned out its hut earlier that day and forgot to latch it up. She always did that – forget to latch it up. I went into the garden in the morning and there was just blood all over the grass. Its head was completely off. Half of its body wasn't even there, but Sheeba had this brown fur and that was scattered everywhere. I just screamed and screamed.'

Jonah regretted asking her immediately. He felt disturbed by the mental imagery and clutched onto Snowy even tighter. 'So what if I said that Dwayne was going to try and kill this rabbit, just like what the foxes did to your Sheeba.'

'He wouldn't,' she responded firmly.

'But he might, like for a joke. Maybe if Solomon asked him to he might.' At this, Genie was silent. 'I want you to hide this rabbit somewhere safe where Dwayne won't find it until tonight. Would you do that?'

She shrugged. 'I don't know where I can –'

'– Yes you do,' Jonah snapped, so abruptly that she recoiled from his voice. 'You could hide Snowy somewhere for just a few hours but you're scared that he'll ask you if you've seen it, aren't you? And then you'd tell Dwayne where the rabbit is, even if he'd kill it wouldn't you? Wouldn't you?'

Genie scratched under the Snowy's head with a dirt encrusted fingernail. 'No. I wouldn't.'

'So you'll do it?' He'd been contemplating threatening her by saying that if she didn't hide the rabbit, Jonah would tell Dwayne not to give her any more powder to sniff and consolidate the gesture by saying, 'and you know he'll listen to me, cos I'm his oldest friend.' At that point, Jonah would've said anything to keep that dopey little rabbit away from Dwayne.

But he didn't have to.

'Fine. I'll hide it. For how long?'

'Just a few hours. I'm planning on going in the morning.'

'Oh. I thought you were leaving on Friday,' she said, scratching her ribs like a flea-ridden dog. It made Jonah itchy just being near her.

'Yeah, well, I might be leaving early if I can.' He remembered his date with Rose and sighed. Was there really any point in pursuing it? He was tired, depressed and sluggish, not to mention that win, lose or draw, it would be a one-date wonder. She was here, he was in Nottingham. 'Do you have the spare keys to any of Dwayne's cars?'

'Which one?'

'The BM. The black BM that he picked me up in.'

She shook her head and her greasy hair ruffled in front of her eyes. It looked like oily spaghetti. 'No. I only had a key for my dad's car.'

'Never mind then.' Jonah checked his phone. It was almost three o'clock. 'Where is he?'

She barked a wet, thick cough without much effort to cover her mouth and shrugged. 'He went out. I think he went to meet up with Solomon.' Genie watched as Jonah's face twisted into a mug of repulsion. It wasn't jealousy any more, it was pure disgust toward the creep. She picked up on it immediately. 'You don't like him either, do you?'

Jonah shook his head, too tired to speak. He leaned back on the bouncy mattress. 'Do you?'

'I can't stand him.'

After her words sank in, Jonah laughed. It started as a giggle then cocooned into something hysterical.

'What? Why are you laughing?' she asked, sitting down beside him on the bed and looking out of the blinds, probably checking to see if Dwayne was close by.

'I'm laughing,' Jonah began, wiping a tear away from his eye, 'because he makes me sick. I think he's the biggest prick going.'

'You do?' She turned to him with a smile that was probably about as rare as her menstrual cycle. The glow of the afternoon light illuminated her haggard face and revealed her rotting teeth. His laughter slowly rolled to a stop as he wondered what she must've looked like before she met Dwayne.

'I don't trust him.'

'Me neither. I can't quite make out what it is about him, but he's just slimy. Something just bothers me about him and I don't know what it is but it's almost as if it's something I can see, right in front of me. I get the impression that he's a liar.'

Jonah sat up slowly and leaned on his elbows. 'What do you mean?'

'I don't know.' She peeked through the blinds like she was spying on the neighbours. It sounded like a bunch of kids were playing football in the street below. 'He gets them all psyched up to do some really crazy stuff, but I rarely hear of him doing any of it with them. It's like he eggs them on but keeps a safe distance away from the danger. He's a very smooth talker. He can talk them into anything.' Her voice hushed into a whisper, like she only intended to say it to herself.

So I'm not the only one, he thought.

Suddenly, Jonah wasn't sleepy any more.

If there was anything that could've been worse for his nerves at that point, it was waiting on the corner of Rose's road. The humidity had thinned to a neutral standstill but his head was still dripping like crazy. As far as he knew he'd never been a particularly sweaty person, but in the last couple of days he'd been growing accustomed to his armpits leaking tears of perspiration onto his torso. His forearms were greasy from where he'd tried to wipe the moisture from his face and upper lip, but at least his t-shirt still looked fresh. The patches under his arms were no bigger than a penny coin, easily disguised if he didn't flap around too much. He just prayed that the restaurant had good air-con to keep the patches from expanding in his shirt like ink from a broken fountain pen.

She said on the phone she would be out in about ten minutes. It was his own fault, he guessed. He'd arrived early in his haste to leave Dwayne's flat, even though he hadn't seen him since they left the allotment. After their little bonding session over their mutual dislike, Genie hovered around Jonah asking him all kinds of questions that he was too tired to answer. It was mostly dumb things like *what was Dwayne like before I met him and do you think he'd like me more if I was more firm with him?* The simple fact was that Genie was so warped on drugs that she actually thought Dwayne and she were some kind of item in an open relationship, and this depressed Jonah. He'd been feeling low all day, like he didn't have the energy or the will power to be happy. The choice presented to him by Dwayne had made a valid point; if he didn't want to risk doing jail time for a life of crime, then he was simply going to be broke for the foreseeable future. He could get all the A grades and praise from all the Mike Ravens of every educational institution he enrolled in, but he would never be wealthy like Dwayne. It seemed like a simple enough equation for him to understand: if you do things by the book, the right way, the *legal* way, then you will scrape by. At best, you might have a nice car by about the age of thirty-five or so. BUT, if you bent the rules a bit, if you dared to *live on the edge* as the old cliché goes, then you could afford all the happiness you ever wanted. With that in mind, he wanted to sleep.

The sky was a patchwork of fabulous oranges and deep reds behind the slowly setting sun, and the view seemed to raise his spirits a little at least. It wasn't often that London could match the paradise picturesque scenery of say, a tropical island, but when the sky bloomed with those *summer* colours, Jonah doubted there was a place on earth that looked better. The air smelled thick with the aroma of barbeque, carrying the baseline from some anonymous house party in the gentle breeze.

But as the evening began to darken, Jonah began to feel more and more like a fish in a barrel. Rose didn't live in the nicest area. If he wasn't feeling so pessimistic and tired, Jonah doubted he would've waited as long as he did. Her house was on an untidy, narrow street that was agitating in its claustrophobia and surveyed by the looming tower blocks that watched over him like he was in a goldfish bowl. The street was so tight that it was almost like a car would have to scrape its wing mirrors against the doors of the houses on either side of it just to drive through.

A few of the residents lounged on their porches, drinking and playing cards and dominoes, while little kids who were barely old enough to be out of nappies ran around unsupervised screaming with unruly glee. Some boys about Jonah's age were being pulled along the street by their angry dogs and studying him with indiscreet, watchful glares. Their eyes said *Intruder! Intruder!* Jonah diverted his attention from their path and stared at the ground. He wasn't feeling macho now that he was sober and friendless and in an area he didn't know. At least he wasn't nervous about his date any more.

Then, coming down the road like slow-motion, he saw her.

He'd wanted to remain cool, and after seeing those boys, give off a tough exterior. But his face cracked into a childish and excited smile that broadened as she got nearer. She wore a canary yellow summer dress that fluttered around her body like it was thin as paper, and carried a little handbag of the same colour. She waved at the boys who'd given Jonah the once-over, and they all muttered familiar greetings back, before stopping to see where she was going. When Rose reached Jonah and said Hi, the boys and their dogs seemed to grow darker and more vexed, at which Jonah smiled – courtesy of their envy.

'You look lovely,' he told her sincerely. He was going to comment on how she looked anyway as he gathered that was what all girls wanted to hear, but when she glided up to him with those bronze legs, the truth just rushed out of him. She'd make a good lawyer, he thought.

'Why thank you,' she said, touching her hair out of habit. 'You look ... nervous.'

'Nervous?' His cheeks burned with embarrassment as they began to walk to the train station. 'No, I'm fine.'

Without warning she linked his arm; the smoothness of her skin making contact with his was so overwhelming that at first, he nearly pulled away. But when he settled, he began to enjoy the feeling, exhilarated by the fruity scent of her hair. They began more getting-to-know-you chit-chat, and indulged in the polite talking-and-listening game – she was an Aquarius, with three brothers and two sisters and was originally from Colombia. One of her brothers, Miguel, was Down's-syndrome, a revelation that at first seemed odd for Jonah to hear and then made him happy that she was letting him into that much of her personal life.

As they walked, a static tingle ran through Jonah's body. His earlier weariness had melted and given way to an almost unbearable excitement; his heart began to palpitate like he'd drunk too many espressos. It was the first time he'd ever felt something so strange – it was almost intoxicating. His tongue lolled around in his mouth when he tried to speak, and it took a good couple of tries before he could form a coherent sentence.

It was almost embarrassing for him to be walking through such dingy streets with such a good-looking girl and he wondered if the restaurant he had in mind would be ... appropriate. He began to get nervous all over again, worrying if she was going to turn her nose up once they got there and sour the evening.

The sky turned a bruised plum colour and the air tickled his face like the breath from a sleeping lover. His confidence grew with every step, and soon enough the jokes began to flow freely. Thankfully, she giggled away and covered her mouth when she laughed in a cute way that made Jonah's bones turn into butter. Euphoria rushed through his chest and he realised that being with her was kind of like taking a perfectly legal drug, without the deathbed-hangover or the serial paranoia.

And right then, he didn't know it for certain at that point, but he guessed that he might just be falling in love with Rose, as nuts as it sounded. It had been a crazy week and he'd encountered a lot of 'firsts', like doing pills, seeing a real gun, buying a rabbit. Falling in love was just random enough to round the week off.

19

The metallic screech of the rusty railway constantly interrupted the flow of their conversation. When they hit street-level it was buzzing with people as gangs of suited-and-booted businessmen and women swarmed the pubs.

Jonah drifted down a side street just off Tottenham Court Road, tactically sidling through the crowd. Rose clung to his arm for stability to prevent tripping over in her high-heeled shoes, her dress rippling around her waist like a yellow flower.

'Hope you're hungry,' Jonah said as they manoeuvred under the red maze of the China-town lights. Familiar oily aromas of duck, soy sauce and fried vegetables wafted through the air like a delicious phantom teasing their nostrils.

'I'm bloody starving!' Rose said. 'I could eat a horse.'

'They'll probably have that on the menu if you like.'

She slapped his arm playfully. 'You're terrible.'

Flamboyant gay couples sauntered through the street in tight-fitting tops, but nobody seemed to care much. Jonah had always liked the centre of town for that (not the gay element so much; that made him a trifle uneasy) because it was all open and to some degree free in a way that the darkness of the estates never were. People couldn't be *gay* where he was from. He'd heard about some kid in the Autumn Street building who got the shit kicked out of him because he told his mum he was gay. His older brother, who was a marine or some kind of army cadet guy, heard the news and hit him with a left hook so hard that the kid blacked out into a coma for nine days. But if he'd announced his homosexuality in London's glitzy West End, the gay community would've probably hoisted him up on their shoulders and paraded him around the street commending him for his courage.

It wasn't just the gays – everyone seemed to be relaxed. In such a cosmopolitan area it was hard to be xenophobic or to waste any energy worrying about being jumped by a skin-head gang (a reccurring fear of Jonah's) or even to worry about unfair police harassment. In the briefest of seconds before he took her through the narrow hidden doorway into the restaurant, Jonah hoped that someday he'd be able to live in an area like this.

The Happy Dragon Inn did exactly what it said on the tin; complimentary smiles beamed at them, from the person greeting them at the door to the waitress who gave them their menus. Jonah asked Rose if she'd like some wine and his stomach leapt for joy when she declined; he didn't think he'd be able to take the acidity of alcohol for the third day on the trot. The walls were a pleasant lilac which complemented the odd yet striking black plates and cutlery. From outside, the Happy Dragon didn't look like much, but the interior was charming and delicate. With the full house of people stuffing their faces, it seemed that the place had a nice little secret cult following.

'How on earth did you stumble upon this place?' Rose asked him, scanning the room.

Jonah smiled sadly, remembering his first time at the Happy Dragon. 'I literally did stumble upon it. I was down the West End with my friends and we'd been hanging around some of the arcades drinking Honey Bears. Do they drink Honey Bears in your area?'

She looked at him, bemused, and shook her head. 'What the hell is a Honey Bear?'

'Well, you don't buy Honey Bear in a shop, it's kind of a drink that you just make yourself, like Moonshine except you don't go blind from drinking it.' She tittered at this and leaned forward, eagerly intrigued. 'How we make it, in my area I mean, is with treacle instead of honey, 'cos it's sweeter. You buy a jar of treacle, pour it into an empty two-litre coke bottle, add some lemonade and fill the rest with Jack Daniel's. Sometimes it's easier to make it in a bowl first so you can stir it all up together better. But the result is a terrifically sweet and thick drink that gets you off your face because you can't taste the alcohol.'

'Oh,' she said sarcastically, 'so you don't go blind, you just lose all your teeth.'

'Yeah,' he snorted. 'And wake up with a hangover that feels like 9/11 inside your brain.'

'Sounds dreamy.'

'What can I say? We were young. Anyway, we were sloppy from these Honey Bears we'd made and after wasting all our money on the racing machines we wanted to get something to eat. We cut through China-town and my friend Billy tripped over the doorstep of this place and fell like an ironing board on his face. The guy at the door, who I think is the same guy that greeted us when we came in, rushed out to see if Bill was okay. And that's how we found it.'

The waitress returned with Rose's orange juice and his mineral water then asked if they were ready to order. Rose decided on the chicken and chilli stir fry with special fried rice and Jonah ordered the beef with ginger and vegetables. The waitress smiled, nodded, and took their menus away.

'So, er ... Don't you drink alcohol?' Jonah asked as she sipped on her orange.

'Yes, but I'm a complete lightweight. One glass of wine gets my head spinning, and I don't think it's incredibly ladylike to get drunk on a first date, do you?' She smiled at him, looking into his eyes waiting for an answer. For a second he forgot how to speak, made stupid by her gaze. He turned to rubber in front of her, aroused and spellbound by her voice. Now that he was sitting opposite her, he was able to discreetly enjoy her round cleavage – which didn't help the progression of the conversation.

'I think you're incredibly ladylike., he managed after a sip of water. 'I mean, I don't know you that well or anything but from what I've seen, I really like your whole ethic.'

'My ethic?'

'Yeah. You work for your money, you're studying, you have great manners –'

Before he could finish, she cut him off with a sentence that almost kicked him off his chair. '– I have a kid.'

'What?' Jonah coughed, the water going up his nose. 'I'm sorry; I didn't mean it like that.'

'It's okay,' she said waving it off. Her happy face had been traded for one of uncertainty, and now, it was s*he* who was the nervous one. With the revelation that she was a mother, Jonah began to see just how *grown-up* she seemed. Contours seemed to magically appear under her eyes from the sleepless nights like she'd just aged fifteen years in front of him. 'I thought I'd tell you so that we get it out in the open before we go any further.'

'Is it a boy or a girl?' Jonah asked, trying to keep his voice from faltering. Disappointment hugged onto him like a miserable koala bear.

'It's a girl.' She went into her purse and showed Jonah a passport-sized photo of Rose holding a baby on her lap in one of those picture booths you find at the post office. The baby stared into the camera with blank bewilderment. 'Her name's Esmeralda,' she told him proudly.

Jonah looked at the mother and daughter together and felt the disappointment begin to ebb. 'What, you mean like the Hunchback of Notre Dame?'

This time, Rose laughed and shook her head. 'No, not like that. I named her after my grandmother.'

'Oh.' Now that the aura of perfection had been blown away, Jonah was less in awe of her, less intimidated. Somehow, she was on *his* level now, no better, no worse. He guessed he should've known something was amiss, because everything seemed to fall into place a bit too easily. In a way, he wasn't even surprised; she was too beautiful not to be tainted. 'So ... are you still with the dad or ...'

'I don't agree to go on dates with people if I'm already seeing someone,' she snapped firmly, but the shift in her tone didn't rattle Jonah.

'So where is he?'

'Just gone. He was a lot older than me. I was only sixteen and he was twenty-five. When I told him I was pregnant, he said he was too young to have kids and that was it. I never saw him again.'

'White guy?' Jonah asked, unflinchingly probing her.

'How did you know?'

'Well, your daughter is about three shades lighter than you, which is a bit of a give-away. So what was he, a businessman or what?'

'Actually, he sold home insurance, but his colleagues tell me he's quit his job and moved to America to work for a digital camera firm.'

'Were your parents pissed?'

She shrugged. 'Of course they were. We haven't got room to swing a cat and to add a baby to a house full of people – one of them being disabled, isn't exactly cause for a party.'

Shouldn't have got yourself knocked up then, he thought. The waitress returned with food and laid it out for them both. As she went to leave, Jonah called her back. 'Can we have a bottle of red wine as well please?' The waitress nodded and left.

Rose looked at the table cloth with her hands by her sides, not even acknowledging the plate in front of her. 'You should've just got yourself a glass, I told you I didn't want to drink,' she said in a low voice that was almost lost behind the murmur of chatter in the background.

'Well, I'll tell you what – I think we both should have a glass of wine.'

'Why?' she asked, looking up. Her eyes seemed glassy like they were about to brim with tears.

'Because I think we could both do with one. You seem like this whole baby business has put you off talking for the evening and I'm not about to sit here and eat in silence. So I'd appreciate it if you joined me.'

She touched the corner of her eye like she was blotting a sneaky tear. 'Does it bother you?'

Jonah took a moment to answer her question. If they were going to be honest with each other he may as well give her the courtesy of wading through the bullshit and picking his words carefully. 'I don't think it does. You seem like a proud mother and a hard worker. I mean, I know a lot of girls who just get pregnant and sit on their arse all day and don't even attempt to raise their little brats. But you're working and at college and stuff, and you're setting a good example for the baby. I can't knock you, to be honest.'

Rose inhaled and exhaled slowly but didn't take her eyes off of the tablecloth.

'I'll tell you one thing,' Jonah continued. 'You got one hell of a good figure for having a baby.'

Her shoulders shrugged up and down as she chuckled. The waitress returned again with a bottle of wine – probably the most expensive on the menu as he didn't specify, and poured them both a glass. Jonah picked up his glass and urged Rose to do the same.

'Let's have a toast,' Jonah said. She looked up at him and bit down on her bottom lip. He motioned for her to raise her glass. 'To Esmeralda.'

Rose's cheeks dimpled with a smile. 'To Esmeralda,' she repeated, as their glasses clinked together.

20

The bill for the food was a lot less frightening than he'd expected, especially considering they had a dessert each and a cup of tea. Even though his stomach was full, the wine hit his head like a baseball bat. When he ordered the bottle he thought that he'd built up a good enough tolerance to the stuff after his last couple of days, but he was obviously wrong. Although she tried to conceal her own drunkenness, Rose stuttered and slurred her mystique away with a series of hiccups.

*　　*　　*

They talked about the food and the service for a while as they wobbled down the road. Rose seemed to enjoy being waited on for a change. Although Jonah suspected but didn't know for sure, she'd never actually been on a real dinner date before. Her previous boyfriend – Alan – the one who'd landed her in the *trouble*, took her to a lot of fancy hotels and felt her up in the back of a few cinemas, but never once bought her a proper meal. There was one time when he bought her a Big Mac Meal as he was getting himself one and his face screwed up with disgust as he had to pay for *her* food like he was using his own testicles as currency. But apart from that, there was nothing quite as ... was it romantic? As her head tilted in the cool evening breeze, she tried to evaluate what kind of date she'd had with Jonah. It wasn't *romantic* as such, sweet yes, but not romantic. There was all the jangling tension of two strangers chatting away with the obvious lust for each other parked at the back of their minds, and to his credit, Jonah had been a gentleman; something she wasn't sure existed in London. But there was something else, too. The obvious shift in atmosphere when she revealed the truth about her having a child, the distinct wariness that comes across a guy when encountering a young mum as if he were about to get her pregnant again just by looking at her for too long. There were also the cluttering insecurities that dug into her as she wondered if Jonah would look at her daughter as baggage. But, as he patrolled along the street with his arm around her shoulder – Dutch courage, she assumed – they both seemed pretty comfortable just not talking about it.

The night had turned surprisingly bitter. Rose secretly thanked the wine for not making her feel as cold as she would have if she were sober, but regardless, her arms turned to gooseflesh and bumped beneath Jonah's fingers. He looked down at her as they crossed the main road heading toward the tube station and said: 'Are you okay?'

A bus approached and beeped its horn at them to shoo them out of the road. Rose clung on to Jonah's wrist for dear life and shivered when his fingers brushed her nipple beneath the fabric of her dress.

'Yeah I'm fine,' she said. 'Apart from nearly getting hit by that bus, I'm fine.'

'Are you cold?'

She looked at the concern on his face and for a second was unable to answer him. Maybe he'd just had too much to drink; she knew how people were when they were pissed, like alcohol was steroids for their emotions, heightening every feeling in their body. But to have a boy seem concerned about her being cold – alcohol–induced or not, was a nice feeling.

'I'm okay,' she nodded back with a smile.

Coin debris fell from Jonah's pocket as he pulled out his wallet. He began to count the remainder of his cash thoughtfully, as if he were doing a complicated math equation in his head.

'Do you want me to get you a jumper?'

'What?' The sheer randomness of the question bemused her. That, accompanied by the fact that she was finding it hard to focus her attention on any one thing at the moment, made his sentence seem like it was spoken in a foreign language. 'What are you on about?'

'One of those tourist souvenir shops is bound to still be open. I can get you a hoody to wear if you want.'

She was struck with a queer amusement and warmth that filled her insides like the tea they'd just drank. Alan, the father of her one-year-old daughter, had never made a gesture as profound as the one Jonah was making in the few hours he'd known her. She could see it in Jonah's eyes that his offer wasn't just another ploy to try and get her in the sack, and the realisation of this felt quite similar to relief. 'No I'm fine, don't waste your money.'

'It's okay, honestly,' Jonah protested, clutching his few remaining notes in his balled fist. 'I got enough to get you a jumper and we can still go to the fair, if you like.'

'You and this fair!' She shook her head with a smile. 'You're like a little kid.'

'I am a little kid. Young at heart!' Jonah grabbed her by the wrists and twirled her around on the pavement. A couple of drunk rugby player-types were leaving a nearby pub and swerved to avoid their dancing, mumbling something as they avoided the collision.

Rose felt dizzy and breathless and turned-on. 'Stop spinning me Jonah, I'm gonna throw up!'

Jonah spun her faster, disregarding the passers-by on the busy pavement. 'Now that certainly wouldn't be ladylike would it?'

'Seriously!' she laughed and tilted her head back 'I'm gonna break my ankles in these heels!'

Jonah hugged her to a stop. They both stood there panting, a gasp of breathless laughter on both their lips. It was just like one of those corny old romantic films, but she guessed they got their inspiration from somewhere because here the two of them were, staring into each other's eyes like they were about to embrace in a kiss – a kiss that would be like a lightning bolt through their bodies and for that one moment in time, be the most majestic and overwhelming feeling of mutual love that either of them had ever felt.

'We don't need to go on the fast rides at the fair,' Jonah said, filling the silence between them and immediately cursing himself for his cowardice of not advancing with the inevitable kiss. 'We could go on those tea-cup ones, or even the bumper cars.'

She gulped the lump of unpredictable tension down. 'I got to get home to my daughter, Jonah. My mum thinks I'm having dinner with some college friends.'

Reality was back like a bitch with a loud voice.

'Oh, okay.' Jonah's nervous smile made her look away; she couldn't stand to think that she'd lost her Hollywood moment.

They walked to the tube station awkwardly. They didn't need to be telepathic to know what the other person was thinking, that they'd come so close to sharing something rare and beautiful, but reality rarely grants those kinds of pleasures.

The electronic display at the platform informed them that it was quarter to midnight. As they waited, Jonah desperately rummaged through his mind to think of something to say. He'd wanted to make her laugh so he could see those dimples again, the way her nose wrinkled up and highlighted the light brown freckles sprinkled across her cheeks. He felt as though something witty was going to come to him, but in the end his brain gave up – tired, abused and sleep deprived. When he was four or five, he'd once witnessed his grandmother turn the whole house upside down looking for her glasses, only to find that they were actually propped on her head. He giggled himself almost into a bladder malfunction on that occasion, but she was puffed out and frustrated. Now, rolling his eyes skyward as if it had some witty anecdote he could relay, he knew how his grandmother felt. It was like he'd been atop a mountain overlooking a magnificent skyline, only to have a strong gust blow him off, leaving him clawing at the crumbling rock face trying to salvage the evening. They weren't even making physical contact any more like they had been doing so brazenly above ground. It was as if a glacier of ice jarred between them, preventing the progression of their flirting. Maybe the alcohol was wearing off.

The train pulled up, much to Jonah's relief; at least the rattling clamour of the train would give them a reason to sit in silence. As the soot-coated doors pulled apart Jonah held out his arm signalling for Rose, the lady, to board their carriage first. She gave him a half-smile, offering only one dimple, and then floated onto the train with weightless grace despite her intoxication. Jonah, feeling as heavy as a bag of medicine balls, stomped aboard and managed to drag himself to a seat beside her.

Neither of them spoke for a few stops. People floated on and off but neither of them seemed to notice. A couple of ugly middle-class women were talking loudly a few seats away, the high-pitched tone of their voices cutting into Jonah like a chainsaw into a tree branch. They were talking some kind of shit that he couldn't help but listen to, something about a man called Edgar and his rude comments about a pregnant woman called Sophie.

'Yah, yah, I agree. He is totally out of order,' the pale one with thin copper hair was saying, her beak nose looking as though it could chip through ice. 'It's like, he doesn't even think before he opens his stupid fucking mouth.'

'I know!' the fat middle-eastern-looking one said, stretching out the words for dramatic affect. 'Another thing I hate about him is the way he *al-ways* talks about his sex life. I mean I know he's gay but that doesn't give him licence to just talk about him sucking off another man he met in a club ...'

The lack of air was making him feel sick. His forehead was a collection of grease and tube dust and it made him want to claw his flesh off. He hung his head drunkenly like a bashed-up boxer on his stool in between one of the late rounds, but kept his vision on the black window opposite them, stealing glimpses of Rose's reflection. At one point, she caught his eye in the window, and usually (sober) he'd look away embarrassed. Now however, relaxed from wine and light from the strain of the week, he looked straight back.

'If I ask you something, will you answer it honestly?' Jonah said, maintaining eye-contact through the window. 'Did you at least have fun tonight?'

She nodded without averting her eyes. 'Did you have fun with a single mum?'

He wanted to laugh but couldn't find the energy. So instead, he smiled, sighed and fell back into the seat leaning his head against the train window. 'What'd'you think?' His voice came out croaky like he'd just woken up from a deep sleep.

She rested her head on his shoulder and they stayed like that until her stop.

Stars flecked the sky like a splatter painting when they made it out of the station. It was cold but needed, and a great deal better than that furnace in hell they'd just been riding in, he thought. Draping his arm around her, she held on to his fingers. Shadows swallowed everything in the failing street lights. Abstract sounds echoed as they walked making Jonah twitch each time he heard a can rattle across the floor or heard a tramp singing to himself somewhere out of sight. They got halfway down the road when Jonah stopped.

'What? What is it?' Rose asked, looking up into his face. He resisted the strongest urge to lean down and kiss her right there in the gloom.

'Your dad. I don't want to get you into trouble.'

She squinted up at him like she was watching the happy ending to some romantic drama, her eyes threatening tears. 'I guess you're right.'

'I'll watch you from here and make sure nothing jumps out at you.'

She nodded. 'Well,' she leaned in and slung her arms around his neck, 'thanks for taking me out.'

He squeezed around her waist and breathed in his last breath of fruity shampoo and perfume. 'You're very welcome.'

'Keep in touch.'

'Definitely.'

Rose waved and smiled sadly, then turned and headed home. Jonah leaned against a parked car and watched her hair cascade in the breeze, fantasising about running up behind her and kissing her neck, licking her collar bone, biting her shoulder –

She turned back, five steps away. 'You didn't even give me a kiss,' she said softly.

He shrugged. 'Didn't think you wanted one.'

'You didn't ask.' She took a step toward him.

All at once she seemed incredibly vulnerable; a young girl impersonating a much older woman. Her edible shoulders slumped.

'Can I ... have a kiss?' Jonah asked her, his voice lacking the kind of courage that the question demanded. Instead of being sure and authoritative it was clumsy and fragile, his face a portrait of nervous uncertainty. With the self-induced highs of the last couple of the days wracking his body and that evening's alcohol slowly wearing off, he felt incredibly edgy, almost as though he'd used up his quota of false machismo and no longer had any left to mask his insecurities about the opposite sex. A part of him was thrilled at the prospect of meeting her lips, of tasting her flavour that was bound to make him convulse with the kind of magical energy that a person only experiences a couple of times in their whole life – if they're lucky.

But another part of him wasn't ready for it. The cowardly lion in him was jabbering away in his ear *'maybe you should just leave it alone, Jonah, she's got a kid. Don't get mixed up with a girl who already has a baby – what kind of shit is that?'* It was that same inner voice that was breaking him away from his childhood friends, that horrible rational tone of reality.

No matter what he thought it was too late; Rose drifted into his arms again and kissed him, gently holding his face with her delicate hands. The shock was so surreal that when he thought about it later – it was convincing enough to have been a dream. Her tongue worked into his mouth with daunting experience, her saliva jolting his heart awake like a tazer. In the seven or eight seconds that it lasted, Jonah was on another planet, transported further away than the ecstasy had taken him. Her fingertips were like electrical currents through his flesh, and that overpowering watermelon fragrance made his insides shiver. He put his arms around her waist, not sure if he should grab her arse but doing so anyway, and the firm grasp of her cheeks turned his slowly stiffening dick into a mallet hard enough to hammer a nail with. Aware of his erection, she squeezed him tighter. Now, that niggling, shaky voice was like a whisper deep inside him, far too quiet to be heard under the rushing of his blood and the frantic beating of his heart. Jonah pressed his lips against hers even firmer, his tongue wrestling and dominating the interior of her mouth.

When Rose finally pulled away, she was panting softly. Jonah was light-headed, thousands of tiny black dots exploding in his vision. Both breathless, they stared into each other's eyes.

It was at that moment that Jonah had what he believed was a supernatural experience. He never told a single soul about it, not even Rose, for fear of being ridiculed, or more specifically for fear of that special moment being *rationalised*. But as he looked into her eyes, seeing his obscured reflection in her pupils, Jonah believed with every fibre in his body that they were reading each other's minds. He believed that she was able to feel what he was thinking – all the confusion of the last couple of days, all of the apprehension, the sheer sadness of being alienated from the only friends he'd ever had. And he felt her agony of being a young mum, of being frightened and immature and being objectified by men who saw her as a nothing more than a sexual Everest. He felt her desperation and loneliness, and somehow, their waves of emotions seemed to flow into each other like two streams between them. He felt a presence that was as real as all of the five senses, and believed this with the conviction of a born-again Christian. Jonah didn't mention it to her, but instead, just nodded. Two tears spilled from her eyes, which had been brimming like a full bucket of water in the rain, and right then he knew, she felt it as well.

'I'm leaving tomorrow. I don't know how often I'm going to be able to afford to come to London, but I would really like to see you again. Please.' He whispered, their foreheads resting against each other.

'I wanna see you again if you wanna see me,' she whispered back.

Breathing out, he felt the curdling strain of inevitability; he was going to have to leave her behind and didn't know when he was going to see her again, and this lodged a pain in his chest that ached like a stab wound. 'I'd love to meet your little girl. Maybe we could all go out one day. If I can save up enough money to come back before the weather gets cold, maybe we could all go on a picnic in Hyde Park.'

Unexpectedly, Rose began to sob. Jonah didn't ask what was wrong.

'I-I'd like that too.' Her sobs turned into full blown bawling. Jonah drew her in and held her against his chest, her tears wetting through his t-shirt. Everything was pouring out of her; negativity she'd kept bottled inside spilled out in wordless despair. They stood and swayed on the spot, caught in the rhythm of a strangely therapeutic dance. Jonah wanted to ask her if she believed in soulmates, but somehow couldn't find it in himself to speak; their moment went beyond words, beyond anything *physical.*

They embraced for twenty minutes against the pervasive chill of the air. Rose's cries slowly dampened into an occasional sniffle, until eventually they ceased altogether. She pulled away from Jonah and wiped her eyes.

'Oh no,' she said quietly, 'I got make-up all over your t-shirt.'

Jonah looked down at the smudges of brown and black and the grey circle from where she'd been crying. 'Doesn't matter,' he shrugged.

Her eyes were bloodshot and puffy, her cheeks shiny from the tears. 'Thank you for taking me out tonight, Jonah.'

He nodded. 'I'm going to try and come back as soon as I can.'

'Please do.' She kissed his lips again, softly and slowly, then turned and made her way home.

21

Except for a red-faced old man who looked like a homeless Hell's Angel sleeping in a seat at the end of the carriage, Jonah's tube ride back to Dwayne's flat was completely empty. He'd managed to catch the last train but wouldn't really have cared if he'd missed it; the evening had been far too meaningful to care about the transport and in a way, he'd have preferred to walk home so that it would give him an excuse to be alone with his thoughts. Did he really care that Rose had a daughter? Probably not. It wasn't an ideal situation, granted, but someone to love was always better than no one. And after what had just happened, that revelatory experience that somehow seemed to fuse the two of them together like some kind of spiritual ceremony, Rose having a baby girl was like a drop in the ocean when compared to how they could grow together, how they could bloom.

Falling in love with her was as instantaneous as a lightning strike. He didn't know if she loved him back or if she was even *in love* with him (for surely the two are quite different, he thought) but he knew that she must've felt something profound for him beyond the subtle alcoholic manipulations of their emotions. Whatever they had, it was worth coming back to London for. Forget the fact that he'd lost his two best friends in the world – hell, the only two friends he had in the world – it was worth it to find Rose, he thought.

A lurking dread crept behind the image of Rose in Jonah's mind. Another confrontation with Dwayne was inevitable, but as far as Jonah was concerned their friendship was over. The whole time since he'd been back he'd barely recognised Dwayne, seeing only flashes of him in subtle facial expressions or unconscious gestures, like he was talking with some kind of identical cyborg that hadn't been programmed properly. There was definitely a wire loose somewhere inside Dwayne's head. His creator, Solomon, had botched something while rewiring his brain to make him believe that the city was his oyster. After the whole fiasco with the rabbit and that dog (sadness tugged at his heart as he remembered Champ being locked away in that shed, almost suffocating in the heat), it was clear that Dwayne was gone, and he was never coming back.

As for Billy? Well, since the first day that Jonah met him when they were seven or so, it was clear that Billy was never going to have a happy ending. The kid had been beaten, strangled, stomped and thrashed with just about every household appliance you could name – and this was all stuff that everyone knew happened to him; there was a catalogue of assault, maybe (probably) even sexual, that went untold, locked behind that vacant stare. In a horrible, guilty way, Jonah knew that Billy was never destined for anything good. He was never going to amount to anything – forget all that talk about 'you can do whatever you want if you put your mind to it,' oh no. It had been all downhill from the minute Billy-Lee was born.

Jonah's mother warned him time and time again to steer clear of Billy. As an adult, she had that aura of wisdom about her that comes with age, and for a kid it can be a daunting and mostly intimidating thing to be in the presence of. When Jonah grew up and learned things for himself, the aura faded around his mother and the masquerade of omniscience deteriorated along with it. But one thing that had always remained faithful to her word even as the years rolled by was that Billy, whether it was his fault or not, was always going to be trouble.

As Jonah sat with his head gently vibrating on the train window, he remembered when he came home from a hard day of playing during the summer holidays when he was twelve. His mother was in the kitchen, peeling some vegetables for dinner, when she calmly beckoned Jonah to her.

'What is it?' Jonah asked her, his voice visibly shaken and with good reason. He knew that tone in his mother's voice, the stern baseline under a disguise of normality. And she knew that tone in his too, the apprehension of the unknown. What had he done? Forgot to clean up after himself in the bathroom? Had his mum overheard him rapping along with Biggie Smalls in his bedroom and heard all the bad curse words he was using so brazenly?

He stood in the doorway of the kitchen, just out of arm's reach of where his mother was skinning a carrot. It may have seemed stupid to be scared of his mum while she was holding a knife, but on the rare occasion when she lost it with him, she'd whack him with just about anything. Her shoe was her favourite, or the TV remote, and she never hit him above the waist, always on the fleshy parts like his thighs or his arse. But if what her voice suggested was correct, Jonah feared that she might just turn around and stab him to death.

'What did you do today?' she asked him without looking away from the sink. It wasn't the general sort of enquiry that a mum might ask her son after a hard day of running around, and she didn't care either. It was a trap. Jonah's mental defences sprang up. His whole body tensed except for his legs – those rubbery things always gave him away in times of stress, probably softened from the thought of getting the shoe or the remote.

Scanning his mind, he searched for anything he might've done wrong that morning. He hadn't harassed the corner shop lady, he hadn't sworn loud enough for his mother to hear. After a suitable pause, he had to tell her the truth. Maybe she already knew where he'd been and was trying to trick him.

'I went to the arcades with Dwayne.'

'What did you play?' she bit back immediately. Now he knew something was definitely wrong. His mother was an ambassador for the campaign against video games. She hated them with the same kind of hatred he reserved for boring religious documentaries and awfully low-budget films about Jesus.

'I er ... I played Super Monaco.'

She stopped chopping. 'What kind of game is that?'

'Motorbike game.'

She continued chopping, slowly and methodically. 'Who were you with?'

'Dwayne and Malcolm from downstairs.' A few years later, Malcolm got attacked on another estate over some girl that he was seeing and got a baseball bat broken over his head. When Jonah heard this he felt sick thinking about how hard someone would need to get hit to make a baseball bat break. Malcolm was in a coma and recovered nine months later, but to his knowledge, Malcolm still couldn't see, talk or walk unassisted.

'Who else was with you?'

'No one.' Jonah shrugged, maybe sounding a little too defensive. He turned to make his way back through the living room but was called back mid-step.

'Where you with Billy?'

'No.'

'Why not?' She still hadn't turned to look at him.

'I knocked for him but nobody came to the door.'

Suddenly, his mum turned around and pointed the knife directly at him. 'Come here,' she ordered, a psychotic glint in her eye.

'Wh-what did I do?'

'Stop stuttering and get over here.'

He took three steps and was by her side but the walk felt a lot longer.

'I saw your friend Billy out there.' She pointed to the window in front of her that overlooked the courtyard below.

'So?'

'So?' His mother repeated, outraged. Jonah gulped hard but couldn't produce any saliva, flinching under the weight of her voice. 'Look outside.'

Jonah craned his neck, hesitant to bring his head anywhere near his mother's reach. Three policemen stood by what had once been a Ford Escort, but was now little more than a slumping hulk of gnarled metal. The burnt, windowless frame of the car showed the smouldering interior that had fused into the metal in an unidentifiable molten black mess. Smoke still rose from the corpse of the vehicle like it'd just been exhumed from hell.

'Billy did that?' Jonah tried to fight a smile. His mum would surely whack the side of his head off if he even dared think that setting fire to someone's property was funny, but Jonah couldn't help it. 'You sure it was him?'

'Of course I'm sure. I saw his ginger hair from all the way up here. He smashed all the windows and set the thing on fire.'

'What with?' Jonah asked, a little too eagerly.

'Does it matter? He set someone's car on fire and he's lucky that the man didn't catch him. The police are probably looking for him now,' she shouted, annoyed at her son's line of questioning.

But Jonah knew that the police wouldn't catch Billy for at least a couple of days. They'd have to look at the CCTV footage because even though there was only one ginger-haired boy that acted retarded enough to set fire to a complete stranger's car in broad daylight in front of security cameras and two tower blocks full of witnesses, nobody would ever cooperate with the police – probably not even the dude who owned the car. Oh no, he'd just catch Billy alone and kill him.

'I don't want you knocking around with him any more. Do you understand me, Jonah?' Jonah nodded absently at his mother's request but continued to stare out the window, squinting to see if Billy was dumb enough to be hiding in one of the trees or in the nearby bushes. 'Are you listening? You better stay away from that boy because whoever's car that is, they're going to kill Billy for that. And if you're with him they're gonna kill you too, do y'understand me, boy?'

'Yeah.'

'I said do you understand me, don't "yeah" me, Jonah.'

'Yes, I understand,' he said, still wanting to laugh and only being able to contain himself with images of Billy lying stabbed-the-fuck-up in a dirty stairway somewhere splintering his mind.

The last thing his mother said on the subject always stayed with Jonah. He remembered it word for word and since that day, every time he saw Billy the words would trail somewhere in the basement of his subconscious like a ghost trapped in the cellar: 'Nothing will ever help that poor boy.'

He'd drifted asleep. When he woke up, the Hell's Angel was looking directly at him with his hands folded across his fat stomach. Jonah gave him a sleepy glance and leaned his head back against the window. The Hell's Angel said something incomprehensible through his wiry beard that looked like a tangle of spiders, his voice the texture of sandpaper. Jonah ignored him, his lids too heavy and his head too light to bother with the aggravation.

The train began to slow and conveniently, pulled up at Jonah's stop. Steadying himself with the poles, Jonah wobbled over to the doors and waited for them to open. The bum gargled something again, before laughing to himself as if an invisible comedian was telling jokes in his ear; the sound made Jonah itch. A flare of heat rose from the crack of Jonah's arse to the nape of his neck, sweat beads springing from his skin like crops for harvest.

'Come on, come on,' he willed the doors to open. The bum tittered, the sound climbing in pitch until it seemed like a little girl was sitting there giggling away. Jonah didn't dare look at him – the pressure of being locked in such close proximity was enough to set his skin on fire. His chest tightened like hands that were clasped around his heart trying to squeeze juice out of it. Vomit crept up his throat. *Another panic attack* he thought.

When the train pulled up to the stop, his t-shirt was wet through. In the light of the platform he was able to see his reflection clearly in the window of the doors before they slowly screeched open; his eyes were wide and unrecognisable like two boiled eggs, harbouring deep semicircles underneath. Drumming his fingers against his jeans, Jonah quickly squeezed off the train as soon as a big enough gap opened in the doors. The sooty air tickled his throat.

'Thank God,' he whispered as soon as he was able to talk. The curved walls of the underground felt as though they were narrowing like a funnel as he made his way down the platform toward the exit, frantically pulling his t-shirt away from his Adam's apple for fear of puking and fainting.

The train spluttered alongside him and began to depart. For some reason that he couldn't explain, Jonah desperately wanted to get off the platform before the train passed him. A craving for cool, fresh air made him desperate for a fix; he didn't care if acid rain was falling, it'd be better than being in that tube station.

The whoosh of the train was in full motion as Jonah reached the end of the platform that led to the escalators. He was almost out. Before he turned the corner to leave, his head sickly throbbing like he had the flu, Jonah took one last look at the train as his carriage passed.

Everything began to slow down and he was quite sure he was going to faint, the unbearable heat blistering beneath his skin. His vision blurred along with the faint line between dream and reality, his grip on rationality rapidly losing its solidity. The carriage he was on was about to enter the mouth of the tunnel, and Jonah felt magnetised by it, compelled to see it leave. The lights flickered in the carriage for maybe a second or so, but in that time the Hell's Angel – who was grinning at Jonah from behind the window – *morphed*. Before the lights went out, his appearance, even from the distance that Jonah stood at, was clearly humanoid. But for that second, it appeared (no, not appeared, *it was*) as if his head were malformed, extended somehow; it was wider and elongated, becoming a snout where the tramp's nose and mouth should've been. The only thing that Jonah could compare it to before he shoved the image away forever behind the excuse of intoxication, was the head of a moose.

The bum looked like a hairless, antlerless moose.

As the train vanished, Jonah's vision and senses realigned. His throat and stomach felt as though he'd just tried to digest a shot-put. Hot puke flew from his mouth and splattered against a poster advertising a new theatre production of Hamlet.

'Oh you dirty bastard,' one of the underground workers said at the sight of Jonah throwing up. 'I'm sick and tired of you fucking kids puking your guts up all over the shop.'

Jonah attempted to stand from his crouched position and fell onto his arse. The angry, pug-faced tube worker stormed toward him.

'You little prick. All you care about is getting drunk isn't it? Yeah, fuck whoever has to clean up after you, as long as you have a good time that's all that matters.' The man's voice echoed off the curved tiled walls. Jonah felt like protesting his sobriety but decided that trying to get some strength in his legs was far more important. He needn't have worried. The train worker yanked him up by his arm with intimidating ease and tugged him toward the escalators. Jonah felt his north and south bearings pull away from each other like repelling magnets.

'Go home and get some sleep. And get a job,' the man

yelled up at him as the escalator carried him toward the sweet, fresh air.

22

It was half past one in the morning. The house was dark and empty. Jonah stripped down to his boxer shorts that were moist from sweat around the crotch, and climbed into bed. He felt something cool against his thigh and reached down to inspect it. It was a piece of torn card about the size of an envelope. He immediately fumbled around on the floor for his phone so he could inspect it with the glow of the screen. It was a note from Genie, the handwriting surprisingly elegant. It read:

> You're bunny is under your bed I didn't know
> where else to put it. Hope it's okay

Almost as soon as he finished reading it he heard the dull scraping beneath him and felt the burden of the creature adding to his stress. He was too exhausted to get out and inspect the animal; there were holes in the box so he knew it wouldn't suffocate and there was a big leaf of lettuce the last time he saw it. It could wait till morning. The pillow felt like a cloud as his head sank through it. He felt himself falling, drifting ...

A knock on the door.

His eyelids sprang open like an elastic band snapping. For a second he thought he might've imagined the noise, or that maybe someone had dropped something next door.

'Jonah?' Dwayne whispered.

He remained silent, his heart not knowing whether to pump or stall.

'Jonah?' The door opened in the darkness, but the horizontal lines of streetlight bleeding in through the blinds revealed Dwayne's silhouette. 'I heard you come in. You still awake?'

Well I fucking am now, he thought. Jonah mumbled that he was in fact awake.

'How was your night?'

'Yo man, I just wanna go to sleep.'

'Okay,' Dwayne said apologetically. 'I just wanted to say I was sorry.'

'Whatever.' Jonah tried to sound more tired than he actually was in an attempt to avoid the conversation going any further. Dwayne fidgeted around uncomfortably, leaning against the door. The rabbit clicked away in its box as if it were nibbling something.

Dwayne didn't respond to Jonah's dismissal immediately. Instead, he kind of just shuffled on the spot like he was waiting in a long queue. The density of the air in the room was quickly angering Jonah. He kicked off the cover and rolled onto his side facing the window, hoping he'd be able to suck in whatever breeze blew, and that Dwayne would see his body language and leave.

No such luck. 'Genie said that you wanted to go home tomorrow. Is that right?'

'Yeah.'

'Is it 'cos of earlier?' When Jonah refused to answer, he carried on. 'Look, I'm sorry about earlier ... with the rabbit, okay? I didn't know you were going to react like that or else I wouldn't have taken you to the allotments. I just ... I don't know. I guess I just wanted you to be a part of what we're doing.'

'By killing a rabbit?' Jonah said dryly. 'I don't know what's wrong with your head, Dwayne. Honest to God I don't. Its bad enough you got a dog that looks more like a fucking bear than it does a dog, but to want to feed it something like a bunny rabbit. It's just sick. No, it's not even sick, it's just retarded.' When Dwayne didn't respond this time, Jonah decided to continue his tirade. He wasn't going to get a good night's sleep anyway, not with everything swirling around in his head and the oppressive warmth of the still night. 'You know something, Dwayne, you want me to tell you something?'

'It's up to you.' He replied – his voice cool and calm, the complete contrast to Jonah's erratic high pitched yapping.

'Okay then. I'm actually jealous of you guys.' Jonah sat up in the bed and leaned against the window, the cool wooden blinds soothing his back. 'I'm jealous of the fact that I had to go and you guys all got to stay. I'm jealous that you guys made friends with this fucking fruitcake Solomon –'

Before he could finish, Dwayne promptly cut-in. 'Don't say that about him, Jonah.'

'Or what? You gonna shoot me in the foot?'

'No. I just don't think you should be talking bad about someone you don't even really know. He's got nothing to do with why you're pissed off.'

'Motherfucker!' Jonah yelled and sprang up from the bed, his fury giving him a surge of adrenaline and waking him up completely. They both stood there in the dark, sweating and agitated. If the lights were on it might've looked like the set of a gay porn flick, but the darkness was enough of a veil to comfort their sexualities. 'It has everything to do with why I'm pissed off. I have to leave London, where I've lived my whole life, and leave my best friends and you replace me with that guy. You say I don't really know him. Well, what do you know about him? Because from where I'm standing, it don't look like you know a thing about your little magician slash criminal mastermind slash Portuguese-speaking English gentleman boyfriend.'

Dwayne stepped forward, his chest heaving. 'Don't go there, Jonah. There's no need. I'm not looking for an argument.'

'You wanna know what else I'm jealous about, Dwayne?' Jonah was yelling, his upper body glistening in the limited light. 'I'm jealous that I have to do everything the hard way. I have to leave my home, my friends, everything I've ever known, just to go to a college where, instead of learning, I'm worried about getting jumped every five minutes, and working in a fucking bakery every Saturday – and you guys are playing around all day long. You got money falling out your arseholes, cars, more girls than you can wave your dick at, and the worst part is you don't deserve it. None of you do. Not you, not Billy, and not that fucking creep bastard Solomon.'

In the next room, Jonah heard Genie indiscreetly shuffling up to put her ear against her bedroom wall. Dwayne folded his arms and took the stance of a person calmly waiting to fire back in an argument, the stance of a man one word short of violence.

'Jonah, I gave you money. I gave you clothes and a place to stay. I offered you the chance to join us. The only one making it hard for yourself is you. I said everything was there to be taken –'

'– Who said that? You or Solomon?' Jonah snapped sarcastically.

Dwayne exhaled. 'Okay. Fine.' He put his hands up and signalled submission. 'I'll drop you to the station tomorrow afternoon, okay? For what it's worth though, I really don't want to lose a friend like you, Jonah. I ain't got many friends and if dropping you to the station a day early is going to salvage our friendship, then I'll do it.'

Something about Dwayne's words didn't seem quite right, like they were rehearsed. Jonah always thought that most intelligent people knew when they were being lied to, especially by a bad liar, and Dwayne's little heartfelt closing speech was about as authentic as a daytime soap opera actor. Even the way that Dwayne bowed his head and went to leave made it seem like he was watching a performance, even in the dark where facial expressions were obscured. Just the outline of Dwayne's body language seemed exaggerated, unnatural.

Before Dwayne closed the door, Jonah had one last request. 'If you want to drop me to the station tomorrow then I'd appreciate the lift. But don't think I'm gonna go with that nigger.' Even though Dwayne was now outside of the room, Jonah heard him stop mid stride, and when he proceeded to walk again, his footsteps were firmer, more like stomps.

Jonah hated to drop the N word. He hated everything about it. He didn't even like hearing it in rap songs or in films where other black people were saying it. It was an ugly, hateful word that just sounded disgusting and if his mum had heard him say it – well, there was no amount of physical restraint that could stop her belting her son with a high heel or the TV antenna. Jonah wasn't even sure that Solomon was black, part black, or black anywhere in his whole bloodline. If Jonah was asked on *Who Wants to be a Millionaire* and didn't have any lifelines left, he'd just take the money and run rather than risking the gamble.

But somehow, in some terrible way, it was the only suitable thing to call him.

THURSDAY

23

Alleyways were always the most iconic setting for anything bad to happen in Jonah's opinion. Especially at night; nothing good ever happened in alleyways at night. Just the look of them conjured up nefarious connotations; the moody lighting, the shadows shrouding the graffiti-strewn walls, the smells of piss, shit and every other rancid waft of abject human effluence. There was something incredibly claustrophobic about being able to hear the muted city sounds but not able to see beyond the ever narrowing walls, the bricks shrinking with every step making the path ever so tight, tight enough to rub against your shoulders. Tight enough to squeeze you into a compromising position of capture.

Jonah quickly came to the realisation that the only way he'd be walking down such a menacing and sinister alleyway – at night – was because he was having another one of his nightmares. Steam blew from a pipe sticking out of the wall above him like a protruding bone, concealing the path ahead. He could only see as far as his hand in front of him, and with it outstretched he used it to make sure he didn't walk straight into a wall and smash his teeth out.

Breath was billowing out of him like he'd just attempted to break the hundred-metre sprint world record and he'd only walked three paces. Scared shitless, he tried to mumble a prayer to God but couldn't gather the rhythm in his mouth, let alone remember one. Instead, he blubbered with wet lips and felt his way through the encroaching mist like a newly blind man in a department store with no cane to aid him. The mist was acrid, seeping into his mouth and scratching his tonsils and tasting like a bag of pennies. It was like rust particles were floating in the air and tearing little gashes deep into his trachea.

His mind was exploding with horrific thoughts:

Something is going to jump out at me any minute I can feel it oh God I just know that it's going to touch me and I'm going to scream but I'm not going to be able to because I can't even breathe and the fright of it might be so bad that I'll just drop down dead on the spot and die in my sleep.

Looking upwards to see if the view was any better, he searched for an escape route. He'd hoped that if he thought about a ladder or a rope dangling for long enough that it would materialise, but instead, he was greeted with a black and featureless sky; the type of blackness that exists when the world is asleep and nothing else is stirring except for that which lives in darkness; the things of nightmares.

Picking up the pace to a light jog but not fast enough to trip over any debris that might be littered about the place, Jonah realised that the further he went the thinner the mist became until after a few seconds he was able to see an exit of sorts.

The alleyway path led to a decrepit house, the shattered windows appearing like the empty eye sockets of a brick-faced zombie. Upon seeing it, Jonah's feet came to an abrupt halt. There was no way on earth, or even in his subconscious mind, that he was going to step one foot inside that place; it reeked of suffering. The alleyway suddenly didn't seem that bad. It was no trip to Spain but compared to that crumbling squat house, he'd take that alleyway with a pinch of salt.

I'll just stay here, he thought. I don't care about waiting around in this disgusting piss and metal-tasting alleyway. I'll do it standing on my head. But you are having an absolute laugh if you think I'm going any further.

Jonah stopped looking at the house. The foreboding vibe made him want to piss on himself. That place had history, bad, evil history.

Then, before it happened, he *knew* it was going to happen, as if he'd just read the future or as if he was actually directing the events of this disaster.

The thing appeared in the windowless void on the second floor of the demon house. It had an oily green face that was haggard and drooping like wet clay, and eyes as white as milk. Its hair was a darker shade of green, knotted and curling in wiry little kinks.

'You down there. Come closer,' it said in a demented, senile voice that made Jonah do the exact opposite of its instruction. 'I said come closer, you stupid fucking moron! Come closer! Come closer! Come closer!'

When he tried to turn, Jonah found that he was physically restricted as if his body wasn't able to manoeuvre in circles. So instead, he back-pedalled as fast as his legs would take him. But this time, he only inched back despite how fast he tried to go.

The witch's head reared from the window, its neck extending like a snake. It clutched onto the bare brick for leverage, digging its nails straight into the dwindling structure. 'You get back here and come closer or I swear I will pull your fucking dick off you and swallow it, you fucking little sack of wretched shit!'

Jonah pushed his heels harder into the ground but felt himself slipping and falling back on an invisible wall that prevented his escape. All he could do was wade in slow motion and listen to the psychotic ravings of the green *thing* leaning out of the window.

'I am much too tired to chase after you, so GET YOUR FUCKING STUPID ARSE BACK HERE RIGHT NOW BEFORE I FUCK YOU LIKE THE DAY YOU WERE BORN!' It closed its eyes to scream and shook its head from side to side like a toddler having a tantrum.

Sharp, shrill panic shot through Jonah from the soles of his feet to the tip of his spine. He could feel himself unable to breathe in his sleep; maybe his face was buried into the pillow. His stomach felt swollen with too much air, turning his innards into a heap of splinters and glass shards. Eventually, he had to release it – like he desperately needed to take a piss. A scream rocketed out of him like a firework shooting into the sky and bounced off of the walls like a bullet ricocheting.

'What do you want?! What do you want from me?!'

The green witch clutched her head like she was trying to stop her brain from combusting, jumping up and down like a petulant child. 'I told you what I want!'

'No!' Jonah shrieked, his voice void of any masculinity, breaking into a crescendo of pure terror.

'Yes!'

'No!'

'Yes I say! Yes! I will give you one more chance to come inside or so help me I'll come out and get you.'

Even in his sleep Jonah could feel the warm urine trickling down his legs, but in this instance he didn't reject it. In fact, he tried his best to relax and help the flow of his pee leave his shaft with the hope that the warmth of the liquid would stir him awake, he spun around against the invisible force preventing his movement, but it was like trying to run into a tornado, constantly pushing him toward the house. The stress of his attempted escape sent arrows through his already frantic heart, pain seething through his chest in icy cracks.

Lord Jesus Christ please have mercy on my soul and wake me up. Please God. Pleasepleaseplease.

His prayers went unanswered. Instead, the hag went even more berserk and yelled obscenities that boomed throughout the hollowed house. It was making its way down the stairs. It was coming after Jonah.

Squeezing his eyes closed, Jonah fell and collapsed on the uneven, lumpy concrete. His lids felt like they were going to bleed from the pressure as he waited for it to come, for the slimy gnarled fingers to reach out and touch him. What could he do? The nightmare was designed for him to lose, to paralyse him from the minute he drifted into the land of nod.

A thought occurred to him like a tiny light the size and brightness of a lit cigarette somewhere deep inside, almost managing to comfort him; *this is a dream.* He wouldn't die, just as he hadn't the previous two nights. He wouldn't even be physically hurt – psychologically it would absolutely rape him, but physically the most it would do is add a fresh stain to the pallet of old ones decorating his sheets.

Impish, maniacal cackling rushed up behind him, sounding like a thousand dry twigs snapping. Just as the laughing seemed to be a few paces away, it stopped abruptly. Jonah was holding his breath in anticipation, dreading the encounter like a firing squad was aimed at him and about to pull the trigger. His whole body was stiff, but when the laughter vanished without so much as an echo off of the alley walls, one feeble, strangled gasp whistled out of him. Then another. When he remembered how to breathe properly, the only thing left to do was open his eyes. He decided to listen out for just a few more moments but could hear nothing beyond his own panting. Opening his eyes at that moment appealed to him about as much as a do-it-yourself circumcision.

'I know you're still there,' Jonah whispered. 'I can feel you behind me.'

Nothing. No stir of madness answered back through the mist.

'I know you're there!' Jonah shouted; his voice didn't echo, but instead just dampened in the air and dissipated, losing its authority. Then at that point it occurred to him that he wasn't going to wake up until he saw it. He knew it. Jonah decided that the first thing he was going to do when he got back to Nottingham was to see a psychiatrist and get these night-traumas removed from his head. If he had to dream about this shit for much longer he was going to end up blowing his brains out.

With one deep breath, Jonah pried his eyes open. Slowly he began to turn around. It was there, he sensed it, almost feeling the rancid breath saturating the nape of his neck.

Slowly, oh so slowly, he turned ...

24

There it was – that disgusting, slouching face. It was an inch away from him and screaming; the eyes, misty white, the sockets watery and peeling. Its teeth, black stumps so corroded they looked like they'd crumble eating boiled rice. But it was the nose again that really troubled Jonah when he jerked awake, sobbing into the pillow. That misshapen, broken, swollen hook nose.

Hansel and Gretel. I'm gonna rip up every copy of that book when I get home, he thought. My kids can eat in all the candy houses they want because they're never going to know the dangers of avoiding it, because they're never going to read or get that evil book read to them. EVER.

Tepid and greasy perspiration slicked his face like he had a fever. 'Fuck this,' he mumbled sitting hunched over on the edge of his bed, tears still streaming down his cheeks despite the fact he was awake. He wasn't hung over but after throwing up earlier, his guts didn't feel right. Maybe it was the accumulation of all the shit he'd pumped into his body over the week. He felt hot and cold at the same time, his brain thumping like trumpet blasts in his head. Then he did something that he hadn't done in a long, long while. He prayed. Not the *Oh God please keep me alive and I won't touch booze or weed or women or white bread* type of prayer. He got on his knees and leaned over the bed, the position actually helping to settle his stomach. The first yellow hints of dawn peeked through the blinds, the birds chirping presumptively. He rested his forehead in his hands, his elbows sunk into the mattress.

'Dear God,' he began, keeping his voice a whisper and feeling embarrassed that he was even saying it out loud, 'please forgive me. Please God, I'm so sorry.' Paranoia clawed at him and he wondered if he was dying, if the stress was making his ticker funny. He worried about the nightmares and what they meant, and felt mortified that those images could manifest inside his head. And what, dear Lord, what in heaven or hell was that moose thing on the train? There was no way he'd imaged that. It was as real as the pain coiling around his crooked neck. Or was it? Now, hours after it had happened, Jonah wondered.

The stress was like being stretched on a torture rack. People had died from stress, hadn't they? His mum had a friend at church called Ms Davids when they lived in Drakeford who would sometimes call in for tea and cake to gossip about other members of the Daisy Lane Pentecostal congregation and disguise it as well-natured *concern*. Jonah didn't like Ms Davids; she was an arrogant fat bitch that always tried to out-sing everyone like she was auditioning for *The X-Factor*. She was always in other people's business, and Jonah just knew that she used to speak about his mother, probably saying things about the dresses she wore or her shoes or some other petty shit like that. But this one time when she invited herself around for cake (and ate near enough a whole chocolate gateau by herself) he was sat at the table in the front room trying to do some math homework for Mrs Wicks (another equally fat bitch), and overheard Ms Davids talking about a man called Edward Michaels. Edward was a fifty-something-year-old widower whose wife died the year before of pancreatic cancer. He always sat in the second row pews wearing his dark green suit, and always looked like he was about to break down, as if he was constantly thinking about his wife Winnie.

Ms Davids spoke through a mouth full of cake, chocolate gritted to her gums. She was never married, probably because she was an absolute snake, Jonah guessed. She was telling his mother about how she'd spoken to Edward after church the Sunday just gone. Jonah was trying not to listen and would've taken his homework to his bedroom, but if he went there then he would've turned on his computer or fallen asleep and it wouldn't have got done.

'And poor, poor Edward,' Ms Davids was saying, her words muffled. 'I went over to him, y'know, I always like to check on little Eddy. And do you know what, Diana?' Before his mum could answer, Ms Davids continued, 'I noticed two of his teeth were missing.'

Jonah's mum gasped and shook her head. 'What?'

'Yeah, I know. I said to him, "Eddy, what happened to your teeth?" and he just shrugged and said they fell out while he was sleeping.'

'Probably the stress.' Diana White said. Now, the rest of the conversation was a blur to him. Jonah realised that Mr Michaels was probably long dead from a broken heart by now. But regardless, his mother's words rang in his ears like a fire drill. *Probably the stress.*

Stress.

'Jesus, don't make me go insane.' He closed the prayer by silently thanking God for everything he believed that He'd benevolently done for him. 'Amen.'

The snakes inside him seemed to stop writhing, or so he tried to make himself believe. It was too quiet in the house, not even Genie was snoring, but Jonah got the distinct notion that Dwayne was still awake and that Dwayne knew that Jonah was also still awake. The thought of trying to get forty winks knowing that Dwayne was still up frightened him.

Jonah didn't feel safe in the flat and was so glad that he was leaving in the morning. The first thing he was going to do when he got back to Nottingham was kiss his mother and tell her just how much he loved her and thank her for raising him, then apologise for being such a selfish idiot. Suddenly, he got the urge to phone Rose but resisted; it wouldn't be fair to have kept her out all night then disrupt her at ... what time was it? He picked his phone off the ground and touched the button. Almost quarter past five. The revelation of the time made his eye-bags weigh even heavier, the red threads pulsing around his bloodshot pupils.

Shrivelled green face. Milky white eyes. That fingernails-on-chalkboard screeching. He tried to shake the images free but his head was a bowling ball filled with liquid and pins. Sleep was all he needed. Just a few more hours, and he could go home, he thought.

He *hoped*. But even then he knew it wasn't going to be that easy.

25

When the front door slammed shut and reawakened Jonah from a fitful, dreamless nap, he rose from his bed and headed for the shower like a sleepwalker. His body was telling him that it was time to leave this place, so he formed a plan of action. First, get clean – wash the sweat off his balls and the piss off his thighs. Secondly, grab every item of clothing that he intended to take from the wardrobe, and stuff them inside an empty duffel bag.

He was ready in half an hour, skipping the luxury of cleaning his teeth. The plaque would just have to stockpile for the morning because the grittiness coating his teeth was overwhelmed by the sudden urgency the rest of his body had to leave, Rushing downstairs, he kept his face stern. In his opinion, all ties between him and Dwayne had been severed on that allotment. Nothing was left to debate or reconcile. He resented having to depend on a lift to the station and would've taken public transport if his bags weren't in the back of Dwayne's other car. But when he reached the bottom step, it was apparent that the apartment was empty.

Well, almost empty.

Genie was in the front room. He heard her begin to rush around when he approached the door, lacking all the discretion a sober person would've harboured when trying to hide something. Jonah swung the door open. Genie was lying on the sofa with a sheet over her, staring up at him like a deer caught in the headlights. Her sneaky behaviour did nothing for his paranoia. Why was she so quick to cover herself up? It was another humid morning despite the gathering clouds, and he was too hot in the denim shorts and vest he was wearing, so what the hell was she doing under a sheet?

'Where's Dwayne?' he asked her, feeling his forehead and nose wrinkle with the words. He was scowling despite his promise to try and maintain a poker face. She looked up at him with a stupid, childish expression of feigned innocence.

'I don't know.'

The nape of his neck burned, the drums pounding in his temples; she was lying to him and doing it deliberately so that he knew it too.

'Genie,' Jonah said, the steadiness in his voice vibrating like a tuning fork. 'Don't play with me today. I'm being deadly serious. Where is he?'

She pulled the sheet up to her neck like she was listening to a ghost story. The room grew darker as the anomalous black clouds drifted on a griseous sea of grey like souls of dead people on a river in purgatory. Looked like a storm was brewing.

'I can't really say,' she said, all mousy and coy.

Jonah rolled his shoulders and clenched his fist. 'Genie ...'

'I'm not allowed,' she squeaked.

That was it. 'Fucking little bitch!' He stomped forward, angry enough to kick her heart out, and grabbed the sheet. She tightened up in a defensive ball and turned away from him, a haggard old woman acting like a disobedient child.

Green Face

Jonah faltered for a second, cringed, then ripped the sheet off her like he was attempting to do that table cloth trick. The bumps in her spine looked as though they were about to protrude through her thin flesh. The thing that really creeped him out about seeing her up close and naked was just how much her body looked like a child's, underdeveloped yet withered like a stack of old sticks. Towering over her as she tried to bury herself deeper into the sofa, Jonah noticed that she was going bald, her straggly blonde hair like fraying thread from a blotchy red pillow.

'Where is he?' Jonah flinched away after seeing her scalp, wanting to rush back into the shower and bleach his hands after touching her naked flesh that probably hadn't been washed in a fortnight or longer.

'He said he was setting up a surprise for you for a going away present,' she yelled into the sofa cushion.

Surprise? The roof of his mouth was like compost.

'When is he coming back?'

'I don't know,' she whined, her voice muffled.

'What are you doing anyway? Why are you curled up like that? Why are you hiding?' His angry voice was quickly plummeting into a shrill drone as frail as rice paper.

'Nothing.'

'Nothing?' his heart pulsed weakly. Fire shot up his back. Sweat leaked through his armpits, coating his upper lip, dripping from his brow. 'Nothing?'

He gripped her arm – it was like touching a cold roast chicken – and pulled her over onto her back. Even though she struggled her lack of weight made shifting her as effortless as handling a department store mannequin.

'Jesus Christ,' Jonah tried to gulp when he saw her body, but couldn't summon the saliva to perform the task. The inside of her left arm was bleeding, red lines covering from her wrist to her elbow like a stripy jumper. Dots of blood flecked the sheet. There were faint scratch marks all over the insides of her arms and across her stomach from where she'd previously been slicing herself. She had a biro clutched in her rabid hand; the most artistic form of self harm, he thought. He stumbled away from her, sickened by the sight.

Now that the veil had been lifted, Genie slowly loosened up as Jonah walked backwards across the room. She turned and leaned on her side, her face a sick shade of lime.

Green Face

'What's wrong with you?' Jonah said, not really looking for an answer. He was so disturbed he wanted to cry. And she just looked at him, her eyes faint yet piercing, her boobs sagging down like two deflated footballs, and then did something bizarre enough to make him bolt from the room like a bomb was about to explode: she smiled. With her black gums glorified, she slithered back under the sheet.

Green Face

She called out to him as he ran back upstairs: 'He said he wouldn't be long. He's just trying to set up a surprise for you before you go!' But Jonah raced away from the living room as though her words were pursuing him with murderous intentions. He escaped to his room, slammed the door behind him and leaned against it.

The box under his bed thudded and he remembered about Snowy, wishing now that he'd freed the rabbit into a park or let it run away in the allotment. He was surprised it was still alive in the heat, and quickly fished the box out to give it some air.

'What am I gonna do with you?' He held the rabbit up and appraised it; it seemed a bit sluggish from being cooped up all night and probably needed some water and something to eat but otherwise, it was a survivor, clicking its teeth absently. *So what are you going to do with me?* the rabbit said back. And then, in his weary mind, it just popped in there.

Rose had been fighting her way through her shift from the minute she pinned her apron on. Though she'd done a good enough job with her concealer and masked the crevices under her eyes, the make-up did little to help the slumping weight resting on her back, pulling her arms down like a cave woman. A combination of yawns continuously swelled in her throat and left her mouth like invisible balloons. Her stomach had been queasy since she woke up, but the pressuring fatigue far outweighed the symptoms of her hangover.

'Here honey, get this down you.' Kayleigh handed her the double espresso before manoeuvring around to serve the customer that was waiting there, while Rose stared into space and watched the interior of the Mocha Inn, grey with exhaustion.

'Thanks,' Rose mumbled before sipping the beverage. She'd already had an espresso thirty minutes ago but all it'd done was make her heart palpitate wildly. She turned and faced the mirror behind the decoration jars of coffee beans and gave herself a quick assessment even though the last time she looked at her reflection the sight that stared back had made her want to cry. She wasn't just tired from the previous evening; she was completely shattered from countless nights of patchy sleep. And even though Esmeralda slept soundlessly for once, it didn't stop Rose from waking up every forty-five minutes to check on her baby. She sighed with the knowledge that she would not know a peaceful night's sleep for a long while to come: such were the pleasures of single motherhood.

Kayleigh had mastered the knack of late nights and early mornings when she was in her thirties, and perfected the robotic art of functioning at unsociable hours in the morning through years of monotonous training in her forties. She rubbed Rose on the back affectionately. 'Not long to go now. Then you can crash on the couch and get some sleep.'

Another yawn left her mouth violently, threatening to dislocate her jaw. 'I wish. Got too much to do when I get in.'

'Poor thing,' Kayleigh said, lacking the condescending tone that most older people used when they knew she had a child. Kayleigh had her first kid at seventeen, and in the following nineteen years she had another four by two different men. She was immune to the grogginess that Rose was feeling, her brain and bones long since hardened from years of work and home keeping, her insomnia accelerated from a general lack of self-confidence and pessimism.

The nine o'clock rush was over and all that was left until noon was washing up and wiping down. Rose rubbed her eyes with the bottom of her palms and gently shook her head from side to side.

'Looks like it's gonna piss down,' Kayleigh said, tossing the tea towel over her shoulder and tucking a stray strand of blonde hair behind her ear. The gloom of the off-white sky added to Rose's looming threat of narcolepsy.

Rose felt her lids chaffing against her eyeballs, and walked to the sink to splash some water in them. Hopefully the cold would startle some life into her and help her through the remainder of the shift.

When she turned back around, Jonah was standing there holding a box in his hand. The shock of seeing him manifested after thinking about him all morning was enough to jolt her awake.

'Can I help you, love?' Kayleigh asked him instinctively, the sentence solidified and identical every time after years of rehearsal.

'I just wanted to say hello to Rose,' he told her, nodding in Rose's direction.

Embarrassment singed her cheeks; she felt way too rough to see him. A large majority of her wanted to run out the back and hide her aching face, or coat another layer of make-up on it.

'Hi,' she managed, blushing.

Kayleigh looked at the boy, then looked at Rose with raised eye-brows and mouthed the words 'Is that him?' as she excused herself from the counter, pretending to busy herself with some odd job in the kitchen area. Rose nodded that yes, it was in fact the boy that she'd spoken of earlier in the morning, the boy who had been a perfect gentleman; the boy who treated her like a lady.

'Hey,' she replied shyly. 'I thought you were going today.'

'Yeah, I am,' he nodded, looking nearly as tired as she felt, his eyes squinted in that familiar way – the way eyes looked when a person hasn't woken up properly yet. 'I just wanted to say bye and stuff, you know.'

Her cheek muscles began to tighten as if a gigantic smile were about to spread across her face. 'That's nice. How're you feeling?'

A cheeky grin crept on his mouth. 'I've been better. What about you? Have trouble waking up this morning?'

'Is it that obvious?'

'No, but I got to lie-in and I still struggled to get out of bed. I feel like I'm gonna collapse and fall into a coma at any minute so you must feel even worse. Am I right?'

Rose giggled then lifted her espresso to salute him. 'I've been taking my morning potion so I should be okay. Want one?'

'No, I can't stay long. I'm waiting for my friend to come back with my bag so I can get to the station.' When he finished his sentence, she looked down at the floor, disappointed. 'Aren't you gonna ask me what's in the box?' He held it up slightly higher.

'I thought it was a pair of trainers.'

'Take the lid off.' As Jonah came closer, Rose backed away slightly, surprised and a little nervous.

'It's not a snake is it?' she asked. The question was so unexpected that Jonah burst out laughing.

'A snake?'

'Well what's inside it then?'

He took the lid off and Snowy's head bobbed up inquisitively, looking around and taking in the new surroundings. Rose yelped in fright. It took a couple of seconds for the image of the animal to register in her sleepy brain. Kayleigh came over to have a look, cooing at the creature.

'Oh he's lovely,' Kayleigh said, 'we used to have a couple of rabbits but they got sick.'

'Why have you got a rabbit, Jonah?' Rose asked him, unable to avert her gaze from it. She was in awe of Jonah, like he'd pulled the animal out of a hat. In an unorthodox way it was a terrific turn-on.

'You could say that I rescued Snowy here from a cruel owner. But I can't take him back to Nottingham with me so I was wondering if you wanted it.'

'Me?'

'Yeah. For Esmeralda.'

Her breath got caught in her throat and she was suddenly overwhelmed with a feeling of profound sadness; *why did he have to be leaving?* seemed to be the question on her mind, but the underlining, deeper issue that would haunt her for many sleepless nights in the future was *why couldn't it be him? Why couldn't he be her dad?*

'I er ... I don't know what to say.'

Kayleigh reached out to pet the rabbit, which responded by sniffing her hand. 'They're so cute aren't they? My Stevie used to love our one; she was called Clover. I don't even remember how we got that name, I think it must've been from the butter we were using at the time, I dunno. I bet your little 'un would love a rabbit wouldn't she?'

244

Rose shrugged, still apprehensive to touch the animal. 'She's only one. All she does is eat, sleep and cry.'

A customer came to the counter and did a double take when he saw the rabbit. He laughed and gave Kayleigh his order, then petted Snowy as he waited.

'Certainly getting everyone's attention.' Rose said, feeling brave enough to touch the fluffy head of the rabbit.

'So what do you say? You wanna take it home?'

As Kayleigh handed the customer his drink, he interrupted, 'They're dead easy to look after aren't they?'

'Tell you the truth, I don't really know,' Jonah replied.

'Of course they are. All you do is feed 'em and they're quite happy to just hop around doing their own thing.'

'Cleaner than a dog,' Kayleigh added.

'And more interesting than a bloody cat,' the customer said before heading off to find a table.

The more Rose stroked the rabbit, the more attached she became to it, the gentle feeling of fur becoming somewhat therapeutic. 'I don't know, Jonah. I mean, I already got a baby to look after, I don't know if I'd be able to manage a rabbit as well.'

'What about Miguel?' Jonah felt an awkward sting of discomfort as he made the unconscious parallel between a baby wanting the pet and her Down's-syndrome brother, but it didn't last long. She, apparently, didn't even seem to notice.

'I don't know the first thing about rabbits, Jonah. Neither does he.'

Kayleigh was wiping the froth away from the latte machine when she called over her shoulder: 'You can buy this special feed for them, it's like muesli. But you can just give 'em vegetables and stuff like that and water. You'll need a hutch for it though cos that box won't do. You got a hutch for it?' Jonah told her he didn't. 'Well I've still got the one we used for Clover in the shed. If you wanna take it I can bring it in tomorrow for you.'

Rose paused, contemplating the offer. 'I don't think I can, Jonah. Thanks anyway for the offer but we already got a house full of people, a dog and a baby. I think a rabbit would be the straw that broke the camel's back. But thank you for the offer, I'm really touched by it, honest.'

'That's okay,' Jonah said, trying not to let the disappointment register. 'Is there an animal shelter where I can take it around here?'

Drying a cup from the dishwasher, Kayleigh turned and perked up. 'You just giving it away?'

'Yeah. I can't take it all the way back to Nottingham with me so I'm just looking to give it a new owner. Why, you interested?'

Kayleigh didn't answer immediately. She kept her eyes trained on Snowy while she finished drying another glass before she answered. 'Okay. I'll take it. I got a five-year-old granddaughter that would probably love a little rabbit. She's got a bedroom full of stuffed animals so I can't see why she wouldn't want one. Hasn't got fleas or anything has it?'

'I don't think so. It only came out of the pet shop yesterday. The guy who bought it wasn't really fit to look after it so I took it.'

'Okay.' Kayleigh reached out for the box and muttered to the rabbit: 'I think little Mica is going to love you, isn't she?'

Jonah felt a great weight lifted off his chest; one less thing to worry about. While Kayleigh took the rabbit into the staffroom out back, Jonah extended his arm over the counter and grabbed Rose's hand, lifted it to his lips, and planted a soft kiss on the back of her palm.

'I'll call you tonight, if you're not too tired,' he said.

Her cheeks flushed red. 'I won't be. I'll wait for your call.'

They looked at each other for a moment, the chatter of the coffee drinkers slowly muting out as they became entranced. Words weren't necessary with their body language doing all the talking, like they were communicating telepathically. When Kayleigh returned, the link was temporarily broken and the background volume turned itself back up.

'Guess I'll be seeing you.' Jonah turned and headed for the door without looking back.

26

The bitter wind began to pick up by about one o'clock that afternoon, the storm clouds growing like black whirlpools in the sky. Jonah welcomed the moist air he was breathing, it helped to somewhat clear the cobwebs. Dwayne had texted him saying he was on his way to the flat, and after reading the message, Jonah's phone bleeped signalling low battery – he hadn't charged it since he got there.

The first spittle of rain fell.

Grabbing his bag with his new clothes, Jonah made the bed (minus the sheet, which he left in the laundry basket in the hallway) and laid down on top of it, still exhausted from the week of disrupted sleep. Although he was traumatised from the disturbing imagery that plagued his dreams and turned him into a trembling bag of nerves, he decided to close his eyes and try to get a bit of rest. There was nothing else to do in the flat. He couldn't go in the front room because Genie was downstairs, probably coked up and still playing connect-the-veins with her biro, and Jonah didn't want a part of it.

His thinking, no matter how illogical it seemed, was that if he fell asleep during the day then he wouldn't suffer a nightmare, hence the name *night*mare. He watched the light rain splash his window in thin beads. The ominous clouds loomed over the estates on the horizon like a tornado was about to form. The hush of the whooshing wind rustling the leaves in the nearby trees slowly lulled him to a gentle and unthreatening sleep, his first in three days.

27

It was one of the most eerie feelings Jonah'd ever had – to be woken by the mere presence of another person standing near him. Before he opened his eyes, Jonah was stirred awake by the hairs prickling on his arms with the distinct notion that someone was watching him.

'Ready to go?' Dwayne leaned against the bedroom door with his arms folded. Maybe he'd just entered the room, but why was he just *standing* there? He could've quite easily called Jonah's name or shook him instead of just standing there like he was studying him.

Blinking rapidly, Jonah sat up. The wind was howling now and for the first time this week, he felt cold. 'Yeah. You got my bag?'

'It's in the car. Shall we?'

Dwayne led the way to the front door and Jonah followed groggily a few steps behind in silence. It was like he was going to the electric chair. Just before he crossed the threshold of the flat, Genie popped her head out of the living room door.

'Are you going?' Her voice seemed hurt, perhaps a little afraid at the reality of his departure.

Without turning, Jonah replied. 'Yeah.' He didn't want to see her and be reminded of

Green Face

Her self-harm, such a savage act of self pity. Everything about her was dirty and negative. He was glad to be rid of her. Jonah slammed the door shut behind him, cutting short her farewells.

As they made their way to the car, the silence between them was deafening. Jonah debated with himself on whether or not to strike up some small talk or to just forget about it and not even begin with such falsities as idle conversation.

They reached the BMW that Dwayne had picked him up in; it still looked like an older, more mature person's car for Dwayne to be driving but there was no need to turn his nose up at it. Right now, that car was his escape vehicle. Once inside, Jonah rubbed his bare arms trying to get rid of the gooseflesh he wasn't certain was a result of the chilly temperature; the tension was icy enough to preserve him in time.

Dwayne started the engine and let it run a while before heading off, flicking the radiator button on to warm the car up. Jonah reached for the seatbelt and clicked it in.

They began to drive through the stark streets that now looked depressing and miserable under the grey blanket enveloping the city.

'So are we gonna just sit here in silence all the way?' Dwayne said, the sudden sound of speech startling Jonah.

'I don't mind sitting in silence.'

'What're you so pissed off at me about, Jonah?' Dwayne asked casually, like he didn't actually care what the answer was.

'Nothing.' To a degree, it was true. Jonah was more tired than he was angry and his lack of dialogue was down to a lack of motivation. He was past caring about mending the soiled relationship. The thing that had really hurt him and pissed him off more than anything else was that Billy hadn't swung by to see him off.

The windscreen wipers got rid of the tattooing rain, squealing as it rubbed against the glass, but the melodic rhythm was making his eyes droopy. He leaned his head against the window and preserved his energy which he gathered he'd need for the hustle and bustle of getting on the train.

'You know, I realise why you're angry,' Dwayne said monotonically.

'So why'd you ask?' Jonah replied, irritated.

Ignoring Jonah's question, Dwayne continued, his face expressionless. 'Things have changed. We couldn't be kids forever. When you left, it was like our brains left with you, Jonah. Do you know what I mean by that?'

When he didn't reply, mainly because he wasn't listening, Dwayne carried on. 'Me and Billy are dumb-dumbs. We couldn't even write and add up a shopping list between us. So when you went, the brains of us went with you. I'm surprised that you're so shocked that we started doing what we did.'

'And what did you do? You still haven't made that clear. All I know is that you got a load of cash, a nice place to stay, and cars that you're not even qualified to drive.'

Before Dwayne answered his question, the sky seemed to darken as if anticipating the morbid truth. 'I've done terrible things, Jonah. Things that I couldn't even begin to tell you about. But everything I ever did, I got away with. And that's all that matters to me. You hate Sol, but –'

'– I don't hate him,' Jonah lied defensively, not wanting to have the word hate tied to a person without a valid reason, which he couldn't think of.

'Okay,' Dwayne said, 'you don't *like* Sol, and I think that's because he's the brains now. And I've been thinking about that a lot since yesterday. It was wrong of me to try and make you kill that rabbit, Jonah. Sincerely, I apologise.' He took his eyes off the road for the first time since he got into the car and looked over at Jonah. 'Do you accept my apology? As a friend?'

The car stopped in a small queue at the traffic lights. Raindrops bounced off the bonnet and roof like a drum roll.

'It's been a crazy week, man,' Jonah said, closing his eyes, drifting. 'It hasn't been all bad. I think maybe we're just two different people now, so maybe there's no need to apologise at all.' He didn't wholly believe that part about there being no need to apologise, but it was less uncomfortable than having someone in close proximity get all sentimental like that. 'That's just how people are I suppose. They grow apart, get older, change.'

Dwayne nodded in agreement. They were never going to be friends like they used to be, that much was obvious, but at least they'd reached some kind of mutual understanding.

The light turned green and the traffic began to flow. Jonah tried to consume as much of the scenery as he could before he had to go, hoping that the flavours of London would stay on his palate for those lonely days in Nottingham, though there was bound to be a nasty aftertaste; ragged, lunatic-looking men with animal eyes strolled along, snarling and ready to bite. A melange of promiscuity, violence, and hyperactivity hung in air like exhaust fumes.

They turned off Burktrom Lane and into Dumpling Avenue; the roads winding like the intestines of the city. A swirling, watery feeling began to rise in the pit of Jonah's stomach as they passed Haidon Park – repressed-memory central. Was Dwayne taking him through this route on purpose? Maybe it was a shortcut, but it seemed like more of an indirect act of malice, whether Dwayne meant it or not.

'I know Genie didn't keep her mouth shut, did she?' Dwayne asked, with a grin that Jonah didn't trust as far as he could throw it. He looked devious, not in a cheeky, jack-the-lad way, but in a sneaky, serpentine way. 'She told you about the surprise, right?'

'She mentioned it,' Jonah replied hesitantly, like he was about to have the world's worst April Fools prank pulled on him.

'That's where I've been all morning. Preparing something for you, a going-away present seeing as we didn't have time to get you one last time you left.' Dwayne turned the corner and looked at him. 'What? What is it?' A bogus smile that desperately wanted to look natural and friendly was plastered across his mug, like a hideous waxwork.

'I don't want it,' Jonah said shaking his head. 'Whatever you got planned, I don't want it.'

Dwayne's grin refused to falter, revealing his teeth and gums. 'Why are you being like that? You don't even know what it is.'

'I don't care. Just drop me to the station. Please.'

'It could be Beyonce giving out blowjobs –'

'– It's fine,' Jonah interrupted hastily.

'– It could be Pamela Anderson with her legs wi –'

Jonah tried to laugh his nerves away hoping the disruption would make Dwayne drop the subject, but the sound came out as a strangled whimper. 'I'm just really tired and I wanna get settled on the train. Thanks for the offer and for thinking of me and everything.'

They passed a group of about twenty boys, Jonah's age and slightly older, standing outside the entrance of a block of flats. They were huddled under the shelter of the balcony to avoid the rain, all of them wearing hooded coats – a bunch of urban druids about to make a sacrifice of the first non-native they see. On the graffiti-decorated wall behind them, their shadows cast a nefarious dark aura. Under their hoods their eyes were strangely black.

That burning feeling returned; Jonah's temperature would've made mercury pin-ball through the thermometer.

'Well I can tell you this, Jonie,' Dwayne sneered, interrupting his thoughts, 'what I got for you is better than both of those things put together. It's something you've always wanted. Trust me.'

Jonah rubbed his throat, softly massaging his Adams apple. He couldn't breathe. 'Thanks but can we just … the train.'

The car turned another corner and parked alongside a row of spacious semi-detached houses with neatly cut lawns; the complete contrast to the twelve-story-eyesores that towered at all angles like a row of walking giants.

'We're already here,' Dwayne said shutting the engine off. 'It'll only take a few minutes. Don't you wanna know what's behind door number one?' He encouraged. Dwayne seemed genuinely excited, gleaming with pride.

Everything in Jonah, right down to the tips of his toes, was repelled by the idea. Just based on Dwayne's body language, he knew that they had two different ideas of what would be a nice send-off. What could it possibly be? Girls? Big deal. Jonah had seen what kind of problems the average estate girls posed and managed to pluck a Rose from the tangled weeds. If it was booze or any other disorientating stimulant, he didn't want it. And the last thing he was in the mood for was a party.

He glanced over at the house that Dwayne had parked in front of. It was nice, window sills and borders all painted white, cobbled drive, neatly trimmed bushes along the paved walk leading to the wide front door. Next to the garage, an alleyway leading to the back yard separated the houses.

'Whose house is this?' Jonah asked him, his voice crackling like twigs in a fire.

'That's part of the surprise,' Dwayne said. 'It's right in there waiting for you.'

Realising that there was no way around the situation other than demanding his bag from the boot and trudging through the increasing downpour, Jonah took time to swallow and breathe before attempting to speak. 'Is there something bad in that house?'

Dwayne's smile faded slowly into a completely stern expression. He leaned on the wheel looking at the house, then turned to Jonah, his face resting on his forearms. 'I know these last couple of days have been a shock to you,

Jonah. I know that you've seen some horrible things. And even if you don't trust me any more, I'm asking you to trust me this one last time. I know you better than anyone, Jone. I'm just asking you to trust me on this. All you gotta do is come into the house.' When Jonah refused to offer any verbal agreement and stared vacantly at the double-glazed windows of the anonymous house, Dwayne leaned back into the chair and continued. 'I wouldn't put you in any danger, Jonah, if that's what you're thinking. Just come inside, for ten minutes. Please.' His smile returned, this time less striking, to rule out any inkling of deception. He got out of the car and walked up the path to the house, rummaged in his pocket for a set of keys and held them up to Jonah, who was still waiting in the car. Dwayne opened the door, waved for Jonah to follow his example, and then disappeared inside the house.

Slowly, against the objections of his screaming head, Jonah undid the seat belt and stepped out of the car. Rain pelted down on him, stinging his ears like cold needles. The fresh air and the cleansing rain felt good, helping to loosen his taut chest. His feet splashed against the puddles in the uneven ground, dampening his socks. Rain trickled down his neck, soothing that aching, sunburnt feeling.

He reached the door and pushed it open, stepping in cautiously after a quick scan of the nice, upper-working-class street. Jonah wiped his feet on the doormat and shrugged off the rain, careful not to dampen the freshly vacuumed carpet. The house smelt like a mix between varnish and fabric softener; a new, clean smell. The deep blue carpet and peach walls would've made the place feel cosy if it wasn't for the vaporous shadows that slunk over the interior, wracking him with a deep sense of foreboding. God, it was almost like the set of one of his nightmares.

'Dwayne?' Jonah called, closing the door behind him, shutting the last of the gloomy light out with it. No answer; he knew there wouldn't be. Dwayne had obviously scarpered upstairs and wasn't about to give him the satisfaction of helping him through this unwanted bullshit surprise. At first, Jonah had visions of a bunch of drunk or drugged up semi-nude girls draped on the stairs or prancing around in the kitchen throwing body language provocative enough to make a giraffe poke its own eye out. But instead, he was welcomed with the distinct, lonely draught of an empty house.

Everything inside Jonah screamed at him to get out of the house. It was so *obviously* wrong: Dwayne parks up on a peaceful little road and hurries off inside a spacious middle class mansion (anything with more than three bedrooms and double glazed windows was a mansion to him), and like a complete dick-brain, Jonah follows him inside. He hadn't even moved from the threshold yet but he already knew the type of person that lived there; rich, probably middle-aged, definitely white, no pets. Jonah knew they had no business being there. It felt like a setup; like the police were about to crash through the windows and blow the door off behind him, thinking that he was trying to rob this rich white motherfucker's house.

As lightly as he could, Jonah crept forward, afraid to put too much weight down in his step in case a floorboard creaked and a neighbour called the cop shop. It was bad enough that two black kids just pulled up in a BMW far too expensive for either of them to be able to drive legitimately.

'Dwayne!' Jonah called up the stairs again in a loud whisper. A tense feeling of discomfort engulfed him like the wallpaper had eyes and was watching his intrusion. There was something deeply disturbing about skulking around in that house uninvited like some kind of seedy burglar. Every instinct in his body was pulling him toward the front door and away from the house, urging him to wait in the car. But how long would he have to wait before Dwayne gave up the charade and came out? An hour? Two? Unless he wanted to make his own way to the station – a possibility he was seriously considering despite not knowing where the nearest tube station or relevant bus stop was – he was stuck, playing Dwayne's game.

Uncertainty seemed to oppress him like a dense humidity as he reluctantly climbed the stairs, taking hold of the banister. It'd dawned on Jonah that Dwayne must've had some kind of link with the owner of the house because he entered with a key, which helped to ease his doubts a fraction ... but that was it, a tiny, infinitesimal fraction. Maybe it was just another rich girl that Dwayne had been able to hook on drugs and simply repossessed her house like some kind of street bailiff monopolising different properties. The logicality of the thought made his ascent up the stairs a bit more fluid, the rickety worst-case scenarios of the house drowning in the back of his mind.

The spacious landing, which was the size of his bedroom back in Nottingham, seemed cold and unwelcoming in the eerie silence. Four glossy white doors faced him like some kind of urban reality game show; *and behind door number one, we have breaking and entering! Congratulations, you've just won four years in Feltham youth prison.*

'Dwayne? For fuck's sake, where are you?' he hissed. No amount of bravery could make him talk louder than a whisper while he was in a stranger's house. It was stupid to think it, but apart from the very real possibility that he was prowling around in someone's house without their knowledge, it just seemed impolite to raise his voice.

He didn't have to call out again. This time, there was an answer.

'I'm in here,' Dwayne replied behind the second closed door.

28

Before he reached out to touch the brass knob of the door a shiver ran through him, starting in his fingertips and wavering through his arm and into his chest. It was Dwayne's tone of voice that worried him now, like slime poured out of his mouth and made words. Almost on cue, thunder erupted in the sky ominously as his hand touched the handle. His stomach vibrated like he was sat on a washing machine, the shockwaves creeping down past his testicles and into his knees. Rain hammered down onto the roof above him, making him feel even colder.

Slowly, he opened the door.

The room was dark because the curtains were drawn, the odd flash of lightning sneaking through in white streaks. The air was instantly heavier and muskier as he walked in. Dwayne's shrouded silhouette stood in the opposite corner of the room by the side of a double bed, a large lump underneath the covers; maybe he wanted a threesome. Jonah's hand went for the light switch –

'Leave them off,' Dwayne ordered.

'Why?'

'It's better that way,' he said.

'What is all this?' Jonah asked him, trying to maintain some level of composure, his voice reeling off with trepidation. He kept his back to the door with his sweaty palms balled into fists. Something about the weighty, stale odour of the room made his head begin to ache; it was not a smell he associated with anything good. The house was so silent it was frightening, amplifying every heartbeat.

In a dry, dead voice, Dwayne said: 'The other day I made a mistake with you. I took you to that allotment and I tried to make you do something you didn't want to do. That was my mistake, and like I said, I'm sorry. What I was trying to do, was make you see what you *could* have in this world if you could take that small step. But obviously, I threw you in the deep end, and I realise it must've been scary for you. You couldn't throw that rabbit to be killed because it was an innocent, furry little animal.'

With the storm howling outside like a herd of injured animals and the room steadily greying into complete darkness, Dwayne's speech took a more courteous, sinister tone. He sounded like –

'Solomon said you'd have trouble taking that first step because you *think* too much. You think things through. You don't act on impulse, which is a trait that Solomon reckons could make you more money than you could even imagine. You could be a very powerful asset.' Dwayne no longer sounded like himself. His words were more articulated, carved with precision beyond his capabilities. It was like someone speaking through him, a ventriloquist's dummy relaying a carefully crafted script from a puppeteer.

Just from the mention of Solomon's name, the first sparks of fury began to rekindle inside of Jonah. His body tensed up, his face hardening into a scowl of distrust. 'Are you going to drop me to the station, Dwayne? Or am I going to catch a bus out there in the pissing rain? Cos I want to leave now. Right this second.'

'You haven't opened your present,' he replied, smiling in the dark, his voice completely alien.

'Well give it to me and then get my bag out of your car. I'll go to the station myself.'

A low, cough-like chuckle left Dwayne's mouth, his shoulders bobbing up and down. Rain battered the window like someone was throwing handfuls of pebbles at it. A crack of lightning lit the room up for a second like the flash on a camera. 'It's right in front of you,' Dwayne told him, pointing at the lump underneath the covers.

Leave. That was the action his brain was telling his body to perform. It was the only logical thing to do in the situation. So why wasn't he obeying his body's command? Because he was morbidly curious, the danger and apprehension mixing into a venomous concoction that surpassed his rational train of thought, that's why. What was under there? Whose house was it? He tingled with the need to know and ached with the fear of finding out.

Jonah took a step toward the bed leaving the safety of the door behind him, immediately missing the solidity of its structure. In the gloom, Jonah could barely make out the contours of a person underneath the quilt, the dry waft of dust and stale sweat growing offensively stronger. He stopped mid-stride, almost gagging. Jonah looked over at Dwayne and the first real stab of horror struck him with the blunt force of a frying pan over his head, completely numbing him and turning his blood to jelly.

'What is it, Jonah?' Dwayne stepped forward, leering. 'What's wrong? Don't you want to see what's under the covers?'

Jonah shook his head, unable to speak.

'Fine. I'll open it for you.' A raspy giggle bubbled in Dwayne's mouth as he reached out for the quilt.

Lightning flashed. Ever so faintly from beneath the quilt, there was a low, whining moan.

'No,' Jonah whispered.

'Yes.' Dwayne pulled back the cover.

It was a man, gagged and bound with his wrists tied to the metallic frame of the bed. His face was covered in so many welts and bruises that he looked like he had potatoes stuck all over his head. Even in the dim shade of the room, Jonah could see the thin crust of dried blood around the pillow behind his head like a halo of death. The sour pang of urine saturated the air.

'Oh my God,' Jonah babbled, unable to fully comprehend what his partially obscured vision was showing him. Another feeble whimper came from beneath the gag like a purring kitten.

'We used to call him Lofty,' Dwayne said, pronouncing the name with disgust. 'Officer Lofty.'

The words echoed through Jonah's head but still didn't register properly. He was too shocked to hear anything, the sight of the man's battered face rendering him speechless.

'Two months ago, Sol and I came back from a party at this girl Charlene's house. She'd just turned sixteen and her mum let her have a house party in that same block of flats we just passed near Haidon Park. The party was shit so we cleaned her house out. Sol got her mum pissed on wine and she passed out. We loaded the car with her TV, her stereo her mum bought for her birthday, her little brother's Playstation, the lot.

'When we were driving away, we spotted Lofty here coming back from an off-Licence with a case of Budweiser under his arm. You remember those things he used to call us, Jonah? Even when I saw him two months ago, with a gun stuck down my trousers, I still got frightened when he walked by. But this is where the funny part comes in. This man, is not, and never has been, a police officer.'

Dwayne paused for effect, letting the information sink in. He stared at Jonah, nodding his head. 'Sol told me that he wasn't a policeman but I didn't believe him. So Billy and me, we staked his house out and broke in when he left. This fucking piece of shit –' Dwayne kicked the man in his shoulder, who responded to the abuse with a long chord of distress, '– works in a PC repair shop. His real name is Robin Maxwell, no wife, no children. Do you get it now, Jonah? This bastard used to dress as a policeman to terrorise us. Remember when he used to search us? We all shrugged it off and didn't talk about it afterwards but we all used to think about it. I know *you* did.'

Jonah felt his lips quiver. Of all the nightmares he'd had that week, the one Dwayne now spoke of haunted him the worst.

'This man deserves to die, Jonah. You should see some of the pornos we found in his garage. Little boys, Jonah. Does it make you sick? It makes me feel sick, and over the last year my stomach's grown pretty strong. I've seen a lot of fucked-up shit that I've been able to handle. But this? He used to fucking touch us, Jonah.'

It was like a hypnotist's instruction. As soon as Dwayne said Jonah's name, his knees buckled and nearly gave way beneath him. His legs were like two foam swimming floats. He began to cry, simply and unashamedly. Covering his eyes with his hands, the fear subsided into something more painful; sadness overwhelmed him. Confusion clouded his ability to string thoughts together. All he now felt was the raw, seething stabs of negative emotion.

'Don't cry, Jonah. We don't need tears. This is your chance to make everything right,' Dwayne cooed. Jonah shook his head, sniffing up snot. 'Come on, Jonah. The man's a paedophile. Impersonating an officer and a stack of kiddie porn is like a golden ticket to kill this man. You'd be doing your community a service.'

'I ... I ain't killing anyone, D-wayne.'

'The man is a pervert. We are victims of his sick fucking hands. You, me, Bill ... everyone.'

Jonah wiped his eyes and tried to regulate his breathing. 'You're talking about murder, Dwayne. You hear what you're saying?'

'This ain't a fucking film, Jonah. Murder is nothing.' Dwayne rooted around in the inside of his hoody and pulled out a knife that was closer to something a samurai would wield rather than a kitchen utensil. Holding it by the blade, he extended it to Jonah. 'Do it.'

Jonah shook his head. Lightning lit up the room, uncloaking the shadows blocking Dwayne's face. His eyes seemed smaller and closer together like a rodents. The person standing in front of Jonah didn't look like Dwayne, instead some kind of maniacal imitation.

'Do it, Jonah.'

'No.'

'For the kids of this area. Do it.'

'No.'

'For the times he called us niggers and grabbed our dicks –'

'NO!' Jonah snapped, the reality of the present horror shaking him out of his melancholy with visceral ruthlessness.

From behind, Jonah heard something creeping up on him.

'I told you he wouldn't be able to do it.' Solomon appeared in the doorway, all traces of distinguished gentlemen gone and replaced with a husky, aggressive tone. 'I told you you were wasting your time, Dwayne.'

A squeal came from the half-dead mouth of Robin Maxwell. Jonah gasped in fright as Solomon finished speaking, but his initial apprehension of Solomon was quickly overridden; Dwayne began to say something, but it wasn't his voice; it was like he was possessed, the words forming with the texture of splinters and glass shards, several octaves lower than how he normally sounded.

'YOU FUCKING PUSSY, COME OVER HERE. TAKE THIS FUCKING BLADE AND STAB THIS CUNT IN HIS FUCKING CHEST BEFORE I PUT IT THROUGH YOUR FUCKING EYEBALLS, YOU SOFT STREAK OF SHIT!'

Another crack of lightning illuminated the room throwing the shadows into disarray, and making Dwayne's ratty face change into something that looked much older, his eyes sagging in their sockets, his complexion strangely green. Jonah's arse clenched with fear, a trickle of pee running down his legs.

'You're weak!' Solomon barked, calmer than Dwayne but no less annoyed. 'I knew you were a sack of useless shit the minute I saw you.' He turned to Dwayne. 'What did you ever see in this pig?'

All the fire Jonah had harboured toward Solomon was extinguished in an instant. Now he knew how his rabbit must've felt looking at Champ as it dangled above its drooling, snapping jaws.

'I don't know,' Dwayne told Solomon, with a sudden calm demeanour. Then, with animal quickness, Dwayne leapt onto the bed and began to plunge the knife up and down into Lofty's chest, blood spraying in all directions like a crimson water fountain. He was screaming as he thrust the knife downward, the wet thumping echoed throughout the room. It was the second most disturbing thing he'd ever heard; the first, Solomon's hideous chuckle as he watched the spectacle.

While Dwayne was on his fifth or sixth stab and in mid-scream, Jonah turned and grabbed the door handle. Solomon reached out to try and prevent Jonah's escape, and would've if he hadn't been so engrossed in Dwayne's performance. Jonah whipped the door open and was making his way down the stairs three at a time, wanting to leap down the whole flight but feared breaking his legs. Flashbacks of his dream about the baby with the tangle of wires hanging out of its head briefly raced through his mind, but the thoughts of survival overpowered them. The adrenaline rush in his body was like electrocution, unbearably stinging every nerve beneath his skin. He was on the verge of screaming as he heard Solomon come out of the bedroom door and make his way after him. Jonah fumbled with the front door latch and pulled it open, wind and rain whipping his face. He could hear Dwayne, or that crazy impersonation of him yelling his name. But above the maniacal ranting of his former friend, something else filled his ears with far more terrifying impact; whispering chanted in his head drowning everything else out, a jumble of words spinning around in his brain like helicopter propellers. It was Solomon speaking; he was still making his way out of the house when Jonah was already a good length down the rain-soaked street and there was no way he'd be able to project his voice that far with that kind of clarity at such a low volume. He was chanting something, and the further Jonah seemed to run the more the words slowed down and began to form a sentence. It said, 'You're going to Hell,' the volume raising on the last word until the hairs on the back of his neck pricked up and an excruciating ticklish sensation bubbled in his groin.

'You're going to HELL.'

Halfway down the street, soaked through, Jonah realised that he was running on a completely straight track that went on for another two hundred or so yards. He quickly cut to the right, in between two houses separated by a fence that led to the back gardens. With all the strength he could muster, Jonah channelled the adrenaline flowing through him, leapt on the fence and clambered over it. His palms burned as the damp wood dug into his skin, filling his flesh with splinters, but he had little time to indulge the pain. He stumbled to his feet and sprinted through the alley leading to the back yards. For a solitary second, he stopped, panting and wheezing and wondering just what on earth to do next. He found himself cornered with the alarming sound of trainers splashing on pavement coming increasingly close.

'Jonah!' Dwayne yelled like a war cry. 'Jonah, you better fucking get back here!'

'Hell. You're going to HELL.'

He jogged over the slippery grass and made an attempt to scramble over into the next garden. It occurred to him that he might just run out of steam playing this game of backyard hurdles. The end of the garden backed onto the houses on the opposite side of the block. This was good because he could get out onto another street and lose his pursuers in the hustle and bustle, but on the flip side, he was walking straight out into Dumpling Avenue – an estate where the young gang-affiliated residents were rumoured to have captured rivals from other estates, tied them to railings, slapped them senseless and pissed all over their clothes and faces, recording the ordeal on their mobile phones.

Jonah scrambled through to the opposite garden, the television set glowing cosy pictures of daytime monotony from behind a shield of double glazing. He could see the silhouette of a person walking across their front room to investigate what all the noise was in the back of their yard, but Jonah was out of sight by the time they reached the curtains. The palms of his hands had deep purple welts from the last fence, but it was a small price to pay to be out of sight from his old friend. When he hit the street, his body seized up with exhaustion; he crouched over with his sore hands resting on his knees, sucking in huge gulps of air.

'Jonah!' Dwayne screamed from somewhere behind him. Then a cackle so wild ripped through the air and made Jonah's legs begin running without his prior consent. It was the laugh of a predator hot on the trail of its dinner.

Unconsciously, Jonah made his way toward the tower block with the crowd of feral boys in front of the foyer, who watched his scared puppy routine with wide, soulless stares. Then, realising he was running for his life, the boys broke up in high-pitched hysterics; a gang of hyenas watching a gazelle running away from a pride of lions.

'Pussy! Who you run from?' one of the boys yelled over. Even though Jonah was certain that the boys weren't going to tag along and chase him too (for one thing, he knew black people hated the rain like cats hated water) Jonah spun his neck toward them to judge the threat. Beneath the glistening curtain of rain, it looked as if their eyes were glowing, ironically like hyenas.

'HELL.'

From nowhere, a car flew out, coming to a screeching halt. Jonah stopped, sure that he'd been struck by the vehicle, then after he realised that he was still alive, continued to run. He looked behind him and saw Dwayne and Solomon climbing over the last back garden.

Houses, tower blocks, cars and streets passed in a blur, the shouting becoming fainter and fainter, but his legs refused to stop. Solomon's voice was relentless in his ears, gentle and unavoidable. Jonah ran in zigzags, winding through the different streets hoping that a squad car or a meat wagon would be rolling by. He'd never wanted to see a policeman so badly in his life. He didn't give a shit if he got arrested at that point, as long as he was away from Dwayne and Solomon, then he was good.

The muscles in his legs throbbed and tightened, rapidly losing their elasticity as Jonah reached a quiet back street. The predatory cries had died down a few streets ago; he'd probably lost them in the maze of identical-looking roads. Jonah slowed to a trot as he analysed the surroundings. There was a row of shops that looked like they hadn't been refurbished since the seventies. Yellowing shop signs missing several letters; a laundrette, an off-licence, The Mouse and Lamb pub –that was it! The pub! It would have a phone that he could use since the battery on his mobile died in the morning, and it was bound to be full of people having a pint away from the rain; it was perfect.

He approached the Mouse and Lamb, checking over his shoulder with every step. Nobody in sight. Maybe the hyenas got into a tangle with Solomon and Dwayne for being foreigners in the wrong part of London, or maybe his imaginary crime-busting patrol car picked them up for looking as though they were on their way to murder someone. Jonah hoped that one of those scenarios was true, but doubted it. The nightmare wouldn't end that easily and he knew it. He pressed his blistered and scabby palms on the slippery glass door, welcoming the chatty ambience and the old-school jukebox playing fifties rock 'n' roll. Still catching his breath, he hobbled to the bar, his thighs and calves like frozen slabs of meat.

The barman was a young, skinny white boy with dyed black hair that made his skin look even paler. A ring piercing circled his bottom lip. Seeing Jonah approach, the boy dragged himself to the bar with the enthusiasm of a slug on a salt trail, and cocked his head upwards.

'Alright mate? Where's your pay phone?' Jonah asked him, keeping his eyes trained on the street through the misty glass window.

'By the toilets,' he replied, looking and sounding like one of those kids who are just about ready to go into work and shoot the place up and then kill themselves.

'Cheers,' Jonah thanked him and quickly headed to the end of the pub. He wiped the oily sheen of mingled sweat and rain off his forehead with the back of his hand and trudged passed the booths and pool tables to the phone. But who exactly was he going to call? The police? He had to think this through. If he brought the cop shop around, he'd have to answer a shit load of questions that could just land him in deeper trouble. After all, whether he liked it or not, he'd just been part of a vicious murder – he was in the house, his fingerprints were bound to be all over it. Then, paranoia thumped into him like a locomotive: what if he got arrested as a suspect? Jesus Christ, he could get sent down and all the GCSEs and teacher references in the world wouldn't be able to save him.

Nah, fuck that, I was tricked into going in there. If I dial the police and explain, I'll get myself off the hook. All I have to do is tell the truth. I'll tell the truth about every single thing that's happened over the week. Fuck it, I'll tell them about the Ouija boards and the ecstasy tabs, the steroid-ridden dog, the cracked-out bitch back at the flat, the guns, the drugs, I'll give everything up, he thought as he held the receiver in his hand, biting on his bottom lip until he tasted the coppery blood. Breathing began to hurt. His throat tightened like a balloon was being inflated inside his throat. He was going to faint. All around the pub, eyes seemed to be on him, judging him with quick glances. Visions of Dwayne thrusting the knife down into Lofty's chest clung to his mind, and a sick, twisted satisfaction lingered inside of Jonah; a part of him was relieved that Lofty was dead. But now, a very real, petrifying thought taunted him – his friend was out in the rainy streets, looking to kill him.

As far as he could remember, Jonah had never suffered a migraine. But he had one now, and it hurt like a bastard. It felt like people throwing furniture against the walls of his head. He still had the receiver clutched in his sore hand, the annoying wailing of a dead tone ringing in the earpiece of the phone. Surely he was safe inside a pub, he thought. He did a quick head count – there were thirteen people including the Goth behind the bar. Oh shit, wait ... Thirteen? Jonah did another quick count. Definitely thirteen. The omens were bad, but as long as he stayed among people they wouldn't touch him would they?

Then, as if to deliberately induce a bout of panic, he remembered the party on Monday. Dwayne shot a kid in the foot and would undoubtedly have killed the guy if he fancied it in a room with twice as many people. If he stayed here and they found him, then this old codgers' haunt would be the place where he would die.

His hands shook. Maybe they wouldn't need to come and murder him, maybe his body would just pack up on him.

'Okay, so who're we gonna call, Jonah?' He tapped the receiver against his shoulder, then dug in his pocket for some change. He pulled out a crumple of notes and a few annoying bits of shrapnel – mostly 2p and 5p coins. When he thought of buying a drink to get some change, Jonah reckoned it was just about the single greatest idea he'd ever had in his entire life. He cradled the receiver and floated to the bar, tapping his fist on the counter to get the Goth's attention.

'I want a ... what's the biggest, strongest drink you can give me?' Jonah asked him over the jukebox.

The boy shrugged, obviously not giving a shit about customer care or any kind of general manners. 'What'dya want?'

'Gimme a whisky. A good whisky.'

The boy closed his eyelids lazily as he asked, 'Single or double?' Not caring that the patchy loose hairs on Jonah's chinny-chin-chin told him that this customer was blatantly under the legal age.

'Don't you do triples here?' Jonah was more than aware that he was sounding a little bit desperate, like an alcoholic getting the shakes and needing a taste of that sweet, sweet nectar.

'Not allowed to do triples. I can give you a double and a single if you want.'

'Just gimme two doubles, no ice.'

The boy shuffled off to fetch the drinks with his knuckles scraping the ground. Jonah pulled a stool out and sat at the far side of the bar, slumping down behind the beer taps to stay hidden, just in case ...

A ringing sound made Jonah leap in his seat and almost topple from the stool. It felt like his skin just tried to snatch itself off his body. He whipped his head around to see a fat old man with a ten-month-old beer foetus under his shirt playing on the fruit machine; he'd just made the bitch pay out and she wasn't too happy, hence the electronic wailing.

Walking at a pace that made Jonah suspect the boy had taken an overdose of sleeping pills, the boy groggily placed Jonah's order in front of him and took the money. Jonah grabbed the first glass of whisky and backed a long swig of the dark liquid that made his throat raw. He coughed, wiped his mouth, and took another gulp. The liquor made the room swell and slow down, that beautiful underwater feeling drenching him instantly. His belly ached slightly as it went down and he remembered that he hadn't actually eaten anything yet.

'Fuck it,' Jonah mumbled finishing the first glass off. The spidery bar-boy with his annoying tight jeans was leaning against the other end of the bar dreaming his day away when Jonah again signalled for him to come over. The boy made his painfully slow way toward him and asked if he could help him.

'I need a cab to King's Cross Station. Can you call me one?'

He nodded, more than familiar with the duty. It was part of his job description to call cabs for all the piss-heads who were too sloppy to get themselves home safely. 'Who shall I say it's for?'

'Tell them it's for Mr Lucky.'

The boy grabbed the bar phone and made the call. When he hung up he said: 'Be about five minutes.'

'That's fine,' he replied, starting on the second drink. His mind was clogged with too many scattered images of death to form a coherent thought, though his body reacted to the atrocity he'd just witnessed with convulsive shivers. He wondered about the police and whether or not he should call them and risk digging a grave for himself that he'd never be able to claw out of. They might, just might believe that he had nothing to do with this bloody mess, that he was an innocent bystander that was duped into breaking and entering and witnessing a murder. But as he replayed the scenario in his own head, the truth became increasingly harder to sell, even to him. Then, as the whisky numbed his head and segregated it from the rest of his jittery body, he decided that the best course of action to take would be to just get out of London and make an anonymous call from a phone box somewhere in Nottingham. He could get his story straight on the train and reorganise himself, but right now, getting out of the city alive was his main priority.

Because one way or another, he was fu –

Déjà vu froze him like a waxwork immortalised mid-sip. Slowly, he put the glass down on the counter and swivelled around on his stool. A new dread pinched away at his skin, but he was still too dislocated to feel it. How on earth could he have walked straight past them, and how the hell did they not recognise him?

Underneath the sounds of *Blue Moon* from the juke box and the clamour of the fruit machine, Jonah had been listening to a conversation in Portuguese without it even registering, like some low-frequency subliminal message. Over at the pool tables by the pay phone, two vaguely familiar boys were locked in a game of nine-ball, sipping on Coronas. Both wore white vests which were still sopping wet from the rain. One was short but meaty, with big shoulders and a pot-belly, and the other was tall and gangly with muscles rippling through his long arms.

Jonah had seen both of them darting out of the back door of the house after Ernesto got shot on Monday. The only reason that Jonah could even recall their faces from the dozens of other strangers at that party was because he'd fallen into them while trying to keep Billy on his feet and suffered the foreign threats and aggressive body gestures. At the time he didn't care. He was too flooded with endorphins and the excitement of carefree promiscuity to pay any attention to a couple of dudes trying to have a Mexican stand-off. But now, in a very real environment where chairs flying and glasses smashing were the norm, the blood seemed to drain from Jonah. If they spotted him then surely they would associate him with the shooting, seeing as he was one of the only British guys there. The consequences could be catastrophic.

As calmly and as casually as he could, Jonah turned back around and finished his last mouthful of whisky. He stood up and was about to make his way outside to wait for the cab, when –

– *Oh dear Lord sweet Jesus why me? Why me God?*

A loud clunk came from behind him and a cue ball flew off of the table where little-and-large were playing pool.

The ball bounced off the hardwood floor and rolled right between Jonah's feet with the menace of a live grenade.

'Oh my Christ,' Jonah moaned, leaning on the bar for support. He was about to just walk off without acknowledging the ball at all, until ...

'Hey man, can you pass the ball?' the little one called at Jonah's back, chalking his cue.

He only had a few seconds to decide on what he was going to do. Maybe they wouldn't recognise him, after all, he'd walked straight by them just five minutes before and they hadn't said a thing. Or maybe they were just too tied up in their game to pay attention to him.

'Yo!' the taller one yelled trying to get his attention.

One second longer and they would've got angry with Jonah for ignoring them when he could quite easily hear their calls. If he turned around now, it would be on. So instead, he lurched forward toward the door, staggering from side to side like he was on a giant see-saw, over-exaggerating his drunkenness; it was so bad it was actually believable. Throughout his performance, he never turned around. The Portuguese boys broke up in laughter at the spectacle. The smaller one fetched the ball as Jonah reached the door, and continued with their game.

Outside, the rain had died down to a gentle pitter-patter, the sky the colour of steel.

Faintly, like the ringing in his ears from the pregnant migraine, Jonah heard that voice again, the words seeming to manifest behind the wet leaves of the trees and from the overflowing drains:

'You're going to Hell, Jonah. Tonight, you're going to Hell.'

29

Headlights shone at the end of the road, two yellow orbs turning rain puddles to piss with their glow. Jonah walked to the corner and observed the vehicle from afar, standing behind the poor concealment of a lamp post. The street behind him was devoid of life, the shutters of the retail shops locked tight like graffiti-scrawled gravestones.

He checked the car again. It was moving too slowly, as if it were patrolling the area. Jonah squinted through his wet lashes but couldn't make the details of the vehicle out any better. He was in two minds whether or not to watch it come any further. If it was the cab then it would stop outside the pub and honk. If it was Dwayne it would creep past and leave Jonah to flee down an empty road with no place to retreat to. He nibbled on his thumbnail trying to decide.

It wasn't worth it. He pivoted on his heels and began to jog down the steep road. Light puffs of vapour left his mouth as he battled on creaky legs, listening out for approaching tyres. He refused to look behind him, not wanting to give the game away. At his leisurely pace (leisurely only because his legs couldn't manage a sprint) he could appear to just be a person trying to get out of the rain. If it was them, then there was the slightest shred of hope that they would overlook him. But the further he travelled down the sloping street, the louder the voice spoke to him, as if the parked cars were humming abuse through their grilles. The decline of the hill made his pace quicken as his head spun around trying to find another bar or pub that would offer refuge so he could call another cab. It wasn't looking good. He passed an alleyway that was roughly three quarters of the way down the road, and chanced a look behind him.

There was no car. He stood panting for several seconds, expecting to see those dull yellow orbs roll over the horizon and start the chase afresh. But he didn't. He was alone in the middle of the street, brimming with a new confidence. Each step was closer to where he wanted to be – away from the ugly jaws of London; away from the blank, corpse-like stares of the denizens on public transport; away from the hideous architecture that jutted out of the concrete like the bottom teeth of some gargantuan monster.

Walking through what seemed like a ghost town, an eerie calm enveloped him. The scene before him was anything but optimistic, the inner-city urban decay festering over every inch of the street like a growth of poisonous fungi. The fog in his paranoia-cluttered mind began to clear, all traces of worry blown away with a draught of revelation; he hated London. He'd been a fool to harbour any feelings for her to begin with, like a lonely man falling in love with a diseased prostitute. In the end it would strip him of everything he had. He could see that now as he hobbled through the concrete jigsaw, with every thread of his spirit frayed to tatters. Completely drained of impetus, even the will to walk seemed futile and pointless as his ankles and knees ground at the joints.

His mother was right all along. She was right to take him away from this place before it chewed up every morsel of decency in his body and swallowed his soul. But in the end it didn't matter what his mother thought, because he was always going to relapse and return to this bitch, craving the jagged caress of the nightlife that he'd been unsuccessfully weaned off for the last year. It had been the place of his wildest dreams and his most worrying nightmares, where he'd experienced real terror, and perhaps true love, and now complete and utter loneliness all in one week. As the rain fell heavier, pounding him like tiny ball bearings, he embraced the desolation.

Then he saw Billy staggering around the corner at the bottom of the street, his ginger hair standing out like a lit cigarette in the dark.

All the breath in Jonah's body left him in one giant surge. He couldn't run and was just about still able to stand. A blaring red-alert siren wailed in his head. The alleyway was only a short jog behind him but his wooden limbs protested.

Billy was walking in a drunken 'S' shape clutching the neck of a wine bottle, his head bowed toward the ground like he was trying to count the pavement slabs. He hadn't spotted Jonah. Yet. And so what if he did? Billy was alone and smashed out of his face by the look of it, and even in Jonah's pulverised state he'd still bet that if push came to shove Billy would end up sprawled across the floor.

So Jonah didn't move. Billy soon stopped wobbling around and held his ground about ten car lengths away when he finally saw Jonah. Nobody spoke. The rain pummelled them both and the wind gasped like the breaths of spectators at a Wild West shootout waiting for either cowboy to draw.

'You trying to kill me too, Bill?'

Billy swayed on the spot, his head rotating like he was exercising his neck. 'I just want to go to the pub really! The Mouse ... just down the road there,' he yelled back in the same neutral, alcohol-induced tone. He began to stumble forward.

'Don't come closer,' Jonah called, to no avail.

'We're all friends ain't we, Jone?'

Jonah took a step backward. 'That's what I thought. But now all I know is that Dwayne just killed a man and now he wants me dead, and so does Sol.'

'What about me?' Billy asked, slowly inching forward.

'I don't know what to believe, Bill. Why should I believe you?'

'Cos I'm your friend,' he said, emphasising the last word. 'We've been mates since before we had hair on our dicks!'

He was five car lengths away, and that was close enough for Jonah to realise something that made his heart stop with complete horror: Billy wasn't drunk. Jonah knew Billy's face when he was pissed, the way his skin reddened and how his eyes gleamed in little slits. But Billy's face was completely alert, with a new sneer of disgust slapped across it.

The next few moments happened in slow motion.

Billy suddenly pounced like a lion closing in on a deer, his mouth twisted in a grimace of hatred.

Jonah found the strength to run, his balance off from the sudden turning motion.

A car screeched down the hill. A black car. A black BMW.

Jonah reached the opening of the alleyway and dived into it, noticing as he did that it led to a brick wall. His stomach was going to explode. His heart was beating in his throat. He couldn't breathe.

'*Oh Jo-nah* ...' Solomon's sinister whisper floated past Jonah, somehow audible above the screeching of tyres and Billy frantically cursing Jonah's mother with every known version of the word *whore*. An explosion that sounded like fireworks echoed through the alley, so loud that Jonah's ears turned watery. He felt a thumping in his back and was pulled to the ground.

Then silence.

30

He lay with half his face in a puddle, unable to coerce his body into movement. It felt as though his back was on fire, but he couldn't speak or even roll over to extinguish the pain. Everything else was numb. Jonah stared at the brick wall and watched as his field of vision slowly began to darken, the black aura eating everything in sight. Tears leaked from his eyes and joined the raindrops splashing down on his face.

Wracked with shock, his bowels betrayed him. He wanted to scream out in agony, to scream out for help, just to scream. But all he could do was think, and all he could think was how much he loved his mother. His beautiful mother who did her best to raise him, who worked all the hours God sent. The woman who always made sure that he had toys at Christmas even when she couldn't afford them, and hugged him when he was upset and told him how clever he was, and how proud he made her.

I love you, mum. Please forgive me. I love you so much, mummy. You were right. You were always right.

The last thing Jonah thought about was the image of Diane White holding him, her hand stroking his head and whispering, 'It's okay, son. You're alright. Come on, stop crying, mummy loves you.'

Then everything faded. With blood pouring from his back, Jonah curled up in the foetal position next to a stack of rotting rubbish bags and died in the rain.

Alone.

EPILOGUE

'At least I thought I was dead. Technically I died twice that night but the paramedics were able to revive me. I spent the next three weeks in a coma, and let me tell you, those bad dreams I was having were nothing compared to being unable to see or move but hearing everything in the room. Now I think that's what Hell must really be like, being alone, being vulnerable, without a single friend to call on.' Jonah sounded like an adolescent with his voice about to break. He paused, sitting on his chair, and began to cry. Not one single person in the audience laughed or made a sound. He was thinking about his mother again and that's what triggered it. Rose rushed onto the stage with a box of Kleenex and crouched by his side, wiping his tears away with one arm around his shoulders.

'It's okay, baby,' she quietly said in his ear. Some of it was picked up in the microphone. 'You take your time. Just take your time, I'm here.'

After a minute or so, he pulled himself together and swallowed back the last of the sobs. He cleared his throat and continued. 'By the way, this is my fiancée, who I mentioned earlier.'

Troy came on stage with another chair for her to sit on, and then rushed off again; he looked as though he'd been crying, too. Rose paid no attention to her introduction, instead, concentrated on comforting Jonah, watching him through blurry eyes.

'All you young men here tonight, let me tell you something right now. There is nothing you can't do with the love of a good woman on your side. I mean that.' He squeezed Rose's fingers. 'When the doctor said I might not walk again I wanted to kill myself. But with her help and the support of my family, I was finally able to do it. Rose here, she held my hand through all of those gruelling months of therapy. It's funny because while I was learning how to walk again, her little girl was taking her first steps too.'

A few polite titters.

'And that's about it.' Jonah shrugged, staring at the floor. 'In a lot of ways my life has been completely ruined by what happened to me that night. I won't ever play sports again, but the way I look at it, I did enough running that night to last me a lifetime.

'I also get chronic back pain. When it's cold, I swear I feel like I'm about to snap in half from the pain. It's unbearable, and it's not going to get any better. And, even though I went to university and managed to get a degree in Business Studies, I'm still yet to get a job. I get as far as the interview but I'm guessing that no firms want to hire a cripple.'

He lowered his voice with embarrassment as he said that last word. Rose lightly swatted the side of his arm for using that phrase and shot him a glance of annoyance; she never let him get away with referring to himself with such flagrant self-pity. She hissed, 'Stop it,' clearly audible to the audience. Jonah chuckled gently and kissed the back of her hand.

'I apologise. I start feeling sorry for myself every now and then, but the point is that it's still going to be damn hard for me to get a fuckin' job, probably as hard as some of you convicts.' The crowd laughed. So did Jonah. 'But on the plus side, I'm still alive. I've still got a lot to live for. I have a beautiful fiancée and a crazy stepdaughter who is constantly running and jumping around and tiring me out.

'Y'know, I told you guys earlier that I'm not here to lecture you. I just wanted to tell you my story. But I hope the message you take away with you tonight is that life is precious. The world is a hard enough place without all the guns and knives, and I'm living proof of that. I hope I gave everyone something to think about.' Jonah got his crutches in place and leaned down on them, using the strength in his arms to stand up. 'Goodnight, guys. Take care and God bless.'

A rapturous applause erupted in the auditorium, the kind of rowdy hollering and whooping only excited youngsters could make. The predominantly male audience were all standing, thumping their hands together aggressively. That was it. Jonah felt like he'd just been to confession and received absolution for his sins. It was almost as if he had his old body back, like he could run off the stage and crowd surf into the hands of his impressionable listeners. For the first time in a long time, Jonah felt no pain.

Some of the kids were stood on chairs even as the officers in attendance yelled from the aisle for them to get down and behave. One boy at the far left of the room was just standing there and nodding among the chaos around him, and with the slightest of gestures, wiped his eyes with the sleeve of his jacket.

'Oi! Oi sir!' A white boy with a hearing aid in his right ear was trying his best to shout above the cacophony. He waded his way through the sea of people and reached the front of the stage. Looking up at Jonah he asked: 'What happened to the rest of 'em?'

'What?' Jonah cupped his ear and leaned on one crutch to try and hear the boy a bit better.

'Your mates and that. What happened to them?'

Jonah put the microphone to his mouth and cleared his throat; it took a few seconds for the hype to die down. 'I almost forgot. My good friend here just reminded me. Sorry what's your name, mate?' Jonah asked the boy, who couldn't have been older than fourteen.

With the room quieter, the boy replied, 'Tommy,' in speech slurred due to his impaired hearing.

'Tommy just reminded me – shit, I can't believe I nearly went home without telling you what happened to the rest of them.' The mob began to sit down again, eagerly waiting for the finale of the story. 'Well, where do I begin? I never saw Genie after I left that night. I assume she's dead or roaming around some shopping centre trying to steal things to support her habit. I doubt she cleaned herself up, and to be fair I don't really care either way.'

Jonah sighed before he continued. 'A few days after that night, Billy-Lee Porter died. Not too far from where Billy was staying, they were building a new set of office blocks. It happened on a Saturday night, but the foreman of the site found him on Monday morning, lying in a broken heap on the floor. The papers put it down to another binge drinker getting carried away, who somehow managed to get over the gate and climb the crane. Billy must've been completely pissed, lost his footing and –' Jonah paused, taking a second to think about his old pal. Even after everything, Jonah still missed him.

Rose gently patted him on the back.

'– Anyway. When I was well enough, I went past the site where Billy died. I don't know what made me go there. When you survive something like I went through, you do a lot of stuff that you can't explain. I guess I just wanted to take a look at the last place where Billy had been alive. You see, I've become a bit religious since everything happened, and in a way, I've become more sympathetic to Billy. I think about what it must've been like for him and ... I don't know. But when I went to this site I saw this huge red crane surrounded by a bunch of yellow cranes, and I thought about everything that Billy had been through in his life. I think maybe he was trying to fly.'

Jonah rubbed the corner of his eyes and cleared his throat.

'What happened to Dwayne is what you could call karma coming back to bite you. When I came out of my coma, the police had a shitload of questions for me and they even asked me about Officer Lofty. I'm not ashamed to say it, ladies and gentlemen, but I gave up everything I knew. I told them about Dwayne stabbing him to death, about them shooting me, everything. And that's when the officer told me that Billy and Dwayne were both dead.

'They found Dwayne in an alleyway, which was ironic I thought. He'd been tortured. Somebody had burned him with an iron, burned him with acid, chopped his fingers off, sledge-hammered his knee caps in, then wrapped him up in a bin-bag and dumped him in an alleyway somewhere in north London. I only learned about the details of the murder in the papers about six months later, but to my knowledge, they never caught who did it. I have a rough idea though. Among his injuries, the coroner pulled buckshot from a shotgun cartridge out of the shattered bones in his foot.

'I only remembered about Dwayne's dog a few weeks after I woke up, because as you can imagine, my head was pretty fucked up from everything. But by the time I got some police officers and the RSPCA down to the allotments, all they found was a decaying bag of bones.

'As for Solomon ...' he paused; the name felt like chewing on a baked bean can in his mouth. 'Well, like the great magician he was, he just vanished. Maybe he went back to his country, wherever that was. But I've never seen him since. One of the detectives investigating the case, Detective Snow, told me that he and several others were compiling a case on Billy for knocking over the jewellery store because they had him on camera, but as it was so dark they couldn't quite make him out. According to this guy Snow, there was only ever one person in the shop; they had detailed files on Dwayne and Billy and were trying to nab them both for possession of firearms, but had never even seen or heard of Solomon as the third party.

'When he told me this, I felt sick. The police had their eyes on Bill and Dwayne and that's how they knew I wasn't involved. Solomon was never documented as an accomplice.'

It sounded like a ghost story. Maybe it was. It was a mystery that'd kept him awake for countless nights as he continuously played out scenarios in his head. But now, as he captivated his listeners with the horrors of his little yarn, he felt relieved, as though he'd finally shared the burden of the mystery.

Maybe they'd lose a bit of sleep over it too.

'I guess that's my whole point tonight,' Jonah shrugged, 'everyone here knows Solomon. He's the guy that whispers in your ear and fucks up your entire life. As of this moment, from the second you leave here tonight, you all have a choice, a clean slate. Make the most of it.'

Jonah propped the microphone back on its stand and nodded to Rose that it was time to leave the stage. He'd finally exorcised the demons that'd tormented him all these years. Now, he could leave the phantoms of his darkest memory in the auditorium to float around in the minds of the impressionable youngsters. Maybe in a few months, the nightmares would come back and kick-start the panic attacks again, and if they did, he'd find a new audience to share his tale with.

More applause ensued as they walked off, not as frantically as before, but modest enough to let him know that at the very least, he was a good storyteller. Behind the curtain by the stage exit, Troy was clapping appreciatively.

'You did so well,' Rose whispered with her arm around his waist. His back was full of sharp pains and his legs had stiffened from sitting down for so long, but he felt good.

'Thanks,' he replied, kissing her head.

Before he reached the end of the stage, Jonah decided to take one last look at the congregation. What he saw almost toppled him.

'Their eyes.' Jonah froze and leaned on Rose. She stumbled under his weight but managed to steady him.

'What is it? What is it, honey?' She was searching his face with that look of concern that he'd grown accustomed to.

'Glowing ...' Jonah squeezed his eyes shut, trying to block it out. It was another hallucination.

He'd been having them ever since that fateful summer. Sometimes, he'd be walking down the street and see a maggot-ridden skull staring out the window of a bus at him, or he'd see a gory, pus-dripping ghoul parading in a shop display window like a mannequin.

'*Daydreams,*' young Ms Angela would tell him when he went in for his weekly talk with her. *'Horrific daydreams brought on by the anxiety you still harbour because of your ordeal. Once you can let go of the past, they will fade, I promise you.'*

'Jonah, look at me,' Rose commanded in her mum voice. 'It's okay. You're safe.'

Jonah released a shaky breath and slowly opened his eyes. Rose held his face with both hands, analysing his facial expression the way a doctor might check a patient's pupils for signs of dilation. Behind her, Troy was gawping over with nervous anticipation. Jonah risked another look at the crowd but they'd already begun to disband, their faces free from abnormalities.

'Well done, mate. Well bloody done.' Troy patted Jonah on his back as they emerged into the bright backstage hallway. 'I'm not kidding you, Jonah. I think you're one of the best speakers I've ever heard. Those kids really looked like they were taking in everything you were saying. Jesus Christ, I was laughing, crying and scared all at once while you were up there. Almost two hours it was! Feels like ten minutes. You're a natural you are. Even when you were swearing, which I don't normally like,' he quickly added, 'I think it was good because you connected with the kids on a level they understand.'

'Thanks,' Jonah said. The tone of Troy's voice, along with his constant plastic grin, was quickly grating on his nerves.

'No seriously, you should write your memoirs. Turn it into a book! It'd be a bestseller, I'm telling you. We could even help promote it. They might even turn it into a film.'

Jonah just nodded. The back door leading to the rear car park was open as the event staff began to file out. A cold air blew through the hallway, chilling them to the bone. Rose adjusted her scarf in preparation for the elements. It was only a short walk to the car but with Jonah's bad back it would feel like a hike.

Rose could see the expression of fright and pain spread across Jonah's face. The cold weather had been bothering him all week.

'Well thank you very much, Troy.' Rose began, 'I know these talks really help Jonah.'

'Oh it's my pleasure. They help the kids as well, that's the main thing.'

Jonah noticed the sign pointing toward the toilet as they approached the exit; he'd been on stage for a while and gone through two glasses of water.

'I'm just going to quickly go to the toilet, Rose.'

'You need any help?' Troy asked promptly, unflinching at how inappropriate it sounded.

'No, I'm fine.' He turned to Rose. 'Go get the car warmed up, I'll be out in a few minutes.'

'Okay.' She kissed him on the cheek, pulled the hood of her coat up, and briskly left.

Just to make sure that Troy didn't actually follow him into the bathroom and offer his shaking services, Jonah extended his hand at the door. 'Thanks for everything, Troy.'

'I should be thanking you!'

Jonah opened the door to the little boys' room. 'Gimme a call if there's anything else I can do,' he said, hoping he wouldn't.

'Will do!'

The bathroom had a cold, sterile feel to it. Everything gleamed, from the back-lit mirrors to the shiny taps. The rubber stoppers at the end of his crutches squelched against the tiles as he slowly hobbled to a cubicle. Although he only needed to pee, using the urinal was just too strenuous. He'd grown accustomed to pissing while sitting because it was more comfortable, plus if he needed to pass any solids the option was there. He bundled his crutches in the corner of the cubicle and relaxed on the icy seat, letting nature take its course.

As his pee hit the water in the bowl, sounding comically like a waterfall, Jonah heard the door of the men's toilets open. The hard soles of a man's boots clunked off the tiles as he took slow, methodical steps to the cubicle next to Jonah. The gushing of Jonah's urine broke the awkward ambience of the man in the next cubicle unbuckling his belt and pulling his trousers down.

Then, unexpectedly, the loudest fart Jonah had ever heard echoed through the room, trumpeting like a wet orchestra. Sloppy plops sloshed into the bowl like handfuls of mud being thrown into a river. Jonah's first reaction was to laugh. He was shocked to say the least, but also a little disgusted that the man hadn't exercised a little more discretion, knowing that someone was in the next cubicle.

Maybe the poor guy had irritable bowel syndrome or something.

When the noise continued to rip and the bowl continued to fill, the offensive smell wafted over and hit Jonah; he could taste the sickening stench of excrement in the back of his throat. He gagged violently, fearing that he was going to be ill. Jonah's penis stopped peeing in mid flow, sending a stinging sensation through his shaft.

The farts began to rev with inhuman volume, like a rhino was letting loose on the toilet. Jonah gathered his crutches, pulled himself to his feet, flushed, and unlocked the door. As he did so, the farting stopped abruptly.

And the person began to cry.

'Oh no ... It hurts so badly. It hurts when I poo.' The voice sounded as though it came from a frail old lady. 'It pains my bum-bum when I shit. Oh dear!' The elderly woman moaned, with almost inaudible whimpers.

Immediately, Jonah felt his chest tighten and the marble walls start to close in on him. She was obviously some kind of nutcase who'd wandered in the building somehow. There was probably an old people's home nearby, or a mental ward, and she'd decided to go for a stroll. Jonah would simply leave the toilet, grab hold of Troy and tell him that an old lady was having 'difficulties' in the Gent's. Then it was their problem.

But as Jonah took his first step past the cubicle, his rubber stoppers sucking the tiles, the woman called out to him. Except it was no longer a woman's voice; it was the eerily resonant voice of someone from his past.

'It hurts when we shit you out in Hell, Jonah. We have mountains of turds and rivers of shit waiting for you in Hell Jonah. We can't wait. None of us can wait, Jonah.'

'Horrific daydreams brought on by the anxiety you still harbour because of your ord –'

Jonah thrust his crutch at the cubicle door, falling painfully on his side with the lack of balance and momentum. The crutches sprawled out from underneath him as his left leg thumped the floor. The whole right side of his body numbed. His back screamed out in agony.

The cubicle door, unlocked the whole time, swung open. Jonah looked up and saw ...

... Nothing. Of course not. It would be too easy to see Solomon standing there, or some red, pointy-bearded troll with a pitchfork.

'You keep obsessing about this boy Solomon because of what he was able to do to you,' Ms Angela's voice chimed in his memory. Every time he had one of his episodes he called on her words for reassurance. *'He was a horrible, manipulative*

person who was able to take away the things that mattered most to you – your friends. He stole them from you and that's why you still hear his voice, Jonah. All the fear from the past and all the insecurities you have now, you associate with him. It's the one chapter in your life you still haven't closed, and until you do, you will never be able to move on.'

On the floor, Jonah clutched his crucifix so hard that the edges pierced his flesh and drew blood. He whispered the Lord's Prayer, because he found that prayer usually helped steady his nerves; not completely, but enough for him to gather his crutches, make it to the sink and wash the tears away.

Maybe he'd tell Rose about what had happened in the toilets. Maybe he wouldn't. Lately she seemed so stressed out, constantly trying her best to reassure him. Some nights, when he woke up from a bad dream, sweating and panting and crying into his hands, Jonah could sense her patience slowly dwindling, her soft words marked with a tired, hard edge.

These days, he felt more and more like her child, rather than the man she was due to marry.

So, no, he wouldn't tell her any more; he'd keep quiet and do his best to ignore everything he saw, even though it felt real enough to strike him dead with terror. He'd lose his sanity but maybe he'd salvage his relationship. He could live with paranoia, but he couldn't live without her.

'Please God. Let it end.'

But somehow, he knew it never would.